The Outlier

The Outlier

R.J. Stanton

Writer's Showcase
presented by *Writer's Digest*
San Jose New York Lincoln Shanghai

The Outlier

Writer's Showcase
presented by *Writer's Digest*
an imprint of iUniverse.com, Inc.

For information address:
iUniverse.com, Inc.
5220 S 16th, Ste. 200
Lincoln, NE 68512
www.iuniverse.com

ISBN: 0-595-13282-0

Printed in the United States of America

To my wonderful wife, Meredith.

Without her, this book would not have been.

Thanks for believing in me.

Epigraph

"The vengeance of history is more terrible than the vengeance of the most powerful General Secretary."

—Leon Trotsky

Acknowledgements

I would like to acknowledge the invaluable assistance of the following people: Bob Stanton for his editorial assistance, Don Labreque, for educating me in the history of mental retardation and making me aware of the Eugenics Movement, Barry Greaney, Chris Cobb, and Chris Hamill for their advice and suggestions, and all the family and friends who put up with my constant bantering and whining while I wrote this novel.

I

"Time to meet with destiny, Bitch."

It's late—after 10 p.m. Late for the little town of Wilton, Massachusetts on Thursday, October 26, 1972. He knows this. He knows a lot about this town and its mostly working-class residents. It was his hometown, or at least it was where he started his life, years ago. After what happened, it is hard to feel "at home" here. Anywhere. It seems long ago. When he thinks about his youth and what has come to pass, he does it as if he were thinking of someone who really doesn't interest him, as if he were watching something horrible happening to a man on the news. Sometimes, however, he gets confused, caught up in the horror, knowing that it is really he who experienced those things. But if he concentrates on the present, it always gets better. The frightful nightmares pass into a part of his brain that will not affect what is going on *now*. It hadn't always been that easy. For years he had suffered before he learned to control it.

Tonight he must think back, to get the frame of mind he needs. Once he begins shaking and sweating, when breathing is difficult and the nightmares take hold, he can re-focus the fear and send it down a different path. That fear allows him—drives him—to do what he needs to do. He'd spent many years training his mind to do all *sorts* of great acts, for himself and for others.

Tonight is one of those nights. He stands in the woods, not far from the edge of the road, where nobody will see him until the right time. And then, the selected people will see him. He's gone over his plan a hundred times and each time it has gone off perfectly. Tonight will be no different. He just has to wait until he sees their car pass under the streetlight, standing sixty yards up the road. It all begins with that.

The last fifteen times or so, he has imagined it happening with these particular people who would soon drive by. He'd picked them over a month ago. He laughs a little as he thinks about how easy this has been. How simple it is to manipulate the time, the place, the people, and even the situation and the weather conditions he needs. Cool and crisp. He can smell the sweetness of leaves decaying at his feet; a gentle breeze cuts through the branches. A beautiful autumn night in New England with a full moon and clear skies.

"Time to meet with destiny, Bitch," he says again, louder this time.

If people saw him now, as he stands among the trees, they would see a man of average height and weight in a dark pair of coveralls. His gray hair, once black or brown, is a bit straggly, sticks out in places, and appears shiny. They would not be able to determine his age or see any unique facial features. He knows this.

He looks at his watch. "Almost time...almost time." He begins to let his mind take him back to that place. The sounds always came back first. The wailing of sad souls, in unison, filling his mind and hurting his ears.

The coldness of yesterday's memories mixes with the chill of night air. He shivers. Instinctively he crouches down. He puts his back against a big oak tree. They can't get at him from behind. He pulls his knees up close to his chest and wraps one arm around them; the other arm bends up and around his head, which he sinks between his thighs. He is little, out of sight. He can't get away from them, though, no matter how well he hides. He knows he doesn't belong here, but nobody else seems to know or care. His breathing increases as he hears her voice—like a knife, cutting into his soft, young flesh. She is coming down the long, lime-green hall.

"Did ya find him?" he hears her bellow.

"In the day hall, back behind the chairs!" someone yells back.

He sees old Billy running past him, away from her voice. His shirt is torn and he is naked below the waist. He holds his penis and testicles as he runs, mumbling over and over again his favorite phrase, "Oh boy, what'd we do, what'd we do. Die now! Gonna die now! Oh boy, what'd we do now? Die now, die now!" Billy runs out of sight, into the room with the beds.

He squirms against the tree, or is it a wall? He's no longer sure. He peers up to see her scowling at him. When she raises her hand to strike him, he flinches, pulling himself inside the shelter of his arms and legs. The blow doesn't come. Instead he hears the words that are more painful than a physical attack. "Take him to the doghouse and leave 'im there for a few days, he'll straighten out." She draws close to him, just above his left ear. "Right, you little fucker?"

Jamming her fingers into his cocoon, she grabs the base of his chin, forcing his face up close to hers. He turns his eyes away, afraid to look at her directly. "You bet your squash head ass you will!" she hisses, answering her own question.

She lets go of his chin and he tucks his head fast. She waits. She enjoys watching him, and the others, too, flinch under her authority. Her brutality. From his tight little cocoon he finds a moment of courage and yells through his arms, "I'm no m...mo...more of a sq...squash head than y...y...you! Squ...squash head!"

Now the blows come. He knew they would. He had nothing to lose in talking back. She would beat him until she was exhausted anyway. She is a big woman. Powerful. Her hand feels like a two-by-four as it repeatedly pounds into the side of his head. "Don't you *ever* talk back to me!" she screams as she pulls away, out of breath. She drags her sleeve across her face to wipe away some spit that had slipped from her mouth. "Get the fuck outa my sight!"

He gets up and tries to run, unable to escape...but that was then.

His head comes back hard against the tree. Broken memories flash like that of a slow strobe light on the inside of his eyelids. He sees a bucket in the corner of a vacant room. It holds his feces and urine. It is piled high. He sees a naked child running in a field; a view of a building through a dusty window partially blocked by crisscrossing metal wires. The images fade out. He rises above that place. He opens his eyes and sees things clearly; everything is in its proper position now and he floats above it all. He is in control. He begins to hear the faint sound of monks chanting. Their voices echo peacefully in his mind as he looks up the road to see the blue station wagon pass under the streetlight. He stands up and then steps out of the trees. He begins walking on the shoulder of the road. Everything is vivid. He hears the sound of his feet crushing the grass and leaves; he feels the cool October breeze on his face. The roar of the car engine drowns out the chants of the monks.

He bows his head as the headlights illuminate his image. The driver and his passenger are looking at him now. It is what he knows they will do. He smiles to himself as they pass by. He hears the change in the throttle as it lets up just a bit, the telltale sign that they have seen him. They drive on and the lonely sound of rubber on pavement fades into silence. Everything is silent now, except for the sound of his calm and rhythmic breathing. Even the breeze has died down. He is at peace and he is ready. Completely ready.

         *   *   *

She waits for him in her house. He continues up the road. He is surprised to hear another car coming around the corner. He dives back into the woods, out of sight. "Fuck! Fuck!" he screams as he gets up and steps back out into the road. This is not part of the plan. He vows to see the driver of that car on another night, but then realizes that this car *was* part of his plan after all. It was a test to see if he could handle surprises. He laughs and shakes his head, wondering how he lets himself be fooled by his own built-in tests, installed to keep him on his toes. He stops briefly to wipe the dirt off his coveralls; then he takes something from his pocket, a plastic bag, and rubs some of its contents on the areas he had just wiped clean. It is time to settle up, time to see what happens to those who have harmed his people.

He turns into her driveway. The house is big and white with black shutters around its windows. There is a wraparound porch complete with a swing and all the other cute little things like flower pots and an old spinning wheel which gives it that real New England look. He remembers being surprised that she was capable of doing something that appealed to him. But that was four months ago, the first time he had come up onto her property.

He quickly realized then that she'd done this to fool people, to hide her ugliness. Could he overcome these little diversions that she created? Of course he could!

He wanted to do it that night, back in the middle of the summer when he first stood outside her window, looking in at her. But he knew it had to be done right. Some unexpected guests had almost stopped him the first time when he hadn't planned ahead. The early tests to his master plan were always the toughest to pass. But he had passed them all, and now he was almost done with his work.

He walks quietly and calmly through the shrouded darkness of the front lawn and goes around to the back of the house. Once he turns the corner, he moves to the third window, just outside the circle of light cast from within. He looks at her. His body begins to tingle. There she is, as always, sitting under a reading lamp, doing crochet. She does this every night until 11 p.m. and then, after watching the news, she goes upstairs to bed. He checks his watch. He has plenty of time. Every ounce of him aches for the moment. He remembers back to last week, the most recent time he had entered her house while she was at the hair salon. He touched her things and smelled her again. It had made him vomit in the toilet. Just for fun, he left the toilet unflushed. She had not called the police. That surprised him. He took a few little things along with him when he left—a handkerchief with her repulsive odor on it, and a little figurine from the center of the mantle in the room where he knew she most often sat. He hoped she would look up and notice this missing item and think it odd while she sat in her recliner, underneath her little lamp, doing her crappy crotchet. Maybe she would lift her vile body up and try to find it. Yes, he knew she would do this.

He had waited until he heard her key sliding into the lock before he left that day.

As she opened the front door, he was just going out the back, moving quietly away through the woods behind her house. He walked almost three miles until he came to a footpath that led back to town. No one had noticed him. That day he had been close to her, but tonight he would confront her.

He does his final check. He reaches into the front right pocket of his pants and feels the knife there. He runs his fingers over his rear right pocket, feeling for the thin, strong wire. The monks are beginning to sing louder now. After making sure the little box is in his shirt pocket, he pulls out the plastic bag one more time and bends down to rub some of its contents on the tops and sides of his boots. He stands up and walks to the back door. He stops long enough to pull on his thin leather gloves and take out the metal wire.

The lock pops open easily and he steps into the kitchen, lighted only by a small bulb above the stove. The light is soft yellow, dreamlike to him. Pots and pans hanging from a rack on the far wall glisten. Glass spice containers sparkle. The monks' crescendo hits its peek and stops. Her smell is suddenly all around him. He's overcome its power. He is doing the work of God now. He walks through the kitchen, not worrying about the sound his boots make on the linoleum floor. She is in the next room. She hears the boots. She begins to panic. He smiles as he hears the sound of her voice.

"Who's out there? Is someone out there?"

He stops and waits, listening to the energized silence. There's no need to rush. She's too fat to move quickly.

Everything begins to slow down. He sees himself outside his body as he walks into the room where she sits. Her large, hideous head is turned towards him. Her face is contorted into a twisted mass of flesh and fear. Her eyes bulge.

"It's just me, vile pig-woman. Are you happy that I've come to see you?"

He hears the Ewan McColl song that would become the song of the year for 1972, "The First Time Ever I Saw Your Face," playing in his head. Or is it in the room? He sits down on the hassock in front of her and smiles. He's so calm.

"The first time...ever I saw your face," he sings softly. "Do you remember," he whispers, "when you first saw my face? I've always remembered yours." Her large, swollen body shakes uncontrollably. She does not answer his question; she will require an explanation of her sins. He will do this later. He stands above her and raises his hand high in the air, squeezing his gloved fingers into a tight leather ball. She pulls her arms up around her head and closes her eyes. He stops. Smiles. He realizes the wonderful irony of the moment, holding back the blow he knows he will soon deliver. After a long moment he leans close to her. He inhales deeply through his nostrils, smelling her stench. He feels no fear, only power. He feels the wonder of it, the serene ecstasy, the magnificence. He whispers something in her left ear and stands back to watch his words sink in. He waits for her to remember. There it is! Her body convulses strongly and she looks up in recognition. The terror in her eyes is apparent. That is what he needed to see. Now he can do his work.

2

Tuesday, September 17, 1940. Miss Wiggam saw them coming through the classroom window. The morning bell hadn't rung yet, so most of her students were still bouncing around outside, yelling and playing, exhibiting the sort of energy that only children could this early in the day. She passed through the classroom into the large entranceway and stood at the top of the front steps. The three approaching women who walked amongst the children carried themselves with great authority. When they reached the bottom of the steps, the leader of their group looked up and offered a quick, official smile. "Miss Wiggam?" She waited for Miss Wiggam's nod. "We are here as requested."

Miss Wiggam, a stout woman well on her way to becoming an old maid, excitedly took the six steps to greet her guests. "I'm so happy that you have come," she said, wringing her hands. "I was-n't sure if Dr. Goldsmith had received my message. I'd sent it at the end of last semester but hadn't heard anything until yesterday."

"The work of the HBS is vast and difficult. We are trying to accommodate as many as possible but you must understand that in addition to testing, we also do all field interviews while trying to maintain the highest standards in our regular jobs at the school. Please, let me introduce the members of my field crew." The woman turned, slowly allowing her arm to pass in front of her as if she were introducing the cast of some great Shakespearean company. "To my left is Miss Colleen Owen, the newest and youngest member of our group. She has just finished her training with Dr. Goldsmith this summer."

Miss Owen was a tall, pretty woman with dark hair pulled back in a tight bun. She bowed slightly in Miss Wiggam's direction. "How do you do, Ma'am?"

"This is Mrs. Mary Crampton. She has been with us for—how long has it been now, Mary?"

Mrs. Crampton looked away and thought for a moment. "Seven years now! My, how time flies when one is doing interest-ing and exciting things." She trailed off into a shrill little giggle and smiled at Miss Wiggam, but a quick glance at her leader's stern face made her take a more serious tone. "How do you do, Miss Wiggam?"

"Very well, now that you are here," Miss Wiggam replied, all the while looking at the powerful woman who was handling the introductions.

"I am, of course, Mrs. Martha Mason, leader of this particular field crew. I have been with the Human Betterment Society for ten years now." She paused a moment to let the power of her words sink in. "We are here, as you asked, to first do the testing, and then, after tests have been completed, we will conduct the interviews with each of the children. I assume you have prepared a room?"

"Oh! Yes, Mrs. Mason. Everything set up just the way you wanted it. The children will take the test and then I send them to you in alphabetical order. I've set up three small tables, one for each of you." She paused, becoming a little apprehensive. Mrs. Mason noticed her hesitation immediately.

"What is it, Miss Wiggam?"

"Well, I was wondering," her words started slow but picked up pace as she spoke, "could I possibly get involved with the field work? I would love to help out in any way I can. I've been a member of the HBS since 1938, ever since I saw Professor Roberts give his wonderful speech in Boston. I know I could do a good job. I've been a teacher now for going on sixteen years. I can tell a lot about kids. I really think I could contribute."

Mrs. Mason looked her up and down as if she were sizing up a piece of livestock. She stood thinking for a moment, then turned to Miss. Owen. "Before we leave today, I want you to take down Miss Wiggam's address. We need people like her."

An old beat-up baseball sailed through the group, startling all, just missing Mrs. Crampton's head. It came to rest at the bottom of the steps. After the women recovered and asked Mrs. Crampton if she was okay, they all turned their attention to the young boy running over to get the ball. Miss Wiggam grabbed the boy's arm as he tried to pass by the group. "Josh! What is the matter with you, boy? Didn't you see how close that ball came to hitting this poor woman in the head?" She pointed at Mrs. Crampton. The boy glanced at her, then back up into Miss Wiggam's face.

"I didn't throw it, Ma'am," he said defiantly. "I'm only gettin' it. Wayne Grady throwed it." Everyone looked over at another boy standing across the schoolyard. He was trying desperately not to pay attention to what was going on. Miss Wiggam glared back at Josh. "Well, you are just as responsible for this as Wayne is. You apologize to Mrs. Crampton. Go ahead, do it now."

The boy turned to the woman, reluctantly apologized, and then ran off to get back to his game. Mrs. Mason looked over at Miss Owen and cleared her throat. Miss Owen looked back at her nervously. "Don't you think you should be studying your traits book? You need the practice if you are going to do this sort of work," she said, shaking her head in disapproval. While Miss Owen fumbled through a large bag Mrs. Mason continued. "Physical characteristics are sometimes the only way you will be able to determine on which side of the fence the borderline cases will fall. Remember, while the intellectual defects may be small in some cases, or for that matter even non-existent, the immoral and criminal tendencies of these types of people will quite often be there. It is your job, Miss Owen, to be able to protect our good society with early intervention. You must sharpen your skills by practicing every chance you get. It will be up to you, with the traits book as your guide, to push past the hidden obstacles, which will most often be a decent score on the test." Mrs. Mason turned her attention back to Miss Wiggam and away from the young woman who was frantically dividing her attention now between the pages of her book and Josh.

"Jew?" Mrs. Mason asked disdainfully, tilting her head in the child's direction.

"Yes," Miss Wiggam replied, frowning. "Josh Koehler."

"I'd like you all to look at him for a moment," said Mrs. Mason. "Two things immediately jump out at me. Can you name one, Mrs. Crampton?"

Mrs. Crampton answered confidently. "Well, the obvious trait is the ears. Notice that his ears protrude out much further than a normal, healthy child's ears. Am I not right, Mrs. Mason?"

Mrs. Mason nodded in approval. "You can see how experience pays off, can't you now, Miss Owen?"

The young girl turned her attractive face towards Mrs. Mason, her cheeks flushed from embarrassment. "Yes, ma'am. I see your point."

"What else can we determine from what we have seen in our brief meeting with Master Koehler?" Mrs. Mason asked.

Miss Owen got up the courage to speak. "I think that, in looking under section 7, covering 'Adaptability to the Environment,' one can safely assume that his defiant attitude and offensive tone towards adults is a prominent feature of somebody whose family we need to explore more thoroughly." She said it with such conviction that Mrs. Mason couldn't help but offer a rare smile.

"Very good, Miss Owen. I see all that training with Dr. Goldsmith has not gone to waste after all. Well done! You are absolutely right. Make a note to yourself—you can have the pleasure of interviewing Master Koehler when he comes to see us this afternoon." Miss Owen glowed in the praise and jotted down her findings in her note pad. "Miss Wiggam, let us move inside now, please. You shall begin the day with any pertinent school matters, announcements, handouts, homework, whatever else you need to get out of the way. Education of our children is our number-one priority. Once this is done, please introduce us."

"Shall I tell the children what the test is about?" asked Miss Wiggam.

"No. No sense in putting pressure on them. Just tell them it is a fun exercise to see how much they know…about words, numbers, and puzzles. That will be sufficient." She and the others moved up the stairs and into the building just as the bell sounded to begin the school day.

∗   ∗   ∗

Victor Gianetti came into the classroom and took his usual seat, shoving his books into the shelf below the desk's surface. He surveyed the room to make sure his brother Jimmy had made it in on time and saw him taking his seat. Jimmy was a big kid with a tuft of wavy, jet-black hair that he was always pushing back away from his forehead. He was not a bad-looking kid, but nobody would call him handsome. Victor was not so lucky, but he was too young to really care about his small stature and the fact that his head seemed too big for his body. Both boys had the traditional Italian noses, Jimmy's a bit bigger than Victor's. Jimmy glanced over at his younger brother and smiled happily. Victor gave him a little wave and settled back in his seat.

Miss Wiggam walked in and Victor noticed immediately that she was excited about something. He didn't like his teacher, mainly because he knew she didn't like him. But he loved learning and she was the only teacher his town had; so he put up with her attitude and tried to show her the respect that a teacher deserved. The class began as usual, all the students greeting her in unison and then turning their attention towards the flag to do the Pledge of Allegiance.

Once these formalities were over, Miss Wiggam took her usual place in front of her desk and began to speak. "Class, today we will be participating in a very exciting event. But before we get to this, I want to get some things out of the way."

Gene Phillips, the boy who sat behind Victor, began to poke him in the back of the neck with his pencil. "Hey st...stup...stupid, how are you today?" he teased in a soft voice.

Victor waited until he thought Miss Wiggam wasn't looking, then turned his large head enough so that he could see Gene out of the corner of his eye. "Cut it out, you goof!" But Miss Wiggam saw him.

"Victor Gianetti! You are not going to start this day by disturb-ing the rest of the class again, are you?" She waited for him to answer, but he turned his face down in embarrassment. "Victor, when I ask you a question, I demand an answer! Are you going to disturb this class today?"

Victor looked up at her. She seemed to enjoy making him uncomfortable. He was getting nervous and that's when it flared up. He set his jaw and tried as hard as possible to prevent it; yet as soon as he attempted to answer, his handicap took over. "N...No, ma'am, I...I...I'm not gonna disturb y...you."

She stared at him angrily for another five seconds or so, but to Victor it seemed like hours. He could feel the eyes of his class-mates on him, some risking a small snicker. They loved to see him in trouble. "If I see you talking or turning in that seat again, you'll spend the rest of the day in the corner! You understand me?" she asked.

"Yes, Ma'am. I'll b...b...be good."

"Okay then."

As soon as she turned to go to the blackboard, Victor was bom-barded with spitballs and other flying objects. Everybody took full advantage of his vow of silence. Victor was used to it.

"I am going to collect your homework assignments from last night, and for tonight I want you to write a one-page essay on the Emancipation Proclamation." She wrote the two words on the board in big swooping letters. "Who knows who wrote this piece of history?"

She turned to look around the classroom. Seeing only Victor's hand in the air she repeated the question, but no one else volun-teered. Miss Wiggam caught the eye of a girl in the front row who at once began to pick at her fingernails. "Jessica, do you know?"

The girl shook her head, "No, Miss Wiggam."

Reluctantly, Miss Wiggam nodded in Victor's direction. "Go ahead."

"Abraham Lincoln," he said with pride.

"Yes," she said sharply, "that's right, Victor. Abraham Lincoln wrote the Emancipation Proclamation on January First, 1863. It called for the freeing of all the slaves in the South. You will find the information you need to write your essays between pages 127 and 134 of your history books. The essay should be a summary of the Proclamation's main points." She paused momentarily. Victor's hand was up again. "What is it now, Victor?"

Victor brought his hand down slowly, hesitating briefly before he spoke. "Well, actually, Miss Wiggam, A...Ab...Abraham—"

"Spit it out, boy!" she interrupted. "Do you have something to say or are you just disturbing my class again?"

Victor felt his blood rising. He became determined and said clearly, "Abraham Lincoln didn't write the Emancipation P...Proclamation on that date! It was earlier." There. He said it.

Miss Wiggam came down the aisle between the desks, stopping in front of Victor's. She was livid. "Don't you *ever* contradict me! That's it. Move your desk to the corner." Victor picked up his heavy desk and clumsily made his way to the corner, almost all the other kids thoroughly enjoying his suffering. His brother watched sympathetically, but said nothing. He had learned not to—not at school or at home. "You can give me three copies of your essay, Master Gianetti, since you seem to know so much."

"Sm...smart move, du...dummy!" Josh Koehler yelled from where he was sitting in the back of the room. Other kids called Victor names, joining in on the heckling. Miss Wiggam waited a bit before she regained control of her class.

"All right. That's enough! We must get on to more important business. Today we have some special guests who are going to spend some time with us. First, you will be doing some fun puzzles and then you will get to spend some time talking with these ladies."

Miss Owen, Mrs. Crampton, and Mrs. Mason entered the room and Miss Wiggam introduced them. Again the members of the class gave their greeting in unison. Mrs. Mason stepped out in front of the other two women and gave the instructions to the students. "You will each be given a quiz sheet, which has been designed by great men to test your abilities with words, numbers, and puzzles. The test is not hard, and your scores will not be part of the grade you will receive from your wonderful teacher, Miss Wiggam." She paused briefly and smiled at all the children. They smiled back. Victor's ears perked up. He loved tests. "Good luck," she said. Miss Owen went down each aisle, handing out the tests. After some brief comments from Mrs. Crampton concerning the time limit, the test began.

Victor found the test to be fairly easy. The words section covered simple questions, such as "America was discovered by...Drake, Hudson, Columbus, or Cabot" and "The pancreas is in the...abdomen, head, shoulder, or neck." One math problem asked, "If Jane spends 30 cents on lunch each day and Mary spends 25 cents on lunch each day, how much do they spend together for lunch during a five day period?" The toughest questions for Victor were those that showed a bunch of blocks—some fully exposed, some partially exposed—and he had to write down the number of the total blocks in the picture. Overall, though, he felt he did fairly well. By the end of the hour, he answered 137 of the 150 questions and he knew he got most of them right.

The interviews began after the tests were collected. Miss Wiggam called the first three students into the room, and then one at a time after that since the interviewing periods varied with each student. Jimmy went in shortly before Victor, and was already chatting with Mrs. Crampton when Victor walked in. Victor ended up with Miss Owen.

"Have a seat, Victor."

"Thank you, Miss Owen."

"I just need to ask you a few questions. Are you comfortable?"

"Yes, Ma'am." Victor was surprised. For the first time in his life, he was looking at a female and thinking she was pretty.

"So, your full name is Victor Charles Gianetti, is that correct?"

"Yes." She was jotting down what he said on a form.

"And your birthday is…?"

"October 21st, 1927."

"All right, so I have that correct." She looked up at him and smiled. "Your birthday is coming up." Victor thought that she was a very nice person. He smiled back in response. He would not stutter around her. "Now, I wanted to get some information about your family. Your parents, what are their names?"

Victor looked away for a second and then back at the beautiful Miss Owen. "I don't know that much about them."

"Oh, and why is that, Victor?"

"Well, my mom is dead, and my father…he went away when I was small."

"I'm sorry to hear about your mom," Miss Owen said sympathetically. "How did she die?"

"Some sort of sickness. I'm not really sure."

"You were little then. It's understandable that you don't remember. What about your dad? Where did he go?"

Victor hesitated a moment. "He went to jail. He got arrested for stealing stuff. And then after he got out, we never saw him. My foster parents said that he didn't want us anymore. I can tell you about them if you want, my foster parents."

"I see. I'll ask you more about your foster parents in a short while, but I think I want to find out more about your immediate family. You have a brother in school, right?"

"Yes, Ma'am. He's right over there." Victor pointed to his brother, who seemed to be quite confused by something Mrs. Crampton was asking him. Miss Owen nodded.

"Do you have any sisters, Victor?"

Victor shifted in his seat, glanced nervously across the room at his brother again then back at Miss Owen. "Wh...Why are you asking a...all th...these questions, anyway?"

Miss Owen ignored his question. "You have a stutter, Victor?"

"Ye...yes, ma'am. But only wh...when I get nervous about so...something."

She took a second to scribble a note on another page. "Why are you nervous, Victor?"

"I just don't know why you are asking these ques...questions—why are you ask...asking all these questions?"

"We're just trying to learn about the townsfolk of Wilton. Every child in all the small towns around here is getting asked the same questions you are. You don't have to be frightened. Now, where were we...oh, yes! Do you have any sisters?"

"No."

The questions went on for a while, exploring Victor's past and his family. Then they moved into other areas that Victor was not comfortable talking about. Questions about religion and sex, things that he thought about when he daydreamed. His stuttering got the best of him. He no longer thought Miss Owen was pretty. Jimmy finished first and waved to his brother. "Hey, Vic, do you want me to wait for you?"

"No, Jimmy," he answered. "You better get home or Uncle Zachary will be mad. I'll be right along. Right, Miss Owen?"

"Yes, Victor." They both waved goodbye to Jimmy, waiting until he had left the room before continuing. "Victor, I noticed something peculiar about your brother. Is he all right?"

"Yes, Ma'am. He's a might slow from gettin' hit in the head a while back."

"How long ago was that?"

"I was little then, too. I think he was eight…yeah, about eight."

"He got hit in the head? By what?"

"Not by a what, by a who. My uncle Zach. He was angry about somethin', I guess."

Miss Owen looked concerned. She wrote more things down. "Does he ever hit you, Victor…this uncle of yours? "

"Well, yes, Ma'am. He's not really my uncle. It's what we call my foster father. He hits me all the ti…time. I don't always do the right things and I g…go…gotta be punished for it."

"Yes, I suppose so," said Miss Owen sadly. "I suppose so."

They finished up with the interview and Victor headed for home. The day moved along smoothly, all the kids having been interviewed by day's end. Miss Wiggam and the other three women met briefly, long enough for Miss Wiggam to remind Mrs. Mason not to forget her earlier promise to get in touch with her about a job as a field worker. They said their good-byes and then the representatives of the HBS left. Miss Wiggam settled in on the homework assignments from the night before. She only got through three or four of the papers when she stopped to lean back in her chair. Taking off her glasses, she rubbed the bridge of her nose, then sighed deeply. She got up and went to check out what was bothering her all day. Shaking her head all the way to the bookcase, she did not want to believe that this little matter disturbed her. But it had. After pulling out her teacher's copy of *American History*, she flipped to page 127 and began scanning the information. "Emancipation Proclamation…Abraham Lincoln…waiting for a Union Army victory to issue...preliminary version issued Sept. 22, 1862...final Proclamation read on Jan 1,1863...written in July, 1862." Miss Wiggam's eyebrows narrowed. "Well!" she said out loud. "For an idiot, that kid is pretty smart."

3

October 31, 1972. Sixty-nine degrees at 8 p.m. The small town of Wilton was experiencing a few days of unusually warm weather. Laurie Grimes strolled along behind her two children, Emily, a ghost, and Paul, Emily's older brother, a magician. They were making their way along Stanley Street.

"Come on, Ma! You're walkin' too slow," Paul yelled.

"Well, then, go ahead," she said picking up her pace a bit. "I'll meet you when you come down from Mrs. Mason's house." She watched them run along and disappear into the darkness as they turned into the long, uphill driveway. Laurie listened to the gleeful voices of children echoing from other parts of the neighborhood as she walked, smiling to herself, remembering how exciting Halloween was to her when she was younger. Drawing closer to

Mrs. Mason's house, she realized that something was not right. Mrs. Mason had always made sort of a big fuss over Halloween, putting glowing pumpkins on her railing and playing funny, spooky music from inside her house. Tonight, though, the house was shrouded in darkness. She got to the bottom of the driveway just as her children came back down the hill.

"What's goin' on up there, tonight? Did Mrs. Mason scare you guys?"

"No, Mama," said Emily, looking disappointed. "Nobody home."

Laurie looked up the hill into the murkiness. She thought she could see a light coming through the long, narrow windows running along each side of Mrs. Mason's front door. Besides that, however, there seemed to be no other lights on in the house. "Come on, kids, let's go back up there for a minute. I want to see if Mrs. Mason is all right."

"Ma! I want to keep going. My bag isn't full yet," Paul whined.

"It'll only take a second, Pauly." She grabbed Emily's hand and started towards the house with Paul following reluctantly. When they got up to the house, Laurie knocked several times. No answer. She moved to the left so she could peer in through a small, oddly cut decorative window that allowed a distorted view down the long hallway leading into the living room. She could also discern the stairs off to the left. The only source of light in the house seemed to be a lamp in the living room. Nothing appeared out of the ordinary, but she knocked again, louder this time.

"See, we told you there was nobody home, Mama," said Emily sarcastically.

Laurie ignored her daughter's remark and tried the doorknob. To her surprise, the door swung open. Laurie caught her breath as a foul odor seeped out of the house.

"Yucky!" Emily yelled. "What's that smell?"

"You guys wait right here—Mommy will be right back. I just want to see if Mrs. Mason is inside here.

"This is breaking and entering," Paul said.

Laurie looked down at Paul and paused. "No, it isn't, honey. That's only when bad people go into a house to steal things. I'm going in for a good reason. Now wait here, I'll be right back." Laurie lingered for a moment. She'd seen enough movies to know that a smell like what she was experiencing might mean something horrible was waiting for her inside.

Paul and his sister watched their mother move cautiously down the hallway, tracing her fingers along the wall for support. "Mrs. Mason, are you in here?" she asked out loud. When she stepped into the living room, she turned her head to the right. Both her hands came up to her mouth. She stumbled backward out of the living room into the hallway again. She slammed into the wall. She fell to one knee, but got right back up and started running down the hall towards the kids. Emily saw the way her mom acted and started to cry. Laurie got to them in full stride and without stopping, scooped both children up in her arms. Paul saw his mom's face just before they ran into the darkness of the yard. She was crying, too. "Mommy," he asked, "did Mrs. Mason scare *you?*"

Mrs. Mason's body lay spread-eagled inside on the couch. Her nightgown had been pulled up over her head and her undergarments had been ripped from her body. One leg was draped over the top of the couch; the other hung down to the ground, the heel of her foot resting on the carpet. Her mid-section and thighs were covered in dried blood from multiple wounds in and around her vaginal area. There was also some blood up around her chest. Her nipples were roughly cut away from both breasts.

*   *   *

Roland Briggs heard the phone ringing inside his house as he walked briskly up to the front door. He was just getting back from his nightly three-mile run. Moving quickly through his kitchen and into the living room, he reached over the top of his recliner for the phone, dropped it, and then finally got it up to his ear.

"Hello...sorry...hello, I dropped the phone."

He was hoping the call was from his so-called girlfriend. He listened for her voice, but all that he heard at the other end of the line was a lot of commotion and garbled voices. "Hello!" he said again, a bit louder.

"Chief, is that you?" asked the voice at the other end.

"Who the hell do ya think it would be, Kroner?" said the chief, recognizing the voice of one of his officers. He was disappointed that it was not Meredith. "What the hell is going on over there?"

"Well, Chief, you're not going to believe this, but we got a murder!"

"Whatta ya mean we got a murder, Kroner?"

"Just what I said, Chief. There's a dead body over on Stanley Street. It's Mrs. Mason," said Kroner excitedly.

"Okay, Kroner, first of all calm down." The chief quickly got his thoughts together. If this was a murder, it would be the first one that Wilton had had in over fifteen years. "Can you calm down enough to talk to me?"

"Yes, Chief, I'm sorry. I just can't believe this."

"I understand, Kroner. Now tell me—wait a minute, who the hell is down there!"

"Just us and Laurie Grimes, the woman who found the body, her two kids, and the neighbors of the victim. They drove Mrs. Grimes down. Oh, yeah! Steve Gamble is here, too."

"Steve Gamble! What the hell is he doing there already? How'd he find out so fast?"

"He said he had been leaving his office when he saw the car these folks were driving come speedin' into town, screeching to a halt in front of the station house. He said he raced right over."

"Well, tell everybody to shut the hell up so I can hear you."

"Okay, Chief, hold on a second...hey!" he yelled, away from the phone. "Chief said for everybody to shut up so's he can hear me talkin'." There was immediate silence on Kroner's end of the line.

"You didn't have to be so literal, Kroner."

"What's that, Chief?"

"Never mind. Tell me where the murder occurred."

"Like I said, Chief, it was Mrs. Mason."

"Kroner," the chief said while fighting hard to control his frustration. Kroner was the youngest and newest member on his force. "I need the address. I didn't grow up here like you did, remember?"

"Oh, shit! Sorry. It's 242 Stanley Street."

"All right then. Now, I want you to call all the off duty-police officers...is Washburn out on patrol?"

"Yep."

"Radio him first and tell him to secure the scene. Make sure you tell him not to let anyone near the place except us. Call county forensics and tell 'em what we got and where to go; then call all the off-duty officers and have them meet me at 242...at Mrs. Mason's house. And make sure you tell Gamble not to print anything about this until I talk to him. We may need his help. Tell him that, too."

"What?"

"That we may need his help," Briggs said tensely.

"Oh! Okay, Chief. Can I come down, too?"

"No. I need you to stay there and take routine calls if we get any."

"Yes sir, Chief," Kroner said disappointedly.

The chief hung up and went to his bedroom to put on a pair of jeans and a sweatshirt. A quick look at his appearance in the mirror and he realized that he needed to do something about it. His hair was dark and short, but at the mercy of many cowlicks that, without a lot of attention from a brush, would do whatever they wanted. They seemed to have a mind of their own, intent on making the chief look as if he had slept in a headstand position all night long. He was not a very tall man, but he was stocky and naturally very strong. He looked much younger than his forty-eight years, even with all the stress he'd had in his life. He grabbed his Notre Dame football cap off the top of his dresser—his solution to his appearance problem—and a light jacket out of his front closet, then headed out the door.

As Briggs drove the three-and-a-half miles into town he passed many of the old textile mills and shoe factories which had long since been converted into condominiums and outlet stores. Wilton had seen its best years between 1820 and 1920, during the time that Massachusetts led the country in the production of textiles. Wilton's population had gone from about three thousand to close to twenty thousand over this one hundred year period, driven up mostly by the immigrant population supplying the cheap labor for the industry. During the early part of the 20th century, though, textile weaving and shoemaking factories began to move to the South to be closer to raw materials needed for production while putting themselves nearer to the expanding markets of the West. Once the Depression hit, the last remaining factories in Wilton closed down.

Now, farming and tourism were Wilton's major industries, the fall and winter its best seasons of the year. People came from everywhere to stay in the cozy country inns, browse the antique shops, and eat in homey little restaurants while they basked in the wondrous autumnal colors of New England. Briggs began to wonder how a murder would affect the twelve thousand plus residents and the tourism trade.

As Briggs passed through the center of town, he saw a group of parents and children milling about the gazebo on the far edge of the common. They were waiting for their turn on the annual "Haunted Hay Ride," an elaborate production that had become quite famous in all the New England tour books. Briggs traveled to the far end of town, where he took a right onto Route 63, which wound its way through the more wealthy section of Wilton before passing into the heart of the Berkshires. He stopped at Dave's General Store for a pack of Marlboro's and then went the last three miles to Stanley Street.

As he pulled up to number 242, he realized how difficult his situation was going to be. Several cars were already there; some were parked half on the driveway, half on the lawn, possibly destroying evidence. Other than Detective Carr, his entire force had never experienced a murder investigation; so he would have to be very careful or there would be a lot of mistakes. He parked sideways at the bottom of the driveway to prevent any other vehicle traffic onto the immediate scene, then jogged up to the house.

Some officers were already inside. The door was halfway open and Briggs could hear some of them talking. "Hey!" he yelled. "It's me, Briggs. I want you all to very cautiously, get the fuck outa the house. Come out here on the porch." As he waited, he heard other officers coming up behind him. He turned to see them starting across the lawn. "Wait! Stop!" The two men and one woman stopped instantly.

"What's the matter, Chief?" he heard one of them say.

"Don't walk all over the place! You could be destroying evidence. Get back down to the bottom of the fuckin' driveway and tell anybody else who shows up to wait for me there. Who is that, Liz or Jen?"

"It's me, Jen, Chief."

"Oh, good! Did you come in the cruiser?"

"Yeah, I'm still on duty."

"That's what I thought. I forgot to put my watch back on after my run. Listen, when you get down there, run some tape and block off the area. There's gonna be a lot of people arriving soon and I don't want anybody up here that shouldn't be." The four others who had arrived before the chief were now out on the porch. One look at their faces and the chief knew it was ugly inside. All of them looked shaken. "Is it bad?" he asked.

Thayer spoke up. "It's horrible, chief. I can't even tell ya...you gotta see for yourself."

"I'll take a look in a minute. Now, listen up. I want you all to go down the sidewalk in single file. Get your flashlights out if you have them, so you don't step on anything that is obviously impor- tant. Oh, and one other thing: did any of you touch *anything* while you were inside?"

Liz Ronan nervously raised her hand up. "Ah...yeah, Chief, I did. When I went in, I was so shocked by what was in there, I stepped back and knocked over this little table thing and put it back on its legs. I'm sorry, I didn't even realize."

The chief shook his head, a bit disappointed, but he under- stood. Twenty-five years ago Briggs had come across his first homicide. The memory of the wino's eyes, staring doll-like, vacant, just beginning to milk over, was still vivid in his mind. It was during his first year while on patrol for the Jacksonville, Florida police force. "It's all right, Liz. Just don't make any more mistakes, okay?" He smiled at her and patted her on the back as she turned to head down the hill with the others.

"Thanks, Chief," she said, taking her place in line. "As soon as I did it, I knew I had fucked up."

The chief watched them walk carefully along the path and down the driveway. "Make sure you send forensics up when they get here!" he yelled.

Although the chief could hear the muffled voices of the officers and the small group of neighbors that had begun to gather, he felt like he then had a moment to himself, and he needed it. This sort of thing was exactly why he had left the Jacksonville police force after twenty-two years, fourteen of those in homicide. He had been a brilliant detective, having one of the highest case-closing rates in the state, but it had almost killed him. He had achieved the rank of lieutenant in only eight years, and during his time on the force had twice turned down opportunities to become a captain because he wanted to stay in touch with the streets. His passion for police work had destroyed his marriage and made him a stranger to his two kids, now both young adults who refused to take his calls. The cards he sent them on their birthdays and on holidays came back unopened every year, a painful reminder of the tragedy that he had brought on them.

He'd physically succeeded in leaving that part of his life behind by coming back home to Massachusetts. Although he'd grown up in Boston, he didn't want to go back to the city. One of his old childhood friends, now a detective who had worked on the Boston Strangler case, told him about a small town in Western Massachusetts in the market for a new chief. He sent a resume, had an excellent interview with the Mayor of Wilton and the retiring chief, Scott Livingstone, and was hired on the spot.

Now, though, as he stepped into the quiet house, he knew he was about to confront a situation that would measure how well he'd dealt with the emotional side of his battle with the past. He took a deep breath and moved down the hall into the living room and began to examine the scene. Whoever had done the crime had first covered the couch with a white sheet. The couch itself was a dark brown. Briggs' first thought was that the killer had used the sheet for effect. The brown material would have hidden a lot of the gruesome bloodstains that were now clearly visible on the sheet. But he quickly got this idea out of his head, remembering that he was in Wilton, not Jacksonville. At first sight, Briggs was guessing that the killer had not planned to kill.

He moved closer to the body, making sure he didn't step on any discernible evidence, and crouched down beside it. He took his flashlight out of his jacket pocket, turned it on, and began a quick inspection of the victim's body, starting at her head. He could only see some of her hair, for the major portion of the head was covered by the old woman's night gown, which had been pushed up to cover her face. He was relieved at this, since he had never been good with the eyes. Ever since his seeing of the wino, he couldn't stand looking into dead eyes, and there had been too many pairs in his past. The fact that the eyes and face were covered by the nightgown gave him an important clue. The killer must have felt guilty for his acts. He must have covered her eyes either while he was killing her or afterward because there was blood on the bottom of the nightgown, which now rested on top of the victim's face.

Briggs fumbled around in his pockets for his notepad. He moved quickly down to the breasts, noting the jagged edges of the wounds where the nipples had once been. There was not a lot of blood in or around these lacerations. "Killer must have cut these off post mortem," he said out loud. This conclusion threw Briggs off a bit. The killer may not have been remorseful at all. Maybe he just tossed the nightgown up to get to the breasts without even thinking about guilt or shame. He jotted all this down on his pad.

Briggs took a quick scan of the right hand, noting many strands of hair entangled in the fingers that did not seem to match in color with those of the dead woman. He double-checked. "No doubt, these hairs must belong to the killer." Briggs got very close to the fingers and looked to see if there was any fibrous material under the fingernails. "Doesn't look like you got at him," he said to her. From what he could see, the nails looked clean, nothing underneath. "That's surprising. I wonder how you were able to get so much hair without catching a little bit of the bastard's scalp?" He turned his attention to the area where the major trauma had occurred. It was too bloody to tell how many wounds had been inflicted upon the woman's stomach and vaginal area, but there were at least ten, and he was pretty sure they were knife wounds. It had been a wild attack. "Probably a first-time killer," he mused. "Came in and raped the old woman, then realized afterwards that you'd have to kill her since she saw your face." Briggs quickly shook those thoughts from his head. He'd begun to violate one of his own rules: you never made assumptions unless you really had to; or unless you thought they could work in your favor. But he'd seen enough of these types of sexual killings to feel pretty confident about what he was looking at.

Nothing outstanding about the legs could be noted other than that they too were covered with a lot of blood. Briggs leaned forward. "Hum, what's this?" Some other material on the sheet looked like dirt or mud. "Looks like your killer was a dirty guy, Ma'am." Briggs leaned back and, just before he stood up, gently pushed the woman's arm with his fingertip. It moved easily. Rigor mortis had passed, so he knew she was dead for at least two days and probably over three. He stood up and looked around the room, taking in everything he could. Just to the left of his feet, the woman's torn bra and underpants lay on the ground in a pile. He was surprised how naturally things had come back to him. Not only did he seem to be handling the death scene with ease, he noticed that he was excited to be back at it again after all these years. He'd worried for nothing. This case would be easy to solve.

Most likely he's a local guy; if it had been a transient, he probably wouldn't have killed her, not worrying about getting identified. He would have most likely just beat her, or tied her up and left town. No, Briggs thought to himself, it's a simple case where somebody probably shows up here for other reasons, maybe collecting for some charity or wanting to mow her lawn, and thinks he sees an opportunity. He rapes her but then realizes that he can't leave her alive. She's seen him, maybe even knows him from town. He has to kill her. "That's probably all this is," Briggs whispered to himself.

He walked back outside. He stood on the porch and pulled the pack of Marlboro's from his pocket. He took one out, looked at it, put it between his lips and lit it. "Three years down the tubes," he said out loud to no one, then he took a deep drag off the cigarette and blew a plume of smoke back into the air as he coughed violently.

"You all right, Chief?" he heard someone ask. Briggs looked out across the yard and saw Ron Adamski, head of the county's forensic crime unit, standing there.

"Yeah, I'm okay. Not everything is going to be as easy as it used to be, I guess."

"What's that?"

"Nothing. I'm gonna have my two detectives, Carr and Palin, give you guys a hand if you don't mind. They need to learn what it is you do at a murder scene."

"That'll be fine," Ron answered. "I never thought I'd be doing one of these in your town, Chief."

"Neither did I, Ronny, neither did I. Listen, just to let you know, I noticed some strands of hair tangled in her fingers and also something other than blood on the sheet that you'll see underneath her body."

"I'll check 'em out, chief. Anything else?"

"Yeah, one of my people knocked over and then righted a little table just to the left of the entrance into the murder room. She wasn't thinking."

"Got it. We'll start then." Ron went back down to get his crew; the chief came down behind him.

A decent-sized crowd had gathered now. They must have seen all the cruiser lights. Somehow they knew there had been a murder. When the chief noticed Steve Gamble on the other side of the police line he realized immediately how they knew.

"Hey, Chief!" a man yelled from the crowd, "What's gonna happen to us? Is there any reason to believe this killer is still around here?" Other people joined in; all voicing the same sort of concerns.

"Everybody just calm down." He moved closer to the crowd. "What you should do is just be a lot more cautious for a while. Lock your doors and don't let your kids out after dark. I'll be having patrol cars coming through here every half-hour starting tonight, and don't hesitate to call if you hear or see something out of the ordinary. I need you to go back to your homes now. My officers will be coming around to talk to each of you tonight to see if you've seen anything unusual over the last week, so please get all your family together and wait for my people to arrive. They'll want to talk to your kids, too. Don't worry, we will work as quickly as possible to get this solved."

"Do you have any leads, Chief?"

The chief didn't have to look around to know who was asking that question. "It's way too early to be talking about leads, Steve. I do want to see you back at my office tonight, though, if you have the time. I'll brief you there."

"Of course I have the time."

"Good." The chief turned his attention back to the crowd. "Okay, folks, head on back now. There's nothing else here for you now."

The twenty or so people started moving away. The chief began to walk back to his officers when he remembered something and spun towards the street again. "Hey! Before you head back, take a look at each other. Does everybody recognize everybody else...that is, is there anybody amongst you that you don't know?"

The people looked around at each other and a few of them pointed to one young man whom they did not recognize. The man noticed them pointing and immediately began to walk towards the chief and his men, arms outstretched. "I just stopped because I noticed the cars. My mother-in-law lives three blocks up on Willow. I just dropped my wife off there, Chief, really."

The chief looked at Lance Adams. He and his brother Mark both worked for the police department. "Talk to him and make sure his story checks out."

Briggs' two sergeants, Pete Applebee and Larry Berson were standing next to Lance. Briggs pulled them away from the rest of the group. "Listen, you guys, I want a thorough canvas done tonight. Nobody goes off duty until everybody in this neighborhood is talked to. I think this woman has been dead for three or four days, so time is already working against us."

"What the hell do ya think happened here, Chief?" asked Berson.

"I don't know, but a few good clues are up there. We'll know more once we get all the forensic stuff back. Get to work, guys, we're losin' him as we speak."

The men moved off and began to direct the others. The chief heard a car pulling up. It was the medical examiner. The crime unit was moving spotlights up the hill behind him, and his officers were going off now to do interviews. Briggs had begun his first murder investigation in almost five years.

4

October 21, 1940. Victor saw them standing at the far end of the schoolyard. He knew it was going to happen again. The first time they did it, he wasn't ready for them and they had caught him. They had ripped his shirt from his body and taken turns slapping him on the belly. They hit so hard he could later see their hand prints on his skin. Still, Victor would have forgiven them, figuring it was just a boyhood prank. But then, while they continued to hold him down, when Victor thought it was over, one of them kicked him in the face and split open his cheek. Since then, he'd been ready for them. Whatever they tried, they only did it when his brother wasn't with him.

Today his brother had stayed home from school, recovering from another one of Uncle Zach's bad nights. Victor counted five of his tormentors. He walked slowly away from the school building, all the while keeping them in his peripheral vision. He put his books inside his jacket. It was easier to run when his hands were free. The group of boys saw him and began walking in his direction. Victor got to the edge of the woods and started running.

"There he goes!" They all started bolting after him.

Victor headed down a path that normally led in the direction of his house, but then he veered off when the trail forked.

"There he is! He went right. Come on!"

Victor put another ten yards between him and his pursuers. He watched for the place where the mountain laurel got thick and the ridge behind them sloped sharply up. It was coming. He looked over his shoulder and saw them running madly after him.

"Come back here, you little bastard! You're not going to get away!" he heard one of them yell.

"We're gonna beat the fuck outa ya today V...Vic...Victor!" another screamed sarcastically. The other boys laughed.

Victor couldn't help smiling to himself as he ran. He loved this part. He ran around a small bend where the mountain laurel loomed up on his left. He turned sharply, diving through an outer layer of leaves onto the path he had prepared for himself earlier that month. Dropping to his hands and knees, he followed the pre-cut trail through the thick, low shrubbery then bolted up to the top of the ridge. Once there, he grabbed a large dead branch from the forest floor. The would-be assailants flew by. Victor waited until they got about thirty yards further, then swung the branch he was holding against the base of a large tree. The sound of the shattering wood brought the boys to an immediate halt. They spun around in the direction of the sound. Victor waited calmly. He observed them as they spread out along the dense laurel, trying to see through to the other side. He picked up a twig and snapped it.

One of the boys stepped back to look above the tops of the upper branches. "There he is! Up on that hill." They all raised their eyes to see Victor, who was pretending to be doing a bad job hiding behind a tree.

"Get 'im!" one of them cried as they plunged into the thick mountain laurel. They tried desperately to manage their way through the twisted branches. Victor watched them struggle. He had picked this spot to put his plan into motion because the undergrowth was thicker here than anywhere else along the trail. It was almost impenetrable. He watched disdainfully while they struggled, laughing a little to himself as he looked down on them. They were idiots. He took his books out from his jacket, then turned and jogged slowly into the woods towards his house on the other side of the ridge. The sounds of the other boys yelling and swearing while they tried to untangle themselves from the mountain laurel faded behind him. Tomorrow he would prepare a new avenue of escape for the next time his brother had to stay home.

*   *   *

Victor approached his house and saw Jimmy sitting on the edge of the small stream that ran between the road and the beginning of Uncle Zach's property. He crossed the small footbridge and walked up behind his brother.

"Boo!" he screamed, but his brother didn't jump. "Hey, big brother, Halloween's coming. Aren't you scared?"

"No," Jimmy said sullenly without turning to face his brother.

Victor sat down next to him. "Let me see how bad it is."

"No, it's okay. I don't want you to see."

"Jimmy, come on. I'm your brother. Let me see what he's done to you."

Slowly, Jimmy turned his head. The entire left side of his face was swollen and discolored. There was dried blood around his nose and mouth, but his eye was the worst. Deep bruises of purple and black surrounded a nasty, yellowed eyelid. Victor winced when he saw it. "Can you open it?"

Jimmy began to cry. "No. I pulled the lid up, and when I did, Victor, I couldn't see right!"

Victor rose to his knees and faced his brother so he could take his head gently in his arms. "Don't worry, we'll get outa here soon. We're not gonna be kids forever." He felt his brother's big body convulsing in his arms as he sobbed uncontrollably. Victor softly stroked his thick hair. It was an odd sight; such a small person comforting someone who seemed almost twice his size.

"I'm scared, Victor!" He almost yelled it, unable to control the pitch of his voice. "I didn't think he was gonna stop last night. I wanted to hit him back, but I was thinkin' he'd a killed me." The last words trailed off into heavy sobbing.

Victor looked towards the house while he rocked back and forth with his brother. A warm feeling was beginning to develop inside of him. He clenched his teeth; every muscle in his body began to tighten. He slowly removed his brother's arms from around his waist, and looked at him again. Jimmy looked even worse, now that the tears were mixing with the blood. He took his jacket off and went down to the water. He hopped out onto a rock and knelt down low so he could soak the bottom of his shirt, then went back to his brother and wiped his face off. "Is he home?"

"Yeah, he's in there."

"Did you do your chores yet?"

"Most of 'em."

"You better finish them. Who knows what he'll do if you don't get them done."

Jimmy gingerly got to his feet. He put his hand to the right side of his rib cage.

"What's the matter with your side?"

"It hurts really bad here, too. After I fell down, he kicked me a lotta times right here." Jimmy pointed to the area just below and to the right of his chest. "It's hard for me to breathe, Vic."

"You'll get better." He didn't know what else to tell him. "I wish there was something I could do." Again, he looked at the house.

Jimmy saw the determined look on his brother's face. "No, Victor! Don't do anything! Look…look at me." He made a weak attempt to take a deep breath and smile. "See," he said, trying to hide his pain. "I'm fine. Please don't do anything. He'll hurt you, too."

Victor gazed at Jimmy. Jimmy was big, strong, and clumsy looking with his puffy hair and pants that were not long enough in the leg, yet he was now more concerned with Victor's safety than with his own pain. Victor relaxed a bit and smiled at his brother. "No…I won't. Don't you worry about it. I won't do anything."

Jimmy smiled. Knowing that Victor would not try to do anything to protect him from Uncle Zach made him genuinely happy. Victor couldn't help but see the irony of the situation. Normally, he assumed people would feel relieved when they found out something *would* be done about a situation like this; but the way his family lived, satisfaction was achieved only by knowing that *nothing* would be done. "Go ahead, big brother, go do the rest of your chores now."

Jimmy loved it when Victor called him big brother. He wrapped his arms around Victor, squeezing him as hard as his bruised ribs would allow, then walked off towards the barn.

Victor waited until Jimmy went inside before he headed for the house. He walked past the rusting barrels of garbage and old car parts, lawn mowers, and other assorted machinery that was scattered across the large yard. His Uncle Zach viewed himself as some sort of mechanic, so once in a while a neighbor or someone from town who didn't have enough money to go to a "real" repair shop would bring some work to him. This set-up never generated enough business, but Zach supplemented his income by working now and then at the lumberyard when it needed temporary help. Because of his excessive drinking, he could never be expected to hold a permanent job; so his wife, Aunt Bess to Jimmy and Victor, worked part-time as a cleaning lady for some of the more wealthy residents of Wilton. She did a good job and was always on time, ready to work a full day. Between all of their part-time incomes and the money they received as foster parents, they just barely made ends meet.

When Victor went inside, Aunt Bess was in the kitchen starting dinner.

"Oh, there you are!" she said harshly, as he came in through the back door. "Where you been?"

"I...I got hung up at school a little while. The teacher wanted to talk to me about my last homework assignment. She said I did a real good job." He knew she wouldn't care anyway that he was having problems with the other boys; she'd probably blame him for doing something to incite them. It was best to lie.

"Well, you gotta finish dinner. Old Mrs. McGinty's maid took sick and she wants me to fill in for her tonight and tomorrow. I gotta leave. I got everything started. Just have it ready by six— your uncle will want it on the table. Don't make him mad now, ya hear. He hasn't worked in awhile, so he don't need you causin' him pains."

"Yes, Ma'am."

The way things went Victor had become his aunt's helper, doing whatever work around the house that she wanted done, while his brother helped his uncle with the more physical chores.

Aunt Bess left the kitchen to finish getting ready. Victor walked over to the corner and got the old wooden box he used to help him reach the stovetop. He looked at the clock on the wall. It was almost five. He relaxed a bit, knowing that he would have no problem getting dinner fixed by the required time. He stirred the stew and checked to make sure that there was enough bread; then he sat at the kitchen table so he could do his English homework, his second favorite subject behind history. He heard the front door squeak open and slam shut; as usual, his aunt left without saying goodbye.

The next time he checked the clock he saw it was almost five-forty. It was getting dark, so he closed his book and flicked a switch, lighting a dirty bare bulb dangling from an electric cord above the table. He laid out all the utensils for the meal and went back to the stove. Standing on his box, he picked up the spoon to stir the stew. To his horror, he found that the stew was cold! He tilted his head down to look at the burner. There was no flame. The pilot had gone out. He scrambled down off his box and searched frantically for some matches. Once he had them, he stopped to look at the clock. Five-fifty! Maybe he had enough time. He jumped up on the box and lit the burner again. He turned the knob, setting the temperature to high. He heard the front door open and slam shut again. His Uncle was home!

Heavy footsteps banged down the hall. His uncle was a big man, with a large belly that hung over his belt line. He wore suspenders. His face was always puffy; and large, dark patches of skin underneath highlighted his gray, watery, bloodshot eyes. He was not a healthy man. He only shaved on Sunday, for church, but the rest of the week he walked around with a dirty-gray scruff that got progressively longer each day. He seemed much older than his forty-some-odd years. When he came into the room, Victor was standing on his box, stirring the stew.

His uncle stared at him, then laughed. "I still can't believe you need that fuckin' box! You ever gonna grow up, you little twerp," he said, not expecting a reply. "Why isn't dinner on the table?" He slowly rubbed his fingers along his suspenders as he spoke.

Victor didn't look at his uncle. He continued to stir the soup, trying to buy some time while he thought of something to say, but his uncle was an impatient man. He walked over to the stove and non-chalantly kicked the box out from under the boy. Victor fell into his Uncle. He tried to catch himself by holding onto his uncle's leg, but his uncle grabbed him by his shirt and lifted him off the ground with one hand. He pulled Victor's face up close to his. Victor could smell his foul breath, felt the heat of it against his skin. "I said, where is my f...fu...fuckin' supper, you little puke!"

Victor was too scared to answer. His uncle's face muscles relaxed and he smiled, revealing his rotten, yellowing teeth. "Oh," he said, "am I makin' ya fr...fr...frightened, Stutter Boy? I'm so sorry. Here, let me let you go." With that, the man slung Victor across the room. The boy crashed into the wall while still in the air, then slumped to the floor. He lay there with his eyes closed. Searing pain shot through his back. He hoped his uncle was satisfied, feared that he might not be.

"Now, why the *hell* isn't the food on the fuckin' table? It's six," he said without looking at the clock, "and I always eat at six."

Victor looked at the clock on the wall above his uncle's head. He was tempted to point out to him that it was not six, but five of. He wanted to tell him that he was a disgusting, stupid, pig of a man who couldn't even tell time; he wanted to tell him that he hoped he would drop dead from a heart attack. "The p...pi...ilot had go...go...gone out. It wasn't ho...hot enough," was all that came out though.

"Well, good, I wasn't quite ready to eat anyway," the uncle said, laughing hysterically. Creating pain and fear in Victor and his brother brought much enjoyment to Zach. He stopped laughing suddenly. "Get it done and on the table in ten minutes. I gotta get this grease off my hands."

He started to leave but then turned to look at Victor again. "Is your aunt already gone?"

"Yes, sir."

His uncle smiled sardonically and left the room. Victor picked himself up and arched his back, trying to loosen it a bit. He went back to the stove to finish dinner.

*   *   *

Jimmy came in from the barn just as Uncle Zach re-entered the kitchen. They all sat down and began eating. The only sound in the kitchen was the noises of their chewing. Zach engulfed his food. Victor watched closely, taking small bites of his own food, waiting for his uncle to get close to finishing. When Zach was on his last bite, Victor got up, went over to the stove and brought another bowl of stew to him. Victor walked back to the stove and started to scoop out another bowl. His uncle stopped eating in mid-chew and stared at him. Victor felt his eyes on him, so he turned to see if his uncle needed something else.

"What the hell do you think you're doing?" he asked Victor.

"I was go...gonna get Jimmy ano...another bowl, too."

His uncle scowled at him. His lower jaw dropped open, his mouth half full with a bite of stew, as if this shocked him. "You're *what!*" He started to slowly chew again; the gravy made his lips shine. He enjoyed making the young boy feel like an imbecile. Victor remained standing, the bowl in one hand and the ladle in the other. He didn't know what to do, for he knew that whatever he chose, his uncle would strike. He was afraid to move. Jimmy was staring into his empty bowl on the table, slowly rubbing his sore eye.

"Do you realize that your stupid brother made me lose a job yesterday? He didn't tell me that that ole' bastard Blanchard stopped by offerin' me a few days work until late. By the time I got on over to his house, he had given it to his neighbor's boy. He's lucky he had one bowl!" He looked over at Jimmy. "Go ahead, tell your idiot brother how stupid you are, Stupid."

Jimmy didn't even hesitate anymore. He'd been through this sort of humiliation too many times. He knew the sooner he did what his uncle wanted, the sooner he would lose interest in him. "Victor, I'm stupid," he said quietly.

"Speak up, boy! We all want to hear ya. Tell the whole fuckin' world! Victor, get your bony little ass down from off that box a yours and get me another beer." Victor jumped down and grabbed a beer out of the icebox and put it down in front of his uncle.

"I'm stupid," Jimmy said louder.

"Louder!"

"I'm stupid!"

"Louder! Tell your brother you're *fuckin'* stupid."

"I'm fuckin' stupid!" Jimmy yelled as loud as he could. He was leaning forward and his head was down. Victor could see that his brother's eyes were closed tight.

Without hesitation Zach slammed Jimmy in the back of the head so hard that his forehead bounced off the table. The edge of the bowl caught him in his bad eye and he winced in pain. "Don't you swear in this house! You're Aunt would kill ya if she heard ya sayin' such filth." Zach shook his head. "I'm shocked and disappointed in you, Jimmy. I try so hard to teach you boys manners," he said, taking a big swig of beer. He was unable to contain himself. He turned his head in Victor's direction and started laughing, blowing beer and spittle all over him. "God! I am a riot, aren't I, boys?"

"Yes, sir," they both said, almost together.

"Well, then, laugh along with me. Go ahead," he said. "I'm not gonna hurt ya."

Both boys did their best to make their laughs sound as real as possible. Zach pushed back from the table, rubbing his large, bloated belly, still laughing. He stood up. The boys were still laughing, looking at each other, both wondering how long they would have to continue.

"Wait! That's enough for a minute," said Zach. The boys stopped immediately. "Vi...Vict...Victor, I want you to clean this kitchen up and then get her ready and bring her up. Clean her good this time; last time she still smelled like the shit she lives in." He looked into Jimmy's battered face. "You help him in here. I don't want to wait long tonight; I'm dog-tired. Okay then...start laughing again."

He waited until the boys were howling again, took a little bow, then left the room. The boys kept it up for a minute or so, just to make sure he was gone. They fell into silence and moved the dirty dishes to the sink.

"Do you want more stew, Jimmy?"

"Naw. I ain't hungry no mores anyway."

Victor noticed that his brother was moving very slowly, still in obvious pain from last night's beating. "Go ahead up to bed and get some sleep. I can finish here."

Jimmy brought over the plate that had held the bread. "Are you sure, Vic?"

"Oh, yeah. I can get it. Go on ahead."

Jimmy shook his head to say all right and left to go up to his room. Victor finished doing the dishes as fast as he could, then headed through the dim house to the front hall where the basement door was located. He went down the stairs. Twenty minutes later, when he came back up to the first floor, he was escorting a female figure wrapped in a dirty yellow blanket. Her hair was still damp from the stand-up bath. It hung down in front of her face. She was resisting somewhat, but not so much that he couldn't get her up to the second floor. She was making strange grunting, growling, and whistling noises. Victor got her to his uncle's bedroom door and knocked. He didn't hear anything inside, so he knocked again and then opened the door. His uncle was sleeping, a pint bottle of whiskey resting on his chest. The girl in the blanket began to move away. Victor chased her down. She uttered a long, shrill, whooping sound when he grabbed her, waking his uncle.

"Victor! Is that you out there? You got your sister?"

Victor was wrestling with the girl in the hallway. "Yes, sir."

"Well, bring her in."

"I'm tr...trying, sir, she...she's fightin' hard tonight!"

"Good!" his uncle yelled. "I like it when she's like that. Get 'er in here, boy!"

The sister stopped struggling when she heard her uncle's voice. She immediately quieted down, almost catatonic. Victor looked up at her. She was about five inches taller than he was. He brushed the long black hair away from her empty eyes. Standing on his tip-toes, he kissed her on the cheek. He looked at her sadly. "See, if you'd a been quiet, I coulda gotten ya outta this tonight. Now we woke him up. You gotta go in." None of this seemed to register with her. He turned her around in the direction of his uncle's sparsely furnished room. It contained a double bed, two small dressers, and a rocking chair in the far corner. Zach smiled in anticipation.

"Take that blanket off 'er, boy." Victor took the blanket from his sister's naked body and let it fall to the ground. He tried not to look, but he couldn't help seeing his sister's large full breasts. She was a shapely girl. If one were to see her from a distance, one wouldn't be able to tell that anything was wrong with her. But when close, one saw the strange patches of scars from the tops of her hands all the way up to her elbows. She had an average-looking face, but it was bruised, and a large red welt marked the center of her forehead.

His uncle stared at her and started rubbing his crotch. Victor could see that his uncle was struggling to get his penis hard. He turned to leave but his uncle stopped him. "No! You stay. At least until I get going." His uncle was looking at her and then back at Victor. "Grab her tits," he told him.

Victor reluctantly grabbed his sister's breasts from behind. He closed his eyes and pressed his head in the small of her back. He wanted this to be over.

"Move you hands around some!"

Victor complied. For a while, the only sound in the room was the noise of his uncle's wrist, sliding back and forth along his thigh and stomach.

"Move one of your hands down," his uncle said tensely. Victor knew what he meant. He put his hand between his sister's thighs and moved it back and forth. She opened her legs a bit, out of habit.

"Give her over!"

Victor removed his hand and came out from behind his sister. He led her to the bed. His uncle was naked now, standing at the side of the bed. His large, white, fleshy gut loomed before Victor. He had to get so close that he could see some of the few sparse hairs that were growing around his uncle's belly button. His penis was purple and red and swollen. "Get the fuck outa here now. I got 'er."

He pushed Victor by his face. The boy stumbled, tripping over his uncle's pants. Victor lay there for a second, looking up at his uncle, who was positioning his sister on the bed. Leaning his sweaty head down between her legs, his uncle spit between them, smearing the saliva on her vagina with his dirty hand to make it moist. Victor left the room to go finish cleaning the kitchen. He heard his uncle grunting loudly as he walked down the stairs.

Nobody had remembered Victor's birthday.

5

November 3, 1972. Chief Briggs sat at his desk, shaking his head, disappointed at what he just read in the *Wilton Gazette*. Even after he took the time to talk to Steve Gamble about what he was going to print about the murder, good old Steve had taken several liberties. For one, his headline on the story was "Rape-Murder Jolts Wilton." The chief never told him anything about the condition of the body or anything about the possibility of a rape having preceded the killing. Briggs realized that he must have gotten that impression from one of his officers. The other thing the chief wasn't thrilled about was that Gamble had included information about the chief's past war record. "Chief Briggs, World War II Congressional Medal of Honor recipient for his heroism on the beaches of Tarawa," it read, "says he will head up the investigation himself. He is confident that this murder will be solved quickly."

He got up from his desk and headed into the officers' lounge, which had been turned into a task force room for the murder investigation. Everybody quieted down when he entered. The chief looked up, noticing the silence. "Well, What the hell are y'all so quiet for?" he demanded.

Detective Carr volunteered to be spokesman. "We didn't know you were a war hero, Chief. How come we have to find out stuff like that from Gamble?"

"Ah, come on, you guys, there's a lot you don't know about me. But today, you're gonna get the chance to find out what your old chief knows about murder investigations." Briggs took a sip from his coffee, winced a little from the heat, and continued. "All right, is everybody here...good. We got the results back from Adamski last night, but I wanted to think about everything overnight and sort some of this out before I gave it to all of you. I gotta sidetrack a minute here, folks." He slowly looked at all his people. They grew a little uncomfortable and started fidgeting. The chief was a pretty easy guy to work for, but when he wanted their attention, he got it. "I want you all to understand something right up front. *None* of you can be talking to Gamble or anybody else about this investigation. It's critical that we keep certain things to ourselves. I'll be the only one who talks to Gamble or any other reporter that comes here. Something like this happens in a little town and everybody gets interested soon. I got a call from a guy with the *Boston Globe* last night and gave him the story. If we don't catch this guy quick we'll have every jerk writer comin' from everywhere, askin' all sorts of questions."

"You think he'll strike again?" asked Officer Pete Applebee.

"I don't know for sure, but there is always the possibility that if we don't catch him, he'll think he can do it again. Anyway, let's get started. First, I want to tell you what we got back from foren-sics, and then I'll give you my feelings on who I think we should be looking for. Oh, Palin, tell us about what you and Carr got from the scene."

Detective Mark Palin stood up and cleared his throat. "Well, we couldn't find any signs of forced entry, so we figured that the vic probably knew the killer, maybe even let him in. But neighbors said that she was not a woman who was likely to lock her doors. Laurie Grimes said the door was unlocked when she found the body, so the perp might have walked right in. There were no signs of any real struggle, and the victim's bra and underwear had been ripped from her body. These items were piled together on the floor at the end of the couch, where the victim's feet were. I've put up all the photos on the bulletin board—you can see them after we're done here."

The chief interrupted. "Don't you think it's strange that the clothes were in a pile like that after being ripped from the body?"

"I don't follow you, Chief."

"In all my years of murder investigation, I've learned to take nothing for granted. Everything at that scene, everything that hap-pened on the night of the murder, that is, will tell you something about the killer. Something stood out when I looked at those undergarments lying there like that. Why don't you turn the bul-letin board around now, so we can look."

Officer Berson, closest to the bulletin board, jumped up and turned it around for all to see. The chief walked over and stood off to the side, so he could point to various photos. "See what I mean? Two things appear out of the ordinary. The first is that the clothes were piled. If you were a perp, ripping off this stuff in a rage, trying to rape an old woman, why would the clothes be piled? Why weren't they flung across the room? That would have been more consistent with this type of crime. The second thing is *where* they are piled. They're up here at the far end of the couch where her feet are, a little ways beyond the end of it. The perp would have had to lean way out and then back to drop them there. See here, in the photo?" The group looked at the picture. The chief waited until he saw some heads nodding in agreement. "There's another thing that is sort of odd, something we got back from forensics. The dirt—it was dirt that was on the sheet—was a type of fertilizer called Quick-Gro. It's only sold in large, industrial-sized bags, to farmers and landscapers they tell me."

"What's so odd about that, Chief?" asked Kroner.

Briggs realized he was getting ahead of himself. "Sorry. You're right, there's nothing odd about that. Like I said, it's where the dirt is on the sheet that doesn't seem right. See?" He pointed to the photo, showing the front part of the couch where the sheet hung down to the floor. "If the perp was going to commit rape, like the scene indicates, we should have found some traces of it on this part of the sheet, down between the vic's legs at the bottom of the couch, but there wasn't any. I asked Adamski to double-check." Briggs' two detectives, Palin and Carr, settled back down in their seats, realizing that the chief was going to run with this. He was on a roll.

"I find this strange. I would have normally thought that this was a rape turned murder, but these things don't seem right. Another thing, a decent amount of hair from the perp was found in the fingers of the victim, but nothing under her fingernails. You gotta wonder how she was able to get that much hair in her hand without scratching him. She had long fingernails." His officers were frantically writing notes, trying to get everything down.

"Whenever we found victims like this back in Jacksonville, if it wasn't a domestic squabble turned ugly, we would usually find the killer to be a young guy in his late teens or early twenties who either didn't know or barely knew the victim. Someone who just happened on what he thought was an easy target. He wasn't sure of himself, so he would pick an old lady or a young kid to do his thing to. This type of killer is usually very insecure, oftentimes a loner who didn't fit in, bitter about something that had just happened to him, like the loss of a job or being kicked out from his parent's house—a stressful event that drove him to his crimes. But there is something not right about this one. The murder scene seems too organized for this to be a first kill, my initial thought." The chief stared at the pictures for a while.

Jen Wright broke the silence.

"Chief, did you spend a lot of time studying crime scenes and killers down there in Jacksonville?"

The chief looked up, realizing that he'd been quietly standing there for a while. "Ah, yeah, I was starting to do research, in my free time. Collecting data about different killers and their methods. I wasn't just studying my cases; I was going through all the files on violent criminals and their acts of murder. I...well, let's just say I got sidetracked and then, the next thing I knew I was up here with you wonderful bunch of cops." He ended with a note of sarcasm and smiled at the group.

"What else we got, Chief?" Washburn asked.

"Not much else about the perp at this time. Only thing troubling me is I was hoping this would have been a simple murder investigation, maybe even get a confession from somebody, but there are things at this scene that make me feel that a lot of this was staged, you know, for our benefit."

"Chief, no disrespect," said Carr, a long-time cop himself, "but how do you know that it won't be an easy case? We got a lot to work with and there aren't a lot of people in this town. We'll get him."

The chief looked at his officers and saw a lot of confused faces. "Oh, I have no doubt we'll get him. I don't know, maybe I'm just getting worked up over nothing." He paused, searching for some notes on the table next to the bulletin board. "You're right, there is more. Let me run through the rest of this stuff. Let's see, what haven't I covered so far…there were thirteen knife wounds found on the body, seven to the lower abdomen, four to the upper thighs, and two that were into the vagina itself." The chief stopped and looked at the two women in the room. "Pretty brutal, I know. Death was a direct result of these injuries. It seems as though the nipples were cut off after death and were not located in or around the house, so it appears that the killer took them with him, probably as a sick reminder of his crime. The weapon used was a knife with a blade of approximately five inches. Forensics guesses that it was most likely a hunting knife. It was not found at the scene. Detective Carr, any results on fingerprints?"

"No, nothing that came up. Most every thing we found belonged to the old lady. She lived alone; her husband passed away about ten years ago, not much family to speak of. She has a daughter who lives in California. We called her with the news. She'd been a head nurse out at Wilton General Hospital but retired about six or seven years ago. There were some other fingerprints there, but most belonged to a housekeeper who came in on Tuesdays. We talked to her but she wasn't able to tell us much. Said the old lady had no enemies. We're still checking on some other fingerprints we found there. We should know in a couple days if they match any on record. It seems as though he left us nothing. There were also no footprints found around the windows or doors, but it had rained between the time of death and discovery of the murder, so we didn't expect anything."

"Canvassing only came up with one possibility?"

"Yeah, Chief. Mike found an old couple, a Mr. And Mrs. Grant that saw a man in dark colored coveralls walking along Stanley street on Thursday night, the night the coroner figures was about the time of death. They didn't get a look at his face, but did say that his hair was, Mike, how was it that they described his hair?"

Mike Thayer stopped writing and checked his notes. "They said it was sort of frizzy, that the street light behind him made him look like he had some sort of weird, see-through halo around his head."

"Whatta ya think, Chief, is that our man?" asked Mark Adams.

"Maybe. Not too many people that are gonna be walking around that area at that time of night." He tapped his pencil on the table a few times, then stood up. "Okay, so that's what we have so far. I got the green light from the mayor to hire as much overtime as needed for this. He was a bit upset, figures it's gonna have to come from the snow removal budget! Ya gotta love the guy. So, anyway, I want y'all on the case as much as possible. We'll keep up normal patrols and anybody who wants to stay on after their shift, can report to Carr or Palin for assignments. Make sure you guys talk to every farmer, farm hand, and landscaper in town. Oh, and make sure you ask everyone you interview if any of their fellow workers have been acting differently the past few days, like not eating or acting really nervous, or complaining about not being able to sleep. See if any of them have cut their hair or shaved off a beard, things like that. Oftentimes, you'll find that sort of post-crime behavior in these sorts of situations." The chief looked at his watch, then put his jacket on. "That's all, folks. I got a meeting." He got up and left the room. The officers began getting assignments.

Palin leaned over to Carr. "Do you think he's going to see her?" he whispered.

"God, I hope so. He's been a little off-balance this last week, and I don't think it's because he's worried about this case, ya know," he said and winked at Palin.

"Yeah, I know. Do you think it's somebody local?"

"Who knows," Carr replied. For some months now, both he and Palin believed that the chief was seeing somebody.

"Oh, well! And what the hell is all this crap about a staged rape? You think he's having flashbacks to the old days or some-thin'?"

"I think it's just a simple case of some guy who went crazy," Carr replied. "He gets pissed off and kills the old bag. Simple as that, ya know."

"That'd be my guess, too. We'll see, but I think he's blowing things out of proportion."

The chief left the old town hall, ducking under some scaffolding put there by the architectural firm doing repairs on the building. He walked around the corner, heading towards the wooded area at the back of the property. After cutting down a path that led to a small, unused picnic table protected from view by some over-grown shrubbery, he sat and waited. A few minutes later, he heard rustling in the woods behind him. He turned to see Meredith com-ing down the path that led from the school parking lot. He stood up and went to her, taking her hands in his.

"What the hell is going on?" he asked. "I haven't heard from you in over a week."

"I know," she answered. "It's been a little difficult. I think he suspects something."

"Oh, come on! All he does is work at that damn bank of his! How the hell could he have found out?"

Meredith released him and stepped back. The chief reached out and touched her short auburn hair; stared at her beautiful, dark, expressive eyes. "I'm sorry," he said. "I didn't mean that to sound so harsh. I just can't take not seeing you for so long."

Meredith paced back and forth, her arms crossed in front of her. "I know, I understand. You have to understand too, though. I want to see you as much as you want to see me, but it's a lot more difficult for me. Especially lately. He's been asking questions, nothing direct of course, but all of a sudden he's been a lot more interested in what I do when he's at the bank. He wants to know what my plans are. He's been calling me a couple times a day to see how I've been, whether or not I want him to pick anything up on the way home. Can you believe that? Eleven years of marriage and now he's suddenly interested in what I do. It's crazy!"

"What does that mean? You're not thinking of giving him another chance, are you? You know he's not going to change. He's a bastard and you know it!"

Meredith stopped pacing and turned to the chief. "Listen. You don't have to be so insecure about this. You know I love you. A little extra attention from him now is not gonna make me forget about all the shit that he's put me through. It's just…well, I don't know what I'll do about Jess. She's only nine years old. It's hard for me to think straight about all this stuff, ya know."

"I know," said the chief. "But you have to realize that leaving her in that environment is more detrimental than any ramifications of a divorce. She'll still be able to see him. It's not like we're gonna leave or anything. You've got your teaching job and I'm the goddamned chief of police for Christ's sake!"

"Roland, this is a small town. You don't realize how people will look at me afterwards. Everybody thinks Tim is a great guy. They haven't seen his moody side. They don't know that he has basically ignored his wife and his daughter. People look at us and we look like the perfect couple. And think about how people are gonna view you afterwards. Have you thought about that at all?"

"Fuck 'em! Fuck 'em all. What's important is that you and I are together. That's all that matters to me."

"Look! I can't help it that you…never mind." Meredith stopped talking and stared off at the shrubbery.

"Go ahead, say it. I know what you're thinking. That I fucked up my marriage and killed my wife! Right. That my kids won't talk to me. I know this; you don't have to remind me. But that's why I know that it is right for me…for us to be together. I understand who you are, what you're going through."

"I wasn't going to say anything like that. You know I wouldn't bring that up." She was standing in front of him with her arms still crossed. She looked at him. He was staring at her. She went to him and put her head on his shoulder. He squeezed her into him. "We'll be together soon. I promise. You just have to give me some more time. Please," she said and looked into his eyes.

The chief softened and nodded his head. "Yeah, okay, how could I say no to that face?" He smiled at her, kissing her neck. She pressed into his kisses, then pushed him gently away.

"Cut it out, Tiger. You're not gonna get me going out here. You know we can't do anything."

"Well, then, you better change the subject, because this place seems fine to me!"

Meredith laughed and kissed him on the forehead. "Soon enough. I think I can get away tomorrow afternoon, right after school ends. Can you meet me somewhere?"

"Of course I can. How about the old mill? We haven't been out there for a while."

"Okay," she answered coyly. "What do you plan on doing with me?"

"It's a surprise. You'll find out tomorrow."

"I can't wait." They both laughed together. "So…what's going on with that murder business? What a horrible thing to have happen here in our little town."

"Yes, it is. I don't know yet. I think we'll catch the guy soon—but to me, things aren't adding up. The more I think about it, the less comfortable I feel."

Meredith tilted her head to one side. "You don't think it was some crazed rapist?" she asked.

"No. To be honest with you, I don't. I think it was *made* to look that way. My guess is that the guy, whoever he is, knew this woman well. There is a lot more to this than what appears." Briggs sighed. "Of course, all my men think I'm crazy, or at least that's how they were looking at me as I left today."

"Do you have any proof to support what you think?"

The chief looked at her and smiled meekly. "No. Let's just call it an old ex-homicide detective's intuition."

"Oh, I see," she said, smiling back. She checked her watch. "I have to go. Lunch is about over and I have a class to teach."

"I gotta get back too. Tomorrow then?"

"The old mill. I'll be there." Meredith leaned over and gave the chief a peck on the cheek. "Love you."

"I love you, too."

6

Middle of November, 1940. Victor was surprised at how well things were going over the last week and a half. Both his foster parents were being very nice to him and his brother. They'd even let Felicia up from the basement to go out into the yard and get some sun. Victor liked seeing the color come back into his sister's cheeks. Today held the biggest surprise of all. Uncle Zach had announced that they would be going on a trip. He didn't say where they were going; but as far as Victor was concerned, anywhere would be a nice.

The day's events were planned out. Victor was told to go to the basement and clean his sister's cage. He washed away all the feces that had built up over the last few days. He had to do it twice. The first time, Uncle Zach told him it wasn't clean enough, but didn't hit or make fun of him. He even smiled at the boy. Once he'd finished in the basement, he then was told to bathe his sister. To his surprise, he was allowed to wash her in the tub upstairs. He had never done this before. His aunt always made him do it in the basement with a rag and a bucket of water. As far as Victor knew, this was the first real bath his sister ever had in a tub. She fought and scratched and kicked, scared and confused by what was happening to her, but they got through it. By the time he was finished putting the girl into one of his aunt's old dresses, she looked fairly cute. Almost normal.

He brought her downstairs and sat her in the kitchen with his aunt, then went back upstairs to pack a few outfits for himself and his brother. He put the clothes and a few of his books in an old satchel before returning to the kitchen. To his surprise, his aunt was attempting to fix Felicia's hair.

"I've already done that, Ma'am."

"I know. I wanted to give it a woman's touch."

Victor looked around the kitchen. "I don't see your bags, Ma'am. Do you want me to go up and pack your things?"

His aunt paused, resting her hands on the girl's head. "No, that's all right. Your uncle will do it when him and your brother come in from chores." The girl began to wiggle her hand back and forth in front of her face. "Sit still, child."

"She does that when she gets nervous."

His aunt frowned. "Make her stop. She's goin' to mess her hair."

Victor walked over, bent down, and gently took the wiggling hand in his, then put his face very close to his sister's. "Look at me, Sweetie. Look at your brother, now," he said softly. "You have to set still so aunt Bess can finish doing you hair. She's making you look nice and pretty."

The girl stopped fidgeting and looked into her brother's eyes for a moment. She stared at him as if she didn't recognize him, then smiled faintly. She leaned close to him and rested her cheek against his.

"That's it, Sweetie. Put your hands in your lap now." He guided his sister's hands into her lap.

Aunt Bess pursed her lips. "You think that child understands what you say to her?"

"Yes, Ma'am. You have to get real close though. Get her attention away from other things. I don't think she picks up on all the words, but she seems to understand what you want her to do if you can sort of show her."

"Well...I think it's a waste of time."

"Yes, Ma'am. But, she's my sister, and I gotta try. She looks very good. You did well by her."

Aunt Bess studied the girl. "It's the best I could do."

The back door swung open and Jimmy walked in. "Whowee! Look at her. Ain't she a sight." He moved over to the girl and went to put his hand on her head.

"Don't touch her! I just done her hair up."

"Sorry, Auntie." He turned to his bother. "I didn't know."

"It's all right. I got all our stuff packed."

The front door opened and the boys heard their uncle talking. They looked at their aunt, who turned her eyes away. Jimmy moved to a spot in the kitchen where he could look into the living room and see who it was his uncle was talking to.

"Who is it?"

"I don't know. There's a lot a folks in there." Jimmy stared for a minute, then turned back to his bother. "I think one of them is that woman who came to the school. And a few men are with her." He looked down the hall for a few more seconds. "Yeah, it's her. That big one who didn't talk much 'cept for at the beginning."

Victor left his sister's side and moved to the other end of the kitchen. The woman who had been in charge of the test they'd been given back in September was with four men. One of them, a tall, distinguished-looking man with a gray beard and thick glasses, was talking in a low voice to their uncle. The two men turned and looked at the boys.

"What do ya think they want?" asked Jimmy.

"Heck if I know."

The man said something to the three other men who'd come with him. They all started walking down the hall. The boys moved back to stand next to their sister as the men entered the kitchen. The distinguished-looking man came forward.

"Hello. My name is Dr. Rhodes." He moved between the boys and knelt down in front of the girl. He reached out to put his hand on her cheek. The girl flinched and in one quick motion leaned forward to bite the doctor's hand. He pulled away and smiled. "She is a feisty one, isn't she?" He stood and turned to the others. "Okay, let's take them and get going. I have a meeting to get to."

Victor looked over at his aunt. "Aunt Bess, wha...what's happening?" His aunt didn't answer. Instead, she pushed her way past him and left the room. "Aunt Bess! Wa...wait. Who...who are th...these men?" His voice was shaking.

One of the men came over and took him roughly by the arm. "Come on, boy. Time to go."

Jimmy took a step towards his brother, but the two other men moved in front of him. The bigger of the two sneered at him. "What you gonna do, boy?"

From the doorway, Uncle Zach's voice boomed. "Hey! You boys listen up. You ain't gonna be livin' here with us no more. Now don't be startin' no trouble for these good people, ya hear me." He stared menacingly at them. "You HEAR me!"

"Yes, sir," they both said.

The doctor said, "Very good, then. Let's go. Get your bag there, and why don't you help out these fellows and escort your sister to the wagon outside."

*   *   *

A half-hour later, they pulled off the main road onto what appeared to be a long driveway. They passed underneath a large stone archway. Victor looked out the window just in time to read the first two words on an ivy-covered sign: Wilton School.

The doctor looked through the wire mesh separating his seat from the boys. "Don't worry. You'll like it here," he said.

Victor continued to gaze out the window while the road began to wind up a hill. He could see the tops of large buildings looming up out of the trees. Well-manicured shrubs lined the drive. He saw a playground off in the distance. Where was he being taken?

They came to the top of the hill and the road bent around to the left, leading to what seemed to be a small village of many Victorian buildings of different sizes. The wagon passed several of these buildings before stopping in front of the largest, three stories high. An expansive set of steps led to a very wide deck. Two immense wooden doors allowed access to the inside.

The doctor, the nurse, and the men got out of the wagon. One man with a round face and soft features opened a door to let the children out. Of the three, he seemed to be the kindest.

"Where do you want them?" he asked.

The doctor turned to the nurse who hadn't said a word the entire trip. "Where to, Mrs. Mason?"

The woman pulled a notebook out of her bag and flipped it open. She ran her finger down the page until she found what she wanted. "The big one there goes to C building, the little one to L, and the girl will go to A building. Let the nurse on duty know they are here and that Dr. Rhodes will be over to do the admissions physicals right after his meeting." She turned to the doctor for confirmation. He nodded. "Very well then."

Mrs. Mason and the doctor moved up the stairs and disappeared into the building. One of the men, the one who had opened the back door of the wagon, spoke first. "I'll take the girl to A. I'm doing overtime there tonight."

The one who'd grabbed Victor at the house spoke next. He leered at the man and smiled. His eyes were fierce and black and his teeth were crooked. "I bet you are, Ray." He looked around to make sure there were no others around. "But I seen her titties, too, and I ain't no fool. You gonna be grabbin' at that shit all the way to A."

"McMann, you're a pig. I don't get my jollies grabbin' some stupid girl's boobies."

"Right, whatever you say, Ray-boy. You gonna take 'er down the back way, down the trail, ain't ya?"

"Yeah," Ray answered defensively. "How else? It's the shortest way to A."

"All I's sayin' is that I know when you get that thing in the woods, alone, you ain't gonna be able to resist those things. It's human nature."

Ray looked at McMann in disgust. "It ain't worth arguin' with ya. You are the pig everyone says you are."

"Yeah, whatever you say, Ray. Go along now, and don't git your dress dirty."

"Fuck you, McMann." The man took the girl by the arm. Because she'd become used to being led around, she went without fighting.

The man who had not yet spoken moved over to the older boy's side. "I'm gonna take him to C. I'm off as soon as I can get done, and my car is out in the big lot. What you doin' later?"

"I'm on all night, Bobby. I'll be rollin' in the dough next pay-day, I'll tell ya."

"Good. I'll help ya spend it."

"The hell you will, Boy Lover!"

"Fuck you, McMann. Everyone knows you was out fuckin' that dog that was wanderin' around the grounds last week. I ain't seen him since. That little dick 'a yours couldn't even please a...what was it, a beagle!"

"Very funny. Your right about that, I did try to fuck that dog. But I was too tired from havin' fucked your wife earlier in the day!"

"Get the fuck outa here. Even the mailman won't give her the time a day, and he'll fuck anything!"

"Oh, you are good, Bobby, you are good. Listen, you better run along. Looks like your boy pissed his pants!"

Bobby glanced at Jimmy's crotch. It was soaked. "Oh, man! Why'd ya go and do that for, son? Now I'm gonna have to clean you up before I leave." He moved to slap the boy, but thought better of it out in the open.

"Don't worry 'bout it. They ain't gonna notice if ya shuffle him in quick," said McMann.

"Yeah, you're right. I better get goin' then. I'll see you around." He reached over and grabbed the older boy by the back of the neck. "Come on, Pissy-Boy. Time for you to go to your new home."

Jimmy tried to resist. But the man shoved him on ahead. "Don't be temptin' me to beat you, boy."

"I don't want to leave my brother! Can't I stay with him?" Tears ran down his cheeks. "What's happening to us?" Victor meanwhile, stood in silence, looking at the ground. He was too small and weak to do anything about what was happening He was powerless.

"Awh, look at the big sissy-boy," McMann said. "Ain't that sweet, cryin' out to his puny little brother to explain things. Don't you want to help your brother, little man?"

Victor looked up into the man's uncaring face, then over at his brother. "Just g-g-g-go with them, we ca-ca-can't do anything about it. I'll se-se-see you later. I promise."

"Yeah, he'll see-see-see you later," McMann mimicked. He grabbed the boy by the arm and spun him around. "Walk. We're goin' over to that first building over there."

They walked back along the road they had come in on. Victor could hear his brother screaming for him, but refused to turn around. He knew it was useless.

"There's a couple ways you can be here, boy. Our way and the wrong way. You keep your stutterin' mouth shut and you'll get by all right. Step outta line and there will be hell to pay, ya hear." It was a statement, not a question.

Victor knew better than to answer. He just kept silent and nodded his head. They arrived at the last building along the arching road, the first they'd passed on the way in. It looked very much like the building Mrs. Mason and the doctor had entered, only smaller. As they approached, a woman came out and moved down the steps. She was very stout, and as she walked her legs rubbed together making a strange, swishing noise. Her nose was long and thin and her eyes were set very close together.

"Who's this?" she asked.

"New admission, Ma'am," answered McMann.

"You can't put him in here now. They're all out in the fields."

McMann rubbed his head. "What should I do with him?"

The woman stood and thought for a minute. "Is Dr. Rhodes doing the physical?"

"Yes, Ma'am, I think he is."

"I'm going to a meeting now with him in admin. Put the boy in...B. Martha's working over there today. Tell her that there's no one who can take him now and that I'll owe her one. I'll let the doctor know where he is."

"Yes, Ma'am."

She walked on towards the administration building while McMann and Victor crossed the large common to B building. They climbed the stairs and stepped through the doors.

"You'll like it here, Boy. You'll get to see how the other half lives." McMann laughed to himself.

A scream ripped down the hallway from somewhere within. Then came the sound of hysterical laughter. The boy slowed his pace. The hall entrance was very wide. On the walls were pictures of circus clowns and one of a smiling giraffe. The floors were highly polished. McMann and Victor moved toward a massive, metal, lime-green door. The paint was starting to peel in spots. The boy stood by as McMann pulled a large ring of keys from his pocket, chose one, and inserted it into the keyhole. A well-oiled bolt slid to the side. He pushed the door open and moved aside so the boy could enter first. Air rife with stench raced to fill the boy's lungs. Smells of human excrement mingled with some sort of strong antiseptic disinfectant. Victor caught his breath. He tried to step back, but McMann urged him forward with a shove from behind.

Before Victor was a sight he would never forget. It was a large room, devoid of any furniture except for a few wooden chairs and benches. At the far end were six windows covered by heavy wire mesh. The light from the sun poured in and yet the room seemed somehow dark. He heard strange sounds. Lying on the floor balled up or crouched on chairs, climbing up and down off the benches were other human beings. Some raced back and forth, seemingly tying to get somewhere, anywhere else.

Near Victor, on the ground, was another boy, a bit older than he was. He wore muffs on his hands. He banged his head slowly against the wall, stopping only long enough to chew briefly at the strings that prevented him from removing the muffs. His face was black and blue, from an assortment of bruises. A large young man in a flimsy nightshirt sat with his legs askew. He had a hideously ridiculous look on his face. There was an emaciated person whose age could not be guessed crying quietly in a corner. He rocked gently back and forth. Still others, many others, did nothing at all. They seemed to have accepted their fate and sat in silence, offering only an occasional, untamed shaking of the hands or a wild arching of the head and neck.

Victor began to cry. He tried to turn and run. McMann grabbed him by the shirt.

"What's the matter, little man? Not happy with your new playmates?"

"Le…Le…Let me go! I don't wa…want to be here."

McMann laughed. "Boy, if they wanted your opinion on this, they'd a beat it outta ya. Don't worry, you'll get used to it. Come on, I'll introduce you."

They moved to a small side room. A fleshy woman with swelling cheeks sat behind a desk. She did not look up from her magazine. "Get the hell outta here," she moaned.

"Martha, it's me, Darren."

The woman raised her sleepy eyes. "Oh, hey."

"Miss Becky told me to tell you she needs this one to stay with you until they get done with their meeting. There's no one in L right now. They're in the fields."

The woman sat back and sighed dramatically.

"She said she will owe you one."

"You bet she will. Let him out there on a bench." She turned her eyes on the boy. "Don't cause no trouble. Remember, you're a guest here." She returned to her magazine.

McMann looked down at the boy. "You heard her. Get out and sit quietly on the bench. Oh, and give me your clothes. Martha here will get you some state issue in a minute." Victor did not move. "Goddamn it, take off your fuckin' clothes." McMann's fierce eyes narrowed. "Do what I tell ya. Now!"

Slowly the boy began to unbutton his shirt. It wasn't fast enough for McMann. He reached down and pulled the buttons open, then yanked the boy's pants and underwear off. Victor stood there, shivering. He moved his hands to cover his genitals.

"There, that's better. Now you're ready for the doc. Go out and sit on a bench or a chair or something."

Victor turned and left the room. He stood in the hall, not knowing where to go. Confused. Scared to death. McMann mumbled a goodbye to Martha and came out, too. "Go ahead. Get over there."

The boy moved mechanically to the bench. He heard the sounds of the lime-green door open and slam shut. He heard the spring-loaded bolt slide into place, locking him within. Another 'student' crouched on the bench next to him; a puddle of brown fluid was forming around his feet, seeping from his nightshirt.

Victor began to shake uncontrollably. He tried to wipe away the tears that streamed down his cheeks, but they kept coming. He lay on the bench and huddled inside himself, waiting anxiously for his nightmare to end.

7

November 5, 1972. It was early Sunday morning. Detective Carr and Detective Palin walked into the chief's office. The chief was sitting behind his desk, anxiously waiting to hear what they'd come up with. "So what have you guys got?"

"Well, Chief, not as much as we had hoped for," said Carr. "We talked to all the neighbors. Teddy Wilson, Mason's neighbor at 244 Stanley Street, said he thought he heard something odd that Thursday night. Said he was reading in his living room. He had his windows open because of the warm night and he was sure he heard one distinct scream. He said he listened further, but heard nothing else. When he mentioned it to his old lady she told him he was crazy, so he let it go."

"Did he remember about what time it was when he heard this scream?"

"No. Said he hadn't paid attention to the time."

"That doesn't help us at all. Anything else? What about the older couple who saw the man on the side of the road?"

"Oh! You mean the 'Bushy-haired' man," Palin exclaimed. "Yeah. They saw this guy, said he was walking along with his head down, wearing some type of coveralls. Average height and build. Funny thing was they said he had this bushy hair that appeared glowing because of the street light behind him. They slowed down a bit when they saw him 'cause they said they're not used to seeing people walking around that area at ten o'clock on a work night."

"Where were they coming from?"

"Bingo. Chief, do you mind if we sit down?"

The chief shook his head. "God, I'm sorry, guys. Of course." Carr and Palin smiled at each other and sat in the two chairs on the opposite side of the chief's desk.

"What's the matter with you, Roland?" asked Carr, the only one of the chief's men who ever called him by his first name.

"I don't know. Lots on my mind, I guess. Between this murder and...a few other things, I'm just a bit preoccupied, that's all." He couldn't tell them that Meredith had again broken their date the night before. "What else have you got?"

"We thought we had something yesterday," answered Palin. "That Quick-Gro is a new product. Only 14 people have bought it on account down at Harold's Hardware, which is the only place in town that sells it. We stopped by this farm, talked to the owner, ya know. He was one of the guys who'd bought the stuff. We cleared him pretty quick as a suspect, but then we asked him about his employees, you know, like you suggested. We asked if any had been acting differently over the last week or so, and sure enough we got a hit. Guy says that this kid, Arnie Branston, called in sick on the 30th and the 31st, and when he shows back to work, he's sporting this five-day beard."

"Yeah, so what happened?" pushed the chief.

Carr picked up the story. "We go over to talk to the kid. He's working yesterday, Saturday, to make up for one of his sick days, but when we call him, the kid starts running away, then he stops and puts his hands up! He walks over to us and says he did it. He couldn't help it. He wanted us to know that he was gonna come in and confess on Monday anyway."

"What was the kid really confessing to?"

"Turns out his girlfriend dumped him on Friday, the 27th. He was pretty sure she was seeing another guy, even though she said she wasn't; so he decided to follow her on Saturday night. He was right. When the girl and this other boy went into the movies together, he ran over to the guy's car and smashed the windshield. That's what he thought we were there about!"

The chief laughed. "Did you bust him?"

"Naw. We took down the name of the kid whose windshield he broke and told him that we'd check to see if he paid the kid. We gave him until next Monday."

"That's everything, huh?"

"Yeah, Chief, pretty much," said Carr. "We do have one other guy, a house painter who was spouting off at his bar a few weeks ago about how he despised Mrs. Mason because she stiffed him on some money she owed him, but both Palin and I feel that there's nothing there. Guy's never done anything wrong, no record, been married for 18 years, two kids, no real money problems to speak of. We think it was just the liquor talking. His wife says he was home with her all night, anyway."

"Shit!" The chief backed away from his desk and walked over to the window. He stared at the scaffolding that blocked his view. "I knew this case was gonna be different."

Carr spoke up, voicing what he and Palin had talked about several times over the last few days. "Chief, you keep saying that, but I gotta tell ya, we don't see why you feel this way. Some idiot went up to her house that Thursday night, saw an opportunity to get his jollies raping and then cutting up an old lady. We just haven't caught him yet, that's all."

The chief turned back towards them and leaned against the windowsill. "Then why didn't we find any semen, and no damage or tearing at all in the vagina, other than the knife wounds?"

"No semen!" Palin let out a low whistle. "So she wasn't raped after all."

"No, she wasn't. Adamski called me last night with the news. But that's not what gets to me. I've seen many murders where young, half-crazed punks try to rape but can't get it up during the heat of the crime. What usually happens is they get crazy and kill whomever it is they're attacking out of anger and rage, maybe even embarrassment. That first night I was feeling that the Mason murder was this type of crime. What does get to me is that nothing has turned up at all since that night. Not one single solid lead to go on. If it really did go down this way, we should have gotten a lot more back. These types of killers are not that careful, guys. I'm telling you, something is rotten about this whole deal."

They sat in silence for a moment. "Chief," said Carr, "I know you worked in the big city, and I know you've had a lot of experience with this sort of violence, but don't you think that that experience may be coloring your judgment a bit now. This is *Wilton*, Massachusetts, not Jacksonville, Florida. I think we'll see a break in the case soon. Whoever did this is probably holding up somewhere, scared to death. Sooner or later he's gonna come out. He has to."

"There is another possibility," said Palin. "There may be a very good reason that we haven't gotten anything since we found the body. None of us have mentioned it since that night, but we may have to face the fact that this was done by some transient. If the guy left town right after, that would explain why nothing's come up. This crime might not get solved, guys."

"That could be," said the chief, "but then, where does that leave us on the crime scene? How many transients do you guys know that don't leave any fingerprints? No signs of any major struggle? And that neat little pile of her underwear bothers me beyond words. When I run the murder over in my head, I just don't see some frustrated rapist leaning way out, off the body, to pile the clothes up at the far end of the couch like that."

The chief walked back over to his desk and took a seat. "So what are you working now?"

"We got Kroner and Thayer out doing follow-up interviews with all the neighbors again, and I sent Applebee down to talk to the daughter, who's in town now. I don't know what we can expect from her, but we haven't met a lot of people who really knew Mason well. Seems like lots of people liked her, but most considered her an acquaintance, not a friend. I guess she didn't get close to too many people."

"All right then. I gotta see the mayor this afternoon. Tell him the news. He's gonna be upset. The last two days he's giving me the 'We can't have an unsolved murder during an election year,' lecture."

"Are you gonna let Steve Gamble know that there was no rape?" asked Carr.

The Chief thought for a moment. "No...I don't think we will. Let's keep that between the three of us. I don't even want the officers knowing. The whole town is buzzing about it; let's see if we can't use it to our advantage later."

"Sounds good," said Palin.

*   *   *

The chief walked outside. The Indian Summer blew out of town the night before and the temperature had dropped substantially. The sky was overcast and most of the hardwoods had lost their leaves. The bleakness of winter was beginning to set in. The chief shoved his hands into his jacket pockets, walked quickly to his Bronco, started it up, and headed over to the old mill. He was meeting Meredith. As he drove the few miles out of town, he recognized his frustrations. Not just the case, but his attempts at getting Meredith to leave Tim seemed to be met with more and more resistance these days. He began to wonder if he was being played for a fool. Right from the start, he thought his getting involved with her was a bad idea, but she seemed so willing to be with him, so wanting to be out of her relationship. Lately, however, she was breaking their dates more often, if he could even call them dates. More like little meetings, he thought.

He was also fighting his urge to get more involved with the case. He had no faith in his men when it came to investigating a murder. But he knew that he'd come up to Wilton to get away from working the big cases. They'd destroyed his life once. He became obsessive when he worked the cases. Driven to catch the killer, like a starving hunter looking for his dinner. He itched to get involved. His first warning sign that he was not ready was the cigarettes. He immediately bought the cigarettes that first night, just like the old days. Chain smoking, sucking down ten to fifteen cups of coffee a day, and chasing killers. All the while ignoring his family. Abusing his wife. Why had he always taken it out on her? Why'd she put up with it? He forced himself to stop thinking about it. He couldn't allow himself the self-pity. He knew he didn't have a right to it. He pulled onto the dirt road that led out to the mill. Meredith was there waiting for him, smiling as he pulled in, as if everything was just fine. Briggs didn't think so. It's fine for her, he thought. She's gettin' it from two guys whenever she wants, playing both of us like idiots. He felt like he needed to end it; but as he got out of his car, she ran to him.

Her mouth was warm and inviting. She kissed him passionately. He held back, but only momentarily; then he wrapped his arms around her, taking her completely into his body. It was cold out but they didn't notice. She stopped kissing him, pushed him away, and moved quickly to the warm hood of her car. She stood there for a moment to undo her long dress, then let it drop to the ground around her feet. Briggs began to move towards her. She slid herself up onto the hood, allowing her legs to open slightly. She leaned back and gently sucked her index finger, hanging her head alluringly. Briggs slid between her thighs. They hadn't said a word to each other. She pulled at his belt, slid her hand in his pants and took hold. She pushed his pants down to his knees and moved forward, allowing him access to her. He entered her and they began to make love: wildly, passionately. For the moment, Briggs forgot about his bitterness, allowing himself to be lost in her perfume. He buried his head in her neck, his face into her breasts. He fed on her nipples.

She stopped moving and turned her head quickly to look at the tree line. Briggs stopped too. "Did you hear something?" she hissed.

"Where? What did you hear?"

"Right over there, where the edge of the old mill building meets the tree line."

Briggs scanned the tree line, but saw nothing. "Are you sure, or are you just being paranoid?"

"I'm not being paranoid!" she responded indignantly. "I definitely heard something, like somebody moving in the woods. Somebody stepping on some dead branches."

"Who would be out here?"

"I don't know, but I heard something over there."

"Well, if you did, we'd see whoever it was. There's hardly a leaf left on the trees. It was nothing." Briggs smiled at her. "Come on, let's get back to what we were doing." He tried to move back between her legs, but she pushed him away. She jumped off the hood and began to get dressed.

"No. I can't now. I know somebody was over there. Whoever it was must have ducked behind the building and took off through the woods. You should have checked it out right away."

"Meredith, who the hell is gonna be out here? We've never seen anybody out here before."

"I don't care. I know there was somebody over there. Probably...never mind."

"Yeah," Briggs said. "Probably somebody your husband hired, right? Goddamn it! I'm so sick of this hiding out and sneaking around. This is it. It's fucking over between us. Let's face it, you're not gonna leave the bastard."

"I am! You just don't understand. I can't...it will kill him. I know he still loves me, he just doesn't know how to act. You know he's had a rough life. He doesn't know how to show his feelings. I can't just hurt him like that. I have to do it my way, which means it's going to take some time. Why can't you understand that, Roland? You know I love you. Why can't you give me the time I need to do this my way?"

I *know* you love me! And how would I know that? I'm just a fucking diversion to you, something to break the monotony of your crappy fuckin' marriage. So fuck you! I'm through with this bullshit. Tell me right now that you're going to go home and tell him that you're leaving him or it's over between us."

Meredith dropped her head. She stared at the ground and began to cry. Briggs waited, not allowing the tears to sway him as they had in the past. He wanted to hug her, to tell her he didn't mean it, but he couldn't. He'd resolved to do this, to be firm this time. She continued to cry.

"Well?"

Meredith didn't look up. "Why can't you understand?" Her hands went to her face. She shook her head, but said nothing else.

"Fuck this!" Briggs turned and quickly walked back to his Bronco. He looked back at her once more, but she didn't move or raise her head to look in his direction. He jumped behind the wheel, slammed the door, started up his vehicle, and spun it around, throwing a cloud of dirt up into the air. As he looked back in his rear-view mirror, he caught a glimpse of Meredith still leaning against her car before she disappeared behind the cloud of dust.

8

Early Spring, 1941. It had been a long winter, but finally spring had come to the school up in the hills of Wilton, to the rolling countryside of Massachusetts. The winter snows had mostly melted away, some dusty snow still lingering in the corners of buildings and other areas that did not catch the rays of the warming sun. The large maple trees that dominated the grounds of the school were just beginning to show off their buds. The rich soil mixed its fresh, earthy scent with the cool breezes that danced and twisted their way across the campus and across the fields below, the fields where Victor now worked.

When Victor got to the school, the teachers determined that he would not benefit from "classes" that were offered. They were not going to challenge him. Normally, graduation was achieved in one of two ways: one could pass sixth grade or one could turn sixteen, whichever came first. Victor was graduated before he ever started. After the students graduated, the females worked in the kitchens, helped with housekeeping, or sewed. The males worked on the more manual aspects of housekeeping, took care of livestock, or worked the farms. Victor was at least two years younger than any of the other "Best Boys," a title given to those who lived in L building. He and twenty-seven others branded with this title worked in the fields, coming down from the "Hill" in a large mulling group when the early morning sun was burning away the last of the ground fog hanging lazily over the newly tilled earth.

It took Victor only a day to realize that he was in a place filled with strange kids and adults. This was not a real school. After a few weeks, he grew used to falling asleep to the sounds of human beings wailing in the night. Their moans and sighs would drift ghostly through the dark, bouncing gently off the walls of buildings, filling Victor's thoughts with sorrow and fear...and a new feeling: Something he was not yet able to identify, a feeling like anger, but stronger.

It had been about six months since Victor's arrival. So far, McMann's comment about his not seeing his brother and sister again was true. No mingling occurred between people living in the different buildings. Victor thought, on a few different occasions, that he'd seen his brother off in the distance, but he could never be sure.

He hoped that maybe he would be allowed to see his family at Christmas, a celebrated holiday at the school. A tree stood decorated in every building and a wreath was placed on every door that led into the dormitories. But even then, Victor saw only the other residents of his building; it was difficult making friends with any of them. Most where older and Victor did not trust anybody. Many had peculiarities that intimidated him. Two fat brothers, in particular, who looked like twins, had chubby red faces and talked in a language only they seemed to understand. They liked to chase Victor around the dorm at night after the attendants fell asleep; when they caught him, they would make him touch their genitals, give them hand jobs, and once in a while blow them. He hated them. The first few times he yelled for help, but that only brought on beatings from the attendants for waking them up. He couldn't win.

Today, things were going to be different. Victor had decided to set his plan into motion. He would sneak away, up through the woods that separated the fields from the school grounds, and find a way to see his brother. He remembered that the nurse had said his brother would be sent to C building, which stood at the edge of the woods at the top of the hill—the one the Best Boys walked down each day to get to the farm.

He studied the building closely each time they walked past it. It had several doors. Victor hoped that one would be open, so he could sneak in without being noticed, find his brother, and see if he was okay. If things went well, he figured he could sneak back by the time lunch break was over and no one would be the wiser. Victor knew how it worked now. The people who caused a lot of trouble received a lot of vicious attention from the staff. The dorms were always short of staff. Usually only one or two attendants worked at each building per shift; so if you were quiet, did the things you were expected to do, they left you alone.

Four men came down daily with their crew to watch over the Best Boys as they worked the fields, but Victor had watched them, too. He got to know how the attendants behaved. They paid little attention to the Best Boys, since no one ever tried to escape. Where were they going to go? Victor overheard a story about one man who left the grounds to go to the fair in Wilton. He came back on his own at the end of the night, but he had to wear a chicken suit and was fed corn and water for two weeks. The man telling the story found it tremendously amusing. Victor found it horrifying. It had made him think more than once about maybe not going through with his plan, but his concern for his brother was too strong. He needed to take the risk. That morning, Victor grabbed a hoe and jogged to the farthest row to work—the row closest to the edge of the tree line. As the morning drew to a close, Victor kept his eye on the attendants. Finally one of the four got up from the crate he'd been sitting on and moved over to the lunch bell. Victor dove into the trees just before the first clang of the bell.

He waited.

No one had noticed his actions. He crawled along on his belly for ten or fifteen yards, moving deeper into the woods. He reached a stand of squatty pine trees. He weaseled his way through them and then stood up, brushing the dirt from his clothes. His heart was pounding. He peered back at the group between branches. They were going through the chow line; some had moved off to various spots to eat. He'd done it! He turned and made the climb up the sweeping hillside then skirted along the top of the ridge until he found himself behind C building. His crotch ached. He'd had an operation right after the New Year. Before the operation, the doctor told him that he had an infection; the doctor asked Victor if he wanted to get better, even though Victor felt fine. He said yes, of course, and the next day he found himself waking up in the infirmary, recovering from surgery.

The first part of Victor's plan had gone well. Now he could only hope that one of the doors that led into C building was open. He crept up to the first door, the one most hidden from the view of anyone who might be walking by. He tried to turn the knob but it wouldn't move. He slid along the rear wall of the building, his face brushing against the ivy that covered most of it. He moved quietly to the corner. He stuck his head out first, checking to see if anyone else was around. Finding the area clear, he bolted to the side door, only to discover that it, too, was locked. He ran back around past the first door that he'd checked to the other corner, stopping long enough to catch his breath. As he stood there, he heard yelling in the distance. He wondered for a moment where it was coming from before he realized that the voices were drifting up through the woods. They must have discovered that he was missing.

"Shit!" Victor yelled, loud enough even to surprise himself. He could hear the voices getting louder. At least two of the men were yelling his name along with threats of what they were going to do to him if he didn't come out of hiding right away. Victor thought for a moment. He decided that no matter what he did now, the punishment was probably going to be the same. Pushing himself away from the wall, he ran to the front of the building. Two nurses were walking down the road and saw him take the steps two at a time. He flew across the porch and in through the main doors. He found himself in an entranceway very similar to the one in his building. His mind was racing. If the building was just like his, then everybody who lived here slept upstairs. In that case, the day hall was most likely straight ahead. He ran to the doors at the end of the hall, bursting through them. Directly across from where he stood was another set of doors. To his left and right were hallways, identical in length and design. Off of each were several doors with nameplates on them. A quick scan of some and he realized that these were offices. The day hall had to be through the doors in front of him. Victor pushed at the doors but they didn't open. There were voices behind him now, just outside the building. The nurses must have given him away.

To the left of the door was a doorbell. Victor rang it. He heard a buzzing in front of him. Pushing on the doors allowed him access. Now what? Ahead and off to the right were large glass windows, those of the nurses' station. The nurse on duty would be looking to see whom she just buzzed in. Past the nurses' station was the day hall. Victor could see some of the residents sitting in chairs or leaning against the wall. Several of them were walking around the room. Where were the others? The noise from behind was close now. Victor heard the buzzer go off in the nurse's station. He was sweating heavily. He thought his heart might burst at any moment. He started running.

Everything from that point on, Victor would think later, seemed to happen in slow motion. He dashed past the nurses' station. He saw a nurse and one attendant staring at him as he ran by. The doors behind him burst open. Two men from his work detail were in hot pursuit. As he bolted around the corner, he saw the bulk of the residents sitting at the makeshift dining room table.

"Jimmy!" Victor yelled at the mass of bodies surrounding the two long tables set to the far right of the hall. "Jimmy! Where are you?"

Just as Jimmy stood up, Victor was blind-sided by the attendant who had been in the nurses' station. Victor hadn't seen the other door at the far end of the office.

For a second, the room was spinning. The next thing Victor remembered, he was looking up into his brother's gaunt, pale face. Jimmy must have lost thirty pounds. His eyes seemed sunken into his skull. A bruise sat above one eye.

"Victor! They said you died!" Just then his brother was pulled away by the two attendants who had chased Victor. The man who tackled Victor switched off with the one holding Jimmy.

"Victor, what happened! Why did we have to come here?" his brother yelled, but Victor could not see him. He was being pulled and pummeled towards the exit, doing all he could to deflect the blows that were coming to his head.

"I'll be back, Jimmy!" he yelled as they went sideways through the doors. Victor's head bounced off the edge of the wall, almost knocking him unconscious. "Don't give up hope!" was the last thing he yelled before everything started spinning.

Victor could hear his brother yelling his name, "Victor, Victor, Vict—." Then he didn't hear his brother yell again. As they came out of the front of the building, the two men dropped Victor onto his back. One of them loomed above him.

"You think you're gonna get away with making us look bad, you little fuckin' squash? See how you like this!" Each man grabbed a leg and began dragging Victor. The men got to the top of the stairs, then sped up, almost running down to the bottom. Victor remembered looking up into clear blue skies just before his head bounced down the steps. He lost consciousness.

✳   ✳   ✳

When he awoke, he found himself lying on a bed in a physician's office in a building he didn't know. He looked around the room. It had the same equipment as the physician's office he spent time in the first day he'd come to the school: the bed he was lying on, a few chairs, and the medicine cabinet; but the view out the window was different. He heard a jingling sound, the familiar sound of somebody with power—somebody with keys—on the other side of the locked door. The large bolt lock slid smoothly and the door opened. Dr. Rhodes, Nurse Mason, and the two attendants, whose names were Steele and Red, walked in. Nobody said anything at first. The doctor came over and rolled Victor onto his belly. Victor's head had been hurting before, but now, when the doctor turned him over, a sharp, severe pain ripped through his skull. He yelped out.

"Quiet," said Dr. Rhodes, as he felt around Victor's scalp. "How'd this happen?" he asked.

Red answered. "We chased the kid out of C building and he, ahh...turned at the top of the stairs when we yelled his name. He musta' stumbled over his feet 'cause the next thing we know, he's tumblin' down the stairs, bouncin' all over the place."

Victor turned his head sideways so he could look at Red. The feeling he felt in bed the other night rose up, the feeling that was more than anger. "You're a fuckin' liar," he said calmly, with no stutter at all.

"Shut up," said Dr. Rhodes. "No one asked you to speak."

Victor turned his head a little more so he could just see the doctor in his peripheral vision. "I'm only trying to tell you th...the truth, doctor. They dragged me down."

"That's enough! I said no one is talking to you."

Victor's rage mounted quickly. Without thinking about it, he spun around and sat up. He grabbed the doctor by his white medical coat before the doctor could react. He pulled him close. His eyes were locked on the doctor's. "Fuck you," he said, with ice in his voice. "I don't give a damn if you weren't. I'm the only one who will tell you the truth." The two attendants raced over and pulled Victor off the doctor. Victor didn't resist. He only smiled at the doctor, oblivious to the jostling he was getting from the two attendants, who were now doing everything by the book in the presence of the doctor.

The doctor was visibly upset. "Listen, you little bastard, you don't *ever* touch me, you hear!" He walked over to Victor, grabbing him roughly by his chin. He squeezed Victor's face into a twisted mass of lips and teeth. "You'll pay for that." Turning to one of the attendants, he said, "Half-head, two weeks in the doghouse." Then to Nurse Mason, "Let's post him after that to your ward. Have him clean shit and piss for a while; see if he's such a wise guy after that." He released Victor's face.

Victor just smiled. "You can't hurt me no more. It must be so easy to be tough like that wh...when you're twice my size. I...It won't always be like that, Doc."

The doctor stared at Victor. He'd never been talked to like this before by any one at the school. "Nurse Mason, make it three weeks with you. You have anything else to add, Victor?"

"Not today," Victor answered.

Nurse Mason walked up to Victor. "So, why did you run away from the farm this morning?"

"I wanted to...I needed to see if my brother and sister where okay. No one t...tells you anything if you ask. That's all I wanted."

"Do you doubt our ability to take care of your brother and sister, Victor?" Her voice was calm and evenly paced. She seemed completely unfazed by Victor's outburst. She turned to see if the doctor was out of earshot, then leaned very close to Victor's ear. "You best think before you answer, Squash-Head," she hissed. "For the next five weeks you're mine, and for the next five weeks you will do as you're told or you will feel the consequences. You will *feel* the consequences, you hear me, Boy." Then louder, so the doctor could hear, "I couldn't hear you. Don't you think we can take care of your brother and sister, Victor?"

Victor looked into her eyes. They were more watery than most other people's eyes; the whites were yellowy. He saw nothing but ugliness and hatred. "I'm sure you can," he finally answered, feeling a certain amount of fear in the presence of this woman.

"Take him," she said to the attendants.

Victor was led to another building. He knew where he was going. He'd seen others who'd received a half-head haircut. They went into a smaller building between the one where his brother lived and the one where he would spend the next five weeks. The men led him down a flight of stairs to the barbershop. The school was almost like a little town. Everything they needed was right on the grounds. "Hey, Nick!" Steele yelled. "We got another bad boy here for you." Nick, the barber, a sad looking man in his late fifties, turned to look at Victor.

"Sit in the chair," he said.

Victor hopped up into the chair. The men each took an arm. "You don't have to ho...hold me. I won't fight."

"Yeah, right. You been fightin' us all day, why should we believe you?"

Nick was looking at Victor with his sad eyes. "Let him go. You don't have to hold him."

"All right, old man, if you say so," said the other attendant. They stepped back as Nick came over with the buzzer.

"I'm sorry about this," he said to Victor, and then proceeded to cut off all the hair on the right side of Victor's head, leaving the left side untouched. Victor looked in the mirror as Nick did his work. He was gentle. He softly ran his hands through Victor's hair as he cut it. Victor could not remember when anyone else had been this gentle with him. He thought how sad it was that the most gentle person he ever knew was this barber, cutting half his hair off, making him look like an idiot.

"Look at that, would ya now," said Red. "Don't you look like a pretty boy."

Nick softly put his hand on Victor's back. "You're all set, Son." Victor stood up, walking over to the attendants. Both men began rubbing Victor's head. "For luck," they said.

"Now comes the fun part, Squashy. Now ya get ta spend a couple weeks in the dog house," said Steele.

"Hey, I'd rather be there than in A building doing what he's gonna have to do."

"Yeah, but look at it this way, if it weren't for troublemakers like ol' Vic here, we'd have to clean up after the idiots ourselves," the other said.

Red thought about this. "Jeeze, that's true. Vic, I guess we should be thankin' ya!" Both men laughed. "Let's get him into the dog house."

"Sounds good ta me."

They headed over to A building, but instead of going up the stairs, they moved around to the side of them. Victor had seen the wire mesh running along the side of the stairs before, but he always thought it was just to keep animals from going under. As they got closer, however, he noticed that there was actually a small hatch in the mesh. Steele moved ahead and reached down to unlock it. The hatchway swung up. Red positioned Victor in front of him, pushing him down to his hands and knees. "Get in," was all he said.

Victor peered into the darkness beneath the stairs. He could see spider webs hanging thick from the underside of the porch; the smell of dampness and mildew surrounded him. He paused too long. Red got impatient. He put his boot to Victor's rear and shoved him in. Victor slid into the hole, his hands mushing through mud and soft moss. He landed on his belly and decided to lie there until the men went away. He heard the hatchway swing down and the key turn in the lock. Footsteps sounded on the steps directly above him and then on the porch. A moment later he heard a single set of footsteps coming back down. Steele's face appeared on the other side of the wire.

"You'll need these." He opened the hatchway again, pushing one thin blanket and an old coffee can into the small cage. "Shit and piss in that," Steele said, pointing to the can. "Every few days, we'll let you out to empty it in the woods around back."

Victor crawled over and grabbed the blanket, which was so thin it felt more like a sheet. "I'm not gonna be warm enough with ju...just this."

"Hey, that's all you get, tough guy. You did it to yourself. You shouldn't a bolted from the farm and you shouldn't a talked back to the doc. You'll learn to behave, or you'll spend a lot of time in the doghouse. It's up to you. Have fun!" Steele slammed the hatch down and was gone. Victor looked around his dank home, reminding him of a doghouse. He couldn't stand up straight. The ceiling was only three or four feet from the dirt floor. Victor wrapped the blanket around his shoulders and huddled into the corner nearer to the hatch where it was a little lighter and he could keep a better eye on the spiders and whatever else he might be sharing quarters with. It was going to be a long two weeks. After a few seconds, though, he started smiling. He'd finally seen his brother.

9

Thursday, November 23, 1972. "When will you be home?" Meredith asked.

"I have a few clients I have to see, I guess around seven."

There was a long pause. Meredith waited for Tim to say something else. He never did. He only used enough words to answer her questions. She hated that. He'd stopped talking to her years ago. Not purposely, of course, it just seemed like he had little to say to her after a time. "Well...I guess I should go. I have a meeting." She didn't have a meeting, but she couldn't stay on the phone with him any longer. She missed Roland. "I'll see you tonight."

"Okay."

"All right...bye."

"Bye."

She put down the receiver and walked across the teachers' lounge to the coffeepot. She poured herself a cup of very old coffee. She took a sip, winced from the burnt taste, then tossed the cup and its contents into the wastebasket. She moved over to the window and crossed her arms in front of her, watching the carefree children load on to the busses. She uncrossed her arms and looked at her watch: 3:15. She shook her head and put her hands on her hips. She knew what time it was; the kids boarded the buses at the same time every day.

She wondered what Roland was doing right now. She hadn't heard from him since he left her at the old mill over two weeks ago. He was so angry that day. His temper was one of the things about him that intimidated her. She was probably the only person in town who knew it, though. He was so reserved in his role as Chief of Police. She'd never seen him even raise his voice in public. Offsetting the temper was his passion for her. She loved the way he seemed to ravish her when they made love. Nothing violent really, but manly. He took control of her and brought her to heights she'd never experienced with any other man. And then he was so sweet and gentle when he kissed her after they made love. He talked to her about her day—her life. He listened. Something she didn't get from Tim. Something she was pretty sure she'd *never* gotten from Tim. But she knew about Roland's past. How the passion he felt for her was the same sort of passion he had poured into his work as a homicide detective in Jacksonville. He told her that he was going to try to stay out of the investigation, let Mark Palin and Chris Carr handle it. He didn't want another taste of it. Like an alcoholic, he was afraid that he wouldn't be able to stay away if he had just a little.

Meredith moved away from the window and headed to the main office. She went in, said hello to the secretaries, and checked her box. She flipped through the usual notices about PTA meetings and inter-office garbage. Stuck between these items was a folded note. She opened it and read it quickly. Then she read it again. A note from Roland! It read:

> *Please forgive me for the other night. I was out of control. I've been extremely ambivalent about our situation, and my love for you drives me to these moments of craziness. I need you in my life. I can be patient. Come and meet me at the horse barn (5 p.m.). You remember...where we took advantage of the loft!*
>
> *RB*

The note was typed, as were the initials. Meredith thought this was a bit odd, but only for a second. She was too excited by the note's contents to worry about how it had been composed. She looked around the office, thinking that someone might have noticed her joy, but no one seemed to be paying attention to her. She looked at her watch again. She had almost an hour and a half to kill. She smiled in anticipation.

*   *   *

Meredith pulled out of the parking lot of the school, taking a left through the center of town. A strong wind was swirling dead leaves across the road. She loved this time of year when the days were growing shorter and colder; when one really felt like a New Englander. She had taken out her family's winter clothes a few weeks back. The first snows would be upon them in less than a month. She passed through the small business section of Wilton and turned right onto Maple Street. Wilton was a typical small town in Massachusetts. It sprung up out of nowhere in the middle of the woods. After a mile on Maple Street, the distances between houses grew larger. As she approached Aaron Street, the road she had to take to reach the horse barn, dusk was descending around her. The western portion of the sky was splattered with strands of bright pink clouds while the eastern sky was shrouded in a touch of darkness.

She took a left, traveling down a long, dead-end street with just a few country homes, each one separated by rolling fields dotted with cows or trees. She neared the end of the street and slowed to take the turn onto a small dirt road that cut up to the horse barn. The barn was a favorite drinking spot of Wilton youth at night and a parking lot for those who wanted to access the Robert Frost Trail during the day. At this time of the day, though, there was usually no one there. She put her directional on, then laughed, thinking how programmed her mind was. How silly it was of her to use her blinker on this old road. She hadn't seen a soul around any of the houses she'd passed much less another car. Just as she began her turn, a movement in her peripheral vision drew her attention to the end of the street she'd been traveling. There, standing in the yard of the house at the far side of the cul-de-sac, was a man. She couldn't make out any features, for he was too far away; but he was definitely looking in her direction.

Without realizing it, she slowed the car down to a crawl, feeling odd that this man would take such an interest in her. He turned, and started limping towards the side of the house. He was in some sort of dark work suit, like those mechanics wore. His dark figure cut clearly against the whiteness of the house. He moved around a large shrub and started jogging. "How strange," she said out loud, as the whole scene passed behind the wood line running along the dirt road. "Oh, well." She drove the last few hundred yards up the old dirt road before finally seeing the narrow turn-off into the parking area by the horse barn. She squeezed her car through the tight entranceway. She'd hoped that Roland would already be there, but neither he nor his Bronco was anywhere in sight.

She watched the beam of her headlights shrink rapidly on the wall of the horse barn as she pulled her car up and parked. She turned the car off. The sudden silence frightened her. Slowly, as the noise of the engine drifted away, the sounds of the late New England afternoon closed in around her. It was too late in the year to hear tree frogs, but the crickets were still hard at work. Bats flew around the perimeter of the small safety light that hung out from the building on a metal pole. The sky was now drained of all its color, and a canopy of stars was beginning to form above. She walked to the back end of her car and leaned against it, wrapping her arms around herself to stay warm. A biting wind was beginning to twist its way through the trees. Meredith remembered that the weatherman had said it was going to get close to freezing tonight. She listened intently, hoping to hear the sound of Roland's truck coming up the dirt road. She heard nothing.

Her mind began to drift to thoughts of the recent murder. It must have been so frightening. An old woman alone at night, thinking she was safe in her big house in a small town where the hottest news in the police log in the local paper usually concerned kids and their adolescent acts of vandalism. Pictures of the old woman flashed in Meredith's head. She could see the woman beginning to panic when she realized that someone was in her house. A chill raced up Meredith's spine and her body shook involuntarily. "Where are you, Roland?" she asked out loud. She looked at her watch. It was almost five-thirty. Briggs was never this late. "Something must have come up."

She decided to wait another five minutes. But something quickly changed her mind. Off to her left, from somewhere deep in the woods, came the gentle sound of laughter. Meredith's body tensed. She looked towards the direction of the sound, but all she could see was a vague darkness where the tree line opened up to allow those walking on the Robert Frost Trail to enter the woods. There it was again! Louder this time and more eerie. Meredith bolted around the back end of her car and pulled frantically at the door handle. Her first attempt failed, her fingernails bending back against the handle as she lost her grip. She got the door open on the second try, then dove behind the wheel. The laughter came again; it sounded closer this time—crazier. It was as if a madman were walking down the trail towards the barn.

She fumbled with the keys before she got her fingers under control. The car's engine turned over with a roar. She threw it into reverse and floored it, sending the car hurdling backwards towards the trees on the opposite side of the lot. She hit the brakes just in time, then spun the wheel hard to the left as she threw the transmission into drive. She could feel her heart pounding. As her headlights swept the entrance to the trail, her eyes lingered a little too long. Even though it was only a second, it was long enough. She looked back towards the narrow exit. She was going too fast to get the car to the correct angle to pass smoothly through the opening. The car first bounced awkwardly off a medium-sized maple tree on Meredith's left just before her front right fender smacked into the old gate that had not been closed in years.

The car stalled. Immediately the laughter pierced the resulting silence. Although she could not see whoever was laughing, she could tell that he was now at the base of the trail. He was in the clearing behind her. She pumped the gas and turned the key. The car started. She jammed the car into reverse again and pulled the car back just enough to get the bumper out of the gate and angle the car so she could drive through the opening. She glanced quickly at her rearview mirror. To her horror, the torso of a man was clearly displayed in the glow of the reverse lights. He was walking towards the driver's side of the car. Meredith blasted the car into drive and hit the gas. Her door flew open but then swung shut as the car plowed forward. For just a moment, the man's laughter filled her ears. She gripped the steering wheel so tight that even in the darkness she could see her white knuckles. She was breathing hard. She found the courage to glance briefly in the mirror once more, just in time to see the man disappear into the shrouded darkness left behind in the wake of her taillights.

It wasn't until she got to the end of Aaron Street, turning onto Maple, that she realized she was crying.

10

Saturday, December 2, 1972. Briggs checked his look in the mirror one more time before he left. He was headed to the mayor's party. He straightened his tie again, even though it didn't need it, then headed out the door. Winter had come to Wilton with a vengeance the day before, one day after Thanksgiving. Temperatures had dropped into the teens. The wind outside his house was biting, and although Briggs could not see the snowflakes in the dark he could feel them hitting his face. The weather report indicated that by morning there would be at least a few inches of the white stuff on the ground.

Briggs was always surprised at how human beings reacted to murder. Only a month ago, his town was in an uproar because of the Mason killing. People were staying in after dark, mothers where not letting their kids out of their sight. The papers reported the gory details and the townsfolk gasped and shook their heads in sadness. "That poor woman," people had said. "How horrible!" But then, with each passing day, the stories about the murder faded further and further away from page one, and people began walking at night again, and slowly, the children were given back their freedom to roam. The memory of that night faded quickly from the minds of those living in Wilton and life got back to normal.

Briggs figured that part of the reason for this fade-out was that the woman had no relatives. She hadn't been too close to anyone, so there were few who were really directly affected by her death. No one was left to grieve. Even the mayor had begun to lose interest in the case. Up until last week, Briggs had to report to him daily on the progress of the investigation. But this past Monday the mayor told him that once a week on Friday would be good enough now. People seemed to have come to believe that Mrs. Mason was the unfortunate victim of some transient. They were sure that none of their own would be capable of committing such an ugly crime. Obviously, whoever had killed her was long gone—and good riddance. Briggs himself was beginning to feel that the case was not going to be solved. The only difference was that this sort of feeling bothered him. He hated the idea of someone getting away with murder while he was the chief of police. And he hated to think that the only two murders that occurred in Wilton in the last fifteen years had both gone unsolved.

He pulled his Bronco onto the mayor's lawn behind a large black Cadillac. He recognized the car immediately as the one owned by Tim King, Meredith's husband. Briggs' disposition, which was already not good, got worse quickly. He sat behind the wheel, watching the snowflakes turning and twisting in the space between the two vehicles. "Fuck it," he said out loud. He'd been dreading the fact that he was going to have to see Meredith tonight. He'd spent Thanksgiving Day alone, brooding about his relationship with her. He thought for sure that his making a stand that Sunday would have forced her to leave her husband, but he hadn't heard a word from her in almost four weeks. "I knew that bitch was stringing me along."

He got out of his car and walked across the yard to the door. Anybody who was somebody in Wilton was at the mayor's. He had to put in an appearance, but he planned on getting out as quickly as he could. Mrs. Tatum, the mayor's wife, opened the door. She was a petite woman in her mid-fifties.

"Chief Briggs," she said warmly. "Come in, come in. Let's get you out of that cold." She took him gently by the arm and pulled him inside, closing the door behind him. "Let me take your coat."

"How are you, Mrs. Tatum?" Briggs asked.

"Very good and all the better now that you're here." She turned to him after putting his coat in the hall closet. "How was your Thanksgiving?"

"Quiet."

Mrs. Tatum frowned. "I wish you had taken our offer up and come here. I was so disappointed when Jim told me you weren't coming."

Briggs looked at Mrs. Tatum and believed that she meant it. She was always very nice to him. She owned a small coffee shop in town, and although she had a couple of women doing all the work, she was always down there socializing with the residents and giving advice and directions to the tourists. Briggs got his morning coffee there, and Mrs. Tatum and he had become good friends. "Am I the last to arrive?" he asked.

"Of course. You always are. Help yourself to a good stiff drink. You're gonna need it to get through this night," she said with a laugh. "All your favorite people are here." She knew that Briggs did not appreciate parties very much. Although he'd never come out and told her the details surrounding his marriage, he had told Mrs. Tatum that his wife had committed suicide. She also knew that even though Briggs was in the public eye because of his position, he preferred to avoid the social events that came with it.

The mayor's house was one of the largest in town. It had been in the Tatum family for five generations. Briggs moved down the large hall adorned on both sides by large portraits of the previous Tatum men and smaller family photos of people completely unfamiliar to Briggs. The Tatums' did all their entertaining in a large ballroom located in the rear of the home. As Briggs approached it, the sounds of human chatter got louder. He got to the door, took a deep breath, and went in. The room was magnificent. Two large crystal chandeliers sparkled above, filling the room with a soft, warm glow. Other lights fashioned to look like old gas lamps adorned the walls. The alternating black and white tiles on the floor were highly polished. It seemed as if Briggs ware stepping back in time as he moved through the room. The long dining table in the middle of the room was piled high with all sorts of food, and a table in the corner of the room was cluttered with a wide array of alcohol and mixers. Briggs spotted the latter table and headed directly for it.

"Roland! What are you doing sneaking around behind my back?" Briggs heard the mayor say, loud enough so everyone at the party turned to look. Briggs stopped and turned.

"Hey, Mayor," Briggs said with a forced smile. "I was just gonna grab a drink."

"Well, let me get you your first one. After that you're on your own." He clapped a hand on Briggs' back and walked him the rest of the way to the refreshment table. "Sorry you couldn't make it for Thanksgiving. Mae really outdid herself this year. What are you drinking?"

"You got any Jack Daniels?"

"Of course. How do you take it?"

"Straight. And could you make it a double?"

"Sure thing."

"I didn't get a chance to talk to you yesterday," Briggs said, "because of the holiday. I wanted to fill you in on the investigation."

"Don't worry about that now. We can talk about it on Monday. Let's just enjoy ourselves tonight. Come on over and join in on the discussion." The mayor led Briggs over to a group of men and women at the far end of the ballroom near the large French doors leading out to the deck. Along the way, Briggs said hello or nodded to various business owners and influential people of Wilton. He saw Meredith, standing with her husband amongst the group that he and the mayor where about to join. The rest of the group consisted of Mrs. Ann Cavanaugh, head of the Wilton branch of the PTA; Buzz Ackerman, the principle of the Wilton's junior high school; Jerry Sicard, owner of Sicard Real Estate; and two men that Briggs did not recognize.

"Everyone," the mayor said, "the chief has finally arrived." Those that the chief knew nodded or said hello. The Chief's eyes lingered on the two men he did not know. The mayor immediately picked up on this non-verbal message and jumped in. "I'm sorry, Roland. You probably don't know Frank Murman. He's the architect in charge of the renovations to the town hall."

Briggs looked at Murman. He was a solid man, about the same height and age as Briggs. His short hair was just starting to show a touch of gray at the temples. He was sharply dressed in a black suit, white silk shirt, and blood-red tie with a touch of dark gray in it. Briggs figured him for a man, like himself, who tried to stay in shape. He also figured that Murman was doing a much better job than he was. Murman gave Briggs a strong handshake.

"Nice to meet you, Chief Briggs," he said, smiling at the chief.

"It's Roland. And it's nice to meet you, too." Briggs thought he recognized the last name. "Have we met before tonight? Your name sounds familiar to me."

"Yes. We met very briefly when I first started working on the town hall."

"Oh okay, that must be it."

"This fellow over here is Mr. John Richards, Roland," said the mayor. "He is in town representing the state of Massachusetts in negotiations involving Wilton's attempt to purchase some of the old state school land."

"Hi, Roland," Richards said quietly as they shook hands. He stood in sharp contrast to Murman. Tall and slender, Richards had a narrow face and small, tired-looking eyes. His suit was a bit rumpled and his hair needed combing. "How's the weather out there? Snowing yet?"

"Actually, yes. It just started really coming down as I pulled in." Briggs sensed that this man was, like himself, fulfilling an obligation by being at the party. "You living out this way?"

"No. That's why I was asking about the weather. I have to drive back to Springfield tonight."

Briggs thought for a second and decided to give the man an easy out if he wanted it. "Well, I hate to spoil the night for you, but if I was in your shoes, I'd start heading back soon."

Richards looked relieved for a second, then covered up well. "That's what I was afraid you'd say. I guess I'll head out in a little while."

"Hey, Briggs," said Jerry Sicard, "what's going on with the Wilton Ripper case? I haven't heard a word about it lately." His tone was filled with sarcasm.

Jerry was an overweight slob of a man who loved his liquor. Briggs couldn't stand him. He stopped Sicard the first week that he was chief when he noticed Sicard's big Lincoln weaving in and out of the lines. Briggs had ignored Jerry's "Don't you know who I am?" and "You'll regret doing this to me?" statements on that night and busted him for drunk driving. When Sicard realized his threats were not going to work, he tried to get physical. In less than a few seconds he ended up face down on the ground in hand-cuffs. Briggs knew that Sicard still held a grudge, blaming Briggs and not himself for the public humiliation that followed the arrest. Briggs could see that Jerry was well on his way to getting sloshed and that he was looking for an argument. He decided to stick to the official response. "Well, Jerry, that's an ongoing investigation. I can't talk about it with you."

"Oh, really," Jerry sneered. "You can't even give us a hint about who killed the old broad?" He was going to push Briggs if he could. "Come on! I thought a big city DICK like you woulda had this thing solved a few days after it happened. Getting a little rusty are we?"

Briggs looked hard at Jerry, but the man was too drunk to be intimidated by a look. Everyone was watching Briggs, wondering how he was going to answer. Briggs chose not to. Instead, he turned to Murman. "So what got you into the field of architecture, Mr. Murman?"

Murman, realizing he could help break the tension, answered quickly. "Ever since I was young I was interested in buildings. I still remember staring up at them as a small child, so impressed that man could—"

"Aren't you going to answer Jerry's question, Roland?"

Briggs turned his head to see who decided to jump into the fray with Sicard. It was Tim King. He was staring at Briggs with a big, 'I want to cause trouble' sort of smile on his face. Briggs looked at Meredith, who was squeezing Tim's arm, trying to get him to back off. He wanted to walk over and slap Tim around. Teach him a lesson. His schoolyard mentality got the best of his thinking. He thought how much fun it would be to show Meredith how powerful he was and kick the shit out of her husband right in front of her and God and everybody else. Briggs remembered that Tim and Jerry were best friends. Figures he'd pick a slob like that for a best buddy.

He was gonna stop this before it got out of hand. He walked over to where Tim was standing, getting uncomfortably close to Tim's face with his own. He stared intently into Tim's eyes. Tim backed down first and stepped away a bit. "You want an answer to that question, Tim? I'll give ya one." Briggs glared over at Jerry for a second to make sure he was listening, too. Out of the corner of his eye he caught sight of his two detectives coming over to see what the commotion was all about. "You see, this big city dick is allowing his men to do their job. Whoever did this was a lot smarter than say...a guy like you. He covered his tracks well, and we're having difficulty catching him. But don't you worry, because if my men don't catch him soon, I'm gonna take an active role in the investigation and help 'em out. Is that good enough for now, Tim?"

Tim looked visibly shaken. Briggs had a crazy look in his eye that Tim had never seen before in a man. Meredith saw it, too. "Yeah, Briggs. That's good enough."

"How about you, Sicard?" Briggs said, turning to look at the chubby man. "Is that a good enough official explanation for you?"

Sicard didn't get a chance to answer. The mayor said, "Roland, please! Let's stop this...situation right now."

Briggs stood in the middle of the room for a moment, still staring at Sicard. Then, as if someone waved a hand in front of his face, his expression changed and he got hold of himself. He looked down for a second, then back at the mayor. "Sorry, Jimmy." He had to think quickly. Time to save face a little. How could he explain his actions? "I...I just can't stand it when people talk ill of the dead. Mrs. Mason was a human being, not an 'old broad', and we're still doing everything we can to find her killer. There is no reason to laugh about this stuff. I don't find it funny at all." He looked around the room at the faces. He might have gained some ground with some, but it looked like there was no getting around it—he'd made a fool of himself.

Mrs. Tatum came to the rescue. "Roland, dear, could I steal you away for a moment? I need to ask you a question about that new zoning ordinance that is going into effect on the first of the year."

Briggs didn't hesitate. He took the out and walked over to talk to Mrs. Tatum, then headed over to freshen up his Jack Daniels. As he walked to the table, he looked over and noticed everyone talking normally again. They'd lost their interest in him, at least overtly. He caught a few furtive glances cast his way, but no one was willing to look at him directly. Except Meredith. As he poured his drink he felt someone come up beside him. It was she. "What were you trying to prove?" she asked him sharply.

"What do you care?" he rasped back, not expecting an answer. "This isn't my fault. I didn't want to come to this fuckin' party anyway. I knew it was going to be a disaster."

Meredith hesitated. "Because of me?"

"Yes, because of you! Who the hell else would get me this upset?"

"Roland, you can't honestly blame me for what happened here tonight." She glanced over her shoulder quickly to check the movements of her husband.

Now it was Roland's turn to hesitate for a second. "No," he said. "Of course you're not directly to blame. It's just that...." Roland let the sentence trail off. He wasn't going to tell her how much he missed her. How he was going crazy without her. She didn't care, anyway. He was getting angry again. It was time to leave.

He put his drink down and turned to go. He looked at Meredith coldly. "The hell with it all."

But Roland, why are you mad at me?" He started to walk away. Meredith checked to see if anyone was paying attention. Mrs. Tatum and another woman were approaching. "I was there!" she hissed. "You didn't show."

Briggs waved her off and was halfway across the room before her words sunk in. He turned to walk back but two women had joined Meredith almost as soon as he'd walked away. He was going to wait until he had another opportunity to talk to her and find out what she meant, but he realized that too much attention to her might bring on curious onlookers. Luckily, he thought, as he walked down the hall to the closet, no one had noticed their little argument.

But he was wrong.

Two people had noticed something odd going on between the chief and Meredith. Steve Gamble, the reporter, for one, and Detective Chris Carr. Carr could not help smiling to himself a little when he saw the two of them arguing. And there was someone else who was watching, too. Someone who couldn't believe how well things were going. Everything was working out as planned.

II

The house was quiet. There were no lights on in any of the front rooms. Briggs sat in his car for a moment preoccupied with other thoughts before he realized that something was out of order. The living room light was usually always on. And through the large bay window of that room, one could normally see the lights of the kitchen as well. But tonight—nothing. Just darkness.

Briggs got out of his car, snuffed out under his shoe the cigarette he'd been smoking, and pulled his 38 caliber Smith and Wesson from its shoulder holster. He moved quietly across the front lawn, ending up with his back against the wall, just to the left of the bay window. He turned his head slowly, peering into the blackness. Nothing was moving inside. He waited a minute, just listening. Hearing nothing, he vaulted the three steps to the front door and swung it open quickly. He'd always told her to lock it, but she never listened. She was much more trusting than he was. Again he listened, thinking that maybe the sound of the door crashing open would cause a stir, but still nothing. "Janet!" Briggs yelled. No answer. Briggs smelled the air. Was it the lingering smell of gunpowder? He wasn't sure. His mouth was dry and the taste of cigarettes was dominating his sense of smell.

Briggs flicked a switch on the wall to his right, just at the base of the stairs. The living room flooded with light. He squinted in momentary pain and rubbed his eyes. Everything seemed in place. "Janet, are you here, Honey?" Silence.

A sudden wave of anxiety swept over Briggs. He had that feeling that he'd come to expect whenever he entered a crime scene—whenever he came upon the dead. Briggs ran around the corner into the kitchen. Nothing. "Janet! Janet!" He flew back through the living room and raced up the stairs into the darkness of the second floor. He turned left at the top of the stairs and came to his bedroom door. Putting his hand on the doorknob, he paused. His breathing was heavy. He put his head against the door. "Janet," he whispered. Wisps of smoke danced around his feet and up around his legs. He pushed the door open. The only light came from the bulb hanging inside the closet. The closet door was open. There, lying on the bed, was Janet. Most of her brains were splattered across the quilt. After she had blown the back of her head off with Briggs' back-up handgun, she must have fallen back onto her own brains. Briggs could barely see her. The fog was filling the room. He moved close. He was crying. "No, Janet! No!" he screamed. He looked quickly. He saw the bruise he'd given her shining brightly on the left side of her face. Her eyes were open, glazed over. The phone rang.

Briggs shot up in bed. He was drenched with sweat. He was shaking. He'd had the dream again. The phone next to his bed was ringing, not the one in his dream. He looked at the clock. It was almost 10:30 a.m. He'd overslept. He didn't even remember the alarm going off. Maybe he hadn't remembered to set it. Briggs leaned over and picked up the phone. "Hello—yes," he croaked.

"Chief, it's Kroner." The tension in Kroner's voice was immediately obvious. "I hate to say this, but they...we...we got a call. They found another body."

*   *   *

Tuesday, December 5, 1972. Gertrude Stiener was staring out of one of the large windows onto the parking lot below. She looked worried. "What's the matter, Gertrude?" Asked Angie Brooks, the young African-American who was working at the Senior Center as a volunteer.

Startled by Angie's words, Gertrude moved her hand away from her mouth and turned her head quickly. "Oh, hello, Angie. I was wondering about Mary. She was out last Tuesday and now, today, she hasn't arrived either." Gertrude shook her head. "This is not like her at all."

Angie thought for a second and realized that Gertrude was right. "Well, I'm sure she's fine. Maybe she's off with her family."

"She hasn't any family, my dear. That's what's bothering me. She lives in that big, old house all by her lonesome, you know."

"No, I didn't know that, Ma'am." Angie stood quietly for a moment, looking at Gertrude. "Well, it's only ten after eight, she may still show up."

Gertrude looked at Angie and smiled. "How long have you worked here, dear?"

Angie did the quick calculations in her head. "Just short of three months."

"In those three months, have you ever known Mrs. Gowan to be late? Any of us to be late?"

"No, Ma'am."

Gertrude looked down for a moment. "When you get to be our age, my dear, you'll understand. You see, we have worked or taken care of our children all of our lives. What happens is you eventually become creatures of habit. After a lifetime of getting up early to send our kids off to school or our husbands off to work, it's hard to stop doing that. The routine, that is. We all still get up, even though most of us have little to do anymore, as if we have a full day's agenda. We still need that routine in our lives—our schedule. So, on Tuesdays, when we all get to come down here to the center…well, it's a big event for a lot of us. Arriving late is not what we do."

Angie thought she sensed a bit of sadness in the old lady's voice. "I see, Ma'am. Do you want I should call her house and see if she's coming?"

Gertrude looked at Angie with relief. "Oh, yes, my dear. That would be wonderful if you could do that."

When Angie came back, Gertrude could tell that she was unable to reach Mary. "No luck, Ma'am. Nobody answered."

Gertrude bit her lip with worry. "Thank you for trying, Dear."

"Do you want to join the others now? They have a speaker coming in to discuss scams being perpetrated against the elderly. I've heard it is very interesting. And beneficial."

"I'll be along in a moment, Love. You go on ahead." Gertrude watched the chubby young girl walk away. She'd already determined what she was going to do and it didn't include listening to any speeches. She got up slowly from her chair, getting her walker out in front of her, and moved to the pay phone in the hallway. She picked up the receiver and dialed the number of her house. Out of breath, her grandson answered on the fourth ring.

"Hello," he gasped.

"Doughboy, come and get me."

"Grams?"

"Yes, it's your grandmother, and I want you to come and pick me up now."

"But Grams! I just dropped you off. I just got back home."

"I am well aware of that, Doughboy. But I have a pressing emergency. I need you to come. NOW!"

Doughboy wasn't a very bright boy, but he could hear the seriousness in her voice. When he arrived back at the center, his grandmother was waiting just inside the glass double-doors. He pulled up in the front, jumped out of his pick-up, and hauled his large body around to help her get to the truck.

"Grams, it's cold out," he said, when he noticed that her jacket was still open around the collar. "Let me button that for you."

He reached out to help her, but she swatted his hands away with one of hers. "Stop it, now, Doughboy. I am quite comfortable. Get me into the truck."

"Grams, I wish you wouldn't call me Doughboy anymore. It was cute when I was a kid, but I'm twenty-three years old now."

"Yes, I know. But you're still fat and I'm still your grandmother. I'll call you what I want. Now hurry up and get me in the truck. We may have an emergency on our hands."

"An emergency?" Doughboy asked as his strong arms lifted his grandmother up into the cab of the truck with ease. It was a funny sight to see the two of them together. This giant of a man doting over this tiny old lady who, although she was sweet as pie to everyone else, teased and tormented the poor man to no end. She'd raised him since he was twelve, right after his parents and her son and daughter-in-law were killed in a car accident. The boy was completely loyal to her. The townsfolk often compared their relationship to that of one shared between a golden retriever and his master.

"Yes, an emergency. Get behind the wheel of this contraption and get me over to Mrs. Mary Gowan's house."

Doughboy, whose real name was Walter, put his grandmother's walker in the back and slid his large body behind the wheel. "Where does she live again?"

"Oh! You infernal child. You've been there before."

"Yeah, I know," he said sheepishly, "but I forgot again."

"Just drive," she answered, her voice filled with frustration. "I'll tell you as we go."

Wilton's next income-producing market came in the form of skiers who flooded the town from December until sometimes as late as May, depending on the weather. Wilton sat twenty-five miles south of one of Vermont's biggest ski areas. The town heavily advertised its fine points in all the ski magazines, playing up the little inns and quaint restaurants while playing down the driving distance to the ski resort. Many of the local business owners had gotten together to create very exciting and reasonably priced ski packages to entice the vacationers; and once they had them the first time, they kept them. Almost sixty percent of those who came once came again sometime later. Gertrude and Walter took some side streets to avoid the hectic town center, eventually finding themselves on Maple Street. "Slow down!" Gertrude barked at her grandson, "Take this left here."

Walter did as he was told, and, after Gertrude filled him in on the situation, they drove the rest of the way in silence. When they got to the end of the street, a dead end, Walter pulled the truck into the driveway his grandmother indicated. The weather gods that had dumped almost six inches of snow on Wilton three days before finished it off with enough light rain to ice over the top layer of snow. Walter's tires were the first to crack into the snow covering Mary Gowan's driveway. He and his grandmother sat quietly for a moment, both staring at the house.

"It doesn't look like anyone has been in or out of this place since the snow storm, Grams. No footprints in the snow on the steps." He pointed to the few steps that led up to the small porch on the front of Mary's house.

Gertrude's concern for Mary grew as she looked at the front of her house. Her grandson was right. There had been no movement at all around Mary's house for at least the last three days. Gertrude turned her head to look out the side window of the truck. She couldn't believe her friend chose to live in such a lonely area by herself. After Mary's husband died, she started to come out to the senior center. Once she and Gertrude had gotten to know each other, Gertrude encouraged Mary to live with her and Walter. Their house was in town. It was very large, Gertrude had told her. Stop living way out there in the woods by yourself. But Mary was stubborn and insisted that she was fine. She liked her privacy. Also, Mary was in much better shape than Gertrude, and younger. Mary's looks betrayed her age, and when she first came to the center a lot of the regulars mistook her for a volunteer instead of a fellow senior citizen. She later confided in Gertrude that she was actually too young to be there, by a few years. Her husband had been her best and really only friend. When he passed away, she sought out the center to find some companionship.

"Hey, Grams."

Gertrude pulled herself back to the present, turning to look at her grandson. "Yes?"

"You know, it's been a while since…" He let his words trail off as he looked back at the house.

"A while since what?"

"Since that last murder. You don't think that—"

"Stop that talk! Of course I don't think that. Mary is probably..." she paused, trying to think of something Mary could 'probably' be doing. "Just go up and knock on the door."

Walter got out of the truck and lumbered across the snow-covered lawn. He climbed the steps to the front porch, swung the storm door open, and knocked gently.

"I didn't raise you to be a sissy," his grandmother yelled from the truck. "Knock like a man, boy."

Walter knocked again, louder this time. It seemed to him that his knocking echoed for a moment inside the house. He listened intently, but heard no one approaching the front door from within. He started walking back to the truck. He felt very uneasy on the porch and was thankful to be headed back to the safety and warmth of the truck. "Oh, well," he said nonchalantly, "might as well get back to town. Nobody home."

"What are you doing?" his grandmother yelled. "Get back up to that house this instant! Look around, boy. See if you can see anything through the windows."

"Awh, Grams."

"Do it!"

Walter turned back to the house. The wind blowing across the fields off to the north of Mary's house was picking up and the few rays of sun that had earlier been piercing through the gray clouds were now obliterated. Walter crunched his way to the south side of the house to get out of the wind. His grandmother watched as he peered in one window and then another. When he walked around back, out of sight, she turned her glance to the far side of the house to watch for him. Seconds later, she heard the crunching of feet running through the snow. Her grandson was flying back around the side of the house from where he'd started.

"What's the matter, Walter!" she screamed.

"We gotta get outa here," he yelped back at her. "There's some guy in the house! He was starin' right at me when I looked in."

"Get to a neighbor's house, quickly!" Gertrude yelled. "We must call the police."

*   *   *

Briggs felt horrible, both physically and mentally. He'd called in sick on Monday, the day before, because he was too embarrassed to show his face around the town hall after Saturday's little episode at the mayor's party. Then, when the *Wilton Gazette* came out Monday afternoon, he got even sicker. Gamble had printed a story—page one—that Briggs was sure would bring all sorts of wrath down on him as well as rekindle the talk surrounding the murder of Mason. The headline read:

CHIEF BLOWS UP AT MAYOR'S PARTY INSISTS THAT MASON MURDER WAS NOT DONE BY TRANSIENT

The article included all the gory details of that night, playing up the part about the chief "insinuating" that if his men did not start turning up some leads, he himself would take over the investigation. He didn't feel too bad about getting on Tim King; in fact, it had brought a few smiles to his face on a weekend not prone to many. He did feel bad about making the comments about his men, but he hadn't meant it the way Gamble had made it sound in the paper. The one thing that was bothering him for the last two days was the comment that Meredith had made to him as he was leaving the party. What had she meant?

He thought about all these things as he drove out to Mary Gowan's home, the scene of Wilton's second murder in less than six weeks. Kroner was able to give him few details about the crime, so Briggs did not know what to expect. He definitely didn't expect to see Detective Carr standing in front of a camera at the end of the driveway, answering the questions of reporters, including one from Channel 22 out of Springfield, as he pulled up. The scene was already cordoned off and Adamski and his men were inside collecting the forensic evidence. Briggs looked down at his watch before getting out of his truck. It was almost 11:20 a.m. How long after the initial finding of the body had it been before he got the call from Kroner?

Carr saw the chief arrive, so he finished up as quickly as he could as the chief came over. The reporters scattered to get their stories in and Carr held up the yellow plastic barrier so the Chief could pass underneath. Then they started walking toward the house together.

Briggs spoke first. "So, let's see, the scene is sealed, Adamski and his men are here already, and news crews from Springfield beat me out here. Was it your decision not to get in touch with me right away on this?" Briggs jaw muscles where tightening as he waited for Carr's answer.

"Hey, what can I tell ya, Chief?" Carr's attitude was flippant. "You were out sick yesterday, Kroner said he hadn't heard from ya or seen ya. I told him to leave you be. We figured you'd come in when you were ready. I mean, after Saturday...I figured you'da taken at least a week off! I know I would ha—"

Carr's words were cut short. The chief grabbed him by the arm, spinning him around. Carr was surprised by Briggs' strength. "Listen, Detective Carr," Briggs growled. "I don't care what you would have done. I'm still the fuckin' chief and you answer to me, you understand. I know you're probably pissed about what Gamble said in that article, but you were at the goddamned party and you know I didn't mean it the way he twisted it to sound. And what the hell were you doing out here, giving a fuckin' press conference. I said no one but me talks to the reporters."

Carr saw Detective Palin walk out of the house and stand on the front porch. Briggs was still squeezing his arm. Carr pulled free, exaggerating the effort, before answering. His actions caught the attention of Palin. "I didn't tell 'em anything you wouldn't have. I've been a detective for a long time, ya know. I just gave them the prelims. Goddamn it, Roland, what the fuck is up your ass?"

Briggs talked through clenched teeth. "Listen, you little piss ant, small-town punk. I have a good mind to write you up and suspend you for insubordination. You've put no effort into Mason's murder at all. I know how you were thinking. You'd convinced yourself that somebody would just fall out of a tree some day and confess. Or that it was some old bum on his fuckin' way through town. All BAD cops think like that. Well, now, detective, as you can see, you were wrong and I was right. Unless of course you think this hobo was returning from his winter vacation up north and just stopped by our little town for one more quickie little murder before hopping a train to Florida. Is that what you're thinking now, you jerk!"

Carr was shocked by Briggs' anger. He did tell Kroner not to call the chief, and he did know when he did the interview that he would be pissing off Briggs, but he never expected Briggs to come on this strong. It was better than he'd hoped. He looked over to see if Palin was catching all this. He was. "Chief, I...I...I'm sorry. I was really angry after I read the paper, like you said before. I guess I was trying to show the press that we, you know, me and Palin were capable cops—cops that were going to solve this case." He paused for a second and looked away. "I shouldn't have done it. I hope you accept my apologies. It won't happen again."

Briggs was in no mood to get mushy. "It sure as hell won't!" He saw one of the forensic team members walking by behind Carr. He was lighting a cigarette. "Hey, bud."

The man turned around to look at the chief. "Me?"

Briggs decided not to get arrogant and point out to the man that he was the only one in sight. Briggs needed something from him. "Yeah. Can you spare one of those?"

"Sure, Chief." The man walked over, handed him a cigarette, then loaned the chief his lighter.

"Thanks." The man walked on and the chief took a deep drag off the cigarette before turning his attention back to Carr. This time there was no coughing. Briggs closed his eyes for a second and relished the quick, calming effects of the nicotine. He opened his eyes and looked back at Carr. "All right. Enough said about this morning's bullshit. What do we have here?"

Carr pointed over to a large man, leaning against a pick-up truck. "See that guy over there?"

The chief looked over at Walter. "Yeah."

"That kid and his grandmother came over here this morning. The victim, a Mrs. Mary Gowan, hadn't shown up to the senior center last Tuesday. When she didn't show up today, either, the kid's grandmother got nervous and had him drive over here and check things out." Carr smiled. "The kid went around looking in windows. When he got to one of the windows in the back, he looked in and without realizing it, saw a reflection of himself staring back at him in Gowan's dressing table mirror. He freaked out, thinking it was some—and I quote—'big ugly guy' roaming around in the old lady's house. They called, and Kroner sent a car over. Found Gowan in her bed, laid out just like Mason on a white sheet."

"Shit."

"Yeah. This one is a lot worse than the other though."

"How so."

The killer appears to have gone into a frenzy or something. The room was all torn up, not neat like the last one."

"What about her clothes? Was she wearing anything?"

"Nope. I mean, she had a nightgown on, we think, but it had been ripped off. Panties too."

"Hmm. That's something. Were the clothes piled like last time?"

"No. This time they were just like you said they should be for a crime like this. Thrown in different spots around the room."

"Really!"

Carr's face clouded. "And another thing was different too, Chief. Well, noticeably different."

"What was that?"

"The killer cut her head off."

12

Wednesday, December 7, 1972. Briggs stormed up the steps of the town hall's inner staircase. He was coming from the mayor's office and he was not in a good mood. He couldn't remember the last time he *was* in a good mood. He'd managed to avoid the mayor the day before by remaining at the crime scene until after 6 p.m. When he finally did return to his office, seven messages from Jim Tatum were laid out across his desk, demanding his presence as soon as he came in. He'd decided to face the music this morning and get it out of the way.

The mayor had nothing good to say. He attacked Roland for behavior he felt was below that of a seasoned detective and a chief of police. He screamed at him for getting the press all fired up about the murder again. Briggs wanted to scream back and say that it didn't matter, since another body had been found. Tatum even started to accuse Briggs of inciting the killer, driving him out to kill again, having been motivated by Briggs' compliments concerning his intelligence. When Briggs interrupted and reminded the mayor that Mrs. Gowan had been dead long before the reports in the paper, the mayor changed the subject and ranted on about how Briggs' inability to catch the killer was going to seriously effect the economic situation in Wilton. No skier in his or her right mind would dare come to a town where some maniac was running around, cutting off the heads of his victims, he screamed. But worst of all, Carr had 'mentioned' to the mayor yesterday afternoon that Briggs had gotten 'physical' with him at the latest crime scene, and as far as the mayor was concerned, this was unacceptable. Briggs tried to tell him that he just grabbed his arm; but again, the mayor did not want to hear it. Now Briggs would have to tiptoe around Carr, too.

Briggs stormed through the station and went to his office, slamming the door behind him. He'd had enough. The chief slumped into his chair and buried his face in his hands. He had tried to stay away from the investigation as much as he could. He was the only one who knew that he'd run away from a lot more than just a bad memory down in Jacksonville. People down there, people he once considered friends, began to wonder out loud that maybe Briggs had done more than just *drive* his wife to suicide. After all, they had said, it was his gun she'd used. He had no real alibi for the time she allegedly killed herself. If anyone knew how to stage a suicide, it would be a veteran homicide detective. Even after his nervous breakdown, doubters still exsisted. They attributed his mental problems not to grief, but to guilt from the stress of covering up a murder. He'd run away from all of that and he ran away from therapy that had only begun to help him. When he left Jacksonville, the next to last thing his therapist had told him was that he was barely ready to go back to police work. The last thing the therapist had told him was that he was definitely not ready to go back to working homicide.

The nightmares involving his wife and other dead people he'd seen over the years, nightmares that he stopped having two years ago, were back with a vengeance. He didn't even want to go to bed anymore. He, more than anyone else, needed closure to this case. The only thing he'd resolved for sure was that he was through with Meredith. He would not, for any reason, get back into that situation with her again. Briggs pushed his head back into the headrest on his chair. He pulled a Marlboro from the pack he had in his jacket pocket and lit up. He needed cigarettes right now. He quit before; he'd quit again after this case was closed. There was a knock at the door.

"Yeah."

Palin stuck his head in. "It's us, Chief. You ready for us?"

"Come on in. Is Carr with you?"

"He's right behind me."

Briggs made his decision. Now that the killer had killed again, there would be more clues. A stronger likelihood that they would catch him. Briggs had gone over everything in his mind the day before when he stayed at the Gowan house long after everyone else was gone. He climbed inside the killer's head, he thought, and he felt that he had gotten a pretty good read on him. Briggs was done feeling angry with Carr. Hell, it was probably his fault that he was having problems with his men. Carr was right. There had been something up his ass lately, but she was gone now. It was time to move on, get this murder solved, and get back to healing.

Carr came in and joined them seconds after Palin sat down. He was quiet, probably waiting to see how Briggs would react to him. No problem. Briggs planned on getting off to a fresh start with these two. It was the first item on his agenda. The second item was solving the murders.

"Listen, you guys. I'm gonna make this short and sweet, 'cause we don't have a lot of time to be fuckin' around with anything other than the murder investigation. But first, I gotta apologize." Carr and Palin looked at each other, then back at Briggs. He continued. "I've been a bear these last few weeks, I know that. This time of the year is really hard for me." Briggs decided to tell them a quick half-truth about his personal life and move on. "Ever since my wife passed away, my relationship with my kids has been deteriorating. It's gotten so bad that they don't even accept my Christmas cards anymore. So between Thanksgiving and Christmas, I'm usually not that much fun to be around. With these murders...well, it really intensified my feelings as of late, and I've been taking it out on you guys and anybody else I can find, as you both saw at the party. So, I hope you'll accept my apology, so we can move on to catching this killer."

"Hey, no problem, Chief," Palin said. "We all have bad phases we go through, ya know."

"Yeah, let's just put all the bullshit in the past and get this guy," said Carr.

"All right. Excellent. Now, with that said, the first thing I want to do, is to force you guys to put up with a little bit more of my theorizing. That thing I said to you, Carr, about waiting around for our criminal to fall out of a tree. I know that you haven't been doing that, but you also haven't been asked to investigate homicides before. Things are getting serious now. We have two victims, and if I'm guessing right, more will follow if we don't catch this killer soon. So, I'm gonna go over some things I've been putting together. I've closed over one hundred murder investigations and I think that I really need to step in and assist. You guys will still be doing all the 'investigating,' but I want to give you some of my observations, my take on this, so to speak. Okay?"

Now it was Carr's turn to concede a little. "That sounds good, Chief. I gotta tell ya, it has been a little tough. I thought for sure that we'd get the guy pretty quick. But as time passed by, I believed that it was a transient and that we probably were not going to catch him. Now, though, I'm a bit overwhelmed and I realize I am out of my league. You were right when you said this guy is sharp, so anything you can give us to get us on track will be great."

Briggs reached into his desk and pulled out a pad of paper. "I've come up with a list of similarities and differences between the two murders and the two victims. My feeling on this is that since this guy isn't leaving us much to go on, we need to start with the victims and work backward.

"What do you mean by that, Chief?"

"I'll let you guys in on a little secret. A couple of years or so before I left the force in Jacksonville, me and two other guys I'd been in the service with had a small reunion at a seminar the FBI held on fingerprinting techniques. Both of them went into law enforcement like myself: one to the Boston police department and the other to the FBI. Completely by accident, we all ended up at this seminar together. The guy from Boston had been fortunate enough to have worked on the Boston Strangler case, and he started talking about the case with us over beers after the first day of the seminar. To make a long story short, this Boston Strangler case got us talking about the similarities we'd all noticed in certain types of violent criminals. We also began to realize that by studying the types of people who fell prey to these violent criminals we could determine what sort of people were more likely to become victims of violent crime.

"The three of us went home at the end of the three-day seminar very excited and raring to get to our violent crimes files and start doing research. We'd developed a checklist of items to make sure that we were all looking for the same sort of things—making sure we were consistent. Our hope was that we would be able to establish some sort of way of predicting the characteristics of a particular criminal based on the type of crime he was committing."

Palin was nodding excitedly. "That sounds really interesting. How far did you get?"

"Unfortunately, I didn't get too far. I'd compiled a lot of research and began seeing strong personality patterns developing for particular types of crime, but then after my wife died…well, I sort of lost interest in the project."

"Are the other guys still at it?" asked Carr.

"As far as I know, Doug Johnson is. Jason Donell, my buddy out in Boston, was too busy to really get into it. I talked to them both right after…after my wife died. But not since."

"Hey!" Palin exclaimed. "So that first day, after the Mason murder, when you were guessing that it was a young kid that had killed her…" he flipped open his notebook. "…Somebody in his late teens or early twenties.' Were you basing that on some of your past research?"

"Yes."

"If you don't mind, Chief, maybe you can tell us how you came up with that so we can see how this stuff works," said Carr. He looked at his notes. "You also said that there was something not right about the scene, made you think that it was too neat. I have to admit, I had no idea what you were talking about when you said that."

Briggs smiled. He had his men interested. "Well, let me tell you how it works. I'll start with why I originally thought it was a kid and then point out the problems with that assumption." Briggs paused to clear his throat, and then continued. "One thing I discovered is that killers mature and become better at what they do, just like a detective becomes better at detecting after years of doing it. As these killers become better, they also become bolder—they are more willing to take risks. In this particular murder, we have Mason, a retired woman, overweight, no one else living in her house with her since her husband died. She presented little challenge to the killer—an easy target, same with the Gowan woman. She was even easier, living way out in the middle of nowhere.

"These kinds of victims are usually the target of someone, some murderer, who was, well, a beginner for lack of a better word. I saw it over and over again when I was on the streets, and later too, when I was going through the files of other violent crimes. Old victim—young kid. Little boy or girl disappears from a wooded play area—young kid. It's not until later, when they've pulled it off a few times, that these guys start going after the prostitutes or the kids in the supermarket or on the city playground. These situations present more of a challenge to the perp. The young prostitutes could put up much more of a fight than any old woman, and to walk into a shopping center and pluck a kid right out of a store takes balls. Oh, one important aspect of the research we were doing was that we were looking at crimes where the victim was not known to the killer prior to the killing. The rules changed a lot if there was a prior relationship. The kind of murder me and my buddies were, well, *are* interested in is known as Stranger Killing."

"All right, so far this makes pretty good sense," said Carr. "But what about the problems you mentioned? If what you're saying is true, then I would agree that we should be looking for a younger person. Why do you doubt that it's a kid?"

"Because of the scene itself. The murder itself appears to be the work of an amateur, but the crime scene is way too clean."

"Yeah?"

"Well, the first scene did not fit with the research I'd done in the past. Put yourself in a young killer's shoes. You're gonna forget a lot of stuff, you're gonna make mistakes. You'll be nervous. Both these murders have strong sexual overtones. Attempted rapes, clothes being ripped off the body. That's all there in front of us. But then the crime *scene* is almost perfectly intact. Nothing was knocked over; the place hadn't been ransacked. There was no malicious damage done at all. No bloody hand prints on the walls or doorknobs. Nothing. All the indications from the wounds to the body, though, indicate a killer in a sexual frenzy. Wildly stabbing and slashing when, supposedly, he can't perform." Briggs paused for a moment to think.

"What's the matter, Chief," Palin asked. He was discovering a new respect for the chief.

"Something that just struck me. I hadn't thought about this yesterday, when I was at the Gowan house. This second murder, if the scenes had been reversed, I probably wouldn't have had so much trouble with things. It would still be a stretch for me to think that the killer matured that quickly, but at least you'd have a progression. The way these crimes occurred, there's regression, which is odd. There was blood everywhere at the second murder. The place was trashed and the traces of that soil were there, between her legs, as if the perp had crawled up between her, tried to rape her, ya know. There were bloody boot marks left across the rug in the living room leading out of the house. The nightclothes were thrown instead of placed. And then that head being cut off—the act of a true, out-of-control psycho. That's what I would have expected at the first scene; and then, like a wish come true, here I have it at the second."

"Maybe you did it!" Carr joked.

Briggs had to look at him before realizing that he was kidding. "It's weird. It's like the killer crawled inside my head and lived up to my expectations for this sort of murder."

So who did do it, then?" asked Palin.

"I think it was someone who knew these women. Someone older. Someone trying to get the murder scenes to appear to us in a certain way."

"Why, though?"

Briggs brought his hands up to his face, interlocking his fingers but extending his index fingers, and placed them against his lips, thinking. After a long pause, he shook his head. "I don't know, and it pisses me off. Did you guys come across any background information linking these two women at all?"

Carr flipped a few pages of his notebook. "None. Mason was a retired nurse, as you know. Gowan was a housewife. Mason's husband was an insurance man; Gowan's was a teacher. We even checked to see if Gowan had been insured by Mason's husband's company, but he wasn't."

"Were you able to get a better idea about the time of death?"

"Most likely it was between the evening of November twenty-first and the morning of the twenty-eighth. The last people to see her alive were those old folks down at the Senior Center. There's a strong possibility that she was still alive as late as the twenty-third because store flyers delivered on that Thursday were inside the house. After that time, the mail had been left in her mailbox. She didn't get much, just bills and such."

"That's good work, guys. What about—"

There was a knock at the door. Then Officer Berson, who was working the desk, stepped inside the chief's office. He looked excited. "Sorry to interrupt, Chief, but we may have had a break in the case."

13

Briggs leaned against the wall of the room used for interviews and interrogations. Meredith sat on one side of the small metal table in one of the three plain wooden chairs in the room. Palin and Carr occupied the other two, sitting across from her. Her hands were in her lap. She looked nervous. One large window allowed the morning sun to fill the room with light.

"I think I saw the killer of that Gowan woman. I was driving by her house on Thursday, November twenty-third, I looked—"

"About what time was that, Mrs. King?" asked Palin.

Meredith had thought out this whole description in her head on the way over. She wanted to act as if she wasn't exactly sure of the time. Make it seem like she was just out for a walk on the Robert

Frost trail, nothing suspicious about that. "I guess it was about five or so. It was getting dark out and—"

"If you don't mind me asking, Mrs. King, what were you doing out in that part of town?"

Before answering Meredith shot a quick glance over at Briggs. He showed no signs of knowing why she'd been out there. "I...I took a walk up the Robert Frost trail, back by the horse barn. There's that entrance there, off of Aaron street."

"Yes, I know the place. Please go on."

"Well," she said, "I pulled out of the little lot at the barn and came to the end of the dirt road. I looked to my right just to make sure that no one was coming and that's when I saw him." She looked at Briggs again to see if she could tell anything from his expression. Nothing. Over the last week, she'd decided that the man in the mountain was probably Briggs. He'd set her up and scared the hell out of her just to spite her, to get even with her for not being able to leave Tim. She was very angry with Briggs and didn't want to see him, but when she saw the picture of the Gowan house in the paper and recognized it as the house where she'd seen the man standing in the yard, she knew she had to go to the police.

"Saw who, Mrs. King?"

"The killer, of course," she said, a bit flustered by Detective Palin's dumb question. "He was standing in the yard, just staring at me. His longish gray hair was blowing across his face in the wind, so I couldn't see his features. Plus he was about seventy-five yards away and it was getting a little dark. But I do remember he had on one of those dark, one-piece uniforms mechanics wear. You know what I mean?"

Carr and the others were excited. There was a very good chance that Mrs. King had indeed seen the killer. "How old would you say he was?"

"I'd guess over fifty. He didn't look like a young man."

"What else can you remember?"

"That's about all. Oh, wait. There was one other thing. After he looked at me for a few seconds, he turned away and started heading around to the back of the house. He broke into this sort of jog, but he had an awkward gait. Like a limp or something. I drove on and he passed out of view behind the wood line." She looked at Briggs once more. He seemed confused, but said nothing.

"That is excellent, Mrs. King. That really does help us out a lot."

"It does? I was hoping I could help. It's so scary with that maniac running around out there." She got up to leave.

"Thanks again. If you think of anything else, come see us. Okay?"

Meredith left. Carr was the first to speak. "Well, Chief, does that description fit more with what you had been talking about?"

"Yeah, it does. I really think it must be an older guy. But I'd still guess that he knows these victims. Listen, guys, I'll be right back." Briggs hurriedly walked out of the town hall. Meredith was just turning the corner of the building, headed for the shortcut through the woods to her school. "Meredith!" he yelled.

She turned and waited while he ran over to her. "What?" she asked, coldly.

"Why did you lie in there?"

"What are you talking about?"

"It took me a minute, but then I realized. You said that the man in the yard passed out of sight behind the wood line as you drove on. You were going *to* the horse barn when you saw him, not coming from it. Why did you lie?"

"You know why I lied! What was I supposed to tell them? That I had a date with you and that you stood me up!"

"What are you talking about?"

She was about to lash out at him, but the serious look on his face made her stop. "You...you didn't send a note to me asking me to meet you at the horse barn?"

"No. Is that what you meant, at the party, when you said that you were there, but I wasn't?"

"Yes. Oh, my god!" Meredith could feel herself getting dizzy. "If you didn't send it, then who did? And who was that man who tried to attack me?"

"What!"

Meredith got a hold of herself. "There was another man. Jesus, probably the same man who killed Mrs. Gowan! I thought it was you getting back at me for not being able to leave Tim." Meredith told Briggs the whole story, from getting the note to being pursued by the man in the mountain.

"Do you still have the note?" he asked.

"Yes," she said softly, turning her eyes to the ground. "It's with the others, in a box in my attic."

"Could you let me see it? It may be a clue."

"I'll bring it by tomorrow." Meredith hesitated. "You won't show it to anybody else, will you?"

"No. Don't worry. I'm not going to let your little secret out."

"Our little secret. You have just as much to lose as I do."

Briggs thought about that for a second. He looked into her dark eyes. "I don't think so."

"What do you think this means? Why did the killer send me this note?" She was getting upset again.

"Calm down, Mer. I'm sure the person who sent you this note is not the guy in the yard," Briggs said after calming her down. But he wasn't so sure. What if whoever spooked Meredith was the same guy who killed Gowan? Briggs might now have a killer on his hands that knew about his relationship with Meredith. How had the killer found out? They'd been extremely careful the entire relationship. No, it couldn't be, Briggs thought, just a very weird coincidence. It had to be. He was trying to convince Meredith of this when he heard one of his patrol cars give a quick blast of its siren as it passed through the main intersection of Wilton, a block away. A few seconds later, Officer Mike Thayer brought the police car to a skidding stop in front of the town hall. "Something must be up, Meredith. I gotta go. Don't worry about this. I'm sure the guy who bothered you was not the same guy you saw in the yard. Some killer is not going to take the time to play hide and seek with you right after he did his thing."

"I hope not," she said, sounding somewhat reassured.

"I'll see you later," Briggs said, and turned to leave.

"Roland, wait. I—"

Briggs faced her. "Don't say anything, Meredith. It wasn't going to work, anyway. We had some good times—some nice memories. Let's leave it at that."

"Chief! Wait 'til you see what I have!" yelled Thayer.

"I'll miss you," she said.

"Yeah, me too."

Meredith walked into the trees and Briggs turned back towards Thayer. "Whattaya got?"

Thayer was carrying a box the size of a laundry basket. The two men went inside, where everyone who was working was already waiting for him with tremendous anticipation. He'd called his find into the station while Briggs was outside with Meredith.

"Show it to us," Palin said excitedly while he cleared a spot on his desk for Thayer to put the box down. We already called Adamski, he's coming over to pick it up."

"What the hell is it?" asked Briggs.

Officer Thayer triumphantly opened the top of the box. He pulled a pen from his pocket and the others watched as he slid his hand out of sight for a moment, hooking the pen on the end of something. He slowly raised a dark blue jumpsuit, covered with dark, brown splotches, half way out of the box.

"Holy shit! Is that blood?" asked Kroner.

"We won't know for sure 'til Adamski checks it out, but it sure looks like it, doesn't it? There's a pair of boots in here, too. They got this same brown staining."

Briggs could not believe how clues were coming out of the woodwork after nothing for almost six weeks. "Where'd you find this stuff?" he asked.

"I didn't. Some kids found them in an old abandoned shed on the other side of the field behind Mary Gowen's house. I guess they use the place as a regular hangout during the winter. These items were inside, lying on the floor. I left Lance Adams out there to protect the scene."

"This is fuckin' amazing!" Carr exclaimed. "First the much more detailed description of a man with a limp running away from the Gowan house, and now this! What next?"

"What did you just say!"

Everyone turned to look at Kroner, who stared, dumbfounded, at Carr. Carr said, "Meredith King, Tim's wife. She saw a guy running away from the Gowan house. She described him as having a distinctive limp when he ran."

"Son-of-a-bitch! Why didn't I think of this before?"

"What!" Briggs yelled.

"The blue overalls, the wispy hair, that professional fertilizer. God, I could kick myself. It didn't fall into place until you mentioned the limp."

"What are you talking about, Kroner?" asked Palin.

Kroner looked excited. "I know who the killer is!" he yelled.

14

May, 1946.

"Victor! Hey, Victor! Get up."

Victor lifted his head off the pillow to see who was yelling to him. It was one of the new attendants. Victor thought his name was Vince. "What is it?" he mumbled. Other patients in the dorm were waking up. Victor swung his legs out and put his feet on the cold, cement floor. He had to shuffle sideways to get out from between his bed and the bed of Willy Rivers, the man who slept next to him. The ward was getting tremendously overcrowded. Willy looked at him as he slid by. "Sorry, Willy."

"That's okay. Where ya goin', Vic?"

"I have no idea. I'll be back. Go ahead and sleep, I'll tell ya about it in the morning."

Willy pulled his blanket up around his neck and closed his eyes. Victor sat on his footlocker and pulled on his shoes. Vince walked down the small alleyway between all the beds. His silhouette cut sharply against the light coming in from the hallway behind him. "Here, Victor, take this. Put all your stuff in it." Vince threw Victor a large canvas duffel bag, much bigger than Victor needed.

"What for?"

"Just do it, okay, Victor? I don't know why for sure. Just load it up with your stuff and come with me. Oh, yeah, you're supposed to stuff your blanket in the bag, too."

Victor looked at him, confused. But he did what Vince told him to do. He could tell that Vince was being honest about not knowing what exactly was going on. Victor had learned to read people's faces very well. He had to. For the last six years, he'd been living in a world where just about everyone lied all the time.

Victor followed Vince down the hall through the locked doors, then out the main door and down the stairs leading out of his building. When they got outside, Victor took a deep breath. The cool night air smelled of the wet earth. The last snows had melted away a few days ago. "Hey, Vince, What time is it?"

"It's late. Around eleven."

Victor was on a first-name basis with most of the attendants now. He'd grown into a strong, intelligent young man and most of the staff had a certain cautious respect for him. Vince was new, but he tolerated Victor like the others. When Victor went off, it took more than a few of the attendants to subdue him. Vince had been warned about Victor within his first five minutes of being on the ward. About how Victor had put out seven men on permanent disability, two of them in one fight. Vince decided he would do like the rest and let Victor call him by his first name. Best to let sleeping dogs lie, he figured.

"Where we goin'?"

"I gotta take you to the superintendent's office."

"Really!" Victor exclaimed loudly. Vince flinched and stepped sideways, shocked by Victor's sudden outburst. "What the fuck does he want with me?"

"I don't know, Victor. I guess you'll find out soon, huh."

"I guess so, Vince. I guess so." They walked the last fifty yards in silence to the administrative building. Most of the building's offices were dark, but light from three large windows on the second floor shined down upon them as they climbed the stairs. Vince led the way up, and soon they were standing in front of a large oak door. Vince knocked lightly.

"Come in," said a cheerful voice from inside the room.

Vince swung the door open and stepped aside so Victor could enter ahead of him. Victor stepped into the largest office he'd ever seen. Along the lower portion of the walls were bookcases stuffed with all sorts of books. On the walls above were photographs of the school, taken from various angles and at different stages of its construction. Victor had entered at the far-left end of the room. In front of him, bathed in the soft yellow light of a small reading lamp were two overstuffed chairs and a cream-colored, comfortable-looking couch. Standing behind a desk at the far right was a well-dressed man, his hands behind his back. Victor guessed his age to be around forty. He peered at Victor over a pair of small, wire-rimmed glasses. To his right were two very large men who were obviously there to enforce order. They were sitting uncomfortably in two high-backed Victorian-style chairs on either side of another doorway into this man's office. After a few seconds, when the well-dressed man was done sizing Victor up, he smiled quickly and stepped forward, resting the fingertips of both hands on his desk. "Victor, please have a seat." Victor moved cautiously to the small chair on his side of the man's desk and sat down. Once he had, the man pulled his leather swivel chair around and sat, too.

The man continued to gaze at Victor for a few uncomfortable moments. He had gray, watery-looking eyes and a sharp, almost delicate nose. Victor cleared his throat uncomfortably and the man smiled again. "Don't be nervous," he said. "My name is Dr. Harold Wesson. Did you know that, Victor?"

"No, I didn't."

He smiled again. "I'm the superintendent of this school."

Victor felt uneasy around this man. "I thought that old guy that I seen around here was the boss of this school."

"He left a year ago. I was asked to replace him, to...make some changes."

"What sort of changes?"

"Well, Victor, with most of the changes you don't have to concern yourself with. But one of them affects you greatly. That's why you're here tonight."

"What are ya talkin' about?"

The man paused for a moment and picked a file up off his desk. He studied it for a moment, then looked at Victor again. "It says here that you have a severe stutter."

Victor waited for the man to say more, but he didn't. "I—it went away."

"Really. How so?"

"I don't know. It just did."

"That's very interesting." Dr. Wesson looked at Victor's chart a little more. Another long, uncomfortable silence followed. "Things have begun to change around here, Victor."

"I hadn't noticed."

"You haven't noticed that the building you live in is much more crowded?" the man asked sharply, as if doubting something he'd previously thought.

"Well, yeah, I thought you meant...something else. Like the place was getting better or something."

Again the man smiled. "You are a smart man," he said, as if confirming something he'd previously read or heard. The man placed his elbows on the armrests of the chair; bringing his hands up, he interlocked the fingers and brought them up underneath his chin. "My job here is to try to do just that, Victor. Make the place better. And one of the things I have to do to get that process underway is to make sure that only the people who *need* to be here, remain here. It is my opinion, based of course on the new standards established by the board of trustees of this school, that you no longer need to be here."

Victor was stunned. The man had said the words in such a matter of fact way that he'd been caught totally off guard. He could feel his heart racing. All he could manage was a very weak "What?"

"I said you no longer need to attend this facility. The standards, which were used to bring you here, have now changed. You no longer fit the profile of a man who needs this school's help."

"I don't understand." Victor had dreamed of the day that he could leave, but he'd never really thought about the possibility of it really happening. Where would he go? He hated to admit it to himself, but the thought of leaving scared the hell out of him. "What are you talking about?"

Again, the smile first. The man glanced down briefly at the chart again. "A long time ago, you were given some tests, back at your school, the school you attended before coming here. Do you remember?"

Victor remembered. "Yes, of course."

"Well, you see, based on the results of those tests—well, actually the results of your brother's tests and the fact that your sister was who she was, you were brought here to this place. Since that time, there have been new, scientific discoveries indicating to us that you no longer have to be kept away…that you no longer need our support. Victor, you are free to go."

"What the hell are you talking about!" Victor yelled. He heard a noise off to his right. The two large men were now standing. Victor checked his tone. "Excuse me. I…it's eleven o'clock at night. What am I doing…I…what am I supposed to do?"

"I can understand that it is a bit overwhelming."

Victor pulled himself together. "Is that what happened to Stevie and Paul? Did you let them go, too?"

"Yes. They've already left the facility, and they're doing fine, I'm sure."

"What about my brother? My sister?"

"Your brother and sister will remain here. Their problems still dictate involvement by the state.

"I don't understand all this. How is it—"

"Victor," the doctor interrupted. "You don't need to concern yourself with that, now. You need to be thinking of your future." The man took a deep breath and began a short, prepared statement. "You will now be going out into the world to start your new life. It is important that you find a place to live and then a job as soon as possible. Idle time is the devil's handmaiden. Stay away from the criminal sort. Stay out of trouble. Work hard and you will do well. There are people out there who will try to take advantage of you. Don't be fooled by anyone offering to help you. Save some of your money that you earn for emergencies. Don't drink alcohol and don't fall in with questionable women." The doctor paused and opened a drawer of the desk. He pulled out a small metal box, opened it, and removed a crisp twenty-dollar bill. "Here Victor, this is yours. To help get you started."

He looked over at Vince. "Do you have his jacket?"

"Yes, sir. It's in the closet downstairs."

"All right then. We're done here." The doctor stood up and offered his hand to Victor, who took it slowly. Was this some sort of weird dream? "Good luck, Victor."

The doctor sat back down and busied himself with some paper-work. Suddenly, Vince was at Victor's side. "Come on, Victor. It's time to go."

In a state of shock, Victor turned and aimlessly followed Vince out of the room. The two large men fell in behind. They went back down the same stairs they'd come up when Victor was still a student, but now he was walking down a free man. When they reached the bottom of the stairs, Vince walked over to a hall closet and took out a winter jacket. "There may still be some pretty cool nights ahead, Victor. This jacket is for you, provided by the state."

Victor allowed Vince to help him put the jacket on. Together they walked to the large double doors that led to the outside world. Vince opened them, then led Victor outside. "Good luck, Victor." Vince patted him on the back and turned away, walking back inside the administration building. He closed the door behind him, leaving Victor standing on the steps alone. What was he supposed to do now? He had no choice. It was time to leave.

Victor looked out into the darkness. From where he stood, he could see out over the edge of the property line of the hospital. Off to places he hadn't been in years. The land sloped away, down a steep hillside. Over the treetops, Victor could see specks of light. He sighed gently, then walked into the night toward the town below.

15

Monday, January 15, 1973. It took the jury only one hour and twenty-three minutes to convict Milton Pike on two counts of murder in the first degree.

The state's evidence was overwhelming. Christian Peters, the district attorney, presented the case in chronological order. Mr. Grant went first. He described how he and his wife had seen a man fitting Milton Pike's general description walking down Stanley Street on Thursday night, October twenty-sixth of last year, the night the coroner approximated the time of death to be in the Mason murder. Then Peters had the coroner himself explain the graphic photographs of the Mason and the Gowan murders, exposing all the gory similarities between the two victims while staying away from the differences.

Once the stage had been set with the photos, Peters had Ron Adamski take the stand to go over all of the forensic evidence that was found at the murder scenes. He also went over the physical evidence collected at Pike's residence during a search warrant, which was issued and executed less than two hours after Kroner's realization. Everything fell into place. Very little effort was needed. All Briggs and his men had to do was collect all the pieces of the puzzle, slide them into their appropriate places, and make the arrest of Milton Pike. It was a dream come true for the townspeople. The sick man who killed two of their own was now behind bars. They could get on with their lives now without fearing that a killer was lurking among them. They were out for blood. Pike's blood would do just fine.

Briggs, on the other hand, wasn't so quick to judge. He watched as the state's case grew and the items on the evidence table piled up. There were items that had been found in an old toolbox of Pike's. A handkerchief with Mason's initials on it. A small religious figurine of the Virgin Mary, identified by Mason's daughter as one of her mother's long-time belongings. In addition to this, the police had found Mrs. Gowan's wedding ring wrapped in a rag at the bottom of Pike's sock drawer. There was the rusty old saw found hanging on the garage wall, stained with traces of blood matching in type to that of Gowan. Peters had dramatically taken this item up, walked over to the jury and, with the photo of Gowan's decapitated body displayed behind him, dramatically reenacted sawing off her head. He presented the jury with the coveralls and boots, pointing out all the horrible blood stains while telling the jury that Pike himself had identified the items as his, but said that they'd been stolen from him a few months back. "How convenient," Peters added, sarcastically.

Other damaging evidence included the nipples of both women, found wrapped in plastic wrap and tin foil and stuck inside a stack of dirty magazines in the corner of Pike's basement. Pike's hair matched in color and length to the hair found wrapped in Mason's fingers. An industrial-sized bag of Quick-Gro, the soil type found at both murder scenes, leaned against the leg of the evidence table. This had been found in Pike's storage shed. Peters saved Meredith King for his last witness. Having a prominent resident like Meredith point to Pike as he sat helplessly behind the defense table was powerful, but probably unnecessary. By the time she took the stand, Briggs could tell by looking at the faces of the members of the jury that they were already convinced. Without a doubt, Pike was a vicious, good-for-nothing killer who needed to be locked up for the rest of his life.

The rookie public defender, Larry Holloway, did his best, which wasn't saying much. He started his representation off with a bang by accidentally driving another nail into Pike's coffin. After a short conference with his client on the day Pike had been arrested, he blurted out triumphantly that his client could not possibly have committed these crimes because he was impotent from a debilitating case of diabetes. Briggs leaned against the wall of the interrogation room that day, watching Holloway's face cloud up as Carr informed the young lawyer that the *Wilton Gazette* had jumped the gun on that piece of information and that there had actually been no rape committed against either woman. "We just decided that we might be able to use that to our advantage somehow. Thanks for allowing us the opportunity to do so," Carr had told Holloway. Pike didn't seem to understand what had happened, much to the relief of Holloway.

Holloway was only able to come up with two character witnesses willing to take the stand in Pike's defense. Pike was a handyman, sort of a jack-of-all-trades type. Most of the work he did, when he worked at all, was painting, but he had a few customers for whom he did lawn care. His ability to work over the last few years had dwindled to only a few hours a week. The diabetes caused a lack of sensation in his feet. He'd lost the two outside toes of his left foot in a lawn mower accident years ago. Both character witnesses were long-time customers of Pike. They claimed he worked hard and did a good job and that they never saw him get angry or lose his temper. He talked very little with them. He kept to himself and concentrated on his work.

In a last-ditch effort, Holloway decided that Pike would take the stand in his own defense. The man was of average height, about five foot eight. He was a good forty pounds overweight. He limped across the floor, wearing an old brown suit that made him look dumpier than he already was. He stared at the jury members with dull eyes from underneath gray hair, cut short in a weak attempt by Holloway to make the man more presentable and less like the man eyewitnesses had described. He testified to the fact that he had never met the victims before and he had no reason to hurt them. He was unable to offer an alibi for the times in question. He said that the Quick-Gro had suddenly appeared in his shed one day, so he started to use it. Briggs thought that Holloway put him on the stand to show how stupid the man was. Maybe the jury would think that he wasn't smart enough to murder anyone and get away with it for as long as he had. He told the jury that he was not on Stanley Street on the night in question—that he hadn't been on Stanley Street in years. He swore to them that he had never stood in Mrs. Gowan's yard and that he had no idea why anybody would say that he did. But it was all for nothing. He was the killer. The jury believed it and so did everyone else. Even Holloway, worried about public sentiment and what defending a man like Pike could do to his future in lawyering, commented after the verdict that it was difficult to defend a man who was so obviously guilty, but that he tried to do the best job he could. He hoped the people of Wilton would appreciate that.

Briggs talked to the press, too, and did his bit of public relations, saying that it was wonderful that the killer had been caught; but personally, he had some serious doubts. Three things bothered him: the first and most obvious was his gut. Briggs could tell by listening to Pike during interrogations that he had a lot of street smarts, but he didn't think the man was smart enough to leave a scene like he had in the first murder. It was just too clean. There had been few clues and, as far as Briggs could see, very little evidence left behind. Then, all of a sudden, the Gowan woman is murdered in a drastically different way than Mason. The scene is sloppy, footprints across the floor, blood splattered on the walls and ceiling, the head cut off. A gloved palm print is left on the doorknob. It bothered Briggs.

The second thing that ate at him was more than a cop's instinct. Two days before the end of the trial, he'd gone out and talked to the kids who found the clothing at the shack. He remembered that the kids told Thayer it was their 'regular' hangout. He asked the kids when they had been at the shack prior to finding the clothes. He brought a calendar to help them remember. He pointed to the twenty-third of November, reminding the kids that this was probably the day that Mrs. Gowan had been killed. He then pointed to the fifth of December, the day the body was found. Both boys nodded. One boy pointed to the sixth. "We found that stuff out at the shack on that night."

"Yes," Briggs said. "Do you remember if you had been out to the shack at all between this day, the twenty-third, and the day that you actually found the clothes?"

Both boys thought for a moment. "Yeah, we were out there on this day." Briggs pointed to Saturday, December second. "The two of us and Pete, Ray, Drooper, and Dave were out there all day. We were playing war."

The other kid was still looking at the calendar as his friend continued to talk to Briggs. "That's weird," he said, expressing what Briggs was thinking. "I wonder why the clothes weren't out there then?"

The third thing that was bothering Briggs, he needed to test. On the last day of the trial, after the verdict was read and the guards were taking Pike out of the courtroom, Briggs asked to talk to the man in private for a minute. He walked a few feet away from the guards and looked hard at the face of Pike.

"Now, Mr. Pike, I want you to answer me one question, okay?"

Pike sneered at Briggs. "Why should I answer any of your questions? You and your boys are framin' me, you bastard."

"I know you're pretty angry right now, but look at me. I may be one of the only people left in this town that still has a little doubt about whether or not you're guilty. Will you answer this one question or not?" Pike glared at Briggs for a moment. Briggs could almost see the wheels of Pike's uneducated, slow-moving mind spinning, trying to determine if Briggs was attempting to trick him. "What have you got to lose, Mr. Pike?"

Pike stopped staring and looked away. Briggs was right. He'd already been convicted. "What is it ya wanna know?"

Meredith, as promised, had given Briggs the letter in which someone had used his initials to get her out to the horse barn. Briggs had decided that the murderer and the writer of this letter were the same person. The killer did it to get Meredith out there as a witness. He'd read the letter ten times before he realized what bothered him about it. "Mr. Pike," Briggs said seriously, "you've been very *ambivalent* about this trial, wouldn't you agree?"

Pike stared back at Briggs. He looked confused. Briggs didn't think he'd know what the word meant. "What's that?"

"Didn't you hear me?"

"I heard ya, I just don't know what you're meanin.'"

"Thank you, Mr. Pike. You've been very helpful."

Pike looked at Briggs as if he were crazy. "What da ya mean, I been helpful? I don't know what you're askin' me." But Briggs was already walking away. "Well, to hell with you then, Briggs! What the hell was that?"

Briggs left the courthouse in a state of confusion and concern. He no longer believed that Pike was the killer; but the alternative meant that the real killer was still out there, and this person was a mastermind who'd just pulled off the perfect frame. He thought about going to Peters but quickly decided against it. He wouldn't be able to tell him about the letter test without revealing his old relationship with Meredith. He would have to get more evidence. The clothes not being in the shack a few days after the killing and then showing up later was odd, no doubt, but not enough to put aside all the other evidence that had been presented proving Pike's guilt. Briggs felt a wave of excitement as he headed back to the town hall. He was pretty certain that the killer had just made his first mistake. He'd written the letter with Briggs in mind, who might very well have used the word 'ambivalent' if *he* were actually writing a note, but not Pike. He didn't even know what it meant. He decided to talk to the mayor about it. Get some feedback from him. There was a lot of work to do. They'd have to start at square one. Look at all the evidence again. Dig into Pike's past. Who would go through all this effort to frame him? Or was he just an innocent fool, targeted because of his reclusive nature, who honestly never had anything to do with these two women before?

The celebration was already underway by the time the chief got back to the town hall. Everyone knew what the verdict would be, so the secretaries had prepped the police station for the triumphant return of Briggs and his two detectives as soon as they got word that the jury was returning from deliberations. Everyone present applauded as the chief came through the office door.

"Way to go, Chief!"

"We knew you'd catch him!"

The chief walked to the middle of the group of city employees. "Thank you all for this, it's very sweet. I think we owe old Kroner a big hand though. He's the one who clinched it for us." The chief pointed at Kroner, then started clapping. Everyone else clapped, too, and Kroner took an over-exaggerated bow. The chief spotted the mayor towards the back of the room, standing next to Frank Murman, the town hall architect. He thanked everyone again, then moved quickly through the small crowd toward the mayor. As he approached, the mayor offered up a warm smile and stuck out his hand.

"Briggs! Wonderful job. Congratulations." He vigorously shook Briggs' hand.

"Yes, sir, it sure was great to hear that you got him," added Murman when it was his turn to shake hands.

"Thank you. Thank you, both." Briggs was anxious to talk to the mayor about his doubts over Pike's guilt. "Jim. Listen, I really need to talk to you. In private." Briggs cast an eye at Murman.

"I was just going over to say congrats to the two detectives anyway," Murman offered.

"What's on your mind, Roland?"

"Well, I don't really know how to say this, but, I think we made a mistake with Pike."

"What!" The mayor was exasperated. "Goddamn it, Briggs. Aren't you ever satisfied?"

"There are some things that don't add up, Jim. I've been doing some checking. We never really talked to those kids in depth because of all the excitement and everything coming together so quickly. But I checked with them a couple days ago. They'd been out to that shack earlier in the week—but after the murder had taken place! Why weren't the clothes out there then? And look at this." Briggs fumbled around in his pockets until he found the piece of paper on which he'd scribbled a crude map. "Look at the location of the shack with respect to Gowan's residence. It's in the opposite direction of Pike's house. You saw him at trial. Why would he walk—or better, hobble the half-mile out to the shack to dump those clothes? I don't think the guy could even make it out there. And then there's—"

"Briggs! Damn it." The mayor's eyes narrowed. "Would you listen to yourself for a second. You're going a mile-a-minute here. What you're suggesting is preposterous! Weren't you at the trial? We could have gotten a conviction with a quarter of the evidence we had. Not one piece of evidence pointed away from Pike."

"Yeah, I know, but that's what I was leading up to. I think he was framed by some genius of a killer! Someone out there led us right down the path and Pike was sitting at the end of it like a big old Christmas present."

The mayor took a deep breath before continuing, and when he did, he talked slowly. He was fighting to control his anger. "Roland, I know things have been rough for you these last few months, but it's over. You've caught your killer. There is no big conspiracy here." He put his arm around Briggs. "Do you realize that we've had more reservations this year than any previous year to date! People are dying—no disrespect to the victims—to come and see the town where the Wilton Ripper stalked his prey. Business is booming. You have to realize that one very sick man committed two very horrible murders, nothing more, nothing less. Look around you, everyone is here to celebrate your victory. Why don't you join them?"

Briggs glanced over his shoulder at his men and women and the other town employees who'd taken the time to share in his glory.

He hung his head for a moment. Maybe he was acting a little crazy. The case presented by the state was unbelievably strong. Could it be that someone else wrote the letter? Maybe it was Tim, Meredith's husband, who wrote the note and frightened her to try to get her to stop seeing him.

He turned back to the mayor. "I don't know, Jim. It just seemed odd to me that the kids—"

The door to the police station swung open, slamming into the wall behind it. Tim King stormed into the room. His face was beet red, contorted in anger. "Were the hell is Briggs?"

"I'm over here, Tim. What can I do for you?"

Tim's eye's fell on Briggs and for a second, he just stood there, glaring. Then he started running. He jumped over the little divider wall and dove at Briggs, who side-stepped and watched as Tim barreled into the mayor. He righted himself quickly, turning and taking a swing at Briggs with his right fist. Briggs caught Tim's wrist as he moved out of the way of the highly telegraphed blow and twisted his arm. Tim yelped in pain and bent forward, trying to relieve some of the torque Briggs had on his shoulder joint. As he did, Briggs delivered three sharp, snapping front kicks to Tim's solar plexus. Tim dropped to his knees and started to keel over, but Briggs hit him with a powerful, downward left cross that sent Tim sprawling onto his stomach before he had a chance to hit the ground on his own.

"Briggs, my god! You might have killed him," the mayor shouted.

Briggs was standing above Tim, rubbing the knuckles on his left hand. "He's not dead," Briggs said angrily. "But he could have been. What the fuck was that all about?"

The Mayor walked over to where Tim lay and knelt down to check his pulse. He was just unconscious. Next to him was an eight by ten photograph laying upside down. The mayor picked it up and looked at it. Some of the others in the room who'd gathered near Tim saw it and gasped.

"Holy shit, Chief. No wonder he came after you," Palin voiced.

"Son of a bitch," someone else whispered.

Briggs couldn't see what the photograph was from where he was standing, but he could see the mayor's face, and he didn't look happy. "How do you explain this?" he asked Briggs, offering him the photograph.

Briggs took it, allowing his eyes to linger on the others for a moment before looking down at its contents. "Oh, no," he said in a voice just above a whisper. He was looking at a grainy, black and white photograph of himself, his pants down around his knees, and Meredith, making love on the hood of her car. The photo was somewhat blurry, and Briggs had to think a second before realizing that it was probably taken out at the old mill. Unfortunately, though, it was clear enough to easily identify the two lovers.

A moan from Tim King brought Briggs back to the moment. He looked up to see everyone glaring at him, most especially the mayor.

"Briggs!" the mayor yelled. "Get out of my sight! I don't want to talk to you when I'm feeling like this. I may do something you'll regret. I want your ass in my office at ten a.m. sharp tomorrow morning to talk about your future here in Wilton. No, make it Friday. I'll need that much time to calm down. I can't believe this! What were you thinking?"

"I'm not the one who came in here throwing punches! Why are you mad at me?"

"Isn't it obvious?" screeched the mayor, thumbing the photo with his finger.

"That whole thing has been over for months. I can't help it if he can't please his wife!"

"Enough! Enough. I don't want any more of this. Go!"

Briggs glared at the mayor. "Fine." He began to walk out of the station. "What the hell are y'all looking' at!" he yelled at the gawking others. "Get outa my way." He pushed his way through the throng and stormed out of the building.

"Detective Carr, where are you?"

"Right here, sir."

"I want you to take over as acting Chief of Police while Briggs is out."

"You can count on me, Sir," Carr answered in his most official voice. "Do you expect that Chief Briggs will be out long, sir?"

"He won't be back anytime soon."

"Yes, sir," Carr answered, frowning, all the while holding back an evil smile.

16

Tuesday, January 16, 1973. Another night of broken sleep. This time it wasn't the nightmares, it was the frustration and the anger that kept him up. He'd had enough of the bullshit. He ended the relationship with Meredith months ago and now, even though it was over, somehow it was getting in the way of his life. Again, with this woman shit. He swore them off. All women. All of them. He got up early and sat around smoking cigarettes and drinking coffee until eight-thirty, then called Eleanor Mason's daughter at the hotel she was staying at. He decided to do more digging into Mason's past, see if he could turn up something that would satisfy…whatever it was that was bothering him. Briggs was hoping that the daughter hadn't left to go back to California. The clerk told him that she had the room through the weekend, but that she had left the hotel very early that morning. He had no idea where she was going.

Briggs got dressed and headed out. He had a hunch and it paid off. As he drove down Stanley Street he looked at all the houses. Nice, upper-middle class Colonials with the occasional ranch-style house thrown in to break up the monotony, all on beautiful wooded lots. He pulled into Mason's driveway. Murder houses always had an effect on Briggs. Violent death seemed to leave a certain energy in the air. A silent hum. A dark blue, 1972 Opel GT sat in the driveway. Both doors were open and there were a few boxes on the passenger seat. Briggs parked the Bronco behind the Opel. He walked up onto the porch and approached the front door, which suddenly slammed shut as he was about to knock. He heard the dead bolt slide shut. He stood there for a few seconds in silence and then said, "Mrs. Buckman? Ann Buckman?"

"Who are you and what do you want?" asked Mason's daughter in a nervous, high-pitched tone. "I can have the police out here in minutes!"

"Mrs. Buckman, I'm sorry to have spooked you. My name is Roland Briggs. I am the police, the chief of police." Briggs pulled out his identification and held it close to the narrow window to the left of the door. Her small nervous eyes looked at the ID, then up at Briggs. She disappeared and seconds later the dead bolt slid back and the front door opened. Ann Buckman was a small woman. Briggs knew from the police reports that she was forty-one. She was about five-foot-two; maybe a hundred pounds. Her hair was very curly and dark, cut short in a way that boxed her face. Her eyes seemed too close together and her nose was too small for her face. Her upper lip was almost non-existent. She reminded Briggs of a poodle. All she needed was a little dark crust in the corners of her eyes he thought, and he wouldn't have been able to tell the difference. She was wearing jeans and a sweatshirt much too big for her. Only her fingertips dangled from the sleeves. She moved one of her hands to her chest and jutted her chin out, closing her eyes.

"God, you scared me. My heart is racing." She opened her eyes and looked at Briggs. "I didn't expect anyone to be stopping by."

"Sorry about that," Briggs said, extending his hand. "I should have yelled out or beeped my horn when I pulled up."

"No, don't be ridiculous," she said, waving him off with her left hand and taking his in her right. Her fingers were cold in his hand. "It's just this place...and what happened. You know?"

"Yes, ma'am. I know exactly what you mean." Briggs looked over his shoulder at the Opel and then back at Ann Buckman. "Getting some stuff together?"

"Yes. Just some small things that I can take back." She looked around the yard and at the old wicker furniture on the porch. "Everything else is going up for sale. The house too."

"Your life is in California now, huh?"

"Oh, yeah," she said, with almost too much enthusiasm. "I won't be tempted to come out this way again. No sense in keeping the house. Who could live here now, anyway?"

"This is a great old house, though. Must have some nice memories for you still."

She waited a little while, thinking. "Not really," she said and turned back into the house. "Come in, if you like. I was just making some coffee." She walked into the house. Briggs followed her through the living room and into the kitchen. The couch where Mason's body had been was gone. The room seemed much larger now. "Would you like a cup?"

"That'd be great," Briggs lied. He'd already had five cups.

"What brings you out this way, Chief?" she asked as she got the coffee out.

"Well, I just wanted to ask you some questions about your mom. Tie up some loose ends. Nothing very serious."

"Oh," she answered. "I don't know how much I can tell you. I haven't been around here in a long time. My mother and I...we didn't talk much. We weren't close."

"I see. Do you mind if I ask why?"

"Well, no, I guess not. Although I don't see how that has anything to do with her murder."

"It probably doesn't. I'm just trying to get a sense of who your mom was."

Ann poured the water into the coffee maker, then turned to look at Briggs. She searched his face for a second. "Really," she said, doubtfully.

"Well...no. I want you to know that I truly believe we have caught your mother's murderer. But I think there was more to this case that hasn't been discovered. I...I've always considered myself a thorough guy, Mrs. Buckman. I want to make sure I have all the facts."

"And asking me about my relationship with my mother is going to help you?"

"Maybe." Briggs stared her down. She looked away. He could tell she was not satisfied with his explanation, but he couldn't risk telling her his true reasons. She might get upset and scream to the mayor or the press, although she didn't seem like that kind of woman. When Briggs thought about it, she seemed rather unfazed by her mother's brutal death. He waited.

Ann leaned against the counter and crossed her arms in front of her. "I didn't really like my mother, Mr. Briggs. I know that sounds horrible, her...ending up the way she did, but..." Ann's voice trailed off. "If you must know the truth, I haven't talked to her in almost ten years."

"That long?"

"Yes. I got married twelve years ago and moved to California two years later. My husband is a major in the United States Army. I met him when I worked out at Fort Devens. When he had the chance to take a new position at the Presidio in San Francisco, we left this place behind." Ann looked down at the ground and moved her white sneaker along the design of the linoleum.

"What caused the big riff between you two?"

"Oh, God! You could take your pick. There were so many things." Ann paused, took a deep breath, and exhaled slowly. "I feel bad—you know...talking ill of the dead." She looked at Briggs. Her eyes welled up a little, but she wiped the tears away quickly.

"It's probably good to get it off your chest," Briggs urged, then waited.

"Yeah, maybe you're right. I don't know. Let's just say that my mother was a very strict woman, very strict. And she was very...limited in her views. I had no freedom growing up and as soon as I was old enough, I got the hell out of here. I mean, I lived in Massachusetts for a while; I still kept in touch. My father was a great guy. They paid for me to go to college, so I came home for the holidays and summers, too. After I got my degree, though, I saw them less and less. I worked at different jobs for several years before I ended up taking a civilian job over at Devens and met my husband. I guess that was the biggest thing. Her not accepting him."

"Your mother didn't like your husband?"

"Not at all. And he's a great guy. He is an instructor at the Defense Language Institute out at the Presidio. He has his master's in linguistics; speaks five languages fluently. I don't think there are too many women out there who have been as lucky as I have in choosing a mate. And he's as sweet as can be to me! We have two great kids." Ann shook her head in disgust. "And my mother hated him."

"Why?"

Anne took a minute to answer. Briggs could see now that she was having problems with her mother's murder but was trying to act as if it wasn't bothering her. Probably a defense mechanism, Briggs thought.

"Because his mother was Puerto Rican."

"That's it!" Briggs said with a little too much enthusiasm. "Sorry," he said.

"No, it's okay. It's nice to know you feel the same way I did. That was the way I saw it way back then—and today. But like I said, my mother was set in her ways...very limited view of the way things should be. She refused to come to my wedding and although I stopped by a couple times to see her and my father during those two years before we moved, she never really looked at me the same way. I was like...dirty to her." Anne turned and looked out the kitchen window. She gripped the counter with her little hands. Briggs heard her catch her breath and fight off tears. He walked over to her and put his hand on her shoulder.

"I'm sorry about you're mom, Mrs. Buckman."

"Yeah," she answered in a shaky voice, "I guess I am, too. You know she never got to meet her grandkids. My dad said she looked at the pictures that I sent them though. At least she knew what they looked like, right?" she asked Briggs, looking for some empathy.

"You bet, Mrs. Buckman. I've known a lot of people like...like your mom, and believe me, even though she was too proud to admit it, I'm sure she loved them. And in her heart, she probably wished she could have dropped her defenses and seen them. I'm sure of it."

"You can call me Ann."

"I'm sure of it, Ann."

Ann turned to face him. "Thanks."

"Could I ask you one more question?"

"Yes, of course. I'm fine now."

"Do you know of anyone who didn't get along with your mom? Maybe someone who she worked with over at the nursing home. Anyone whom she might have had problems with?" The questions seemed stupid even to Briggs. If the woman hadn't talked to her mother in ten or twelve years, how would she know if she'd had any problems?

"God, no. That was years ago. And she wouldn't tell me if she were. All those years my mother worked, and I never heard one word about her jobs."

"Jobs? Where else did your mom work?"

"She worked up at that old Wilton State School for many years before taking that nursing home job. Yeah, let me think." She paused and tapped her finger on her chin for a minute. "If I remember right, she'd already done twenty years up there by the time they closed the place back in the fifties."

"Do you know if she knew the other woman, Mrs. Gowan?"

"Gee, I don't know, but we could check her address book. I found it in a drawer up in her bedroom. Wait here, I'll go get it." Anne left the kitchen and ran upstairs. When she came back down she was flipping through a small, multicolored book to the G's. "No, doesn't seem like it. At least she wasn't listed here. Didn't you check all this stuff out way back when?"

Briggs smiled rucfully. "Well, Ann, to be honest, we didn't have to. Before we even got going on an official investigation into the Gowan murder, the case almost solved itself. You saw the evidence." He waited until she nodded. "There was little need to explore the connection because Pike insisted that there was none. We had no need to question that."

"And now you are?"

"No! Not at all. Like I said, I just like to be thorough. You know, for my memoirs," Briggs said with a smile, trying to break her interrogation.

She still didn't seem convinced, but decided that it wasn't worth the energy to pursue it any further. "Okay. Well, if you don't have any more questions for me, I really should be getting back to this," she said, sweeping her hand out in front of her. "You haven't touched your coffee. Would you like me to put it in a to-go cup?"

Briggs looked down at the untouched mug. "No, that's all right. Must not have needed it after all. Thanks though. Are you going to be around for a while?"

"Yes, through the weekend at least. As you can see, there is a lot to be done here still. You see anything you like? Tag sale this weekend. I can set it aside for you."

"No, that's okay. I've got more stuff than I know what to do with already. Would it be all right with you if I stopped out again—just in case I need to ask you a few more questions?"

"Sure. I'll be out here all day the rest of the week. Not after dark, though. I couldn't stand the...I'd be too..."

"Say no more. I totally understand."

*   *   *

Briggs drove away, not sure if his visit had amounted to anything. He was still frustrated. He lit up a cigarette and inhaled deeply, then sent two plumes of bluish-purple smoke out of his nostrils. He rolled the window down a bit and watched the smoke get sucked out quickly through the opening. He shook his head and banged his fist on the steering wheel. There was something out there to figure out. He knew that much. What he didn't know was where to start. He turned off the road into a small parking lot and pulled up in front of a gas station. He needed another cup of coffee.

17

Friday, January 18, 1973. His meeting with the mayor was still an hour away, but Briggs decided to go uptown early. He needed cigarettes. He needed a very big cup of coffee. After Monday's fiasco, he figured he was out of a job. But it didn't bother him. He was sick of Wilton and all that had happened to him while there. Briggs had decided one thing for sure—no matter what the Mayor chose to do he was going to stick around long enough to catch the real killer of Mason and Gowan. He had a major problem though: where to start? After his meeting with the mayor, he was going to call someone whom he felt would be able to give him some insight into the type of person that he would need to start looking for. Last night, as he lay in bed trying to fall asleep, he'd come to the conclusion that Pike was not the sort of guy who would have done

something to warrant this sort of revenge. He was having difficulty coming up with a motive for the frame. And why would anybody have reason to kill these two old birds? He had no idea that
his first real clue was right around the corner and that it was going
to come from the most unlikely of sources.

Briggs first went to get a coffee at Cal's Diner. As he expected,
he got nothing but cold stares and quick little hellos from people
who couldn't avoid him completely. He knew the "station" story
had been spread all over town. He was now—Briggs the bastard.
Briggs the home wrecker. He thought briefly about sitting down at
a table just to piss everybody off, but then decided that sitting outside would be wiser.

The weather had grown surprisingly warm for January. A misty
drizzle hung in the air, pushed about by a gentle, balmy breeze.
Briggs' walked the half block to his next stop, Ernie's Smoke
Shop. As he went in, he was immediately overwhelmed by the
booming voice of P.J. Boyington. "There he is!" Boyington bellowed. "Where ya been, Chief? We thought you'd found somewhere else to get your paper and your smoke." The other patrons
in the store quickly folded up what they were reading, paid P.J.,
and left. P.J. watched them with a mischievous, boyish smile. He
was a huge man, six-foot-three and around three hundred pounds.
He always had a smile on his face, ready to tell a joke or laugh
heartily at someone else's. Although he was overweight, he looked
young for his age. Briggs had thought he was only around forty-
five, but P.J. felt he was closer to sixty. He stopped counting years
ago, he told Briggs.

"What are ya doin' to my customers, Chief," he teased, knowing full well what was going on. He'd heard the story at least ten
times already. But to P.J. there were no topics too delicate to make
jokes about. Nothing was sacred. He whiffed the air dramatically
as the Chief came closer. "Hmm, doesn't seem to be a lack of

deodorant." Then he cast a playful eye at Briggs. "So ya got caught. Who cares? That Mr. King, he comes in here all the time, never even says hello. Pays for his paper and leaves. You were doin' that lady a favor, Chief."

Briggs shook his head and laughed. P.J. seemed to know everybody's business, sometimes even before they did. He'd managed the tobacco shop for as long as anyone could remember and was king of the gossip. "You seem to be the only one to see it that way, P.J."

"Ah, hell, Chief, you know these sort a folk. They all act like what ya done is so horrible, but this little bedroom town is filled with people sneakin' around doin' lot worse than what you done. They just ain't been caught at it yet. Givin' you dirty looks and whisperin' about your...situation, it makes 'em feel less guilt 'bout their own little nasty secrets."

"Well, we'll see how it goes."

"So your meeting with the mayor is at ten, huh?"

"You askin' or tellin', P.J.?" the chief said with a smile.

"Hey! I got one for ya that'll bring a smile to your face," P.J. bellowed, quickly changing the subject. Briggs was waiting for this. There was at least one joke per visit. "This old fella and this old dame's in a nursin' home, and, after a while, the two a them starts talkin'. After a few months, the old fella finally gets up the nerve to ask the old dame to his room. When they gets there, things turn hot and heavy pretty quick. The old fella, he has her shirt off when the old dame stops him for a second. 'Before we get much further, I should tell you that I got acute angina, to which the old fella replies, 'God, I hope so, 'cause you got some really ugly titty's.'"

P.J. laughed at his own joke as if he'd heard it for the first time himself. Briggs shook his head, a gesture which he found himself doing often in Ernie's shop, and chuckled. "That's a good one, P.J.

Better than that last one you told me about the cop and the hooker."

"Yeah," Boyington says, thinking hard. "You're right. The cop-hooker joke wasn't that funny." A brief silence fell as P.J. rang up Briggs' purchase: two packs of Marlboro's and a *Boston Globe*.

"I gotta get goin'. I'm gonna get a few smokes in before I go see the mayor. I'll see you around, P.J."

"Yeah, okay, Chief. Good luck." Briggs had his hand on the door when P.J. yelled to him. "Hey, Chief! I heard yesterday that this Pike guy said he didn't know the Mason woman. Is that true? Did he really say that in court?"

"Yes, that's true." He glanced at his watch, trying to send out the non-verbal signals. P.J was a hard man to get away from.

"Ain't that somethin'. I coulda sworn…"

Briggs saw the serious look on P.J.'s face, a rare thing. He was intrigued. "What. What's 'something,' P.J.?"

"Well, it's just that…naw. It couldn't be."

"What! What is it?"

"I'm probably wrong, but I think I remember that guy. From way back when. But his name ain't right. And the guy I'm thinkin' about he'd a known Mrs. Mason."

Briggs walked back to the counter. "P.J., people can change their names. And you know that everybody lies. Tell me what you know."

"Well, Chief, if it's the guy I think it is, his name was somethin' else, but I can't remember it right off. But he worked at the old state school, up on the hill. Nurse Mason worked there, too."

Briggs was stunned. What if P.J. was right? Briggs could kick himself. Why hadn't he been more thorough? Why hadn't he dug deeper into the women's backgrounds? "P.J., think hard. This could be very important. What was this guy's name before?"

P.J. concentrated hard. Briggs could see that he was trying to call up very old memories. "You know, Chief, I'm a lot better with faces than names. That's why I thought I recognized the guy. He's a much older version of who I'm thinkin' about, but I know that face." P.J. concentrated some more then shook his head. "I can't remember it. I think it was something like McGuinn or Miguire. I know it was Irish, though. That I'm sure of."

"Holy shit!" Briggs exclaimed. "P.J., I wish you'd told me this a few weeks ago."

"I haven't seen ya since the trial started!" P.J. boomed. "I figured it wasn't that important, or you guys woulda brought it up at the trial. How was I ta know that it mattered," he said defensively.

Briggs could see he'd hurt P.J.'s feelings. He softened his tone. "I'm sorry, P.J. I'm just upset because I didn't do as good a job as I should have. Mason's daughter told me yesterday that she thought her mother worked up at Wilton."

"Does it matter? What I told you just now?"

"It might. If you remember anything else, you call me. Anytime." Briggs scribbled his home number on a piece of paper and thanked the big man. As he was leaving, Briggs realized he'd forgotten another important question. His detective skills were rusty. "P.J., one more thing. When was this? How many years ago was it that these two worked there?"

"Oh, boy. Let's see. We're talkin' almost thirty years ago!"

Briggs' hopes sank a little. He knew the school had been closed years ago when a larger, more modern facility was built out in the eastern part of the state. But he didn't realize that P.J. had been referring to such an old connection. "Wow! That's a long time ago. Did you work there, P.J.?"

P.J. hesitated a moment before answering. "Yeah...I worked on the farm."

"They had a farm up there?"

"Yep," he said, proudly. "It was the largest product-producing farm in the state during its heyday."

"One more thing."

"That's two more things. You already said 'One more thing' before you asked the last question." The twinkle was back in P.J.'s eyes.

"Yes, well. It's been a while since I did any real police work. You gotta cut me some slack. Do you remember if Mrs. Gowan ever worked there, up at the school?"

"No. I never seen her around. But the other one, Mason, she was a bigwig nurse up there. As mean as they come, too. That's why I remember her so clear. She was so quick to punish uh...the students up there. She'd smack 'em around and beat on 'em for the littlest things. She was a horrible woman."

"Really. The people we talked to said she was a very sweet and generous woman. Did a lot of work for the church."

"She was probably trying to make up for what she done to those folks. They didn't know the real woman. I can tell you. I seen her at work. Most of the time, it was like a Nazi camp up there. And she was the main reason for it."

Briggs looked at his watch again. It was five after ten. "Awh, son-of-a...I gotta go, P.J., I'm late. Thanks. I think you may have given me some really important stuff."

"That guy, Pike. He did it though, didn't he?"

"I'm sure he did. But I just wanna check out some things."

"He's the type to do something like that. I remember him, too. He was one of Mason's bad boys. He loved doin' her dirty work for her."

"Thanks, P.J. You've been a big help." Briggs left the tobacco shop and raced across the street. The mayor was gonna be angry.

*   *   *

"So this is the way you planned on showing me how sorry you were for doing something so stupid. Showing up ten minutes late."

"I wasn't trying to be disrespectful. I got caught up following a lead in the case."

"What case! Roland, get it through your head! There is no *case* anymore. It's over. The man has been convicted."

"Just hear me out. Give me two minutes."

"We're not here about the case."

"Just two minutes. Please."

The mayor stared at Briggs for a moment. He saw the intensity in Briggs' eyes. "Two minutes," he said, reluctantly.

Briggs smiled and dove in. "Well, now that you're aware of the relationship between Meredith and me, I can show you this." Briggs pulled out the note, showed it to the mayor, and explained how he'd tested Pike's understanding of the word "ambivalent." Then he told him that he felt that whoever it was that killed Gowan had also written the note to get Meredith to drive by so she would be a witness. He also explained his gut feeling about the murder scenes being staged. "I'm gonna call my friend Doug Johnson after this meeting. He's developing a program to study the murder behavior, if you will, of a killer. How a killer acts at a crime scene can tell you a lot about who he is. I was involved with the research up until a couple years ago. I'm sure he's going to concur with me. This is all a big frame." The last thing he shared with the mayor was the new information he'd just gotten from P.J. about the connection between Mason and Pike, if that was his real name.

Briggs shut up and watched as the mayor took off his reading glasses and rubbed the bridge of his nose. "Listen, Roland. I've got to tell you. This whole business has taken its toll on me. As the mayor, I of course want you to be thorough in your investigation.

I no more want an innocent man in jail than you do. But, well, I'm not going to lie to you. I'm also a businessman. Our town is on the verge of its best economic year ever. I hate to say it, but we are now benefiting financially from this whole thing. I know it's morbid for me to even talk like this, but what's done is done. I can't bring back those women. The American public loves this sort of thing. They are coming in droves to see...to drive by the murder sites. And when they do, they stay in our inns, eat in our restaurants, and buy souvenirs and antique furniture from our shops. You can't expect me to just step out and tell the public that the man that had stacks of evidence against him might *not* be guilty. That'd be crazy."

Briggs looked indignant. "That's right, I forgot," he said, snidely. "Rumors say that you're the big silent partner in half the fuckin' businesses in town."

"Now, Roland, don't jump to conclusions. I let you talk; now you let me. This is my third term as mayor of this town. I was uncontested in the last two elections. I don't see that changing in the near future, so I'm not afraid of public opinion. But I am a public servant. I have to do what's right for the town. Just for your own knowledge, my ownership in many of the town's business ventures is a matter of public record. I have no secrets. But Tim King is also involved in a lot of the same businesses that I am. What you did was wrong, Roland, and we, you and I, have to figure out a way to save face a bit.

"I knew you weren't going to relent about wanting to dig deeper into this whole mess, so last night I came up with something that I think will satisfy everyone involved. Have you taken any vacation time at all since you've been here?"

"No, I have a little more than six weeks on the books."

"Good. You're going to take three weeks off. The town will split the time with you. You use a week-and-a-half, and I'll get the bookkeeper to add a week-and-a-half. Sort of a suspension with pay. But, before we do this, are you going to stay away from Tim's wife?"

"Yes, that's been over for a couple months, like I said." Briggs was trying to sound a little reluctant, but it was hard. He was fine with what the mayor was saying. He'd love the time off, away from the bureaucratic bullshit, to do some real policing. The more he thought about it, the more he liked the mayor's plan. "You don't have to worry about me doing anything with her again."

"So you're okay with this?"

"Do I have any choice?"

"No."

"Then I'm okay with this."

"One last thing. I want serious low profile on the investigation. I don't want to hear about you at all for the next three weeks—not a peep. I want you out of the public eye, give this affair thing some time to die down."

"I'll do my best."

"You'll do better than that. Don't push this, Roland. Most everybody wants your head, but you've done a good job here and I think the attitude will change with time. It always does."

"Time heals all wounds?"

"Something like that."

*   *   *

Briggs left the mayor's office feeling a lot better than he thought he would. He'd gone in thinking that the decision on his future had already been made. But the mayor was willing to ride out the storm for a few weeks, and that was fine with Briggs. It would give him time to decide if he really wanted to stay.

He drove out of town on old State Road 63. It wound its way up the side of a long sloping hill. At the top, just before the road turned north toward Vermont, Briggs pulled his Bronco onto the shoulder of the road, turned off his ignition, and got out of the truck. He walked around to the passenger side, then leaned against the front quarter panel. He was at the edge of a large, sweeping field, filled with slowly moving ground fog. The misty drizzle had turned into a light rain, but the air was still warm. Together, they were turning the snow to slush. The smell of wet earth and melting ice hung in the soft breezes that danced around Briggs as he stood there. The tall hardwoods, mostly elm and maple, stood guard on the far side of the field.

Looking through them, Briggs could just make out the grounds of the old Wilton School for the Feeble-Minded. Above them, a few spires that sat atop the higher buildings scratched at the low-hanging belly of a dark gray sky. Off to Briggs' right, dead, reddish-brown leaves still clinging to a small oak shivered slightly in the wafting air. He turned a moment to watch them shake. He pulled a cigarette out, lit it, and then looked back at the ominous buildings. He could feel it. It was mild, just a light tug right now, but it was there. The secret to what brought about the Mason-Gowan murders had its roots planted firmly in the wetness on the other side of the field. The real investigation was about to begin.

18

"Briggsy! Is that you?"

"Yeah, it's me, Doug. How ya been?"

"I've been great. Just great. Things are going really well here."

The first thing Briggs had done when he got home was put in a call to his old friend, Doug Johnson. After a few minutes of small talk and catching up, Briggs got to the heart of the matter. "Listen, Doug. I was wondering if you'd kept up with the research on stranger killings?"

"Oh, yeah! After your...after—"

"It's okay to say it, Doug. After my wife died and I lost touch with you..."

"Yeah. Afterwards I hooked up with another guy here at the bureau, named Wes Roberts. He'd been doing the same sort of research as us, but he had about a two-year head start. We started sharing info and we found a lot of comparable data. Of course, the bureau hasn't sanctioned what were doin' yet, so we do what we can on our own time. But we've got a lot of stuff. Found a lot of patterns. We're still a year or two away from being able to organize it all into anything that could be considered conclusive, but a lot of it is adding up just like you and I thought it would. You can tell a lot about the minds of these killers by looking at their crime scenes. I'd go as far as to say that the crime truly reflects the thinking and the actions of these crazies."

"Doug, I can't tell you how happy I am to hear that you're still involved with this 'cause I really need your help with something."

"Those two old women?"

"Yeah, how'd you know?"

"I read the papers. I thought you caught the guy?"

"That's just it. I have, but I don't think he's the guy."

"Wow! That's a surprise. Everything I've read about the case made it sound like the evidence was irrefutable."

"I know. The case was tremendously strong. Everyone around here is satisfied that we got our man."

"Except you."

"Except me. There are a few strong discrepancies in the case, and I have that old gut feeling, ya know."

"I know about your gut feelings. And if I remember right, they were usually pretty accurate."

"Do you think you could help me out?"

"I can sure as hell try. Tell me all about the case, every detail, and I'll do what I can."

Briggs filled him in on everything and Johnson listened intently, offering a few 'I see's' and 'That's very interesting' here and there. A low whistle and a 'Wow!' came after Briggs told him about his involvement with the bank owner's wife. Once Briggs finished, he waited for Johnson to review the notes he'd taken.

"All right. There are some very interesting things about this case, and if I were working it, I'd be very suspicious, too. I think you're right in assuming that these murders were staged to make it look a certain way."

Briggs breathed a sigh of relief. "I was hoping you'd say that. What are your thoughts?"

"I'll try to do this point by point; but remember, Briggsy, this is still all very hypothetical. This shit we're doin' ain't a science, and it's still very much in its infancy."

"I understand," Briggs said, impatiently. "But tell me, anyway. I've got to know what you feel."

"Okay, there are several things about the crime scenes that most definitely throw up some red flags for me. First of all, they differ too much. Remember the idea we had about the disorganized vs. the organized types of killers?"

"Yes. I was just telling my detectives about that the other day."

"Well, there are tendencies of both at these scenes. In both murders, the guy brought his own weapon. He picked very submissive victims, in the sense that they were old and couldn't fight back much. Both scenes reflect a control element and both were, from what we can tell, well planned. In other words, they were not spur-of-the-moment killings. He also took items, little trinkets from both scenes. The fact that both women were seriously mutilated indicates someone who is very into power. The white sheets under both like that, he wanted to see the blood spread out slowly beneath his victims. And another thing, these victims were definitely chosen, they weren't random. All these things point to an organized type killer. A person very well aware of what he's doing—concerned about and fully conscious of the risks he was taking.

"On the other hand, both bodies were left at the crime scene. There was no attempt to hide them, or cover up the acts. This is the work of a disorganized sort of killer."

"Or someone who is trying to stage a crime scene to frame somebody," Briggs cut in.

"Yes, that's quite possible. There were other disorganized traits as well. The choice of victims, the fact that they lived in isolated areas made them easy targets. The killer would not have to use tricks or talk much to subdue his victims."

"What do you mean?"

"What we've noticed is that the organized killer likes to kill a particular target group. There is something about his victims that stands out to him. For instance, the victims may remind the killer of someone who abused him, or it may be as simple as they all wore the same type of shoes."

"Wow! It goes that deep psychologically, huh?"

"Yes. Thing is, this type of killer has to be able to lure his victims. Trick them into coming with him, to get in the car, to take a walk. In order to do this he has to have good communication skills and a sharp mind. He has to be able convince the victims that he is the sort of person who wouldn't hurt them. And let me tell you, these guys are good at it."

"So you're saying that since Mason and Gowan were attacked out at their isolated houses, the killer didn't need to communicate at all to do his deeds."

"Yes, exactly. Remember, a disorganized crime scene, usually a disorganized mind. A disorganized type killer is not capable of convincing anyone that he's okay. They usually exhibit some sort of visible psychosis, which in most cases would scare people away. They have to literally snatch their victims, or, like in your case, march right into their isolated houses."

"Any other disorganized traits?"

"At both murders, you said there was a lot of damage done in and around the vagina, but no signs of rape, right?"

"Right."

"Well, oftentimes, a disorganized killer will not be able to perform the sex act with a live victim, and many times not even with dead ones. Sometimes we'll find semen on or near the bodies in these cases. You found no semen anywhere, but there were the knife wounds to the vagina. If I were looking at a scene that was not staged and saw this, I'd make the leap and guess that the killer was using the knife as a surrogate penis.

"Of course, the biggest sign of a disorganized killer is the sloppy crime scene, which you have at the second murder site. These types of killers can get really nasty. We just got crime scene photos in the other day from a police force out in Oregon. Guy walks into a house only three blocks away from where he lives with his parents. Kills and eviscerates the woman who lives there, *and* her three-month-old baby. He made no attempt to keep them quiet and it was the middle of the day. Neighbors heard some screaming so they called the cops. By the time they got there, this guy is standing in the kitchen, covered in blood, with a frying pan in one hand and the lady's heart in the other. I don't have to tell you what he was planning to do. He gave up without a fight. Didn't even know he'd done anything wrong."

"My god, that's horrible! Did he say why he did it?"

"Yeah. He'd gotten a telepathic message from his dead grandmother that the woman down the street with a white car in her driveway was planning to avenge her own death in a previous life. The killer's great-great-great grandfather had been a Seminole Indian. The deer, which was now reincarnated as this woman, had been his great-great-great grandfather's first kill and it was, he told the police, customary for hunters to eat the heart of their first kill, which the grandfather had done. His grandmother told him to act before the woman did. So this guy walks out of his house and down the street until he comes across the first white car in a driveway. The woman's husband was at work. She just happened to be unlucky enough to have a white car. He saw himself as a warrior, defending his family. This was his first kill, he'd told the police, and that was why he was preparing the heart for eating."

"That is sick."

"Tell me about it. Now in the Mason-Gowan murders, you have a weird twist. The first murder scene was very neat. Nothing really out of place, even the clothes were piled neatly like you said, instead of thrown. Yet at the second murder scene, you have the complete opposite: blood everywhere, palm smears and footprints in blood, clothes strewn about. This is exactly what you'd expect from a disorganized killer. And you said that you'd hinted about your confusion over the differences between the crime scenes to your officers?"

"Yeah," Briggs said hesitantly. "Are you thinking what I'm thinking?"

"That someone purposely lived up to your expectations based on something he'd heard from you or one of your men? Yes."

"But why?"

"Whoever he is, he's a cocky bastard. He's playing with you." Johnson paused for a minute, then added, "And I think he is very close to you."

"Damn it!" Briggs yelled into the phone, his frustration rushing through his body. "Not only does that scare the hell outa me, it also pisses me off!"

"One more thing. At the first scene, which is very controlled and indicates an organized killer at work, this guy left the nightgown on her. Usually, clothes left on the victim, but pushed up to expose the sex organs is a trait of a disorganized killer. At the second scene you have the exact opposite. Wild, disorganized scene, but the body completely nude—organized trait. Very odd."

There was a long silence. Briggs spoke first. "All right then. Do you have any suggestions as to where this all leaves me? I mean, what can we take away from these crime scenes that goes beyond staging and indicates traits or characteristics of the real killer?"

Johnson hesitated. "Briggsy, listen, you've got to keep in mind that I've only been at this part-time for four years or so. That's not a lot of time to try to establish any real definitive answers to a very bizarre bunch of people who exhibit a wide array of very strange behaviors."

"Come on, Doug. This is me, Briggsy. I'm not gonna hold it against you if you're wrong about some of these things. I won't even breathe a word of your helping me to anyone—unless I catch the guy. The right guy."

"It has to be that way. At least for now. Wes and I have put a lot of work into this research and we're getting ready to propose our ideas to the new deputy-chief. We're gonna ask him to allow us to do some more work on this, in an official way. Maybe get some help on organizing all the notes we have crammed into boxes in our basements. Bad publicity could kill us. What I'm doing for you now is only loosely theorizing, just semi-educated guesses. Okay?"

"Okay, Mum's the word. Make some guesses," Briggs said, anxiously.

I'll go from what I'm most sure of first. I have a strong feeling that this guy is very conscious of his goal. He's on some sort of mission. Whatever that mission happens to be is only very clear to him, and it will be difficult to find out what it is. If you do, though, you will find that all the things he is doing make sense from his perspective. He will show no signs of psychosis. On the contrary, I think he's probably quite successful and very social. He is methodical and very controlled. He will be a mature man, who is probably very concerned with his appearance and is very neat and orderly.

"His upbringing will have included a pervasively violent culture, the origins of which will have begun very early in his childhood and probably existed within the family setting. He will have also grown up in an environment where there was a continuous risk of change; in other words, he would have had no sense of security."

"You don't have a name to go with all that, do ya!"

Johnson laughed. "Unfortunately not."

"What about the relationship with these victims? Do you have any idea as to how they could have been connected to cause such a tremendous amount of rage?"

"That's a tough one, but it's probably the key to your case. We feel that by looking at the victims' lives—who they were, how they acted—we can tell a lot about the motive. We call it victimology. Remember you and I talking about it?"

"Yes I do," answered Briggs. "Like it was yesterday."

Well, I found two great books about this, *The Criminal and His Victim,* by Hans Von Hentig, and *The Victim and His Criminal,* by Stephen Schafer. Both were enlightening and gave me a great start in shaping my ideas about these types of killers. As I said, the answer of how this all fits together lies within the mind of the killer, but I would venture to guess that the victims either directly or indirectly held some sort of power over him at one time. He definitely knew them, or knew some people very much like them. My feeling is that these people are directly responsible for whatever it is that brought out this anger. So you should see if you catch him, a direct relationship between him and his victims. I don't think it will be that these people are substitutes for somebody else from the killer's past. But that's a pure guess. I also think that—and this is really going out on a limb—that the relationship between the killer and Mason was very much different than the one between the killer and Gowan."

"How come?"

"Well, even if he was living up to your expectations, playing with you by making the second scene look more like what you expected, he still chose the way in which he wanted to do that. By going that extra step and decapitating her like that—didn't you say that her face had been severely beaten as well?"

"Yes. Her face was beyond recognition. Pulpy."

"Well, that to me shows that he really wanted to obliterate her for some reason. What that reason is, I have no idea, but he had a different sort of resentment towards her than he did Mason. Your coroner determined that Mason's wounds would have brought about a slow death. Gowan's wounds indicated a quick death, but a much more brutal attack post-mortem. All these things represent something about the relationships, I'm almost certain about that. He had different agendas, different 'lessons' for them to learn."

"So where would you start looking if you were me?"

"In the completely opposite direction in which he wants you to."

"God, that could be anywhere. Do you think this guy could have held a grudge for such a long time? Do you think that it might have some connection to the school?"

"Well, the fact that he chose to frame this other guy Pike, *and* if the connection between Pike and Mason did exist *and* it was established way back then during the time they worked together, I'd say it's as good a place to start as any. Remember, the idea behind victimology, more than anything else, is to figure out ways in which particular victims may have contributed to their own demise. This may sound a bit callous, saying that victims *did anything* to cause some act of violence to be committed against them, but they often do. Whether it's some street hooker contributing in the sense that she is in a profession that puts her at great risk, or several people who did something, whatever that something is, that is perceived by the perpetrator as bad or threatening or wrong—something he has to take care of.

"For instance, we interviewed a guy about a year ago who was in jail for killing three women. Didn't seem to be any connection between these women at all until after we talked to the guy. Turns out they all ate lunch at the same place and they all, as the killer put it later, "flirted openly with the man who owned the place." Now, to us sane people, this may seem ridiculous. But to him, it was an act that caused some very powerful and meaningful emotions to be stirred within his soul. When we talked to him more about it, we found out that his mother was in many ways like these women, both physically and in the way she flirted. They looked and acted in a way that reminded him of something he saw his mother do while poor old dad sat at home. But you have to be careful with this. You have to look at all the facts to make your decisions about what this guy is all about. If there had been only the two old women who were the victims, you might venture a guess, just to get you started, that the guy had it in for old women. That's one thing that is very obvious between these victims. But now you have three victims. If you can find a strong connection, like that they all worked at the school, then you'll have a much stronger basis to proceed with your investigation.

"What do you mean 'three'?"

"Well, you have to start looking at Pike as a victim of this guy too, now. Assuming that what your buddy P.J. said is true. Personally, I haven't run across any killings yet that have thirty-year-old motivators, but I've run across enough bizarre shit to believe anything is possible. Just start with the victims. They will tell you a lot about the killer."

"Listen, Doug, thanks again for your help. And I won't say a word about our discussion unless you want me to—after I catch this guy."

"Thanks, buddy. Good luck."

"I promise to keep in touch."

"You better. Oh, Briggsy, one more thing. It could be very important in solving this case."

"What's that?"

"Whoever this guy is, he's handling himself very well. I'd bet a whole lotta money he's killed before, and probably more than once."

19

Briggs waited in the interrogation room at the county jail for the sheriff to bring Pike in to see him. After getting off the phone with Johnson, he decided to interview Pike immediately. If anyone had first-hand knowledge of what went on back at the state school, it would be Pike himself. It was seven p.m. and the sheriff's department wasn't thrilled about late night interviews. It meant a few of the guards would actually have to work. The door to the small, unadorned room with no windows swung open and Pike was led in in handcuffs.

As soon as he saw who it was that wanted to interview him, his face twisted into a mass of anger and frustration. "No!" he yelled. "I don't want to talk to this guy. He's fuckin' crazy!"

"Shut your mouth!" said the guard. "He's the chief of police. If he wants to talk to you, he's gonna talk to you."

Briggs nodded his head at the guard. "Thanks. You can take the handcuffs off him."

The guard looked a little hesitant. "Are you sure, Chief? He seems a little worked up."

"Yeah, well, he has a right to be. I asked him a few strange questions the other day and he probably does think I'm a little crazy. But I'm sure the matter will be cleared up now and he'll calm down."

"All right then," said the guard. He led Pike to the chair near the interview table that was bolted to the floor, sat him down, and took off the handcuffs. "He's all yours, Chief. Ring that buzzer over by that door when you're done and I'll come get 'im."

"Thanks."

The guard left and Briggs stared at Pike for a moment. Pike stared back but broke away before the chief said anything. "What the hell are ya lookin' at me like that for? What the hell do ya want from me?"

Briggs walked slowly over to the table, grabbed one of the chairs on his side of the table and brought it around to Pike's side. He put the back of the chair against the table, then pushed its left side up against the left side of Pike's. The chief sat down, took a deep breath, and exhaled slowly. "Milton, may I call you Milton?"

"It's your jail. Why do you have to sit so close to me?"

"Milton, I am so confused about so many things, and I think you are the only person who can help me. You know what I mean? It's that I got this uneasy feeling about all these issues and I believe that you are the man who can solve my problems." Briggs turned his head to the left and leaned forward, staring into Pike's eyes again. "Are you willing to help me, Milton?" Briggs asked sternly.

Pike was a little shaken by the change in Briggs' voice and his closeness. He wasn't used to people being close to him and he didn't like it. Especially when it was a stocky, crazy chief of police in a room with no outlets, no windows. "Back off, Briggs." Pike squirmed uncomfortably, trying to create some space. Briggs didn't move or say anything. Pike tried to get up but Briggs grabbed him by the forearm and squeezed hard. Pike was amazed by his strength. He settled back into his chair. Briggs moved even closer. He had hoped a man like Pike would become nervous if another man moved into his personal space. Briggs' face was only inches away from Pike's.

"Are you going to help relieve my suffering, Milton?"

Pike shook his head in disgust. "Your suffering! What about my suffering? I'm the one someone decided to screw over. I'm the one sittin' in this here jail for somethin' I ain't done."

"But, Milton, what about all that evidence? And who would see you as someone worth screwing over? You're a broken-down old man who lives in an old house all by yourself. You have no friends. No one came to that courtroom pulling for you. Tell me, why would anyone even waste their time setting you up?"

Pike felt the words Briggs spoke cutting through him. He dropped his chin onto his chest and closed his eyes for a minute, trying to shut out the truth. "I don't know," he said quietly.

Briggs wasn't going to let up. He had Pike going where he wanted him to go. "Come on, Milton! Why should I believe that anyone in his or her right mind would bother with you? You're gonna have to convince me."

"I don't know!" Pike yelled. "All I know is that I ain't done nothin' to those ladies. I don't know why they was hurt that way."

"Did they screw you over somehow? Back in the old days?"

"No!" Pike answered defensively.

"Did you try and go out with them way back when, but when you asked them, they just laughed in your face? Did they tell you that you were nothing, that you were garbage—street trash? Is that why you did what you did?"

"No! I keep tellin' ya, I didn't do this! I thought you said you didn't think I did it?"

"I want to believe you, Milton. But it's all that evidence, you know. That's hard to overlook. And the fact that you are, well, maybe you are worthless. Just a piece of white, backwoods trash, ya know."

"Screw you, Briggs! Get outa here, I don't want to talk to you no more. Guard! Guard!"

"He won't come 'til I call him, Milton. You're not tellin' me anything to change my mind. I guess you did kill them." Briggs started to stand.

"I didn't! Goddamn it, I didn't.

Briggs sat back down, moving even closer. "I think you did."

"I done nothin' wrong!"

"They screwed you over. You wanted revenge."

"No!"

"You wanted to see them suffer."

"No! You're wrong.

"You hated them for turning you away."

"No."

"You cut them and sliced them up so they would pay for hurting you!"

"No! I didn't do this."

Briggs had him answering quickly now. He decided to move in for the kill. "When did it happen?"

"What?"

"When did they turn you away?"

"They didn't."

"Make you feel like nothing?"

"They didn't! You're crazy."

"Was it when you were younger? In school maybe? Is that when your hatred for them began?"

"I didn't know them."

"Even when you were a kid? Do you remember back when you were a kid?"

"Yes."

"You hated those fucking bitches!"

"No! No, I didn't."

"Did you go to school?"

"Yes."

"You lived in Wilton?"

"Yes."

Now or never. "You worked at the state school?"

"Yes—I mean no! You tricked me! I didn't work up there."

"I tricked you how? You would only say I tricked you if you felt that you had something to be tricked out of." Pike was looking down into his lap, but Briggs could see his eyes. He watched them closely as he asked the next question. He knew it was a real shot in the dark, but he figured he had nothing to lose and everything to gain. "How did I trick you…McGuire?"

Pike cut his eyes at Briggs quickly and then looked away. He swallowed hard and put his hand to his mouth. This time, he took his time answering, but Briggs got what he wanted. This man definitely had a past that connected him to the school and most likely to at least the Mason woman. "Who?"

"McGuire. That's your real name, isn't it?"

Pike was flustered and confused. The things Briggs had said to him were sinking in. All his regrets about his life and the loneliness, the emptiness of it, were filling his heart. But his defenses were going up, too. No one had ever done a nice thing for him in his life. This guy wasn't trying to help him. He just wanted to torture him. Make him feel horrible about what everyone in town thought he did. He began to hate Briggs, to see him like all the rest. And he sure as hell wasn't gonna tell him about his days at the school. No way would he give Briggs even more incriminating evidence. Maybe that was what Briggs was looking for. Just more fuel for the fire. Pike crossed his arms in front of himself.

"Why did you change your name, Pike?"

"I didn't."

"Why would a guy like you think he needed to change his name? Were you hiding from someone?"

"No."

"Have you always lived in Wilton?"

"Yes."

"Pike, believe me, it would be much better for you if you told me your real name and what the reason is for your having changed it."

"My name is Milton Pike. I never worked at the State School and I didn't kill no women. That's all I'm gonna say to you, so get the hell outa my face, Cop." He set his jaw and stared at Briggs. This time he wasn't going to look away. His power had returned. His hate for men like Briggs welled up and gave him courage.

Briggs had gotten what he'd come for, but he had hoped that he would break Pike completely—get him to tell all he knew. But that was wishful thinking. A man like Pike wasn't going to trust anyone let alone a cop. He pulled the letter out of his breast pocket and put it on the table in front of Pike. He softened his tone. "Mr. Pike, did you write this letter to Meredith King, pretending to be me?"

"I said no more questions, Cop."

"Could you just look at the letter and tell me if you wrote it? There's nothing difficult about that."

"I don't have to look at it. I ain't written a letter to no one in years. I don't know as I ever wrote a letter in my life, in fact."

"Look at this here." Briggs pointed to the word ambivalent. "See that word? That's why I asked you why you seemed 'ambivalent' at the trial. I believe that the writer of this letter is the killer of those women. I tested you yesterday morning because I felt that you didn't write the letter. You don't know what that word means, do you?"

Pike was still on the defensive, but he was a little curious. He glanced at the part of the letter Briggs was pointing at. It could be another trick. "Maybe I do know what it means, and maybe I don't. And I don't own no typer writer neither."

Briggs slowly folded up the letter and put it back in his pocket. "So you're not going to try and help yourself here. Is that what you've chosen to do?"

Pike tightened his crossed arms. "Yep."

"So you never knew these women?"

"No."

"You never worked at the Wilton School for the Feeble-minded?"

"No."

"And you're telling me that Milton Pike is your real name?"

"Yes. Is that all? I gotta get back to my cell. I got a bunch a letters to write to all the people who love me," Pike said, sarcastically.

Briggs walked over and pushed the buzzer. The sound echoed loudly on the other side of the locked door. "Yup. That's it. I know you're finding it hard to believe, Mr. Pike. But I don't think you killed these women. And I do believe that you were framed. If you decide to tell me the real story—who the hell you are and why you changed your name, I'll probably be able to get you out of here quicker."

The guard opened the door and Pike hobbled over to him. He turned and looked at Briggs. "Fuck you. There's your story, Briggs."

20

Friday, January 19, 1973. Briggs woke up with a start. It took a moment before he realized that he'd fallen asleep in his recliner. He wiped the drool off the side of his face, then looked at the clock. Eight o'clock. Only a two-hour nap. Then he looked outside and realized that it was daylight. He'd slept right through until the next morning! He felt rested. He hadn't had any nightmares. His therapist had been wrong. Getting back to what he loved to do had freed him of the horrors he'd left behind in Florida. After getting off the phone with his buddy, Doug Johnson, Briggs had felt a major adrenaline rush. But it had subsided pretty quickly when he realized that, although he had gotten what he was after when he interviewed Pike, he still had a long way to go. He may or may not have a gotten a little closer to the killer. He was still left with no real direction to take. Pike was unwilling to talk, and now that they'd already convicted him, Briggs had no carrot to dangle in front of him. The man had been screwed over too many times in his life; so Pike wasn't about to trust anyone who said he was trying to help him.

Briggs thought about the way he chose to interrogate Pike. Maybe he should have just played it straight with him? Maybe he shouldn't have tried to trick him, but rather act like he really cared, sort of acted like he wanted to become Pike's friend. That could have been the way to get what he was after. The guy didn't have any friends. Maybe he needed one. Maybe it was time Briggs thought about changing his approach to doing interrogations. He'd sat down in the recliner to think about all this and fell asleep.

Now that Briggs had confirmed, or at least strongly believed that Pike worked at the Wilton School, he was going to have to find a way to prove it by finding out Pike's real name. Briggs figured it would be a simple matter to check out. Just get in touch with the state and ask them to check the records for a guy with an Irish name who worked closely with Mrs. Mason. At the same time, he figured he could get a lot of information on Mason herself. This way, if P.J. were right, he could close the gap between Pike and Mason and hopefully figure out what the motive was behind all this.

But Briggs didn't take into account that he was dealing with the state, a huge bureaucracy where the name of the game was "Pass the buck." After two frustrating hours on the phone—mostly on hold—with the regional office in Springfield, Briggs found out that all the records pertaining to the Wilton State School were still on the grounds, in storage. After another hour, Briggs was able to find somebody with enough authority to grant permission for him to go on the grounds and check the records out. They didn't have the extra personnel to be able to do this for him. It took another hour to find out who was in possession of the keys to the buildings; and another hour waiting for the guy to get back from his lunch break and confirm that he did indeed have the keys that Briggs needed.

Briggs had to threaten the guy with obstruction of a police investigation before the guy would get off his ass and meet him in Stockbridge, a town that fell about half-way between their respective locations. The key-keeper gave Briggs the keys and a small map of the school with the location of the building where the records were kept. Finally, by three in the afternoon, Briggs found himself pulling off State Road 63, onto the grounds of the Wilton School. The rain stopped during the night but the sky was still filled with dark clouds. The rain had saturated the snow and it was now more gray than white. The tires of the Bronco splashed through the virgin slush, leaving two very distinctive tread marks behind. Briggs followed the road up as it arched its way around the edge of the field.

An old stop sign leaning severely to the right was the only indication that Briggs had reached the intersection he'd been looking at on the map. He took the left, as indicated, passing by the first of at least ten—Briggs guessed—large buildings that he could see located on the grounds. The road he was on quickly narrowed as evergreens on either side of the road had, over the years, taken advantage of the open space between them. Briggs got another hundred yards before he had to stop. A twisted, dead maple tree had finally succumbed to its own weight and fallen across the road, completely blocking any chance of getting by. Briggs sighed deeply as he looked down at his feet. He had contemplated wearing his rubber boots that morning but decided his feet would get too sweaty on the ride to Stockbridge; so he had opted for shoes. As he got out of the truck and started sloshing through the wet muck, he ruefully regretted his decision. According to the map, he didn't have too far to go. He walked past what appeared to be an old storage shed. One of the large wooden doors was hanging off its hinges and Briggs could just make out the ghostly silhouettes of some old farm equipment inside. A skinny, sickly-looking barn cat scooted out from underneath an old state truck. The cat stopped for a second to stare at Briggs and wiggle its feet madly, trying to shake off the slush; then it ran to the opening in the shed to disappear into the darkness.

The next two buildings were much larger. They reminded Briggs of dorm rooms, possibly where the students had lived. He was surprised to see heavy wire mesh, now red with rust, covering each of the windows. Many of the windows were broken, undoubtedly by kids throwing rocks. The smell the mildew and the rot floated in the air around him. He looked up at the top floor windows of the second building. He looked away quickly, not sure why; then laughed to himself when he sensed that child-like fear. What if a pale face was staring back? Or a misty figure dressed in dark clothes skirted from one side of the window to the other? What then? He shook his head while walking on, but decided not to look up again. No sense risking it.

Another fifty yards and he reached his destination. The old administration building seemed to have weathered the passing years better than the other buildings he'd seen so far. The steps were still intact and the building itself, although crowded by many large trees, appeared unfazed by the passing of time. Briggs climbed the steps and turned around to get a look at the grounds that lay beneath him. It was very desolate. Briggs shivered. Across a large common, a hill sloped away and he could see the tops of some of the buildings of Wilton below. He turned and fumbled in his pockets for the keys. The one that opened the administration building had been marked with a piece of black electrical tape. He found it amongst the others, slid it into the lock, and after a little wiggling, got it to turn. The door was stuck, so Briggs had to push it three times before it finally swung open. The bang it made as it hit the wall behind echoed through long empty halls and lonely rooms. Gray light flooded in over his shoulders and filled the entranceway with an eerie glow. "Why couldn't Pike just have told me who the hell he really was?" Briggs mumbled as he stepped inside.

He made his way down a large hallway, passing to the right of stairs leading up to the second floor. "Last room on the right, just before the stairs that lead to the basement," Briggs said out loud to break the oppressive silence. "Here we are...hmm, that's strange." He was looking at the ground. The dust that lay everywhere else was missing from in front of the door. A wet path had been cut, leading away and down the back stairs. Briggs was told the door would be locked. He pushed it open without needing to use the key. Except for several small tables and a few metal chairs, the room was empty. There were no files to be seen. Briggs froze. A noise came from outside, the sound of scraping metal. He instinctively pulled out his gun and slipped to the end of the hall. He looked cautiously out the large window. There! One of those dark figures he'd hoped not to see was stepping through a doorway leading into a smaller building on the other side of the courtyard.

Briggs flew down the stairs. He peered out of a door that had been propped open by a piece of wood, saw no one, and dashed across the yard. He stepped into the smaller building. Someone was whistling in a room at the end of a narrow hallway. Briggs crouched, gun at the ready. He slid along the wall quickly, stopping for a moment at the entrance to get a feel for where in the room the guy might be. His body was tingling. "Freeze!" he yelled as he jumped through the doorway. The whistling stopped and Briggs saw a man facing away from him beginning to raise his hands. Then the room turned upside down and everything went black.

*   *   *

"Mr. Briggs. Mr. Briggs, wake up. Are you all right?"

Briggs' head was killing him. He opened his eyes slowly. His vision was blurry. He was slumped against a wall. Kneeling in front of him, holding Briggs' gun, was a man. Briggs pushed back as the reality of the situation came home. The man noticed Briggs' fear and looked down at the gun he was holding. "Oh, Jesus! I'm sorry. I didn't mean to point this at you." The man turned the gun up, so the barrel pointed to the ceiling and extended it towards Briggs. "You dropped this when you slipped and fell."

Briggs slowly reached out and took the gun. The man's face came into focus. He knew him. "Richards!" Briggs yelled. "What the hell are you doing up here?"

The man who Briggs met at the mayor's party smiled at Briggs' gruffness. "It seems as though you're your old self. Can I help you up?" He stood and extended his hand.

Briggs hesitated, but then took it, realizing that he'd probably have trouble getting up on his own. He changed his tone. "Sorry. I'm just surprised. What *are* you doing up here?"

"I told you at the party, remember? I am working with the Mayor on transferring a piece of land from state ownership to town ownership."

"Oh, yeah," Briggs answered. But what has that got to do with employee records?"

Richards glanced around the large room at the piles of boxes and files. "You mean all those? Those aren't just employee records. In fact, most of them aren't. Is that what you're up here for, the records?"

"Maybe."

Richards didn't understand Briggs' cautious attitude. "Well, if that's what you're after, all that stuff is over there, in the far left corner."

Briggs glanced in the same direction Richards was pointing. There were ten or twelve large boxes segregated from the many other boxes and file cabinets in the room. "What's all this other stuff?"

"Student records."

"Wow. All this is on the students?"

"Yup. It looks a little chaotic—"

"A little!" Briggs interrupted.

"Okay, a lot. But believe it or not, I've got most of the stuff in order." Briggs looked at him curiously, and Richards realized Briggs was still waiting for an answer to his first question. "I wear a few different hats in my job with the state. One of them is sort of...well, I guess you'd call me the self-appointed historian of this place."

"Why did you move all the records over here?"

"I don't know if you noticed, but there was a lot of water damage to the ceiling in that room in the old admin building. In a month or so, I'll be transferring all this stuff up to Springfield where I've begun to establish a library, but until then I figured I'd keep them here away from the water damage."

"How'd you get up here?"

"There's a back way in. It's not blocked by any dead trees." Richards smiled softly. "Now, if you don't mind, I'd like to ask a question." He waited for Briggs to nod. "What are *you* doing up here, disturbing my solitude?"

Briggs looked at Richards for a moment. He had a very gentle way about him that Briggs admired. He had none of the characteristics Doug Johnson predicted would belong to the killer. It was easy to trust a man like Richards, and he realized quickly that he could use his help with the employee records. He decided to take him into his confidence. "If I tell you, you have to promise to keep it to yourself. Maybe you can even help me."

Richards smiled. "Does it have something to do with the murders?" He couldn't hide his excitement. He liked his job with the state, yet, it could get very dull at times. The possibility of helping out with a police investigation made him tingle.

"Yes. But it's a very unofficial thing. I'm sure you've heard about my situation with the King woman."

Richards nodded. "Anyone who has passed through Wilton has!"

"Yeah, well," Briggs said ruefully, "it sort of got me on an unofficial suspension. Anyway, I've had my suspicions about Pike's guilt from the moment that we caught him. And without going into all the details with you, I convinced the mayor to let me do a quiet follow-up on some of the details that have bothered me."

"Sounds very interesting. How can I help?"

Briggs tilted his head in the direction of the piles of employee boxes. "I'd like you to help me go through those and find a man with an Irish name who worked with Eleanor Mason."

Richards' brow furrowed. "Mason worked up here?"

"According to a source of mine she did. And her daughter confirmed it. I guess I need to verify that too, though. And I also need to find out if the Gowan woman worked here."

"Anything else?"

"Well, one other thing. If we find out that they did indeed work together, I need a list of names of the other employees who worked on a regular basis with them."

"How far back are we talking?" Richards asked hesitantly.

"About thirty years ago. Maybe between, say, 1940 and 1945."

"God! Why? You don't actually think that these murders have some sort of tie to something that happened that long ago, do you?"

"I know it sounds far-fetched, but right now it's the only thing I have to get started."

Richards looked over at the boxes. "This might take a while. And, of course, you realize that there were a lot of Irish people who worked here back then. There may be—"

"I know that. But we're only interested in the Irish men who worked closely with Mason." Isn't there any way to narrow the search? This school must have some sort of structural or organizational aspect that would help us in looking. It's a pretty big place."

Richards brightened. "You may be right! How was Mason employed here?"

"I assume she was a nurse."

"Excellent! That will make it a lot easier. The students here, if you can call them that, where broken up by sex and by intelligence. If she were a nurse, she probably worked in one particular building with one particular population. That will narrow the search for this Irish man to those who worked in her particular building. If she had been in administration or supply, we might have had to consider many more men."

"What do you mean...about the kids? What were they if these kids weren't students?"

Richards looked at Briggs for a long moment. "You don't know about this place at all, do you?"

"I guess not."

"This wasn't really a 'school.' It was a place to put the unwanted. The retarded. Everyone refers to this place as the Wilton State School, but when it was in operation, its name was Wilton School for the Feeble-Minded. Once you came, you didn't leave. There was no graduation in any real sense, like a regular school. It just meant that you didn't get to spend the first part of the day in classes. You 'graduated' to a job on the grounds."

"Jeez, I didn't know that. I just thought this was some sort of...well, I guess I never really gave much thought to what this place had been."

"Come with me." Briggs followed Richards back through the administration building and onto the front steps. He pointed off to the right. See over there, where you came in?" Briggs nodded. "See that first building—that was L building. These grounds were laid out to allow the brightest students' buildings to be closest to the entrance. This way, for those who were coming to visit for whatever reason, they would see the more normal students on their way to the administration building. The students in L building were the brightest. Oh, and they were called morons."

"Morons!" Briggs looked at Richards, waiting for him to smile or laugh. He didn't. "What, are you saying that that was actually an official term?"

"Oh, yeah. It went like this. Those students who had a mental age equivalent to that of normal mentally healthy seven-to-twelve-year-olds were called Morons.

They—"

"What do you mean by mental age? I'm completely confused."

"Oh, I'm sorry. Getting ahead of myself. Each of these kids was given a test before or upon their arrival here. The services and placement of each of these kids was determined by their score on the test, which equated to a measure of 'mental age.' So, for example, say a woman of nineteen—her chronological age—took the test. She might test out to have a mental age equivalent to that of an eight-year-old. She would be labeled a moron and receive appropriate services entitled to those of her class."

"What other classes were there?"

"If you tested and had a mental age of 0 to 3, you were labeled an idiot. You were not considered 'trainable,' had no opportunities to attend school, and you were placed into one of the back wards. You can't really see those buildings from here but they're back there, far away from the admin building and out of sight." Richards pointed off towards the trees to their left. "If you tested between 4 and 7 years old, you were deemed an imbecile, trainable but not educable. The morons were considered trainable and educable, and did receive primary education up through sixth grade or until they turned sixteen, whichever came first. Oh, and each class had sub-groups of low, middle and high grades."

"God, this is amazing! I never knew about this stuff."

"Most people don't. Anyway, as you hoped, the school was broken down quite nicely—from building A, for the low-grade idiots, through L for the high-grade morons. There was another building, M, for the severe cases and the medical needs kids. That one, of course, is way out there in the woods! If Mason was a nurse out here, she probably worked primarily in one of the buildings. She may have floated to other buildings, but only for overtime purposes. That's how they did it back then."

A silence fell between them for a moment as they both looked out across the darkening grounds. Briggs' head was killing him. Richards noticed him rubbing it gingerly. "Listen, it's getting late. Why don't you let me start the digging. You go home, take some aspirin, and get that head back in shape." He stopped talking and started laughing.

"What's so funny?" Briggs asked with playful defensiveness. He knew he was about to get teased.

Richards was laughing harder. "You wouldn't believe how hilarious you looked, flying into that room all official-like and yelling 'freeze'. I turned around just in time to see you sailing through the air, legs and arms flailing helplessly! It was really pretty funny."

Briggs looked down and shook his head sheepishly, then started to laugh, too. "Yeah. It's sometimes hard to believe that I was once a hard-core homicide detective, isn't it?"

"I guess we'll have to let time determine that, won't we?"

"Yeah. Are you sure you don't mind doing this alone?"

Richards patted Briggs on the shoulder. "No offense, Chief, but I don't want somebody as clumsy as you near my records!" Briggs flashed him a sideways smile. "No, I don't mind. I'll get started and if I'm not done tomorrow, you can come out and help me. Actually, I'm very excited about doing this. This job of mine doesn't come with lots of high points. Pretty run-of-the-mill stuff, you know. This will be an interesting change of pace."

"You remember what we're looking for?"

"Yup. Confirm that Mason did indeed work here. If so, try to find the name of any Irish men she might have worked closely with. You're looking for a connection between the two. Also, you want me to get the other names of all those who worked with them on a regular basis. Right?"

"Right. And, also, we need to find out if a Colleen Gowan worked here. She got married during those five years in question, I think in 1944, so she might be listed under either name or both. Her maiden name was Owen."

"Okay then." Richards hesitated. "You know, of course, that this *suspect* list that I might end up compiling is gonna be filled with a bunch of people who are in nursing homes and the geriatric wards of various hospitals!"

"Not necessarily. Think about it. If this someone was, say, 20 years old back then, he'd be around fifty or so today." Briggs looked at Richards. He was shaking his head. "Believe me, Richards, I know. But we've got to start somewhere, right? It's the only somewhat solid lead I've got. Maybe it will point us in the right direction."

"I guess."

"Call me in the morning. At my house, okay."

"You got it."

*   *   *

Briggs left the state school and drove home. His head was pounding and he wanted to go to bed. As he pulled into his driveway, he was surprised to see Detective Palin and officer Kroner sitting on his porch in the dark. "What the hell are you guys doing here? Don't you know it's risky to be seen in the presence of the town's homewrecker?"

They both smiled nervously. "Well, to be honest, yes," Palin said. "But we...we were—"

"What is it!"

"We wanted to help you," Kroner blurted out.

Briggs stared at them. "What do you mean, you want to help?"

"We knew you had some doubts, and we heard what you had to say. We kinda agree with you."

"You do!"

"Yeah. In an unofficial capacity, of course," added Palin. "Carr said you're off limits. He's runnin' around like he owns the joint down there. I tried to talk to him about some of my feelings about the case yesterday. He almost bit my head off. He thinks those photos of you and Mrs. King were a disgrace to you and the department."

Briggs turned to Kroner. "I thought you were going on vacation with your girlfriend next week. Ski trip or something?"

"Yeah," Kroner answered with a painful smirk. "I was gonna, but she dumped me. Kinda dull going on those romantic getaways alone."

They all laughed. "You guys are serious about this?"

"Very much so, Chief."

"Okay. Well, then, I've got a few things that are really starting to develop. I think by tomorrow I will need some help. Lots of digging into the past. Probably a lot of interviewing. You still interested?"

"Yes, sir," Kroner said.

"We'll talk to you tomorrow then," Palin said.

"Yeah." They started to walk away. Briggs felt a little warm inside. "Hey, guys." They stopped and turned. "Thanks."

2 1

Saturday, January 20, 1973. Briggs came in breathing hard. He decided when he woke up to quit the smoking again, so the half pack of cigarettes that were left went under the faucet and into the trash first thing. Then he headed out for his three-mile run that turned into a two-and-a-half-mile run and a half-mile walk. His lungs were burning. He lamented over his lost youth as he walked back. He thought about the days when he could run a 4:57 mile, how he used to run mountains for fun as a kid, and how he was always the first one in on all the five-mile woods runs he used to do in the Marines. The good old days, he thought. He got back to the house and went immediately to the basement, where he kept his weights. His heavy bag hung from a support beam. Because he hadn't been down to his gym in almost a month, he decided to punish himself. How could he have thrown all his training away so easily? He loved to train.

First he lifted. He usually did a four-day split routine: Monday and Thursday—chest, triceps and delts; Tuesday and Friday—back, biceps and forearms. He did legs only once a week on Wednesday, most of their pounding came against the heavy bag. Since it was Saturday, he decided to make it a 'free' day, doing whatever he felt like doing. He worked his chest first: a warm-up with one-hundred and thirty-five on the flat bench, then right up to two-hundred and forty-five for two sets, first eight reps, then six. He was shocked at how difficult it was to push the last two reps of his final set. "God, I'm gettin' old." He did two sets of pullovers and then two sets of incline. Next was triceps. He did a simple workout for his hinge muscles, altering it only for variety—today he decided to do three sets of pushdowns on the cables and three sets of extensions on the flat bench. He was feeling good.

Another six sets on his biceps and he was ready to hit the heavy bag. After twenty minutes of stretching, he moved over to the heavy bag, which dangled in the middle of the area he'd matted out to be the equivalent of a competitive sparring ring. He slipped off his sneakers, threw on some light foot and shin guards, and went to work. He did some footwork first; just to get the blood flowing, then moved to the bag to work his punches. After twenty minutes of this—what seemed like a lifetime for Briggs today—he did fifty front kicks, round kicks, side kicks, and hooks with each leg; then he worked combinations for ten minutes. Just as he finished, drenched in sweat and ready to pass out, the phone rang. He took the steps two at a time and bounced across the living room floor, flopped into the recliner, and swept the phone up into his hand. "Hello."

"You sound a bit out of breath, you okay?" the voice at the other end of the line asked.

Briggs sat bolt upright. His muscles tightened. "Charlie... Charlie, is that you?" he asked incredulously.

There was a moment of silence. "Yeah, Dad. It's me."

The tears welled up in Briggs' eyes. The voice on the other end of the line was his son's, but even more than that: Briggs could hear a certain niceness, a happiness in his son's voice. What to say now?

"Well, jeez, Kid, how the hell are ya?" Briggs grimaced as soon as he spoke the words. That's not what you say to your kid that you haven't spoken to in years, he thought to himself. Three years to be exact. It sounded too phony, too unfeeling. "I mean...how are—what are you doing with your—Listen, I can't tell you how great it is to hear from you, Son."

Briggs heard his son exhale hard on the other end. He was struggling, too. When he spoke, he sounded relieved. "I'm doin' great, Dad. How 'bout you?"

Briggs smiled broadly. "I'm doing great, Chuckie...So..."

"So! I was calling—I saw your name in the paper down here. Good work on that murder case."

"Thanks. I—we solved it, but now I've had some reservations about it. We're doin' some follow-up on a few points, just making sure we got the right guy."

"Really. Wow! Sounds interesting."

"Yeah! You mean that?"

"Yes, I mean it. I—"

"How's your sister?" Briggs interrupted. "Oops, sorry, what were you about to say?"

"That's okay. She's fine. Finally settling down a bit. She's still out in California, but she's not as crazy as she was. To be honest, I don't talk to her as much as I'd like to. Maybe a few times a year on the phone and five or six letters each a year."

Charlie's sister, Sarah, was twenty-five, almost five years older than her brother. She'd run off to the west coast in '68 when she was twenty, about six months before their mother committed suicide. One Sunday morning Sarah came out of her room, wearing a beautiful sundress and carrying a backpack stuffed with clothes. She found Roland, Janet, and Charlie sitting at the breakfast table. She told them she needed to be free of the Southern oppression and racism and the dictatorship that existed in the family. "I'm moving to California, where people are people, decent, loving people." She got in a car with four other friends and left.

"That's it, huh?"

"Yeah, but she's doing better now. She graduated from college and is working as a social worker, 'Helping to free those who have been subjugated by our government' is how she puts it."

"Well, at least she's working!"

"Yeah, that's true." There was a moment of silence. "Listen, Dad, I called to tell you something. I...I wanted to say that...that I forgive you—that it wasn't right for me to blame you about...about the things that happened, you know? I'm sorry that I blamed you. I know now that it was a lot of things, not just you—it was all of us, and Ma, too. How could you have known that she was gonna do what she did?"

Briggs was fighting back tears as he stretched the phone cord out and walked into the kitchen. "Hey, Chucker, you don't have to apologize. It's been hard on all of us. We all dealt with it the way we saw fit." Briggs dug the half-wet pack of smokes out of the trash, pulled a slightly damp cigarette out, and lit it. "God, you don't know how great it is to hear from you. It's been a lonely few years up here."

"I can imagine."

"How are your grandparents?"

"They're fine. Dad, I wanted to tell you something. I've got sort of a surprise for you. I think it's good. I hope you think so, too."

"What is it?"

"Well, you know...or maybe you don't, but I'm graduating from college—I'm going to the University of Florida, remember?"

"Of course I remember. That's great news, kid. How'd you pull it off so quickly though? Didn't you take a year off after your mom died?"

"Just one semester. Then I went back and buried myself in my studies. Winter and summer sessions, too—defense mechanism, I guess. But anyway, I'll be graduating this spring and I was hoping you'd come."

Briggs wiped the sweat from his upper lip. His fingers were shaking. "Yes," was all he could manage.

"Fantastic! But that's not the *really* good news. I wanted you to know that I'm starting with the FBI in August of this year!"

"What! Are you kidding?"

Charlie laughed. "No, Dad. I'm serious."

"Well, I'll be—I can't believe it. How did this all come about?"

"I know it's kind of a shock. You remember how I used to watch people all the time? I could sit there watchin' 'em all day long. Well, I ended up going into psychology and I love it. I can't get enough of the stuff. I'm graduating summa cum laude, dad. Third in my class."

"Ah, jeez, Kid, I'm so fuckin' proud of you. You don't know how much."

"Well, Dad, I want you to know that I'm proud of you, too. Believe me, I tried to fight the urges. The thought of 'following in the old man's footsteps' kept eatin' at me, but I finally gave in. I...I wanted you to know that even though I wasn't able to handle talking to you, to understand things right off, you still had an influence on me. And I want things to be right for us now."

"Thanks, Charlie. I want that, too. You're sure about this? This isn't some dream I'm having, is it?"

"No, Dad. I've been giving this whole thing a lot of thought, and this morning I woke up and realized that I couldn't let things go on like they have been any longer. But...I hate to dump all this on you and run, but we have this football game; it's just a pickup game, but I gotta get over there. Anyway, I know I've kinda knocked you for a loop. Maybe we can talk again next weekend, Sunday night maybe?"

"That'd be great. What time do you want me to call?"

"I'll call you. Say around sevenish?"

"I'll be here."

"Okay then, well...I'll talk to you soon."

"Yes. We'll talk Sunday, and Charlie?"

"Yeah, Dad?"

"I love you."

There was a momentary silence on the other end of the phone. "I love you, too."

Briggs hung up the phone. He was overwhelmed. He didn't know what to do with himself. He dug into the wet cigarette pack again and found another semi-dry one, lit it, and sat down at the kitchen table. Suddenly he noticed that he was smiling. A big broad, shit-eating grin. He shook his head. This was great. Before he could think more about it, there was a pounding at the front door. Briggs scooted across the living room. He peeked out the window to see Richards standing on his doorstep.

"Richards! How are you?" Briggs asked as he swung open the door.

"Briggs! Guess what? Great news!"

"Nothing could be as good as the news I just got on the phone."

"What's that?" Richards asked as he pushed his way past Briggs, pulling himself from his own euphoria long enough to notice that Briggs was in fantastic spirits.

"It's nothing," Briggs said. "I just got a call from my son." Briggs blushed a bit. He was embarrassed by the overly proud way he said it. "He's going into the FBI."

"Like father like son, aye?"

"Yes," Briggs said, smiling. "So what's going on?"

"Oh! Wait 'til you see. I think I've got what you were looking for. Can I lay this stuff out somewhere?"

"Yeah, bring it into the kitchen here and we'll spread it out on the table." They moved into the next room, where Richards proceeded methodically to lay out several old yellowing folders and what appeared to be lists of names.

"All right. Let's start with this." He opened up one of the folders and pulled out a faded 8x10 black and white photo of what looked like a class picture. There were about thirty-five people, all of varying ages who appeared to make up the body of the class. Around the edges on both sides of this group were several men, dressed in white shirts and white pants, and several females in white nurses' uniforms. "This is a picture of the residents and some of the staff who worked at C building. Look closely at this woman here, standing towards the back on the right side of the photo." Richards pointed to a stern-looking woman, standing with her hands clasped behind her. She was looking over the class rather than at the camera when the photo was snapped. "She look a little familiar?"

Briggs looked at the woman for a few seconds. "Yeah, she could definitely be a young version of Mason. Is it her?"

Richards ignored his question. "See that man standing on the other side of the group, this one here?"

Briggs looked at the man. "Son of a bitch, Richards, you did it. There's no doubt that that man is Pike."

Richards was beaming proudly. "McMann," he said.

"What's that?"

"His name is McMann. Darren McMann is his full name."

Briggs turned and stuck his hand out. "This is great, Richards. Good work." Richards couldn't help but smile. He wasn't used to the praise. "Who are these people?" Briggs asked, pointing his finger at various individuals in the large group.

"Those are some of the residents."

"But they're so old."

"You need to stop thinking of Wilton State School as a 'school.' It really wasn't. Most of what went on here did not include learning. As I told you the other day, it was a place for the unwanted, a place for people with various mental and physical problems. So, obviously, some of these people were pretty old. Remember, not too many people ever really left this place—unless it was to go up to Turkey Run."

"Turkey Run?"

"That was the name of the cemetery were they buried these folks when they died. It was also one of the attendants' favorite threats."

"How so?"

"Well, if these folks started acting up, it wasn't uncommon for the attendants to whisper in their ears that if the behavior kept up, they might find themselves 'going up to Turkey Run in the middle of the night.'"

"That's horrible. They were basically threatening to kill them."

"Yes. Common practice back then. Corporal punishment was used on a regular basis to keep these people in line. The staff-to-patient ratio was very unequal. Sometimes as few as two attendants would be caring for up to fifty patients. The easiest way for them to 'manage the wards' was to make the patients live in a continuous state of unrelenting fear. Sort of a step out of line and we'll kick your ass attitude, ya know. Flip over the photo."

Briggs did as he was told. On the opposite side were the last names, along with the first letter of their first names, of all the patients and the full names of the staff. Sure enough, amongst these, were the names of Martha Mason and Darren McMann. "Fantastic!" Briggs was nodding his head in approval. He looked at the remaining items on the table. "What's all this other stuff?"

Richards picked up a long list of names. "This is the entire employee roster for the hospital during the last year that McMann worked there. I can get you other years if you need them, but I figured this would be a good start. There are a lot of names here." He handed the list to Briggs.

"Wow! A lot of people," he said, as he flipped through the seven-page list.

Richards picked up another list of hand-written names. "This is a list that I compiled from the records of the individual staffing for each building. This first sheet includes all the names of the people who worked at C building with McMann—all the direct care staff. This second list is the professional staff who came there on a regular basis. It's a short list, as you can see. Ten or twelve doctors, psychologists, and other floating medical personnel and various social workers. The third sheet is the remainder of all the professional staff for the entire school. There was one thing that could pose a possible problem."

"What's that?"

"It appears that this guy McMann did overtime all over the place. He worked about two overtime shifts a week and he'd take them wherever they came up. The last list there is of other attendants whom he might have worked with on an irregular basis. I did the best I could at narrowing the names down and breaking them into manageable groups. And Mason, although she worked primarily at C building, took overtime shifts as well. She was what you'd call, 'senior staff.' She was on several committees and was very involved in the politics of the school. Very committed to her work."

"Damn! So that means that the possible reason for their 'victimization' could have come from a lot of places." Briggs flipped through the lists. "Almost anywhere."

"Yeah, but at least you've got somewhere to start, right?"

"Definitely. Any luck with Miss Mary Owen or Mrs. Mary Gowan?"

"Luck on both accounts. She did work up there as Miss Owen and after her marriage as Mrs. Gowan. But she had nothing to do with patients as far as I can tell, so I don't see how she could have been connected to Mason and McMann. She was a secretary for several of the doctors there. She may have come across Mason during some of the meetings, but for the life of me I couldn't think of any way that they could have worked together to bring about such violent actions against them."

"There's no doubt that this is quite the puzzle. But that's what they pay me the big bucks for." Briggs looked at Richards. For the first time he noticed how tired he looked. Then Briggs noticed that Richards was still wearing the same clothes he had on the day before. "Hey! How'd you get this stuff so fast? You didn't stay up there all night, did you?"

Richards lowered his head sheepishly and smiled. "Yeah."

"Why? I would have helped you today."

"I sorta got into it," Richards said, not looking up. "It was exciting."

Briggs smiled. "Hey, Richards, thanks a lot."

Richards looked at Briggs. He was filled with pride. "No problem. If you need anything else, just give me a call. I mean it."

"I will, believe me. Why don't you go home and get some sleep?"

*   *   *

Briggs puffed on a cigarette as he watched Richards pull out of his driveway, then he got back on the phone. The phone rang three times before Kroner's sleepy voice rasped from the other end. "Hello, hello...what time is it?"

"Kroner, it's the chief. What the hell are you still doing in bed? I think it's after noon already."

"Oh! Hey, Chief," Kroner said, perking up. "I went out with a few of the boys last night. Good thing I wasn't driving, huh."

"I'd say so. Listen, are you up for some leg work?" Briggs asked as he flipped through the pages of McMann's fellow workers. There were well over a hundred names. "We got a lot of work to do if we're gonna solve this case."

"You bet. What do you want me to do?"

"Thanks to the work of a friend of mine, we got the connection we were looking for between Pike, whose real name is Darren McMann, and Eleanor Mason. Seems they both worked at the old school up there on the hill."

"Wilton?"

"Yeah. I got a list of names of fellow workers that is pretty extensive. We need to try to find out what these people remember about McMann and Mason, and also about the Gowan woman. She worked up there, too, but not with the patients—a secretary."

"Patients?"

"Yeah. It's a long story, but I'll fill you in when I see you. Can you get in touch with Palin and set up a meeting? I'll give you guys a copy of the list and we can get started on finding these people."

"You gonna have another go at Pike—or McMann?"

"Not yet. Let's find out as much as we can about him first. When I go back in there I want to be able to blow him away—get everything out of him in one sitting."

"Good idea."

"So you'll get in touch with Palin?"

"Sure thing, Chief. I'll call you back in a bit with the where's and the when's."

"Thanks, Kroner. I'll talk to you."

Briggs hung up and sat back in the recliner. The day was still young and it had already been fantastic. The case was getting interesting, and they finally had something real to work with. That smile was back on his face. He couldn't fight it. He didn't want to fight it. He pushed the lever on the side of the chair and the footrest came up. He stretched out and pulled another damp cigarette from his resurrected pack. He lit it, crossed his legs at the ankles, took a deep drag, and then laughed out loud. He couldn't believe it. He had his son back.

22

Wednesday, January 24, 1973. It was three o'clock. Briggs was just about to leave to meet with Palin and Kroner to discuss the early results in locating the people from the list that Richards had compiled for them, including part of the 'professionals' list and the entire 'attendants' list of those who would have worked closely with McMann. After long hours on the phone, running into lots of dead ends, he finally came across two people who worked with and actually remembered Darren McMann. He'd made appointments for the following day to talk with both men, a Bobby Mitchell and a Sammy Ruskin. Others he talked to thought they remembered a Darren McMann, but weren't quite certain. Briggs took their names down just in case. He grabbed his keys, closed and locked the door behind him, and was headed towards his truck when he heard his phone ring. After a moment of indecision he turned back towards the house and got inside in time to grab the phone on the fifth ring. He'd left over twenty-five messages with kids or spouses who promised to have their loved one return Briggs' call if they felt they could help him, so he thought he better take the call.

"Hello, Briggs here."

"Mr. Briggs—Chief Briggs is it?" asked a weak and tired voice on the other end of the line.

"Yes, sorry. This is Chief Roland Briggs."

"Chief Briggs, my name is Mrs. Bellingford. I believe you were trying to find my mother, Marcia Grey. You just left a message with my housekeeper?"

Briggs pulled out his list to double check. He'd talked to too many people. The names were running together. Marcia Grey's name was on the 'professional staff' list. This staff worked primarily in C building. She'd been a social worker. "Was your mother a social worker up at the old Wilton State School back in 1946?" he asked, just to verify the information.

"Why…yes, she was. That was a long time ago."

"Yes, I know. But I'd really like to talk to her if I could. Would that be possible?"

"I'm afraid not, Chief Briggs. My mother is dead. 1967."

"Oh, I'm very sorry. I didn't know."

"No, that's okay. We've all come to terms with it now."

Briggs became curious. *We've all come to terms with it now.* "Come to terms with it, Ma'am?"

"Yes. Well…you see, my mother committed suicide. She…hung herself from a crossbeam in her basement."

"Oh, jeez. I'm sorry. I'm sorry to have stirred up bad memories for you, Mrs. Bellingford."

"Is there anything I can help you with?"

"No, but thank you for calling back. We were just trying to get some information on a person who might have worked with your mother back then. No big thing."

"Bye then."

"Bye. And thanks again."

*   *   *

Briggs drove out to Sullivan Brook Conservation area where Palin and Kroner were meeting him. Snow flurries danced around, hung briefly, and then zipped off in all directions. A blustery wind was kicking up out of the west. The sun had been trying to break through the clouds all day but was losing the battle. The small dirt pull-off for Sullivan Brook came up on Briggs' right and he turned in. Palin was there waiting, but not Kroner. Briggs pulled the truck up next to Palin's car so their driver's side windows lined up. Palin didn't appear happy. He looked up at Briggs.

They rolled their windows down. Briggs spoke first. "Hey, Mark, how's it going?"

Palin had gotten the major portion of the list containing the attendants who worked at the hospital: all those who'd worked with McMann while he pulled overtime in other buildings besides his own. "Not great, Chief. Whenever I could sneak away, I ran names through the Teletype—that fuckin' machine is a pain in the ass. Yesterday, for some reason, I kept gaffing up the entries so I had to keep doing them over. And that bastard Carr is runnin' around acting like a little Hitler. It's been hard to get to this stuff like I'd like to." Palin shook his head in disgust. "Nothing's been coming up. Nothing major at least. A few of the names on the list turned up with criminal records, petty stuff mostly. One guy, a Ned Cane, established himself as a lifetime criminal, but he's been in jail—Walpole—for the last five years. I don't know, Chief, this seems like a wild goose chase."

"Hey, come on. What kinda attitude is that?" Briggs asked with a smile.

Palin was surprised at Briggs' tone. He sounded...chipper. He looked quizzically at the chief, tilting his head to the side. Briggs noticed and couldn't help but laugh.

"What's the matter, Mark? Lose your tongue?"

"No, it's not that, Chief. You just sound different. You feelin' okay?"

"I'm feelin' great. Why do you ask?"

"I...I don't know. You seem different, that's all."

"That's 'cause I'm happy for the first time in about six months, me boy," Briggs said loudly, adding a toothy grin. Briggs suddenly realized that this was the first time he and detective Palin had ever really spent time together—just the two of them. He watched Palin smile and then turned away. He never noticed Palin's small yet delicate features. Almost like a woman's: eyebrows that looked plucked, soft eyes, smooth jaw line, and thin lips all tucked under straight, sandy-brown hair that he was always pushing back or off to the side. He was easy to look at. Quite a contrast to the hard-boiled Carr: squatty and built low to the ground with hard features and a face set with a smirk on it. "How's things going for you these days, Mark?"

Mark looked back at the chief. "Huh?"

"I'm serious. How are you? I know I've been pretty self-absorbed lately. I...I was just wondering how you've been."

Mark smiled at the chief. "I don't know if I can get used to the 'new you,' Chief. I've grown accustomed to that gruff, distant guy who's stomped around the office for the last few years."

"Well, hopefully that guy is gone." Briggs reached out his window and put his hand on Palin's arm. Then he patted it and gave it a squeeze. Palin squirmed in his seat then looked up gratefully as Kroner pulled into the parking lot.

"Where the hell ya been?" Palin yelled as Kroner got out and jogged over to their vehicles, sliding into the gap left between them.

Kroner cupped his hands together and blew into them vigorously, stamping his feet a few times. "God! It's fuckin' cold out today."

"Why don't you jump into my truck?" the chief asked kindly.

Kroner stopped blowing on his hands and shot the chief a quick glance. "No, that's okay, Chief." He looked at Palin who closed his eyes and shrugged his shoulders. "I can't sit still. I got some stuff I'm findin' out, but nothing earth shaking. This process is gonna take forever. There are a lot of names. How'd you guys do?"

Palin said, "I got very little so far. The only one with a serious criminal record was in jail during the murders."

"You don't think he got somebody to...no, never mind. Too tv-ish."

"What? Someone else to come up here and kill people for him for some reason? No," Palin laughed, "this guy's an idiot. Not only that, he'd have to have a lot of clout to pull something like that off. No way."

"Did you come up with much running the names though Social Security and the IRS?" Briggs asked Kroner.

"Yeah, I got a lot of addresses and phone numbers of the people still kickin.' Called a lot of them, too. Lots of the direct care attendants—the ones who probably worked with McMann—didn't remember him. A few did, but once I started asking questions you could tell they didn't remember enough to really help us out. Some of the older attendants had passed away. That was one sorta weird thing."

Briggs glanced over at Palin, who was lighting a cigarette. "Gimme one a those, would you?" Palin handed him a cigarette and his lighter. Briggs lit the cigarette, then turned his attention back to Kroner. "What was weird?"

"A lot of those people on the professional staff list, the ones who were in charge 'a that place, a lot of them were gone."

"What, moved away?" asked Palin.

"No. I mean dead."

Briggs ears perked up. "How many?"

"I don't know. I probably should say that different. It's not so much 'how many' as how many of those who would be...let's see." Kroner looked down at his fingers as he totaled up some numbers. "1946, it's '73 now. That would be...twenty-seven years. Yeah, so a lot of these folks woulda' been in their late fifties or early sixties. I got several names of people who were dead before the age of fifty. I guess, in a sense, that only makes our job easier. Less people to try and contact." He smiled wryly.

"Hmm. I don't know," Briggs answered. "Tell you what, just for our own good, get in touch with vital statistics in Boston and find out what the cause of death was for these folks." Turning to Palin, he said, "And if you could, try to find out what you can on a suicide that occurred back in 1967 over in Jessup. I got a call back on one of the names on the list of professional people who worked in C building, a Marcia Grey. She supposedly hung herself in her basement."

"Whoa! You don't think that our boy had anything to do with that...or these other people, do you?" Palin blurted out.

Briggs shrugged his shoulders. "No, probably not, but you never know." He looked back at Kroner. "Check that out as soon as you can. Get whatever info you can on these people."

"Okay, Chief. What about all these other folks?"

"Try to touch base with as many as you can. We gotta keep digging. I know it's a lot of work, but we gotta talk to these people.
Find out what they remember about McMann and Mason, and
maybe Gowan. There's gotta be something in their past that adds
up to a motive. And, Kroner, I gotta dump some more names on
you. I need you to work on my list, too. I'm going over to talk to
two fellas that seem to remember McMann fairly well. I think it'd
be best to talk to them in person." Briggs pulled the lists he had
from his jacket pocket, unfolded them, and held them out for
Kroner to see them. "I've gotten through the G's on the professional staff list and I've done all the direct care staff. At least I've
done what I could with it. Don't worry too much about them.
Concentrate on working this shorter list. Let's see if we can find
someone with a little bit of authority out there that remembers
our Mr. McMann clearly."

"You got it, Chief." Kroner took the list from Briggs.

"Anything else for me, Chief?" asked Palin.

Briggs thought for a moment. "Yeah, actually, maybe you can
do a better background check on these women's husbands. See if
we missed something. That should do it, for now. I'm gonna head
over to see Gertrude Stiener. See if she remembers anything that
Gowan might have said about working at the hospital. Maybe she
shared her dark secrets with her."

"I doubt it," said Palin. "I can't see how these women 'contributed' to their own deaths."

"Remember what I told you, Mark. My buddy Doug over at
the FBI said that this sort of crime might not make any sense at all
to us. Could be that the whole motivation for these crimes exist
only in the killer's head, but we gotta explore all possibilities.
Didn't realize how much work went into doing homicide work,
huh?"

"No. It seems so futile. I mean…there must be close to five hundred names of people who worked up at that old school—thirty years ago! Some of those people died, moved away, who knows. I mean, what could be the motivation for knocking off these people so long afterwards?" He shook his head and then rubbed his eyes. "I think it's highly unlikely that we're in the right ball field here. There's gotta be an angle that we're missing—something more recent."

All three men sat still for a moment, thinking their own thoughts. Then Briggs spoke. "You may be right, Mark; but for now, all roads seem to be leading up the mountain to that school. I'm always open to other suggestions, though. If you think of something, I'll certainly consider it."

Mark threw up his hands, then slapped them both back down on his steering wheel. "I can't, that's the problem."

"Well, then, let's keep working at this angle and see where it takes us," said Kroner.

"Definitely. I'm gonna head out to Stiener's house, then. I'll talk to you guys tomorrow, okay?"

The chief drove back through town and turned onto Old South Road. Gertrude Stiener lived about a mile up on the right. She and her grandson owned an old house that was built, as the placard nailed to the front of the house indicated, in 1783. Three stories high with lots of angles, windows and porches, the old place needed a new coat of paint in the worst way. Old South Road was the first 'official' street in Wilton, formally named several years after the town was settled.

Briggs had called Mrs. Stiener earlier in the day and made the appointment. She became very sad when Briggs mentioned Mary Gowan's name. "Mary was such a sweet, caring woman," she had told Briggs. Briggs pulled up to the curb in front of the house, which sat upon a slightly elevated lot. The lawn rolled down towards the street, coming to a stop at a craggy-looking cement retaining wall about three feet above the sidewalk. Briggs took the six steps two at a time, then ambled along a broken walkway to a well-worn front porch. He noticed as he waited for someone to answer his knock that the white curtains that hung in the windows were yellowing along the edges. After a moment, Walter, Gertrude's hulking grandson, opened the door. He smiled nervously, quickly looked over his shoulder, stepped out onto the porch, and quietly closed the door behind him.

"Hi, Chief Briggs, remember me? Walter."

"I remember you, Walter." Briggs shrugged his shoulders slightly and stared up into the big man's soft, round face. "What's up?"

"I wanted to talk to you for a second before you talk to my grams," Walter whispered. "I think you should know that this whole thing has been very tough on her. She's not been herself lately. She stopped calling me Doughboy and everything. She...seems to have lost her will a bit, if you know what I mean."

Briggs smiled up into the big man's gentle eyes. "I understand completely. I won't press her on anything. I just wanted to know about Mary Gowan and I think your grandmother could really help us out."

"Oh, okay. All right then, let's go in." Walter turned and reached for the doorknob. It looked quite small in his beefy hand. He led Briggs into a wide entranceway, stopping long enough to take Briggs' jacket and hang it in a small hall closet. The interior of the house was dark and gloomy. Briggs figured that even on a sunny day, it was probably not much brighter inside. The house smelled like grizzle. It brought back memories for Briggs of his own grandmother's house, when, on Sunday, he and his family would visit and have a big roast with potatoes and corn and biscuits—all the fixings. He smiled to himself. Walter led Briggs into the living room, where his grandmother was propped up on the couch, wrapped in an old, multicolored shawl. Her frail bony fingers were interlocked and rested in her lap. She looked away from the television as Briggs entered.

"Chief Briggs! How wonderful it is to see you," she said smiling. Then she scowled at her grandson. "Breaks up the monotony of having to spend eternity with this overgrown giant."

"Awh, Grams," Walter said, grimacing, "you said you'd stop talkin' like that in front of people." The man Briggs had talked to on the porch had suddenly regressed to a small child.

Briggs smiled, remembering the sort of relationship these two had. He also found it both funny and sad that the unexpressed meaning of Walter's words was that he'd accepted being talked to 'like that' as long as no one was around. The old woman ignored him.

"You said that you wanted to ask some questions about Mary, is that right?"

"Yes, Ma'am," Briggs answered.

"Why?" She stared at Briggs.

Briggs was going to give her the 'I'm a thorough guy,' line, but then he hesitated. Gertrude's eyes were sparkling. He turned to Walter. "Could you give your grandmother and me a few minutes alone?"

Walter cast a concerned glance at his grandmother, who waved him off. "Go ahead," she told him. "Go eat something. Lord knows you love to do that."

Walter left and Briggs kneeled down in front of Gertrude. "What if I told you that I thought you could really help me out— that you could possibly help me solve another crime?"

"What kind of crime?" she asked, her curiosity brimming up.

"I can't tell you that, but what I can tell you is that I believe that there's more work to be done involving the Mason-Gowan murders. But you have to keep this little meeting to yourself."

Gertrude leaned forward and patted Briggs on the wrist. "You can count on me to keep a secret. Now, what's going on?"

"I need to ask you about Mary Gowan's past. Did you two talk about the old days much?"

"Chief Briggs, when you get to be old and crotchety like me, talking about the old days is one of the main things that you do." Then she winked at Briggs.

He smiled softly. "Do you remember her talking about the days when she worked up at the Wilton School for the Feeble-minded?"

Gertrude frowned. "Oh, that place," she answered sourly. "What'd they do with all those strange people after they closed that place?"

Briggs thought for a minute before he remembered that Richards had told him that the state had opened another school somewhere out towards Boston. "They moved them to another school out in the eastern part of the state."

"Oh," Gertrude sniffed, "good riddance!"

"Why do you say that?"

Gertrude's eyes widened. "Why do you think! Buildings full of all those deviant creatures. What do you think would have happened if they escaped? There was a whole slew of sex perverts up there. Two or three buildings dedicated to 'caring' for sex perverts just miles from our quiet little town! Do you even have to ask why I say *good riddance?*" She brought both hands up and slapped at the air in front of her.

"Did Mary tell you about these sex perverts?"

"Oh, no. Not Mary." Gertrude softened for a second. "She was too sweet to say a bad word about anyone. She said that those were just stories about the sex perverts being up there. But I think they were all told to say that to any of us that didn't work up there. It was that they were sworn to secrecy about it. But we all knew about it anyway. You can't hide the fact that there were all sorts of deviants up there. Misfits and miscreants."

"What did Mary say about the people who worked up there?"

"The people who worked up there?"

"Yes. Did she ever say anything about some of the other workers? Was there anybody she mentioned more than once?"

Gertrude brought a finger to her mouth, as if to silence herself while she thought. "No," she said slowly. "Not that I can remember. That was a long time ago though. She stopped working with that sort when the place closed. Settled in and made the most of her marriage." Gertrude brought her voice down to a whisper. "She was barren, poor child."

"Oh," Briggs thought out loud, realizing now why there'd been no kids to call and inform about their mother's murder. "Did she have any other friends, people who might have known her from her days up at the school?"

"No, I don't think so. At least she never mentioned any in particular. We mostly talked about those devils she took care of. She was so...I don't know?"

"So what?"

Gertrude searched for the right words. "I guess she was so...almost sad about them. She seemed to talk about them as if they were...like real people. It always surprised me."

Briggs fought off saying something. The hair on the back of his neck was standing up. He was feeling the same way about Gertrude as he did about some of the racist pigs he'd busted back in Jacksonville. "Is there anything besides the stories about the kids that you remember? She didn't ever talk about the other workers? The bosses?"

Gertrude's lips tightened for a second. "Chief Briggs, I may be old, but I'm not stupid. I heard your question the first time you asked it. She did not, to my recollection, make any comments about her fellow workers. She did not, as far as I know, associate with anyone who used to work up there. She came to the center like the rest of us."

"Sorry, Mrs. Stiener. I didn't mean to insult your intelligence. It's just that it would really help me if she had said anything about them."

"Well, she didn't."

"Okay then. Well, I really appreciate your time." Briggs stood up just as Walter trudged into the room.

"You all done, Chief?"

"Yes, Walt, all set. I can see myself out."

                *   *   *

Briggs turned his truck towards home. He didn't like the way Gertrude had made him feel. He knew those sorts of people needed separation from the rest of society, but they were still people. He thought about what Palin and Kroner had said about this being a case that seemed buried in the past. He thought about how it didn't seem like they were getting any closer to finding out what might have happened up at the school to bring on these murders. Briggs opened up the glove box and pulled out a new pack of cigarettes. He remembered back to his days as a homicide detective in Jacksonville. Many of the murders that he worked were solved within days. The family disputes, one lover killing another, a robbery gone bad. But it was the cases like this one, the hard ones with no easy answers that Briggs loved. He'd made his reputation on them. Unfortunately, tonight, he couldn't for the life of him remember why he'd loved them so much.

23

Thursday, February 1, 1973. Briggs drove out to Cortland to meet Bobby Mitchell. Although the distance was only twenty-two miles, the towns were totally different. Where as Wilton was able to adapt to the changing economic times over the years, Cortland tried to remain the same. As Wilton became a tourist town when many of the mills were shutting down, Cortland tried to hold onto its industries. Cortland was not completely successful, although some of the metalwork and paper mill plants had remained. Glancing down the side streets as he drove along Main Street, Briggs could see many vacant stores. The big plate glass windows were dusty from many months or even years of emptiness. A few still had 'For Rent' signs in them, but there were many others where the owners, realizing the futility of it, hadn't even bothered.

Bobby Mitchell was one of the fortunate few who still had a job at one of the metalwork factories. He'd promised to meet with Briggs on his lunch break at a bar called Remmies II. As Briggs drove along he couldn't believe that any business in Cortland could be successful enough to justify a 'II.' He found the place with little problem, parked on the opposite side of the street, and then let the wind push him to the bar. The tinted, dark-green glass door swung shut and sealed him in a vacuum of darkness and smoke. The smell of stale beer and whiskey was everywhere. The gray shades of a few souls broke the line of hazy light cast across the edge of the bar by the neon Bud and Miller signs hanging on the wall, just above the murky bottles. Briggs slid onto the first stool he stumbled into. A man with swollen cheeks and large broken blood vessels strewn like spider webs across his nose turned and took notice of Briggs, then turned back to stare into his beer.

"You must be Briggs."

"Yeah. How'd ya know?"

The man snickered. "Look around. You think we get a lot of new faces in here?"

Briggs eyes were beginning to adjust. There were two pool tables at the far end of the bar and a few other tables here and there. A too bright light shown down on a dartboard so old and used it was hard to see where one number's boarders ended and another's began. The bar itself widened at either end; and just as Briggs realized he was in a strip bar, a squatty-looking woman with long dark hair, narrow shoulders, and wide hips came slinking out from behind a curtain. She climbed a set of stairs that Briggs could not see and took the stage, stopping long enough to bend down and press a button on a cheap cassette player. After a few seconds, the distorted voice of Mick Jagger screaming about not being able to get satisfaction was echoing off the walls. The squatty-looking woman began to sway her hips and swing her arms in an awkward, uncoordinated way. Briggs fought the urge to jump up and tell her to stop embarrassing herself. He turned to Mitchell.

"No, I guess you don't get too many new faces in here, do ya?"

"What you see is pretty much what you get, Chief."

The bartender, an emaciated blonde who was probably near fifty but looked more like seventy walked over to where Briggs was sitting but said nothing. She repeatedly pushed back the corners of her mouth with her thumb and forefinger while she waited for Briggs to order something. "Could you get me a Michelob?" he asked. She brought it to him in silence and then slipped back into the shadows.

"So you want to know about Darren McMann, huh?"

"Yeah, I was hoping to fill in some blanks about the case."

Mitchell shook his head and smirked, still staring into his beer. "Come on, Chief. You and I know that McMann wasn't capable of killin' those women. What are you doin' here?"

Briggs looked at the side of the big man's face. Mitchell had lived a hard life. Signs of it filled every one of his wrinkles. The stripper was slinking her way down the bar towards them. "Do you still talk to him?"

"Naw. We haven't talked in years. A lot of years." Mitchell paused and held up a finger in front of his face, tilted his head. "Well, that's not totally true. I ran into him once, a few years back. Up in Wilton. I forget what I was doing up there, but he was walking down the sidewalk. I almost didn't recognize him, with that limp and—well, I shouldn't talk. I probably looked pretty ancient to him, too. We talked for a few seconds, but he didn't seem interested in rekindling an old friendship. Couldn't figure out why he was acting that way; but now, seein' as he's changed his name and all, I guess it makes sense. He told me to take care and wandered off. He was nothing of the guy I hung out with back in the old days."

"How's that?"

"You keep asking me questions and you still haven't answered mine, Chief. What are you really after?"

The stripper had moved in front of them now. Mitchell lost interest in the chief momentarily. He looked up at the chunky little thing. She'd taken her top off, revealing small, sagging breasts. She had unusually large nipples.

"Hey, Bobby, baby. How ya doin' today?" she asked Mitchell.

Mitchell's lips fell away from his teeth and revealed way too much of his gums. His eyes bulged out even more than they already did. "Precious, my love. You're lookin' lovely as ever."

"Only 'cause you're here, Sweetie-pie." She turned and leaned forward so she could wiggle her ass in Mitchell's face. Briggs could see what appeared to be a rash of some sort developing between her thighs. Mitchell pulled a one from a stack of money on the bar and slowly pulled her g-string away from her hip. He slid the dollar along the outside of Precious' leg and then, once the dollar was in place, let go of the string. It snapped back into place with the dollar underneath. Briggs looked at the few others occupying the barstools. None were taking notice of the stripper. "Who's your friend, Bobby?"

"Oh, this is *Mr.* Briggs. He's a friend come down from Wilton for a bit."

Precious was looking over her right shoulder, smiling at Briggs. She reached down and looped her thumbs around her g-string and pushed them down a little, showing him her ass. She aimed her rectum at Briggs. "Welcome to our little town, Mr. Briggs." She bent closer. Her ass was only inches from Briggs' face. He leaned back and almost bumped into the side of Mitchell's head, who'd leaned over to get a good view of Precious' privates. She smiled sarcastically at Briggs. "What's 'a matter, there, Mr. Briggs, you the shy type? Can't take it when a woman shoves her pussy in your face?"

Briggs wanted to tell her that it wasn't so much 'a' pussy, but rather 'the' pussy that was making him shy away. "Yeah, I'm a shy one," he answered, leaning back all the way.

"What about you, Bobby? You too shy to look at my pussy?" she asked, trying to sound seductive. Briggs was fighting back a laugh.

Bobby was now moving his head back and forth with her ass, hypnotized by her swaying. He looked like he was saying the word 'pow!' over and over again, but nothing was coming out. He finally said, "Not me baby, bring it on!"

She turned away from him, still wiggling her ass slowly and pulled her g-string away from her leg again. Bobby quickly complied, supplying her with another bill, this time a five. She noticed and slid down on her hands and knees, spreading herself wide open and leaning back into Mitchell's face. He leaned in and took a whiff, exaggerating the motion, then pretended to faint from the aroma. Precious giggled like a child. She stood up and moved away, but not before accepting Bobby's offer to visit him after her set. Bobby watched her slink away, then turned back to Briggs, the gummy smile finally starting to fade.

"Sorry about havin' ta call you Mister Briggs," he said. "I don't need her knowin' I'm helpin' out the cops. Bad for my reputation, ya know. If things go well, I'm hopin' that'll be the next Mrs. Mitchell. I been workin' on 'er for about six months now. I think she's gonna go out with me soon."

Briggs thought about how beauty definitely lay in the eye of the beholder. "How many would she make?"

"She'd be the third." He looked back over his shoulder at Precious. A man who looked about a hundred years old was getting the same treatment Mitchell had gotten. "See how she's different with them. There ain't no feelin' in those hips 'less they're wiggling in front 'a me," he said proudly.

Briggs couldn't see the difference, but nodded in agreement. "Yeah," he said enthusiastically. "I see what you mean. Listen, Bobby, I really need to get some answers here. You're right, I have my doubts. I need to know about who McMann might have pissed off back in the old days—back at the school."

Mitchell smiled. "I knew it! I couldn't believe it when I read it. I knew it. There's no way that old bastard could have pulled off these murders. But who the fuck would bother settin' him up?"

"That's what I need to find out. Can you tell me much about him?"

"Ain't too much to tell. We worked together in the same building for a while, got close enough to start hangin' out together after work and all. After a year or so I transferred to another building—better hours—and we sorta drifted apart some. The next thing I heard, he was gone. Some sort of nonsense about him being insubordinate! Humph."

"Why do you say it like that?"

Bobby drained his mug, then exhaled loudly. "This talkin' is makin' me thirsty."

Briggs waved to the bartender and she brought Bobby another beer. He continued. "Because McMann was a coward. Chicken shit son-of-a-bitch. He'd never talk back to any of those bosses up there. He was a real suck up. I mean, he was tough around us and the retards, but he was a pussycat around those higher-ups."

"There was no one who had any problems with him?"

"Not that I can remember. Like I said, he was too much of a pussy around the bigwigs to ever talk back or anything. He was funnier than hell; I remember that real well. Used to make fun…"

Bobby turned to Briggs. "I can't get in any trouble for shit I tell you about stuff I watched McMann do, can I?"

Briggs leaned forward. Maybe he was finally going to hear something that could be a hint to what happened. "No, you can't."

Bobby glanced quickly at Briggs and noticed his intensity. He smiled and shook his head. "No, Chief, it was nothin' like that. Nothing serious. He just used to come up with all sorts of ways to pass the day…by makin' fun of the squash heads, that's all. But I tell ya, he used to do some fucked-up shit. Keep us laughin' the whole shift."

Briggs was disappointed. "Oh, I see," he answered, glumly. Then he looked quizzically at Bobby. "What's a squash head?"

"Yeah, you wouldn't know what that was. A squash head was what we used to call those retards up there. Fuckin' bunch a freaks is what they were, I tell ya. All's I'm sayin' is that McMann used to tease 'em in the worst way, sorta take advantage of their stupidity. Nothin' serious, most of it was just if the retards was bad, ya know. Stuff to keep the order of the place. I'll never forget how he had 'em trained. He would sit up against the wall in the day hall and all the freaks would have to sit or lay around in a circle in front of him. They wouldn't dare move. Then he'd yell, 'Time to get your exercise,' and clap his hands. They'd all get up and walk around the edge of the room 'til McMann would clap his hands again. Then they'd all drop down where they was until he clapped again. He was like a hero to a lot of us younger guys. None of us could get the backward little fucks to respond the way he could.

"Other times he left a few of the best boys in charge and he'd fall asleep in his chair. I remember walkin' in and there he'd be snorin' away and the 'best boys' would be whackin' at anybody who even looked like they were gonna make noise." Bobby backtracked a minute to explain. "The best boys was those retards that weren't so fucked up. They could work and do chores and shit like that." He got silent for a moment, then continued. "He kept those fuckers' in line, I tell ya. And you know what the fucked up part of that was?" He looked at Briggs and waited until he shrugged his shoulders before continuing. "Some of this shit he pulled off was in buildings where the retards were supposed to be...what was the word— untrainable! Tell ya what, you put the fear of God into those little bastards and they learned quick. They made a mistake when they got rid a Darren McMann, I tell ya."

"What do you remember about that?"

"Not much. Like I said, we'd sorta stopped hangin' around on a regular basis by then, me havin' moved and all. One day he was there, the next he was gone. I asked around, find out why he'd had to leave, but no one was talkin'. "Bout two weeks later, I went over to his house—he was livin' with his mother still—and she said he'd left town. Wasn't comin' back for a while as he'd gotten work somewhere's else. She told me where, but I don't remember. Somewhere's out near Boston. One of those suburbs, ya know."

"Do you remember the nurse, Mason?"

"Hell yes! She was tough as nails, boy. Fuckin' Darren and her, they ran C building like there was no tomorrow. There were never any problems there, I tell ya."

"She was aware of this treatment, this way that McMann controlled the kids?"

"Yeah. Why?"

"Just curious. Can you think of anyone she might have rubbed the wrong way?"

"You mean can I think of anyone who she fucked over so bad they would come back thirty fuckin' years later and whack her. No! Come on, Chief, this was a goddamn state school, not the pentagon."

Briggs rubbed his head with his hands. "I know it sounds far-fetched, but I gotta ask. These people did something way back then to piss somebody off."

"I couldn't tell ya what that'd be, Chief. I don't remember either a them getting anyone upset with them. All's I remember is that the bosses loved Mason and she loved McMann. They did their jobs very well."

"Any guesses as to why McMann would have changed his name to Pike?"

"None."

Briggs looked over Bobby's shoulder. Precious was heading in their direction. "Looks like you're about to have company."

Precious swung around and slid herself between Bobby's legs putting her butt against his crotch. Bobby snuggled his big head up against her cheek and offered Briggs a gummy smile. His eyes were bugging out again. "Sorry I couldn't help you much, *Mr.* Briggs." He gave the chief a wink. "Maybe next time, okay"

"Yeah, all right, Bobby."

The chief threw a five-dollar bill on the bar and headed towards the door. He turned back to see Bobby shoving another single into Precious' bra. Ain't love grand, Briggs thought as he left.

24

Briggs headed back to Wilton to interview Sammy Ruskin. As he drove back, he thought about how Mitchell and Stiener viewed the folks who had lived up at the school as less than human. If he hadn't been trying to get information out of them, he'd have told them off. What could be so bad about mental retardation? In Jacksonville there had been a retarded kid who lived down the block from him. Kid seemed sweet enough. Harmless. He also wondered whether the story he heard about McMann was true. Who in his right mind would allow such treatment? And the State of Massachusetts?

Sammy Ruskin still worked for the State. His title, he'd told Briggs the day before, was program director. He'd asked Briggs to meet him at a group home cluster—several homes in the same area where mentally retarded individuals lived—at three o'clock. Briggs had just enough time to stop for a quick bite to eat before their meeting. At five minutes of three, Briggs turned onto Dyer Circle, a small side street in back of an industrial park. Briggs traveled about a hundred and fifty yards, pulling up in front of the first house on the right, a small brown ranch with a wide front porch. A wheel chair ramp led up to the front door. Briggs couldn't help but notice that the six houses located around the circle seemed like a miniature version of the old state school on the hill.

As Briggs got out of his truck, he saw a young man walking over from the house across the street. He was short, about five feet tall, thin wispy hair cut short. His eyes were small and slightly slanted. He facial features were flattened. He had an average build but a little potbelly protruded out from within his leather jacket. As he walked up to Briggs he stuck his hand out. He had short little pudgy fingers. He smiled, his whole face cracking into broad lines. Briggs believed he remembered that this man's type of retardation was called mongolism.

"Hello," the little man said. "How are YOU today?" He had a strange, singsong sort of voice that hit high notes at the wrong time, yet somehow was very pleasing to the ear.

"I'm fine, and you?" Briggs answered, smiling back. He reached out and started to shake the man's hand.

"Good. What's your name?"

"Roland."

"Yes."

Briggs paused. "Yes what?"

"Yes. My name is Roland."

"Oh! *Your* name is Roland, too. So is mine."

The man stuck an overly large tongue out while he thought about what Briggs was saying. He had no teeth. "You're Roland, too?"

"Yes, I am."

The man, Little Roland, gave the thumbs up with both hands and said, "All right!" then smiled broadly again. When Briggs gave the thumbs up back, Little Roland closed the gap between them and wrapped his arms around Big Roland, burying his head into his chest. At first Briggs put his hands up in shock and thought about pulling away, but then smiled and hugged the little man back. He too suddenly felt the camaraderie of the 'Rolands'. A hug was okay. He'd almost forgotten how good they could feel and the young man's pure innocence and willingness to show his emotion moved him. The little man pulled away, looking very serious all of a sudden.

"What's the matter, Roland?" asked Big Roland.

"Roland, do you have a jelly sandwich for me?"

Briggs couldn't help but laugh a little at the perturbation he saw in the little man's face. "Why, no Roland, I don't have a jelly sandwich for you right now. I'm sorry about that."

Little Roland looked completely dejected for a second. He dropped his head and stuck out his tongue. He was the complete pathetic creature. Briggs caught himself aimlessly smoothing his hands over his pockets in a vain search for a jelly sandwich.

"That's okay," Little Roland said in the sweetest, saddest voice Briggs had ever heard. "I'll get one one day." After a few seconds, though, little Roland brightened and looked up at Briggs again. "Maybe, then, do you have a dollar for me?"

This time it was Briggs' turn to smile broadly. "Why yes! Now there I can help you, my friend." Briggs eagerly pulled his wallet out of his pocket, plucked a single out, and handed it to Little Roland who looked at it as if it were the first dollar bill he'd ever seen.

"Thanks...ah, Roland!" he shouted and hugged Briggs again, squeezing even tighter than before. Briggs hugged back and patted the man on the shoulder.

The front door to the brown house swung open and Briggs turned to look. Little Roland pivoted around and looked up, too. "Sammy! Sammy! Roland is here. He's got the same name as me! And he gave me a dollar!"

Sammy Ruskin gave a weary but loving smile to Little Roland. "You didn't work him over with that jelly sandwich routine of yours, did you?"

Briggs looked at Little Roland, who was already hanging his head and pouting for Sammy. "No," he said, quietly.

Sammy waited a second and then said, "All right, Roland. Why don't you go back home then. See what your friends are doing, okay"

"Okay, Mr. Sammy." Little Roland wandered off without saying goodbye to Briggs.

"Mr. Ruskin?"

"That's me. You must be Chief Briggs."

"Have I just been conned?"

"By one of the best," answered Ruskin.

"Come on in," Ruskin continued. "I hope you don't mind, but we'll have to do this while I do rounds, I'm short staffed today and I decided to pull a shift myself. I like to do that once in a while. Keeps me in touch with the patients and the employees."

"That's fine with me."

"Come along then."

Briggs followed Sammy into the house. Sammy was a man of average height and weight. He had a long, kindly face, tightly trimmed mustache and hair pulled back into a short ponytail. He wore silver, wire-rimmed glasses. The house itself was different than what Briggs had expected. Almost the entire front part of the

house was open; one large room with a television set on a high
stand, a couch, and two recliners pushed against the far wall.
There were plants hanging in the windows and pictures of flowers
and New England landscapes on the wall. As they moved into the
hallway, Briggs was surprised at how wide they were.

"Puzzled by the layout of the house?" Sammy asked.

"Yeah, it wasn't quite what I expected."

"You are standing in a model home for mentally retarded
human beings with severe medical needs."

"All these houses in the neighborhood are medical?"

"No, just this one. There are all sorts of different folks with different types of needs living here, and there are even some, like
Roland, who need very little assistance at all. This is what you
might call an experimental neighborhood, an attempt to begin
exposing these guys to living in the community. And, of course,
exposing the community to them."

"Oh," Briggs said, raising his eyebrows.

"You seem surprised, Chief."

"Well, I am. I thought that these folks were supposed to
be...well, I don't know. Separated."

Sammy smiled. "You sound like you feel guilty for saying that.
Did Roland get to you a little?"

"Well, it's not that. I just...maybe he did, but that's...it
shouldn't be—"

"Don't worry, Chief. You're not alone in your ignorance. Our
goal is to try to get the average person to realize that these people
are wonderful. Beautiful. They're no different than you and I;
they're just more challenged. Mentally challenged."

"There, but for the grace of God, go I, huh?"

"Exactly! Maybe we'll use that as a slogan."

"You seem very involved with this. At it a long time?"

"You could say that. Ever since I saw the bullshit these people had to endure. About thirty years now, I guess. This little neighborhood experiment took me almost ten years to get approved. Wouldn't have been able to, but some good souls donated all the building money. Once the state realized that they wouldn't have to foot the bill for construction, they went ahead and gave me the staffing."

"Who donated?"

"Mostly family members. A few generous business owners. This land is owned by one of those large corporations you saw on your way in. Most people don't want these people in their neighborhood. They think they're all deviants and sickos: psychos and killers and rapists. Let me tell you something, Chief. I consider some of these guys my closest friends. They're great and loving people. Innocent and sweet and giving. But nobody knows because society has been locking them away forever. Let me ask you something. How many people do you know that are mentally retarded?"

Briggs thought for a minute. "None, really. There was this one kid in Florida. I guess I knew him."

"Would you like to take a guess at how many mentally retarded people there are in this country alone?"

"Jeez, I don't know. What is your definition of retarded? I know a lot of pretty stupid people!" Briggs joked.

"Somebody with an IQ below 70 or 75, has two or more limitations in adaptive skills areas, like that."

Briggs scratched his head. "Maybe a hundred thousand or so."

"Try around seven million!"

"Are you serious! I'd a never guessed that high."

"I am serious. How many people do you know who died of heart attacks?"

"God, there have been several. Charlie, down at the VFW; George Jones, the guy who ran the police motor pool. He died at forty-six. Then there was my grandfather of course. I can name plenty, why?"

"Only around one hundred thousand folks a year die of heart attacks and you can name a bunch of people who you know who died from them, but you can't name one mentally retarded person that you know. Doesn't that seem weird to you?"

"Yeah, I guess. A little."

"That's because we've shoved them away—out of society as if they were criminals—and they're not, Chief. They've done nothing wrong. Nothing that they could help."

"I see your point."

"Come along with me. I have to do bed checks." Briggs followed Sammy down the hall to the first room off to the right. Inside was an old man with a barrel chest and stumpy legs with feet that looked more like balled-up fists. He was lying on a bed. Briggs cringed when he first saw him. Poor guy. He, like Little Roland, had no teeth. He also had big ears that looked even bigger with the short crew cut he wore. "William, this is Chief Briggs. Is it okay if I tell him a little bit about you?" Sammy was yelling. It was obvious that William was hard of hearing. William looked at Briggs and raised a twisted, arthritis-filled hand. He waved it at Briggs, who smiled and waved back. William looked at Sammy and nodded yes.

"William suffers from epilepsy. He is not really officially retarded, although after spending his whole life in state-run facilities, he has become what is called *institutionally* retarded." Sammy stopped for a second and looked at William, then put his hand on the man's shoulder, rubbing it gently. "It comes from being ignored mentally for years and years. Later in his life, it was discovered that he had rheumatoid arthritis, which has now progressed to the point that William can no longer move around like he used to, huh, buddy?" Sammy was still shouting, making sure that William could hear everything that he was telling Briggs. William tilted his head to the side and frowned, to show he confirmed what Sammy was saying. "Chief, if you could excuse us for a few seconds, I just want to see if William needs my help with going to the bathroom."

"Oh! Of course. Yeah, let me give you some privacy. William, it was nice meeting you." Briggs smiled at William who smiled back and mumbled something unclear.

Sammy said, "Could you shut the door behind you, Chief."

Briggs waited in the hall. There were two other staff members working at the house, attending to what Briggs guessed were at least two other bedridden patients. There were two other bedrooms that he could see. After a few minutes, Sammy came back out. "Let's go out on the porch, Chief."

Once out on the porch, the chief said, "What is it, something in the water?"

"What do you mean, Chief?"

"Their teeth. Roland doesn't look that old, but he's got no teeth. William in there is what, fifty-five or so, he has no teeth either."

Sammy turned away from the chief for a second. "One of the more common practices from the grand old days of institutional care." He turned back to Briggs. "Both he and Roland were biters. That is, when they stood up for themselves or whatever, they bit. They probably bit staff, and so their teeth were removed. Happened to a lot of 'em back then."

Briggs shook his head. "Come on, Mr. Ruskin, who the hell do you think you're talking to? You trying to tell me that some dentist *pulled* perfectly good teeth out of their heads?"

"Mr. Briggs, I'm not trying to *tell* you anything. The shit that went on at Wilton—in any of those sorts of 'schools' back then was horrible."

"Look, I just talked to Bobby Mitchell, and he did say that—"

"Bobby Mitchell!" Ruskin snorted. "Both he and his friend there, the man you came here to ask me about, that bastard McMann, were some of the worst human beings I've ever come across! It still bothers me that I did nothing about what I saw them—and especially McMann—do to those kids. But...I was only one man back then. I couldn't stand up to the system alone. It took me almost twenty-eight years to get a few of them some decent housing. Imagine what would have happened to me if I stood up to those sons-a-bitches back then. You know what they used to do? And not just those two! Half the fuckin' school was filled with these fanatics who believed that we basically had to try to torture the retardation out of these kids. Corporal punishment was the rule, not the exception. If these kids stepped out of line, and it didn't take much, they could spend the day walking the stairs. Up and down all day long. Or they would be put up against a wall, like you guys do when searching a suspect, with their legs spread, leaning forward, hands out. Only they'd get left there for hours until they fell to the ground from exhaustion.

"Imagine, Mr. Briggs, what it must have been like to be a small child, maybe ten or eleven years old—you're mentally ill or retarded and you have to go to the bathroom, but it's quiet time on the ward. You're supposed to be 'resting.' You can't hold it any more; so you get up to use the toilet and suddenly you find your-self in a closet, kneeling on a box of ball bearings. Punishment for disturbing the ward. The circulation in your legs is gone from the ball bearings pressing up against your knees. You can't control your bowels any more and you shit all over yourself. If you dare try to explain what happened, you're beaten and sent out to the doghouse, a little pen under the front stairs of the huge building you live in."

"Jesus, Mitchell didn't tell me about that stuff."

"Of course he didn't! Would you go around telling the chief of police that for years you tortured human beings for a living!"

"How come you let that stuff go?"

"I didn't let it go! I tried to do something about it. I'm trying." Ruskin moved away from the railing he'd been leaning on and paced the porch. "Look, you came here to ask me if I knew anything about Darren McMann. Let me tell you what I know and then I have to get back inside, okay? I don't have much time." He stopped pacing and stood in front of Briggs.

"I feel pretty shitty about lots of things that happened back then, Chief. I should have done more—should have stood up in some way. But I didn't, not right away. And I have to live with that. Maybe it was because of my own need to be...part of something. To be accepted, I don't know." Ruskin dropped his head. "Shit! There was no excuse. Look, Chief, I'll tell you about this, but you gotta promise that you won't make it public. Legally I know I can't get in trouble for it now, but I could lose this whole project if people find out, that I...well, the state covered up a rape."

"It did what!"

Ruskin turned away from Briggs, unable to face him. "Believe me, Chief, I'm not proud of myself. For having known about it and not telling someone. When you first called, I...I wasn't going to say that I knew him, McMann. But as I started speaking, it was as if I had no control over my mouth. The next thing I knew I was telling you to come out here and hear the truth. That bastard McMann raped one of those kids, a young girl. They caught him. He was out behind one of the buildings. All I can tell you is that few people knew about it and somehow it got covered up. The one thing that did happen was that McMann was fired. They told him that if he ever tried to be rehired by the state they'd press charges. They also told him to get the fuck outa Wilton. He was too stupid to realize that the minute they let him walk out of that room they were as guilty as he was. Last I knew he was long gone until I saw his picture in the paper, for killing that bitch, Mason."

"Did she know about the rape?"

"I'm sure she found out about it. She was one of the enforcers. The sicko, self-righteous fucks who believed that they were doing the work of God! She was in on all the dirty shit. If I had to guess, I'd say that she knew about it."

"Who busted him on the rape?"

"I wouldn't know that."

"How did you hear about it?"

"I don't remember. Somebody told me."

"Bobby Mitchell said everyone he tried to talk to—to find out why McMann left—was real hush-hush about it. He said that people thought it had something to do with insubordination. Why would they tell him something like that and then tell you that it was a rape?"

"Come on, Chief. You met the man. Would you confide in him about something that could cause such damage to the school?"

"No, I guess not. Briggs paused. "What about Gowan? What do you recall about her?"

"Now that was a surprise. I didn't know the woman. I mean, I knew who she was—seen her around the school—but I was shocked when I heard about her being killed."

"She had no connection to McMann or Mason? None at all?"

"None that I know of. Why would they? She was some secretary and they worked in the buildings. No. I don't think they had any direct connection."

"Why did the school cover up the rape?"

"Why do you think? Politics. Remember that the retarded were nothing to these people. At least not when it came to their job security. The scandal that would have caused! And, if you remember, the school closed about ten years later. There were a lot of problems already. The news that rape was going on up there would have been a devastating blow to the school."

Briggs moved to the railing and sat. He couldn't believe what he was hearing. Finally some of the pieces were falling into place. But maybe in a direction he didn't expect. "So who do you think killed these women?"

Ruskin spun around and looked at Briggs in shock. "What the hell kind of question is that! You got the guy sitting in your prison right now!" Ruskin paused. "Wait a minute, you don't think…I thought you came out here to fill in some facts about why McMann did it."

"So you think he did?"

Ruskin's face contorted into anger. "My god! Do you have any doubts? If I'd known that you were trying to see how he might *not* have been the killer, I don't think I would have wasted my time talking to you. The man was a monster. That Mason was a monster. I think what happened was that he saw her one day, in town maybe. And he started thinking about how it was all her fault, him having lived such a shitty life. It kept eating at him and eating at him and he finally went up there to her house in a rage and killed her."

"Hey, look, Mr. Ruskin, I never said to you that I thought he wasn't the killer. I'm just making sure we've got the right man."

"The right man! Wasn't it your men that collected that onslaught of evidence! The blood on the clothes and boots. The fucking body parts—for the love of Christ—in the man's garage! What the hell else do you need?"

"How about why he killed Gowan?"

The energy and emotion seemed to drain out of Ruskin. He rubbed his arms and shook uncontrollably for a second. "It's cold out here." He looked at Briggs. "I don't know. It was probably like what your district attorney said. You know…rage or something. He'd gotten a taste of killing and he liked it. It's not a far stretch when you think about who we're talking about."

"So he just happened to kill another woman who worked in the same place he did, thirty fuckin' years ago! That to me, is a stretch, Mr. Ruskin. And that is why I'm checking a few loose ends out."

"Well, I think you're wasting your time. McMann did it. It's not that surprising when you think about how many of the older women in this town worked up there. That school employed a lot of people."

"Many of the older women?"

"Well, maybe not *many*, but a lot. More than a few. It's not inconceivable that he struck out at this woman without knowing that she was once a fellow state worker."

For a second Briggs wanted to believe that Ruskin was right, but then his phone conversation with Doug Johnson flashed through his mind. "*So you should see, if you catch him, a direct relationship between him and the victims.*" If Johnson was right, and Briggs believed he was, then whoever killed them knew them very well. But Briggs kept these thoughts to himself. The two men sat in silence for a while before Ruskin stirred. "I gotta get back in. These folks need my help."

"All right then, Mr. Ruskin. I appreciate you telling me about McMann. Your information has been very helpful. Have a good day."

25

Monday, February 5, 1973. Briggs was just finishing lunch when the phone rang. He was hoping it was his son, who'd neglected to call him the night before.

"Hey, Chief, thank god. It's me, Kroner." His voice was shaking. "We gotta talk. This stuff is getting spooky. It's getting to the point—I'm afraid to open up any more files—every time I do, I find another one."

"Another what?"

"Another record of somebody dying."

"Are you home?"

"Yeah."

"I'll be right over."

*   *   *

As the chief drove over to Kroner's house under heavy gray skies, he couldn't stop thinking about his son. Why hadn't he called last night? Was last week's conversation just some bizarre dream that he'd had? After his interview with Ruskin, the chief had little else to do. He wanted to see McMann again and pound him about this new information he'd discovered, but the man had gotten into some sort of fight that landed him in solitary until today. Briggs set a meeting up for the next day at 2 p.m. He spent the first part of the weekend waiting for his son to call and the last part wondering and worrying why he hadn't. Had Charlie changed his mind again? Did he again not want to have anything to do with his father?

By the time Briggs pulled up in front of Kroner's apartment he'd convinced himself that his son had again decided to have no contact with him. He got out of the Bronco, slammed its door shut, and stomped up to Kroner's front door. The house Kroner lived in was small, but nice. He lived in it in exchange for upkeep. A deal with his grandfather. Before Briggs could knock, the door opened and Kroner pushed open the screen to allow Briggs to enter. The living room was sparsely furnished, an old yellow couch encased by two nondescript end tables, an overstuffed, brown Lazy-Boy in the corner and a fairly large, oak desk under the window. Scattered all over it were files and letters, a few pencils and two notebooks, both open. A small bookcase stuffed with paperbacks stood against the wall next to the desk.

"Boy Chief, I'm glad you're here."

"Yeah, well, that's great," Briggs said quickly. "Whatta ya got?".

Kroner shot a quick glance at Briggs and noticed the tension in his face. "You okay, Chief?"

"Yes! I'm fine. Now what do you have?"

"Sorry, Chief. Well, I got a lot. I've done tons of digging into the past here, and I found some unbelievable shit. Do you want the weirdest stuff first or last?"

"Goddamn it, Kroner! Just tell me if you came up with anything. Please!"

Kroner shrunk back a little bit. "Ah, well...I was going through the records of all these folks like you told me to do. And a strange pattern started to develop. Remember that the hospital closed in 1956?"

"Yes, yes, I remember. Go on."

"Well, right after that, people started dying."

"Son of a bitch, Kroner! Stop being so fucking dramatic. Spit it out!"

Kroner sighed deeply. He walked over to his desk, took a pencil from behind his ear and threw it on top of one of the notebooks. He turned to face the chief again. Briggs noticed the serious and determined look on his face.

"Listen, Chief, I...I know you're the chief and all, and I know that when you come back, saying what I'm about to say could get me in a lot of trouble, but I gotta tell you something. I took this...this responsibility on voluntarily—during my vacation and, well, you can yell at me and treat me like shit at the station, and you have the right to think of me as some punk kid who doesn't deserve to be treated with the least amount of decency—you're the chief and you're the guy with all the war medals and the career as a great detective, but I'm trying to help you. I'm trying to work with you, sir. And you are in *my* home. I've been busting my butt on this shit for almost two weeks and these last two days I've hardly slept. But it paid off. By yesterday afternoon everything was coming together. I have something to share with you that surprised the hell out of me as it began to take shape. To be honest, late last night, while I was going over all this shit again and that wind was blowing and whipping around outside, well, it sort of scared me a little—I'm sorry if I'm taking too long to tell you about it."

Briggs watched Kroner shift his weight uncomfortably a few times before he spoke. While Kroner was standing up for himself, Briggs thought only about his wife. Was this how he made her feel all those years? Why had she never said anything? Stood up for herself. Why hadn't she yelled at him?

Briggs was finding it hard to swallow. He cleared his throat. "Well, Bill, I...I was outa line. I'm sorry. You are right to stand up for yourself. And I do appreciate what you are doing on this case. Go ahead and take your time. Tell it your way."

"Chief, if something is bothering you, you can tell me. You've been through a lot these last few weeks, with the trial and the, um, the Meredith thing and then getting suspended—"

"I wasn't suspended!" Briggs caught himself and softened his tone. "I wasn't suspended. And I appreciate your concern and, like I said, I'm sorry for yelling at you, but don't start trying to become a fuckin' therapist now. It's nothing. I was just expecting a call from my son last night and he didn't call. I was a little worried is all. Nothing major."

"Oh! Were you home last night?"

"Yes."

"Well, then, it must have been your phone." Kroner pointed outside, then waved his hand around in front of himself. "Remember the wind yesterday and last night? Must have screwed up your phone lines. I tried to call you three or four times about this stuff last night but never got through."

"Well, fucking-a! Ain't that something."

"See, you were worrying over nothing. He'll probably call you tonight. Now," Kroner changed his tone to a playful seriousness, "can we get back to business?"

"You bet," Briggs said, smiling. "What you got?"

"Unfortunately, nothing to smile about. Now most of our ex-employees checked out okay. I spent a lot of time on the phone, calling and talking with as many as possible—by the way, do you think the department will reimburse me for these long distance calls?"

"I think I can manage that."

"Phew! Thank God. Anyway, most of the people either didn't know any of our people or knew one or two but couldn't remember much about them. A few people I talked to did in fact work with or know them but couldn't recall anything that would help us out. I took notes on every call." Kroner paused.

Briggs said, very kindly, "All right, I'm with you so far, but what is so strange about that? Did you expect them all to remember? There were around five hundred people who worked up there."

Kroner snapped back to attention. "Oops. Sorry, Chief, I was just thinking about something. Ah, where was I? Oh! Yes, no, it wasn't the people I talked to that got me curious. It was the people I didn't talk to. Listen to this list of names of people who are now deceased. Now keep in mind that not one of these people, at the time of each death, was over fifty years old. And by the way," he looked up at the chief with a smile, "I decided to save the best for last. In 1959, a woman named Julia Waite committed suicide in her apartment in Boston. She slashed her wrists. Not too deep, though. Coroner's report said that it would have taken her over two hours to bleed to death. She had once been a social worker at the school."

"That's weird. That woman Grey, the one who's daughter called me. She committed suicide, too. Hung herself."

"Yeah, don't I know it. Then, it 1960, this guy here," Kroner handed the chief a picture, "died in a horrible car accident.

Skidded off the road and hit a tree, but that didn't kill him. The car caught on fire and York, John York was his name, burned to death in the blaze. He was an accountant up there.

"In January of 1961, a Brian Plummer, who had been the personnel manager for the school, was found dead up in the White Mountains. He'd apparently broken his leg in a cross-country skiing accident and froze to death trying to get back to his house. This guy was an excellent cross-country skier, though. He was one of those fanatics who always trained and pushed himself to get better at whatever he was doing. That's why he got a job up there, so he could train constantly out in the country. His family told me so. They couldn't believe it when they got the news. Worst part for them was, it snowed the night he was out there and his body was buried beneath two feet of snow. They didn't find him until the Spring thaw."

"That's too bad."

"Yeah, I know. Just listen. The list goes on and on. Later that same year, in late November, a Patricia Bonnett, another nurse, bought the farm. She went out to Worchester after the school closed and worked at the city hospital. Seems as though she slipped and fell down a very icy staircase that led up to her second-story apartment. Managed to break her neck. They ruled it accidental but the report says that the investigating officers couldn't figure out why the steps were icy."

"Is it me, or are you seeing a pattern developing, too?" Briggs was getting excited.

"Oh, I see it! There was another guy, lived in Lenox. He too fell down the stairs, but inside his house. His name was Goldsmith. Dr. Goldsmith. Made a lot of money writing books and there was already some family money. They say it was because he was unstable on his feet. He'd had a stroke the year before his death. I guess it left him sort of wobbly. Oh! He was the only one over fifty that

I included in our list."

"Why?"

"Because of the similarity between his death and Bonnett's."

"Excellent! You're gonna make one hell of a detective one day, Kroner. Is that all of them?"

"One other—well, two. There was a woman, Henrietta Crampton, who was murdered in New York City in 1970. Police report says it was during a mugging. And then there was one other."

"This is where you get dramatic on me again, right?"

"Right! You are not going to believe this. One other person who worked up there was murdered. Do you want to take a guess as to who it was?" Kroner watched the chief's face and quickly realized that he did not. "The guy's name was Rhodes—"

A pounding on the door interrupted them. Palin didn't wait until Kroner came over to open it. He walked in. He looked frustrated. "Hey! Did you tell the Chief yet?"

"I was literally just about to." Kroner turned to face the chief. "This Rhodes guy was a doctor up at the school, too. He was murdered almost sixteen years ago. Guess where?"

It took Briggs a few seconds to run the name through his head. "Wait a minute! Was he the victim in our old unsolved murder here in Wilton?"

"The very one," said Palin jumping in. Listen, something has happened."

"What now!"

"We gotta get over to the prison. It's McMann. Guess that fight he got into last week wasn't quite over. He hadn't been out of seclusion for more than a few hours when they found him laid out on the floor in the shitter. He'd been stabbed. They don't know if he's gonna make it."

"Son of a bitch. Let's get over there then. Oh, and hey, before I forget. Kroner, can you get the paperwork on all our victims? The complete files, including any insurance paperwork?"

"I already called and set the wheels in motion, Chief. We should have everything within a week."

"Good work."

26

They decided to ride over to the jail together. For the first five minutes no one spoke as each tried to put things in perspective. Finally, Kroner broke the silence from the back seat.

"Well, I don't know where you guys are on this, but I don't get it. Usually as ya dig deeper into an investigation things get clearer, but with this case it seems that it's the fuckin' opposite. Why are all these people dead and who the fuck is killing them? And, how the hell has the killer been able to get away with making everything look like an accident or a suicide?"

"He did murder a few of them without trying to hide the fact," Palin answered as he drove. "Didn't make any effort to cover those ones up."

"Well, remember, everything this guy is doing should tell us a little about the way he thinks. Maybe from his perspective they each did something that justified a *particular* way to die—one that ended up looking like an accident, a suicide, or a murder."

"That could be," answered Kroner."

Palin said, "One thing that might result from us finding out about all these deaths, if in fact they are related—and I think we'd have to be idiots not to believe that they are, it might make it easier for us to discover the connection between the victims."

"Yeah, but it might make it harder," said Briggs. "Look at the mixed bag that we have. There are two doctors, two social workers, two nurses, an accountant, the personnel manager, a secretary, and, if you count McMann as a victim, one direct care attendant. That's quite a collection."

"Very diverse," added Palin. "Did your interviews with those people last week turn up anything that might hint at a connection, Chief?"

"Not really. The old lady, Stiener, turns out that she's a pretty vicious old bitch. Everyone in town knows she's tough on that goofy grandson of hers, but once I got to talking to her I realized that she's like that about a lot of folks. I think that if she could have it her way she'd have all mentally handicapped people put to death! Mitchell is white trash. He seemed to think that it was a riot to torture little kids. And he's a fuckin' pig. When I met him he was slobbering all over some stripper, hoping that she'd marry him one day. From what I could see, she was just playing him for the tips.

"The last guy I talked to was Sammy Ruskin. He was interesting, the exact opposite of Mitchell. Said he hated both Mitchell and McMann and as far as he was concerned we have the right guy behind bars. I'll tell you, after hearing some of the crap this

McMann did, I don't blame Ruskin for feeling angry. Turns out our boy McMann was up there raping little retarded girls."

"What! Are you serious?"

"That's what he told me. That's why he was canned. Said there was some sort of cover-up to prevent it from getting out to the public."

"That explains the name change then."

"Yeah. He was told to leave town and never try to work for the state in any capacity—really tough punishment for a rape, huh?"

"I guess," Palin answered sarcastically. "What made him come back then?"

"I did a quick check after I found out his name was really McMann. His mother passed away around 1960. He inherited the house. He probably figured that there was nothing to fear anymore, since the school had closed. All I can say is I hope the bastard lives long enough for me to talk to him. He's got some explaining to do."

"Do you think that all these deaths are in some way connected to the cover-up?" asked Kroner.

"Well, it would be nice if they were. Then we'd have our motive. But for me that's quite a stretch. I think it'd be hard to get that many people to cover-up something like a rape. And if the rape was the motive, who is it motivating?"

"I don't know," said Kroner. "Do you think McMann will tell us?"

"He might as well, he's got nothing to lose if he's about to die," said Palin.

*　　　　　*　　　　　*

Twenty minutes later they were entering the infirmary. The doctor, a long, lanky man with a sad face and wavy brown hair was just coming down the hall.

"Hello, gentlemen. What can I do for you?" His voice betrayed his looks. He almost sounded jolly.

"Hello, Dr. Henke, right?"

"Yes."

"We're here to find out how Darren McMann is doing. Is he still alive?"

The doctor smiled and looked down at the ground. "Ah, you must have gotten one of the early reports, based on the *victim's* assessment of his condition."

"How's that?" Briggs asked.

"When he came in, he was screaming like a banshee. Telling everyone that it was all over for him. His attacker had cut into an artery—so there was a lot of blood—but his life was never at risk. I think what probably happened was that whoever called you guys based the report of his condition on all the blood and yelling."

"Can we talk to him?" asked Palin.

"Yeah, he should be coming around any minute now."

"Hey, Doc! Briggs barked. The doctor jumped. "Sorry. I just had an idea. Let me ask you something. Does McMann know that he's gonna make it?"

"I couldn't say for sure. He passed out before I could explain his situation to him though. Why?"

"Could you do me a favor?"

The doctor tilted his head and raised his eyebrows. "What are you thinking, Chief?"

*   *   *

When Darren McMann woke up he saw the silhouette of a man's head and shoulders leaning above him. Before he could focus, the man gently put a hand on McMann's chest and said, "And God be with you, my son." The man kissed a big cross that hung from his neck before he turned away. McMann watched him walk over to where two other men were standing: a doctor, with his back to McMann, and Chief Briggs, whose face he could see.

Briggs turned and addressed the man who had been leaning over McMann. "Thank you, Father. I'm so very sorry we had to pull you away from your…bowling night to get you down here."

"That's okay, my son," the man answered. He had a strong Irish accent. "There isn't any planning when it comes to giving the last rites, you know."

Briggs grabbed the man's hand and shook it vigorously. "Well, thank you anyway." The priest left and Briggs spoke to the doctor. "Is it okay if I talk to McMann real quick, Doc? He's the only man in the world who can help me catch a killer."

"Well, in that case," said the doctor, "go ahead. And good luck. I'm sure that now, since he's been absolved of all his sins, he'll be able to speak freely."

"Hey! Wait, Doc!" yelled McMann. "What the hell is happening to me? Doctor! Say it ain't true. I don't want to die." The man in the white jacket stopped, but didn't turn around.

"Go ahead, Doc. I'll explain everything to him," Briggs offered. The doctor left the room. Briggs walked over and pulled a small wooden chair next to the side of the bed. Sitting down, he took a deep breath and let it out slowly. "Hey, McMann, how ya feeling?"

"I'm feeling fine. I can't be dyin'."

"They gave you a lot of pain killers. Make it easier for you to go."

"But I don't want to go, Chief."

"I know, Darren. None of us do. But there is a time that God has picked out for all of us, and this just happens to be yours. But listen, you could put yourself in a better light with Him if you tell me the truth about some things. Since we talked before, I've found out a lot about you and the school. For instance, I know your real name is Darren McMann and that you worked up in C building at Wilton. I know that you were probably pretty worried before about us connecting you to that place, and that's why you didn't tell me the truth at first. But now, you need to be very honest with me. What I want you to realize is that by telling me the truth, you could clear your family name."

"What did you find out?"

"Briggs stared directly into McMann's eyes. "I know you raped that little girl, Darren."

McMann seemed to deflate right in front of Briggs. "Damn it! No one has ever found out about that! How did you…"

"That's not important. What is important is that you tell me everything you remember about that day. Free yourself of that sin."

"What do you mean? Tell you about what?"

"Well, for instance, who was involved in your being…let off, without being punished?"

McMann looked away for a second as he thought back. Then he turned back to Briggs with a disgusted look on his face. "There were the people that caught me, the inspector and the superintendent."

"That's all? No Mason or Gowan?"

"No. Just that bastard, Tatum, his cousin the inspector, two nurses who I didn't know, and another attendant…Dante."

"Tatum? The mayor worked up there back then?"

"No, not the mayor, his father. His old man was the superintendent. And the inspector was the old man's cousin or something. That's how they was able to keep it so hush-hush."

"What about those nurses? They were willing to keep it a secret, too?"

McMann snorted. "Of course they was. You gotta understand. We was only talkin' about a retard. Wasn't any real big thing. Plus, that old Tatum promised them that if they worked with him he'd move their careers along."

"You actually heard him say that?"

"Well, no. But I'm sure he did. I think there was a lot of favors goin' around in that room on that day. Hey, listen, maybe you could go get that doc back in here. I'm feelin' pretty good. Don't you think they should be tryin' to save me some more?"

"Look, I told you, Darren, it's because they gave you a lot of medicine. They wanted it so it wouldn't be painful for you. So you wouldn't suffer in the end. Who was this Dante fellow?"

"You mean, who was the Benedict Arnold? Dante was his nickname. Little pussy named Sammy…Sammy something?"

"Sammy Ruskin!"

"Yeah, that's it. He's the one. He used to work with me back on C building sometimes for overtime. I remember how he used to tell me about how he loved doin' the hydro treatments to the women."

Briggs wasn't sure they were talking about the same man, but he figured he'd play it out. "What are hydro treatments?"

"That was so that the women would stop havin' fits. You put them in a tub, then pull this canvas over 'em. Then you rope 'em all up with a big rope—tie the damn thing nice and tight. Once you had them in there good, you started pourin' the ice cold water on 'em. You were supposed to start at the bottom and work your way up, but he liked to dump the shit right on their chest first. Watch their nipples stand up real fast. Fuckin' things would turn into little rock-hard pellets that'd stand up even through the fuckin' canvas." McMann cracked a smile as he thought back.

"Dante used to say that the treatments weren't as effective if you didn't dump the ice water right on them. Used to like to see their faces twist all up into shock. Then the bitches would scream and wriggle around a bit, but then they'd calm down after a while. I never liked doin' them 'cause while they was in the tubs they'd shit and piss themselves. I hated cleanin' after that. Tell ya what, though—wouldn't have any problems outa that bunch for a while! Then all of a sudden this Dante, he gets to thinkin' different one day, expects the rest of us all to change our thinkin', too. The fuckin' bastard turned me in like I was some sort a criminal."

"Real asshole, huh?"

"Yeah."

Briggs took the list of names out of his pocket and presented it to McMann. "Darren, do you recognize any of the names on this list?"

Darren scanned the names slowly. "Yeah, I recognize a few. None of 'em was my friends, though, if that's what you're about to ask."

"No. I was wondering if you had any reason to work with these people? Serve on any special duties with them? Anything at all?"

"Naw. Most a those people I think didn't work in the buildings regular. They was the doctors and such. I never worked *with* them. Sometimes I used to have to do things *for* them, though. Like that Rhodes guy. He'd take me and a few of the fellas along with him when he went to pick up folks sometimes. And sometimes I would help out on admissions for both Rhodes and that Goldsmith."

"Admissions?"

"Yeah. When new people would show up to be let in we would do an admissions process. Check 'em out for lice and bugs, clean 'em up, and then the doctors would do the physical; then some of 'em would have the mind test done by that Dr. Goldsmith. He was the head shrinker up there. Bigwig guy. He never came down to the wards, though. We'd always bring the people to him."

"What about these other names: Plummer, York, Grey, Waite, or Bonnett? Any of them ringing any bells?"

"I think that one, that Waite woman, used to come around the building. If I remember right she used to be one a those social worker women. Very high-and-mighty bunch those types. Thought they were doin' somethin' so special. Always actin' like their shit didn't stink. I don't remember any of the others."

"Have you told me everything there is to tell about Mason and Gowan? You had no special ties with either woman?"

"Well, I sorta lied about Martha. She and I, we worked pretty good together. Lots of years in C building. But I guess you know that now."

"Yeah, I know that now. One more thing, this girl, the one you raped, do you remember her name?"

McMann laughed. "Are you serious, Chief?"

"Yes. I want you to think real hard. You've done very well so far. Think for a minute."

McMann closed his eyes and remained silent for a moment. "Naw, Chief, I can't remember for sure. I think it was something like Alicia. That was probably it."

"And a last name?"

"Jeez, I don't know. I'm not even sure about the first name."

"Okay, McMann. That should do it. You take care now."

"You mean you're gonna leave me! Here on my death bed?"

Briggs smiled at McMann. "You still not feeling any pain?"

"Well, a little now. Down here where I got stabbed." McMann put his hand down on the right side of his stomach.

Briggs moved his hand to the spot McMann had indicated. He gently patted the bandages. "Listen, McMann, I gotta tell ya," Briggs pressed his thumb deep into McMann's wound. The pain drove McMann up into a sitting position. He emitted a deep, gut-tural scream. His face was knotted in agony. "You're not gonna die, you piece of shit! But thanks for the information." Briggs twisted his thumb a bit. McMann screamed again. "Don't worry, after you wriggle around a bit, you'll calm down." Briggs released his hold on McMann, who fell back onto the bed. "Nothing is gonna prevent you from rotting in hell."

Briggs turned and stormed out of the room. He almost ran smack into Detective Carr. Carr was standing with Kroner and Palin, who were still in their respective priest and doctor costumes.

"Briggs! What are you doing here? And why are my men here with you? The mayor told you to stay away from anything official for at least two weeks—if not longer."

Briggs stepped around him and started walking down the hall. "Stay the fuck outa my sight."

"Hey! Don't you talk to me that way. I'm not the one who was out at the old mill fucking the shit out of Tim's wife. You've got no one to blame but yourself. Now what the hell were you doing in there?"

Briggs stopped walking and turned back to look at Carr. "Let me tell you something, you squatty little bastard. What I was doing in there would be something completely unfamiliar to you. It's called investigating a crime. Police work, ya know." Briggs moved very close to Carr.

"Oh, what are ya gonna do now, *ex*-Chief? Ya gonna hit me? Rumor has it that's how you used to settle everything with your wife."

Before Carr could blink, he found himself pinned against the wall. He could barely breathe. The chief's fingers were digging in around his Adam's Apple. Carr tried to pry the hand away, but it wasn't until the chief released him that the pain began to subside.

"Now you've gone and...done it," Carr squeaked as he gasped for air. "Your job is as good as mine."

"How do you figure?" Briggs growled.

"You just attacked me in front of witnesses." Carr pointed to Palin and Kroner.

"I didn't see shit," said Kroner in a heavy Irish Brogue. He turned to Mark. "How 'bout you, Doctor Palin?"

"Who, me?" I don't know what you're referring to, Father Kroner."

Carr glared at them. "Oh, I see how it's going to be." He looked beyond them, at the real doctor who was leaning against his desk. "I don't need you, anyway. The doctor saw what you did, right Doc?"

"You know, it's funny. I heard you insult the chief a few times, and then the next thing I know you slipped and fell. How'd that happen?"

Briggs looked at the doctor and winked, then turned and walked down the corridor. Kroner and Palin followed him out.

27

Tuesday, February 6, 1973. Briggs spent the night rolling from
one side of the bed to the other. He'd been bothered by memories
from his days in the war when he'd gotten caught up in the
moment. There had been only a few times when this happened,
but they happened and they stood in stark contrast to his winning
the Congressional Medal of Honor. He wouldn't look at the
award for years after receiving it. All that time proudly standing
up for the United States wiped out because of a few indiscretions.
An hour or two of weakness during which Briggs acted unlike
himself—at least that's what he told himself—that became magni-
fied in his memory. The glare from those moments was so bright
he refused to think about anything else that happened back then,
even the good times, because no good times existed. He let himself

get caught up in 'group thinking' and he had to put aside years of his life because of it. He kept saying to himself, "In war, men do things they might not normally do." But that was some sort of Band-Aid statement that never really worked. And now the rolling around and the preoccupation were back. Another aspect of Briggs' life was left unresolved, and it bothered him. He had a lot of work to do.

He was glad to see Richards standing at the entrance to the municipal parking lot as he pulled in. Talking to another person would prevent him from continuously beating himself up. Briggs wanted to tell Richards about the new circumstances involving the other people who were dead and see if he might be able to shed some light on what it all meant. The weather had broken and there were sunny skies and temperatures in the fifties. Their plan was to start at the far end of town and walk their way to Tatum's coffee shop.

"Chief! How are you?" Richards was wearing a tan overcoat, unbuttoned to reveal a gray suit, white shirt and black tie, which he'd already loosened. It was only 10 a.m. and he already looked rumpled.

"I'm doin' all right. Still trying to catch the bad guy."

"Anything new?"

"Well, that's what I wanted to see you about. I think you're gonna be pretty surprised at what we've uncovered. But we have no idea where it's taking us. It seems that the more information we get, the more confused we become. I thought maybe you could shed some light."

The chief caught Richards up on everything that had been happening. Richards remembered hearing about the Crampton mugging-murder. She worked out of Springfield, too, but he knew her only enough to say hello. He was amazed that someone had been capable of pulling off so much violence without being detected.

"So this one guy may have killed all those people?"

"It seems highly likely. We're getting all the files so we can check out the specifics in each case. Maybe we'll be able to look at the facts in a different way, ya know. See the big picture. To the original investigators, these incidents appeared to be isolated events. We will look at them knowing that most likely one man was responsible. Something may turn up."

"That sounds like a good idea."

"Well, right now it's all we've got. I was wondering if you could dig through the school's records again, see if these people were connected in any way." Briggs added the next sentence before Richards could voice the obvious. "I know, I know. If there wasn't a connection between Mason and Gowan, why would there be a connection between all these people? But to me, there's gotta be something. I can't believe that these people are dying for the simple reason that they all worked up at the school. There has to be something more. Could you check?"

"Hey, I promised I would help. I don't know where I'll start, but I will dig around and see if I can come up with something."

The two men had walked into the center of town. Briggs found himself in front of Ernie's Tobacco Shop, felt the almost empty pack of cigarettes in his breast pocket, and said, "Hey, do you mind if we run in here real quick? I just gotta grab a pack of smokes."

"Not at all."

Briggs held the door open for Richards and then followed him in. Before the door swung shut, Briggs heard the all too familiar voice of P.J. Boyington. "Hey, Chief! This time between visits is getting to be enough to make me concerned about our relationship. I'm gonna start thinkin' that you don't like me," he bellowed.

"You know that will never happen, P.J." Briggs waved his hand in Richards's direction. "This is my friend, John Richards. John, P.J. Boyington."

The men nodded to each other. Briggs grabbed a *Boston Globe*. "Pack of Marlboro's, too, P.J."

"You got it, Chief. And I got one for ya."

"I knew you did."

"Mr. Richards, you mind a slightly dirty joke?" Richards shook his head and smiled. "Good then. These reporters go up to a psychiatry hospital, one that is supposed to be curing everybody that comes up there for help. They're goin' around with the director of the hospital, taking a look at some of the patients. The first room they come to, there's this woman who is playing the violin. She'd doin' a wonderful job, and the reporters ask her how she's feelin'. She tells them that she feels much better and that she's learned how to play the violin so she could find work with an orchestra when she leaves. The next room, there's this guy who's got his room turned into a chemistry lab. He tells them that when he leaves, he's gonna continue his work on curing the common cold. The reporters are very impressed and they start to go to the next room, but the director tries to steer them back down the hall. They insist on seeing the man who is in there. The director opens the door and there's a guy layin' there on his bed with a big huge hard on. Balanced on the head of his purple penis is a cashew. They ask him what's up and he tells them, "I'm fuckin' nuts, and there ain't no way I'm leavin' this place!""

P.J. roared with laughter, and Richards and Briggs shook their heads and smiled. "That's a good one, P.J.," Briggs said. "But it's not one of your best. I think that one about the woman with acute angina was better."

"Oh, yeah. That was a good one, wasn't it!"

P.J and Briggs finished their ritual and said goodbye to each other. "Nice to meet you, Mr. Richards!" P.J. yelled, as the door swung shut.

They continued to walk in the direction of the coffee shop. Richards was very quiet. "What's the matter, John?"

"It seems to me that I recognize that name, Boyington, from somewhere. He's quite a card, huh?"

"Oh, Yes! That he is. But think, if it weren't for him, this whole investigation may never have happened."

"How's that?"

"He's the one who told me about Pike—or better, told me that Pike was not Pike. He told me he thought he recognized him from when he worked up at the school."

"P.J. worked up there?"

"Yeah, on the farm. I guess they had a big farm up there."

"Yes...they did," Richards answered slowly. "Maybe..."

"What?"

Richards stopped walking. He stroked his chin with thumb and forefinger while he looked down at the ground. "Jeez, that would be something."

"What! What would be something? God, between you and Kroner I spend most of my time asking what and why questions."

Richards stopped stroking himself and glanced at Briggs. "Sorry, it's nothing. Just a crazy thought. I'd feel stupid explaining it."

"Are you sure?"

"Yeah. It's nothing."

Briggs stared at Richards for a minute. "Okay." He used his thumb to point over his shoulder at Tatum's coffee shop. "We're here."

"Oh, good. Let's get some coffee."

They moved across the sidewalk and climbed the two steps to the door. Through the glass they could see the mayor and Tim

King sitting at one of the small round tables, where they sipped on coffees and ate Danish. "Oh, fuck!"

"You still want to go in?" asked Richards.

"Yeah. I have questions for both of them," Briggs answered tensely.

"Hey, listen. You wouldn't mind if I passed, would you?"

"Why? I'll only be a few minutes. Hey, did you know that the mayor's father was once the superintendent of the Wilton School?"

"It came up during our walk of the property your town wants to buy. Before that I'd heard the name 'Superintendent Tatum,' but I'd never put the two together." Richards paused for a moment. "So, listen, I'm gonna go and check out a few things. Plus I'll start on that list of names—see if they come up together somewhere." He held out his hand.

"Oh! The list. Here it is. And thanks again. You sure you're all right? You look a little distant."

"Yeah, I'm fine. I just have to check some things out. I'll call you tomorrow, let you know if I've come up with anything."

Briggs walked into the coffee shop. The mayor and Tim noticed him. Briggs could sense the change in the atmosphere as he walked over to where the two sat. Mrs. Tatum and the girl working the counter looked over.

"Chief Briggs," the mayor said, "how are you? I was going to call you today. We have to talk about…"—he glanced uncomfortably at Tim—"your situation."

"Yes. I was hoping to come back today, but I figured we should talk first." He turned to face Tim. "Listen, Tim, I know you and I are never gonna be friends, and I don't expect you to forgive me; but I do apologize for the way things went." Tim didn't say anything; he just glared. Briggs guessed that the mayor had spent a good amount of the last three weeks trying to smooth things over.

"I...I also wanted to ask you a question. Please understand, I'm asking for professional reasons, not personal. How did you get that picture?"

Tim's hand came down hard on the small table. He looked at the mayor. "You said I had to accept the fact that he was going to be staying on as chief—for now. You didn't say I would have to tolerate this." He turned back to Briggs. "How dare you! Listen, how I got that picture is none of your business. Nothing I do is your business. Understand. And if you come near me, for any reason, I'll sue you for...for something." His face was turning red. He stood up and left the shop, purposely brushing against Briggs shoulder with his own.

"How could you ask the man that? Are you crazy? I've spent the last week in meetings calming everyone down and in less than five seconds you stir everything up again. God, Briggs! You know he's going to run to all the others and tell them about this."

"Hey, I'm sorry, Mayor. It really was important. Do you know?"

"No, I don't know. Why would I know?"

"Could you find out? Just ask him if he hired somebody or if it showed up out of the blue."

"Briggs, I gotta hand it to you, you sure have a set of brass balls. Are you hearing what I've said to you? Back off! That's it. I gave you your three weeks. You haven't come up with any killer. So it's over. Understood?"

"Goddamn it. This is like some bad movie where the hard-working cop is onto something big only to be stymied by the powerful politician whose values are all in the wrong place."

"Don't!" The mayor glanced at his wife and the employee. He lowered his voice. "Don't push me, Briggs!" he hissed through tight lips. "Believe me, it isn't *that* hard to start a new search for a police chief."

Briggs thought quickly. Fuck this place, he thought. Time to move to Florida. "Hey, Mayor, I found out that your father covered up a rape while he was superintendent for 'the good of the schools future.' Ten years later, the school closed anyway. You trying to follow in his footsteps?"

"That's it! The mayor stood up and got in Briggs' face. He was a few inches taller than Briggs was. "I want your resignation on my desk by Friday. Make the last day of February your final day."

"You gonna answer me, Mayor? There is a killer running around out there and my guess is he isn't through. I hope and pray he is, but if he isn't, at least I can go to bed each night realizing that I tried my damnedest to stop him. How are you gonna sleep, Mayor, if he kills again, huh? How will it feel, knowing that the death of that person lies on your head?"

"The killer is in jail, Briggs. Remember? You put him there. If this guy kills again, it will be on your head, not mine."

"You'll never get away with putting it on me. Too many people know that I've still been working on this. And believe me, the right people will know that I wanted to continue the investigation and you stopped me. It will be in my official resignation. And I'm gonna get it notarized and then I'm gonna get it copied and send it to several of my friends. So go ahead, make all the threats you want. Make any decisions you want; you're the mayor. If we all luck out, he'll never kill again. But don't think for a minute that I'll be your fall guy if something goes wrong. Good luck."

Veins in the mayor's head were thick and pulsing. Briggs cut him a quick smile and turned to the women. "Have a nice day, ladies." He walked out the door and headed over to the town hall.

28

Thursday, February 8, 1973. "If you don't like the weather in New England, just wait five fuckin' minutes and it'll change," Bobby Mitchell mumbled to himself as he walked out of his house. After two days of unseasonably warm weather, the temperature had again plummeted and the winds were blowing out of the northeast. It was early, six a.m. Work at the mill started in an hour and although Mitchell lived only five minutes away, he liked to get out early so he could stop for his coffee and hang out with 'the boys' at Dunkin' Donuts. It was still dark, but the skies to the east were beginning to turn a steel gray. The morning would be breaking soon.

The door of the old and heavily dented pickup truck screeched and resisted Mitchell's attempts to pull it open; but finally, after three good hard yanks, the door swung free. He jumped in, put the key into the ignition, pumped the gas a few times, and tried to turn it over, but the engine would not even moan. It was dead. "Fuck!" Mitchell yelped. He turned his gaze out the window of his truck and upon the long stretch of road that sloped away from his house. He lived at the top of a bluff that overlooked the town. In the right person's hands, the land could have been developed into a prime site, but Mitchell had bought it years ago and had done nothing but clutter it with old car parts and lawn mowers, as well as broken-down snowmobiles and other large things that no one else wanted.

He pushed the door open as far as he could, squeezed out, and then slammed it a few times until it caught. It was one of those mornings when you could hear the wind building and rolling towards you as it rumbled through the trees. Then it would hit you and bite through your clothes, pass by and fade away, leaving you in a state of strange silence and calm. Mitchell pulled his collar up around his neck, then rubbed his arms a bit to get the circulation going before he began the long descent into town. When the wind wasn't roaring he could hear his boots crunching the frozen snow beneath them. He looked to his right. A steep drop-off slipped away beyond the cement barriers placed every ten yards or so along the shoulder of the road. Through the leafless hardwoods, he could see the lights of Cortland below. The city was just coming to life. He unzipped his jacket enough to slip his hand in and pulled a bent cigarette from his pack in his breast pocket. He fumbled around in his other pockets, looking for his lighter. His fingers were numb from the cold. He waited for the wind to pass before he stopped to light up.

As he walked on he looked ahead and saw the silhouette of a man, at least it appeared to be a man, standing in the middle of the road about two hundred yards ahead. "What the fuck is that?" Mitchell whispered out loud. He watched closely as he walked towards the man. The wind was not blowing and he could see the man's misty breath as he exhaled.

Mitchell walked another hundred yards. The man started up the hill. In a few seconds, he was only fifty yards away, moving along the opposite shoulder. Mitchell slowed his pace and watched the man. The hair on the back of Mitchell's neck began to rise. The gap between them was about thirty yards. Suddenly' the man veered in Mitchell's direction.

"What the fuck do you want!" Mitchell yelled. He wanted to turn, but it was too late. He brought his hand up to his mouth, pulled the cigarette from his lips, and flicked it away. The man was ten yards away.

"What the FUCK do you want!" Mitchell put his hands up. He would fight. The man was right in front of him. He tried to sound brave. "Come on, fucker! I'll kick your ass!" Mitchell strained to see a face. Nothing.

In one sweeping move, the stranger dropped to one knee and swung his arm quickly. There was something long and black in his hand. Mitchell saw him drop, but didn't know how to defend against it. Mitchell wasn't fast enough. The black object smashed into his knee. He screamed in pain, but the winds had roared again. No one could hear. The attacker drew back and swung again. He shattered the other kneecap. Mitchell dropped to the ground in agony. The attacker stood and walked the few feet to where Mitchell lay. He bent down and grabbed the lapels of Mitchell's jacket, lifting him up. Mitchell's eyes had rolled back into his head from the pain.

The attacker scooped him up onto his shoulder in one powerful motion. He carried him to the edge of the road. The drop-off was steep. He tossed him over and calmly watched as Mitchell bounced like a rag doll for about one hundred and fifty feet before smashing violently against a tree.

The attacker smiled. He was sure he'd heard the snapping of Mitchell's spine above the wind.

*   *   *

Three days passed before Briggs heard from Richards. Then, like a whirlwind, he showed up at Briggs' door at three o'clock on Friday morning.

"You kind of run on your very own schedule, don't you, Richards?" Briggs said as he let the man in.

Richards looked like he hadn't shaved since the day Briggs walked with him to Tatum's coffee shop. He was carrying a very large box, stuffed with folders of varying thickness. Briggs helped him bring it to the dining room table.

"Sorry about the time. I just felt that you would want to know about what I've found right away. I think I found the motive for these killings."

Briggs stared at Richards and smiled. He admired the man's interest and his zest, but he didn't believe him. "So, you think you found the motive. For these killings?"

"Yes," Richards answered, ignoring the sarcasm in Briggs' voice. "So you better sit down. It's gonna take a while to explain all this. Could we have some coffee?"

"Sure." Briggs busied himself in the kitchen and got the coffee going, then he came back and pulled up a chair, ready to hear what Richards had to say. "Tell me."

"Okay this is going to be a bit jumbled. It's a lot of info and I haven't slept much these last few days. Do you remember when we came out of that tobacco shop, I told you that I thought that man's name, P.J., sounded familiar?"

"Yes."

"Then you told me that he was the one who got you thinking that McMann might have worked up there—Boyington told you he remembered him from when *he worked* up there...on the farm."

"Yes, John, I remember our conversation. What about it?"

"The only people who *worked* on the farm were the students."

"Well, that couldn't be, Boyington...what are you saying, that Boyington used to be...he's not retarded, is he?"

"I know it's confusing. But it could have happened."

"I thought you said that the school was for retarded people. The unwanted."

"It was, primarily. The range went from severe retardation to mild retardation. But there were a few who fell through the cracks, back in the old days when the view of the mentally retarded was different than it is today. Some were in for a while and then they got out."

"I don't get it. You're saying that a guy like Boyington *fell through the cracks?* A person's either retarded or he's not, and Boyington's not retarded. A little slow maybe, but not retarded. I thought they had tests to measure for that?"

"Yes, they do. But the tests were different back then."

"When is then? What time period are we talking about?"

"Through the forties. Maybe into the fifties in some states."

"So how were these tests different?"

"There was an additional component. A sort of morals test. But that isn't the only way that a person like Boyington could have gotten sent to the school. He could have been put in there because of the Eugenics Movement."

"The what?"

"Eugenics. It means 'good birth.' I'm gonna ramble on here and give you a very quick history lesson, so maybe we could get that coffee."

"Oh! Sure. I almost forgot." Briggs went into the kitchen, poured two cups, and brought one of them to Richards.

"It all started with Darwin—"

"Whoa! Are you talking about Charles Darwin? 'Cause if you are, Richards, I think I need to remind you that this case does probably involve situations that go back a bit in years, but not that many years."

"Oh, but it does, Chief. When Charles Darwin published his *Origin of Species,* in 1859, he set off a chain of events that would effect millions and millions of people. You see, what happened was his cousin, this fellow named Francis Galton, saw some serious problems with respect to the human race when he looked at Darwin's 'survival of the fittest,' theory. He began to worry that man, unlike the creatures in nature, was creating ways for the weaker of the species to survive and propagate, and thus poisoning the gene pool. He believed that if left unchecked, this situation would lead to the demise of mankind. He proposed that society should eliminate all the 'unfit' and, by doing so, it could actively assist nature in assuring only the survival of the highest quality of human being. Basically, Galton believed that man could control his own evolution and guide it towards a population that would have little or no mental or physical defects.

"The cry for control of the gene pool was taken up by several influential people here in the United States right before the turn of the century. Articles and books came out documenting various studies that seemed to support the eugenicists' fears. In 1877, Richard Dugdale, a New York prison inspector, published his *The Jukes: A study in Crime, Pauperism, Disease, and Heredity.* He discovered that there were often several members of the same family in jail at the same time. He dug deeper into their families' past and found that other members of the family had been incarcerated as well over the years.

"Other reports followed, all by very powerful men. Three in particular carried a lot of weight: *The Kallikaks,*' by Henry Goddard, *The Hill Folk,* by Charles Davenport, and the *Burden of Feeble-Mindedness,* by Walter Fernald. Goddard's study was very interesting. He explored the family tree of a revolutionary soldier who, during the war...well, wait. Let me quote this." Richards fumbled around in his box until he found an old, hard cover book. He read:

> *The Kallikak family presents a natural experiment in heredity. A young man of good family becomes through two different women the ancestor of two lines of descendants, the one characterized by thoroughly good, respectable, normal citizenship, with almost no exception; the other being equally characterized by mental defect in every generation. This defect was transmitted through the father in the first generation. In later generations, more defect was brought in from other families through marriage. In the last generation it was transmitted through the mother, so that we have all combinations of transmission, which again proves the truly hereditary character of the defect.*
>
> *We find on the good side of the family prominent people of all walks of life and nearly all of the 496 descendants owners of land or properties. On the bad side we find paupers, criminals, prostitutes, drunkards, and examples of all forms of social pest with which modern society is burdened. From this we conclude that feeble-mindedness is largely responsible for these social sores.*

Feeble-mindedness is hereditary and transmitted as surely as any other character. We cannot successfully cope with those conditions until we recognize feeble-mindedness and its hereditary nature, recognize it early, and take care of it.

"Jeez, what does he mean by 'take care of it'?"

"He probably was hinting at the same thing that Fernald actually said in his article. Listen to this." Richards pulled out a copy of the article. "'Certain families should become extinct.'"

"Didn't they take into consideration the environmental factors effecting these people?"

"No. It was all about genes and heredity. These articles and books stirred up a feeding frenzy. Hundreds of books and articles followed. The alarm had been sounded."

Briggs sat back in his chair. "This sounds like something you'd hear during the war, you know. Something that Hitler and the Nazis would have published, not citizens from the U.S."

"A lot of these articles and books were also published in Germany. The Germans were very big on eugenics. In fact, at one point, they were quite jealous of the United States because they felt that the next great battle for the life of the 'chosen' people would be fought in America."

"Why would they think that?"

"Because we had all the laws in place. The United States had passed laws preventing people with mental retardation, epilepsy, and those of different races to marry. The Germans had not yet achieved these kinds of measures of control. They did eventually, of course, but they were way behind the United States when Hitler and his boys came to power. And don't think Hitler and Germany weren't grateful for what the Americans were doing. There was a convention at Heidelburg University—celebrating high intellectual achievement and learning. Eugenics was the hot topic and representatives from eight universities in the United States attended. This guy, Charles Davenport, had this huge research facility in Cold Springs, New York. The Carnegie Institution and Mary Harriman funded it. A guy named Foster Kennedy, a physician who called for the putting to death of the 'utterly unfit,' they both got honorary degrees from Heidelburg University for their work in eugenics."

"I don't get it. How could intelligent men believe that this sort of thinking had any merit?"

"Well, that I can't answer, but I can tell you that they were out there...everywhere. Another crazy bunch running wild in the U.S., only this time they weren't wearing the white hoods. They sat in public office and hung out at our universities, in plain view, funded by some of the richest people in America. The people they were attacking had no voice, no power, just innocent victims who were at the complete mercy of their benefactors. Look at the difference. Nobody knows about eugenics or about how it affected so many human beings in this country and in others. I found out that more than a million mentally retarded, mentally ill, and other handicapped human beings were used as guinea pigs to test the gas chambers and other methods of killing that the Nazis had invented even before one Jewish person was killed."

"That's horrible. It really is. But I still don't see how you're gonna bring this back home. How do you think this situation creates motive in our murder investigation?"

"Look at this list," Richards answered. He searched his pockets for a crumpled up piece of paper, which he handed to Briggs. "These are the names of the people who worked up at Wilton who were members of The Human Betterment Society. They were our local branch of the Eugenics Movement."

Briggs glanced down the list of names. Among them were Mason, Gowan, John York, Julia White, Brian Plummer, Marcia Grey, Patricia Bonnett, Ronald Goldsmith, Michael Rhodes, and

Henrietta Crampton. "Richards! You fuckin' genius. You figured out the connection. They're all here. That's fantastic." Briggs patted him on the back. "I can't believe it."

"Thanks. I think these people all died because one of the students wanted revenge."

Briggs stopped smiling and thought for a moment. "I don't know about that. You think some slightly retarded patient had the wherewithal to kill all these people for putting him into Wilton. I can't buy it, Richards. I mean, a guy like Boyington...now that you've brought it to my attention, I guess I could see some, I don't know, problems. He's a little slow with counting change, gets a bit confused when several people ask him to do two or three things at once, things like that. However, I would never have thought that he'd been in a school for the mentally retarded when he was younger. On the other hand, if you asked me, 'Do you think a guy like Boyington could get away with these murders, with their level of planning and sophistication, I'd probably laugh in your face."

"I agree with you. But there's more. Remember that eugenics was all about genes. The idea was that mental retardation, alcoholism, pauperism, and a lot of other negative aspects of the human being were passed on through the genes."

"Yes, you'd said that."

"Yeah, well, I told you I was tired. Sorry. This is how it would work back then. Let's say you and I were brothers. I was fourteen and you were twelve. These would be our chronological ages. They would come in and test us—give us IQ tests. The results would be tabulated and we would get a score value in the form of a 'mental age.' If your mental age came back and matched your chronological age, you were theoretically okay; but if, say, my mental age score came back at, oh, I don't know, eight years old, I would then be deemed mentally retarded and most likely institutionalized."

"All right, I'm following you. What's so wrong about that?"

"You have to remember about the idea of the dominant and recessive genes. Just because you weren't actually retarded didn't mean you were off the hook. You had the potential to pass on the gene for mental retardation to your kids—the next generation, so you would be institutionalized, too!"

Briggs leaned forward. "So you're saying that there were people who were not really retarded, yet ended up in the institutions anyway?"

"That's exactly what I'm telling you. Here, take a look at this." Richards reached into his box again and dug around until he came upon an old, faded black-and-white picture of three young girls. They were standing outside, in front of one of the buildings on the Wilton grounds. He handed it to Briggs. "See the little hand-written scribbles under each of the girls?"

Briggs looked at the picture and found the writing. "Yeah, it looks like numbers: 57 under the first girl, 73 under the second, and 94 under the girl to the far right. What do they mean?"

"Those are their respective IQ's."

"Didn't you tell me that 70 to 75 or below was considered retarded?"

"Yes. Fifty percent of the population falls between 85 and 115. The normal range." He waited for Briggs to state the obvious.

"Well, that means that the girl to the right isn't really retarded."

"Yet she has spent her entire life in facilities for the retarded. She's out in the Yarlborough facility, near Boston. She's seventy-three years old. She's considered 'institutionally' retarded now. After years of being denied even the most basic educational and social learning, of love and affection, they become stunted. Even though there are no organic problems, they appear stupid next to the average American, ignorant of most everything except knowing how to achieve the most basic of needs. It's very sad to see, but there are thousands and thousands like them out there. And remember, these tests included a morals component. Even if you and your siblings all tested within the normal range with respect to IQ, they could still put you in based on the very subjective interpretation of answers to these questions. Basically, if the social worker giving the test didn't like you, you could soon find yourself up at the state school. "

"God, that is amazing. But I still don't see how someone like this could pull off these murders."

"What I think is that our killer was a special case. Someone who was, well, maybe what the statisticians call an outlier."

"What's that?"

"When statisticians plot score values on a scatter plot—a type of graph—each value is represented by a dot within the graph. If you were to plot all the IQ's of the people who were in Wilton, almost all the dots would fall between, maybe, 30 and 70, with a few dots above and below. But I think our killer's dot would fall way outside the expected range, well above 100."

"Wouldn't he have become institutionally retarded too, though?"

"Not if he were let out. After WWII the eugenics movement lost its punch. The institutional standards were changed and many of those individuals who didn't meet the criteria anymore were...well, set free onto the streets with a quick pep talk and a 'Good luck.' Many ended up in jails, or worse yet, ended up homeless and dying in the streets. Some, like Boyington, did okay. What if our boy was very young when he was put in and then, before the ill effects of living in the institutions could really take hold, was put back out?"

"Holy shit! If you're right, then you did come up with a motive."

"That's what I told you."

"Yeah, but I didn't believe you when you came in! Wow, that really works! All those killings over the years to get back at those who institutionalized him." Briggs frowned. "But how will we know? Were all the IQ scores recorded? And if so, are we gonna have to go through all the records to find the ones who were…outliers?"

Richards smiled and looked at Briggs. "You should know me better than that by now." He turned to the box and ran his hand over the tops of forty or fifty folders. "I figured that the only place that our man could have resided was in L building, that's where the high-grade morons lived." He pulled the box of folders closer. "I think our killer is one of these guys."

Briggs' mind was moving quickly over the events of the last few months. Whoever it was, would have to have a reason to frame McMann. "Richards, does one of them have a sister? Her name would be something like Alicia."

"Let's check. I haven't looked at any of these yet. They pulled the folders out and spread them on the table. "These admission forms were all the same." Richards opened the first one. "See here, third line down. This is were siblings would be listed."

Briggs began to anxiously flip open folders. Richards joined him. They opened one file after another. Each folder contained at least one black and white photograph of the person whose life was laid out within. Briggs came across a young boy who stared emptily at him from the photograph. The boy's eyes were filled with sorrow and despair. Briggs followed his finger to the spot were siblings were listed. 'Brother, James, imbecile, mid-grade. Sister, Felicia, idiot, low-grade. "Goddamn it, Richards! I've got him. Look. Felicia. This has got to be her."

Richards stepped quickly to Briggs' side. He looked at the frail-looking boy in the picture and then to the line that Briggs' finger rested on. "Son of a bitch. How'd you know?"

"McMann told me he thought Alicia was the name of the girl he'd raped."

"There's a motive for you."

"I'd say so. He was avenging his sister by framing McMann and eliminating all the people he felt were responsible for their being institutionalized in the first place."

"This feels great. We figured it out. It's amazing how it all fits together so clearly now."

"Yeah, but we still have to catch him, this…" Briggs looked up to the top of the page in the space for the students name," "…this Victor Gianetti. And look here. Here are a few familiar names. What's this?"

Richards looked at what Briggs was pointing to, a block that named the people who tested him. It read, 'School Committee Members.' Typed in the space were the names Martha Mason, Mary Owen, and Henrietta Crampton. "Oh, man! The people who were responsible for all that testing I told you about made up the 'Traveling School Committee.' They got their name because they would go out into the communities and do the testing in the schools."

Briggs looked further down the page. Another box that contained the names of the admitting attendants: Darren McMann, Robert Mitchell, and Raymond Newton. "This guy was efficient. He's gotten almost everybody who was involved. I better call Mitchell and see if he knows where this Newton fellow is. Our killer may target them next."

Richards took the file from Briggs. "I wonder what this Victor's IQ was." He flipped through a few sheets until he found what he was looking for. "Son of a…these people didn't know who they were messing with. Look at this."

Briggs peered over Richards' shoulder. In the box for IQ was the number 131.

29

Sunday Morning, February 11, 1973. It took Detective Palin almost an hour to drive to the small town of Snowdon. Heavy, ominous gray clouds hung in the skies above. The forecast was for snow and a lot of it. A Noreaster was headed down the coast and the weatherman was predicting that it would hit New England the next day. He pulled into the vacant parking lot of the long-closed Snowdon Medical hospital. He followed the road around the main building to a smaller parking lot in front of Snowdon Home for the Mentally Retarded; a long one-story building snuggled into a stand of pine trees. The place had been bought from the state by a group of wealthy families with mentally retarded members in 1970. The facility was completely funded by money from those families. Briggs, Kroner, and Richards were standing in front of Briggs' truck, waiting for Palin to arrive. He parked and joined them.

"So what's going on?"

Briggs said, "Did you see the article in the *Gazette*?"

"No, I hadn't had a chance to look at it."

Briggs handed him a copy. "Hopefully that will draw him out."

Palin scanned the article in the lower right-hand corner of the front page:

Mentally Retarded Woman Badly Scalded in Shower Mishap

Felicia Gianetti, a mentally retarded resident at the privately owned and operated Snowdon Home for the Mentally Retarded, was badly scalded during a bath yesterday. According to a source from the home, a malfunction in the temperature gauge led attendants to believe that the water was the standard 110 degrees for bathing, when it was actually much hotter. Miss Gianetti began to react violently as she was lowered into the water, but attendants believed she was just resisting her bath, which, the source said, was a normal reaction for her. Officials would not comment as to the extent of Miss Gianetti's injuries, but did say that an investigation into the accident is underway.

"Looks good. How'd you get the paper to print it and the hospital to go along with it?"

Briggs smirked. "Steve Gamble was easy—all he thinks about is exclusives. Chief Murphy of the Snowdon Police Department helped me get the home to go along with it. I had to write a full letter of explanation for them to send out to the families when this is over."

"Think this guy'll fall for it?"

"Hopefully. There was a call that came in late yesterday afternoon from a man wanting to know what had happened. He wouldn't identify himself. The only staffers who know that this is actually a sting operation are the doctors and the attending nurses. Everybody else believes that Felicia was actually injured. They've all been instructed to give no information out over the phone. Oh, by the way, Mark Palin, this is John Richards. He's the one who's been helping me piece all this history together."

Palin and Richards shook hands.

"Do we know how the woman ended up here in the first place?" Palin asked.

Briggs looked at Richards. "Why don't you go ahead?"

"Once we'd identified Victor Gianetti, I dug up his brother and sister's records. The brother died at Wilton in 1949. Apparently he fell from a third-story window. According to the report, he somehow managed to get the lock pried open and climbed out. To me, that seems fairly unlikely. Those locks were very sturdy, but the explanation was accepted without question. Anyway, the sister, this Felicia, she was transported to another state-run facility and remained there until this place was opened in 1970."

"I thought this place was private—and expensive. Who's paying the bill?"

Briggs jumped in. "That's the curious part. We're sure that Victor is paying the bill, but we don't have any idea where he got that kind of money. He paid with a bank check back in 1970, enough to cover the cost for her to stay here through 1980."

Palin let out a low whistle. "Wow! That had to be a lot of money."

"It was."

No one spoke for a moment, then Kroner said, "Hey, did any-one see about papers Victor signed when he brought her here? Maybe he signed the name he's going by now on the documents."

Briggs shook his head. "No, we checked that. The signature on all the paperwork is illegible. Just a few scribbles. He's covered his tracks well." Briggs looked at his watch. "We better get into place. Mark, you're gonna sit at the front desk. The nurse on duty has a uniform for you, make you look like you're an attendant. Richards and I will be sitting in my truck keeping an eye on the parking lot. Kroner, you gotta see the nurse, too." Briggs smiled at him. "You're going to be a janitor. You'll be mopping up and down the hall where Felicia's room is."

"What! Why does Palin get to sit on his ass all day and I end up pushing a mop?"

"Rank has its privileges," Palin answered. "I'm the detective, remember."

"Oh, hell."

Palin and Kroner went inside and Briggs and Richards climbed into the Bronco. Briggs pulled a thermos from out of the back seat and poured Richards and himself a cup of coffee. After a few sips, he turned and asked Richards, "Have you given any thought as to why something like the Eugenics Movement actually came to be?"

"I have thought about it and I've done some more reading over the last few days. Over the last few centuries, there has been a continuous ebb and flow in the way these people have received treatment. The Eugenics Movement represents another downturn in the cycle."

"How so?"

"Well, these people have never received *great* care, but at times the conditions in which they lived have improved, always in direct response to how society viewed them at the time. Between 1840 and 1880, there was a belief that the mentally retarded could be trained and taught to live a clean and decent life. The leaders within this movement felt that although they could never actually 'cure' these people, they could at least get them to a point where they could contribute in some way to society. Money was allocated, schools were built, and the training began. Many of the 'idiots' benefited nicely, but the trouble was that once they finished, most families didn't want them back! They felt that the environment at the schools was better than what could be offered at home. That wasn't what really changed the tide against them, though; it was society's misconception of what the schools were all about. The belief was that these schools would somehow eliminate mental retardation from those who attended. Rapid results were expected and when they didn't come, the schools were considered failures.

"Right around that time, the Eugenics Movement took hold and the school facilities were quickly dismantled in favor of the institution. I remember reading a quote from a speech made by Governor Butler of Massachusetts back in 1883. He said to the legislature, "Give them an asylum, with good and kind treatment; but not a school." The idea changed from protecting the mentally retarded individual from society to protecting society from the mentally retarded individual." Richards mimicked a voice from the past, "We must do everything in our power to protect our gene pool."

"Do you think things are better now?"

"That's hard to say. I think things are getting better, but it's taken a long time. Parent groups are starting to gain some strength now and establishing quite a voice. The National Association for Retarded Citizens has over 250,000 members now. Last year around this time, family members of people living in a state-run institution in Western Massachusetts filed a class action lawsuit. They're claiming that the Department of Mental Health is violating the constitutional rights of its residents. I think that is going to result in a much-improved living environment within the institutions across this state. We may even see a drastic exodus of the mentally retarded out of the institutions and back into the community."

Briggs looked at Richards. "Yeah, but should they be out?"

"Why not? They're not going to hurt anybody. I can tell you this much. Most of the mentally retarded folks I know are some of the sweetest and kindest people in the world. It's like the mental retardation left them without the capability to be mean. The few that are aggressive are usually only responding to frustration from not having their needs met. I see it all the time. The residents are trying to communicate a need, the staff are too busy or don't want to be bothered, and then the resident gets angry and everybody gets bent out of shape. They're just like you and me in that way. Imagine what it would be like if when you needed to go to the bathroom, or eat, or get a glass of water, you had to get permission; and when you tried, your requests were ignored. Don't you think you'd get upset?"

"Of course I would."

"Well, they have to ask for permission for just about everything they do. They live like they are in jail and yet they've committed no crime. I think it would be great if they got out into the communities. Maybe they could teach their neighbors a thing or two."

"Maybe."

The next several hours went by slowly. The only people who came and went were staff. Then around noon, an old blue Chevy drove into the parking lot and slowly pulled into a parking space. "Think this could be him?" asked Richards excitedly. "Did you observe the difference? He wasn't moving like the employees."

Briggs laughed. "Aren't you the detective now." But as he watched the man get out of the car and glance around, his smile faded. The man had a long face, mustache, and short pony tail. He wore wire-rimmed glasses. "Shit! What the hell is he doing here?"

"You know the guy?"

"Yeah. His name is Sammy Ruskin. He's a program director for the state." Ruskin closed his car door and began to walk to the entrance of the home. Briggs picked up his microphone. "Palin, you there?"

Palin's voice crackled on the intercom. "Yeah, Chief, what's up?"

"We may have something. Tell Kroner to stay on his toes. That guy I talked to, Ruskin, he's here. It doesn't seem right, so watch him close."

"You got it."

"Do you think he could be Victor?" Richards asked.

"No," Briggs answered hesitantly. "I doubt it."

"Why would he come all the way out here to see Felicia then? It's an hour's drive from Wilton."

"I talked to this guy ten days ago. He knew McMann back in the old days. He came off as this caring, very dedicated guy, but when I went to question McMann again he painted a very different picture for me. Said that Ruskin was one of the guys, like himself, that really abused the kids. According to McMann he had this huge change of heart and started regretting his abusive behavior. He said that Ruskin was one of the folks who turned him in for raping Felicia. Maybe, for some reason, he saw her name in the paper and wanted to see how she was. All that guilt came rushing back."

Richards furrowed his eyebrows. "Seems a bit far fetched, don't you think? Why would a guy who hadn't really even known the girl, hadn't seen her in years, drive all the way down here to check on her? It doesn't work for me." Ruskin stopped in front of the entrance, looked around, and then went inside. "Did you see that! This is our guy. He's acting way too suspicious. With all this shit

Victor has pulled off up until now, you don't think he could have somehow knocked off Ruskin and taken his place?"

Briggs shook his head confidently. "No. Think about what you're saying. Even if the 'real' Ruskin had quit and moved away, and then Victor tried to come back a few years later and start working as Ruskin for the state again, the people who knew him before would have immediately realized that Victor was an impostor. You're letting your imagination get the best of you. This Victor is clever, but he's not a magician."

"Oh, yeah, I didn't think of that. But, then, why is this guy here?"

Briggs reached for the door handle. "Let's go find out."

He and Richards started towards the building. Suddenly the front door flew open and Ruskin came running out with Palin and Kroner right behind him. Briggs fumbled inside his jacket and pulled his gun. "Freeze, Ruskin!"

Ruskin stopped abruptly and threw up his hands. "Thank God! Chief Briggs, what the hell is going on here?"

"Why don't you tell us."

Kroner grabbed Ruskin from behind and brought him to his knees. A quick search revealed no weapons. "On your feet!" Kroner demanded.

Ruskin stood up and brushed the dirt from his pants, then faced Briggs. He was angry. "How dare you do this to me! What have I done?"

"What are you doing here?"

"I came to see Felicia."

"Yeah, that's what he said when he came in, Chief," said Palin. "I told him she couldn't take any visitors, and then he asked if we had heard from Victor Gianetti."

"That's when I came up behind him and told him to put his hands on the counter and spread 'em," Kroner said. "He turned and looked at me and bolted out the door."

"Why did you run?" asked Briggs.

"Why do you think! A janitor tells me to throw myself against the counter and spread my legs, and this one," he pointed to Palin, "starts running out from behind the nurses station—what the hell was I supposed to do? What would you have done?"

Briggs looked at his men. "Did you identify yourselves as policemen?" Both men looked down at the ground. "Goddamn it!" He looked back at Ruskin. "How come you came out here to see her? She's not a relative. Why would a guy who hasn't had anything to do with Felicia for years be so concerned about her all of a sudden?"

"I wouldn't have come out, but I got a call from Victor and he begged me to come out here and check on her."

"You got a call from him!"

"Yes. I was shocked as all hell to hear from him. I didn't know who he was at first. Then I remembered." Ruskin looked off for a moment. "It all came rushing back. He was just a little kid back then, living in L building, where I worked. There was a school picnic, a big production to impress the state officials. The school was being inspected. All of a sudden little Victor comes running over and tells me that he saw smoke coming from one of the basement windows of a building up on the hill above the field where the picnic was. I went running up along with a few others and instead of finding a fire we found McMann hunched over Felicia, raping the hell out of her. It was horrible."

"So McMann was right. You *were* one of the ones. How could you not go to the police with what you'd seen?"

Ruskin's face clouded. He said quietly, "I should have. I know that I should have. But I didn't. I haven't to this day forgiven myself. I guess...when Victor called I...I felt obligated."

"Did you ever go by the name Dante?"

Ruskin shot Briggs a quick look and then he turned away. "Yeah, that was my nickname back when I was a kid."

"So it's true. McMann told me that you were just as tough on those kids as he was." Briggs shook his head. "You disgust me."

"I was young when I started," he said defensively. "I...I didn't know what I was doing—the harm I was inflicting. I changed!"

"Yeah, right. Did Victor tell you why he couldn't come out here and check on her himself?" asked Briggs.

Ruskin looked at Briggs and tilted his head. "He is coming out here. At least that's what he told me. He was gonna meet me."

"What!" Briggs looked at the others. "Ruskin was a decoy. Let's go!" They left Ruskin standing in the parking lot and raced into the home. They ran down the hall and into Felicia's room. She was in a rocking chair, asleep. On the bed was an envelope with Briggs' name on it.

Palin said, "Son of a bitch, he set us up!"

Briggs moved to the bed and opened the letter. Inside was a typed note to him. It read:

Chief Briggs,

You must think I am a fool. Did you really believe that your little scheme would work? Just when I was beginning to find within myself a certain respect for your capabilities as an investigator, you go and pull this ridiculous stunt. I'm disappointed in you, Roland. I have to tell you, I wasn't going to even bother coming out here, but I couldn't resist the game. Please offer my apologies to Mr. Ruskin for using him in such a way, but I thought it would be fun watching you get excited when, for that brief moment, you thought he might possibly have been me! Admit it, that is what you thought, isn't it? Anyway, I had a short but enjoyable visit with my sister and now I must be off. I'll be out of your way soon, as my work here is almost finished. Have a good day, won't you,

Victor

"Has the reader gone wandering, hand in hand with me, through the inner passages of my being? And have we groped together into all its chambers and examined their treasures or their rubbish? Not so. We have been standing on the greensward, but just within the cavern's mouth, where the common sunshine is free to penetrate, and where every footstep in therefore free to come. I have appealed to no sentiment or sensibilities save such as are diffused among us all. So far as I am a man of really individual attributes, I veil my face; nor am I, nor have I ever been, one of those supremely hospitable people who serve up their own hearts, delicately fried, with brain sauce, as a tidbit for their beloved public."

Briggs slowly lowered the note. The others looked on, waiting for him to say something. "He's been here all right."

"How the hell did he get past us?" asked Richards.

Kroner said, "Should we go out and look for him?"

"No. He's long gone. He's way ahead of us. Look at this note." He handed it over to the others. Richards took it and Palin and Kroner read over his shoulder.

"What the hell does all that shit in the second paragraph mean?" asked Palin.

"I'm not sure," Briggs said, "but I think he's quoting from something. See the quote marks around it?"

"Looks like a bunch of crap to me," said Palin."

Briggs reread the second paragraph again. "No, it's not crap. It means something. He wouldn't have written it otherwise."

Felicia moaned and began to stir. She was wearing a wool skirt and plain white shirt, covered by an unbuttoned blue sweater. The sleeves were pushed up to her elbows and Briggs could see scars along both wrists from where she had gnawed on herself in frustration. The scars were old and thick. Maybe things had gotten better for her, he thought to himself. Or maybe she'd just given up. Her gray hair was pulled up into a bun. Briggs looked at her soft facial features. The wrinkles were beginning to gather around her eyes and the corners of her mouth. She might have been pretty once. He thought for a moment what her life must have been like moving from one huge institution to the next, then ending up here, alone with no family left except for some faceless man who was running around killing anyone who had ever harmed her. He clenched his fists and turned. "We should get out of here and let this poor woman sleep."

30

Monday, February 12, 1973. Briggs was on the phone all morning and most of the afternoon. He'd been talking to teachers and professors at the University of Massachusetts, asking them if they were familiar with the passage that Victor had left in his note. He'd talked to people in the philosophy, psychology, sociology, and English departments. No one could figure out from where the passage had come.

Briggs was worried. Victor said that his work was almost finished, which implied that he hadn't finished killing and that he was going to kill again. Briggs thought about the things he and his friend Doug Johnson from the FBI had talked about back in January. This guy Victor was a cocky son of a bitch. *'I couldn't resist the game.'* He would leave a message like that only because, in his mind, he felt Briggs and his men weren't smart enough to catch him. That's why Briggs believed that Victor was leaving him some sort of clue with the passage he'd chosen. He was trying to tell Briggs about himself without being too direct, even if Victor himself didn't realize it. Briggs decided that by discovering the meaning of the passage he would discover another important piece of information about Victor. Maybe enough to figure out who the hell he was now.

Briggs put the phone down and took a break for a minute. He swiveled in his chair and stared out the window. The scaffolding that had been up and around his window was gone. The renovations to the town hall had been completed. The snow was beginning to fall—they were expecting up to a foot or more. He got up and walked to the window to get a better view. He'd missed the snow when he lived in Florida; and although he was exhausted, he found himself smiling. He was looking forward to a good, old-fashioned blizzard.

He brought his hands up to his face and rubbed it vigorously. He had to get back to making calls. Just as he moved back to the desk, the phone rang. He picked up the receiver.

"Hello, Chief Briggs?" There was someone coughing violently on the other end. Briggs waited. Finally the coughing subsided.

"Chief Briggs, sorry about that. These cigarettes, you know. I was just in the hall and I overheard a few of my colleagues talking about that passage you've been asking them about."

"Oh, really. They talking about it?"

"Oh, yes. You've got the whole department buzzing. Not that often that a bunch of old, stodgy English professors get to try and solve a 'police' puzzle. I—excuse me."

There was a pause on the other end and then another violent round of coughing. Finally, the professor got back on the line. "Yes, so you were saying?"

"Actually, you were 'saying' professor. But first, maybe you could tell me your name."

"Oh! My, my. That would be helpful, wouldn't it? It's Professor William Blake. You can call me Bill."

Briggs thought for a minute. "I think I know that name."

"I'm sure you're thinking of the poet, William Blake. It's been the curse of my life, living under the shadow of a poet I don't even particularly care for. And that never ending question, 'Oh, professor, any relation to...' drives me mad. Anyway, as I was saying, I believe I might be able to solve your little puzzle. Could you read it to me? All I got were bits and pieces in the hall."

Briggs was picturing a little white-haired old man with a pot-belly, sitting in front of a tremendously cluttered desk surrounded by his books. "Sure, Bill. Let me get it out." Briggs read the passage and waited for the professor to comment. After a moment of silence, he said, "Professor, are you still there?"

"Yes." More silence.

"Do you have any idea where this passage comes from?"

"Hold on please."

Briggs was expecting another bout of coughing but instead he heard the faint shuffling of papers. The professor was obviously digging for something. Five minutes later, the professor got back on the line.

"You know, Chief Briggs, it is completely serendipitous, you calling me about this. I probably would not have been able to help you, except that by pure chance I just recently read a book by Frederick Crews that isolated this very passage."

"Who is Frederick Crews?"

"He's a Hawthorne critic. Nathaniel Hawthorne was a writer back in the 1800's."

"Yeah I know him—*House of the Seven Gables, The Scarlet Letter.* I never read any of his books, but I know who he is."

"Good! Good! That's wonderful." More coughing followed. "Excuse me. As I was saying, I had read Crews book when it came out in 1966, and only recently picked it up to reread it. That's why I was able to identify the piece. Now let's see, Crews actually comments on the passage himself. He says, and I quote, oh shit!" There was a clattering sound on the other end. "Oh, Chief, I'm sorry. I'm afraid I've dropped the book. Hold a second while I find my place."

There was a sharp knock on Briggs' door. Kroner came in and triumphantly shook some papers over his head. "Wait to you see what I've found, Chief," he said excitedly.

Briggs covered the mouthpiece on the phone. "Just a second."

The professor got back on the phone. "Okay, here we are. This is from page twelve of Crews's book. 'Here we see an ill-concealed animosity toward those who would presume to know the author through his works; yet the very expression of immunity begs us to guess at what we have not been told. If we are standing just inside a cavern, and if the author's face is veiled, then surely he has something worth hiding from us....With one arm Hawthorne strikes a cold pose of dignity and holds us at bay, but with the other he beckons us forward into the cavern of his deepest soul.' Does that clear anything up for you, Chief?"

Briggs was trying to think but nothing was coming. Kroner was pacing rapidly in front of his desk. "Sit down and wait! I'll be with you in a second."

"What's that, Chief?"

"No, not you, professor, one of my men. He was pacing and it was distracting me." Kroner sat down in a chair and fidgeted "No, it doesn't clear anything up. It does support the position the man who quoted it is taking though. Is there anything more about that passage."

There was quiet on the other end as the professor scanned the page. "Nothing directly. But I don't know exactly know what you're looking for. This book should be in your library, though, so why don't you get a copy and take a look at the chapter? Maybe then you'll find what you're looking for."

Briggs was doubtful. "Maybe you're right, professor. What's the name of the book?"

It's titled, *The Sins of the Father*, and it was—"

Briggs sat straight up. "Wait a minute! *The Sins of the Father*, that's the name of the book!"

"Yes. Hawthorne was from Salem, Massachusetts. One of his forbears was a judge during the Salem witch trials. Hawthorne was sometimes known to say that in some way the retribution for those judgments would somehow fall upon him. The theme of the sins of the father coming down upon the son could be found in several of Hawthorne's works."

Briggs waved at Kroner excitedly. "Listen, professor, I think you just helped me put a huge piece of this puzzle into place. Thank you very much." Briggs hung up before the professor could answer. "Kroner, I know who Victor is after. I don't know why I didn't think of it before."

"That's great Chief, but—"

"It's the mayor. The superintendent of the Wilton school was the mayor's father. Victor must see him as the 'judge' who made the ultimate decision that led to the destruction of his family. The superintendent must have died before Victor could get to him. Now he wants the son to pay for what the father has done. We gotta call him and warn him." Briggs picked up the phone.

"Goddamn it, chief!" Kroner yelled. "I found out who Victor is."

Briggs put the phone down. "Are you serious?"

"Yes, yes! I'm serious. I've been pouring over the records and reports we got involving all the suicides and murders of the

Human Betterment Society members. I was just about to give up 'cause nothing was turning up when I flipped open the insurance paperwork on Dr. Goldsmith. He had no family when he died, only a caretaker who had been with him through the last few years of his life. He left everything to the guy, almost two million bucks, the house, everything. Look at the name, Chief." Kroner slid the paperwork across Briggs' desk.

Briggs looked down at the name. Frank Murman, the architect hired by the city to do the repairs to the town hall. "Holy shit! I can't believe it." He picked up the phone and started dialing the mayor's number. "We gotta warn him. Get out there and get an APB out on Murman."

The mayor's secretary answered the phone.

"Marcy, this is Briggs. Let me talk to the mayor immediately."

"I'm sorry, chief, he's not here."

"Fuck! Where is he?"

"Chief Briggs! I would appreciate your not using that tone of voice with me."

"Damn it, Marcy! Just tell me where he is. His life is in danger!"

"Oh, my lord! He's gone out to the old state school to meet with Mr. Richards."

"No, that can't be. I was with Richards yesterday. He told me he was taking his wife to—oh shit! That's were he's gonna do it." Briggs slammed the phone down and ran out of his office. Detectives Carr and Palin and Officer Kroner were waiting for him. "Let's go. I think he's got the mayor up at the state school."

They all started to move towards the door. Briggs grabbed Carr by the shoulder. "Not you, Carr. You stay here and man the phones. Get in touch with any off-duty officers you can and tell them to head up to the state school. I'll have Lance and Gina in position at the front and back gates. They'll send them off onto the grounds as needed.

"You've got to be kidding!"

"No, I'm not kidding. You fucked up the other day. Remember? You told me that it wasn't you who got caught out at the *old mill* with the bank owner's wife. There were no identifying landmarks in that picture. I had to think for a while before I remembered were we'd been photographed. Nobody but myself, Meredith, and the photographer would know that that picture was taken out there. So sit your ass down and man the phones. I'll deal with you when I get back."

Briggs, Palin, and Kroner headed out in the Bronco. Briggs got on the microphone and told his two officers on patrol, Lance and Gina, to take up positions at the front and rear gates. "Carr with be sending anyone he can get hold of to you. I want you to put those who show up in position around the grounds. This place is fuckin' huge, so we're gonna be spread thin. Do the best you can."

The Bronco sped up Route 63, then took a right onto the long road that led up the hill. They passed underneath the archway and took the left at the stop sign. Briggs brought the vehicle to a skidding halt behind the mayor's Cadillac, which was parked in front of the fallen tree. It was covered with two or three inches of snow. The three men ran over to the car and wiped the snow from the windows. Palin shown his flashlight inside. Nothing.

"Damn it!" Briggs slammed his fist down on the hood of the car. "We gotta search the grounds, and fast. All this snow on the car, they've been here for a while. I hope it's not too late."

All three turned to look upon the grounds. The wind was blowing stronger now. The snow twisted violently around them. Barely visible off in the distance were the looming spires and rooftops of the buildings. Their dark, uninviting silhouettes cut into the blue grayness of the snow-filled sky.

"Shit, Chief, there must be twenty or so buildings out there. He could be anywhere."

"Maybe we should wait until the others get here. Do a building by building search. Victor could kill the mayor ten times over before the three of us find him," Kroner said quietly.

"No, no time to wait. Let's go. We don't even know how many people Carr will be able to reach. We can still do a building by building search. We'll each take a building and work our way around the perimeter."

They started out along the road that arched its way through the buildings. They came upon the first building, building A, Briggs remembered. "Okay, Kroner, you take this one. Work your way around, try to look for any doors or windows that are open or have been open recently. If you find anything, don't go in! Come back down the road and find Palin and me. We'll check it out together. Understood? We'll meet in front of the forth building along the road here."

"Got it, Chief." In seconds, Kroner had disappeared into the snow.

"You take Building B, Mark. I'll see you in front of D."

"All right. Be careful, Chief."

"You, too." Briggs watched Palin head out and then moved quickly down the road until he came upon building C. His mind was racing. He tried to think like Victor. "Where would he go...where would I go if I were he?" Briggs whispered to himself. He started up the stairs, then stopped in his tracks. Suddenly, it hit him. "Of course! That's got to be it." He looked briefly back in the direction he'd come, but decided not to wait for the others. Spinning around, he headed towards the old administration building.

The huge structure seemed to creep out of the night as Briggs ran towards it. He stopped and stood in the road. He tried desperately to shade his eyes from the unrelenting snow and wind whipping down from off the roof. The storm was getting worse.

Briggs cupped his hands around his eyes and slowly scanned the windows of the second and third floors. Something caught his attention. In a window on the second floor, just above the entrance, he thought he saw the faintest trace of light. He wiped the snow from his eyes and looked again. Something moved. A shadow reflected onto the ceiling. They were up there.

"Chief!" a voice hissed from his left. It was Palin. Kroner was right behind him. "What the hell. I thought you were gonna meet us in front of Building D. Luckily we saw your footprints in the snow."

"I'm sorry. It suddenly came to me. Victor wants to punish the mayor for what the mayor's father did to his brother and sister. Where better to inflict that punishment than in the office once occupied by the superintendent, the place where all the decisions were made. They're right up there. I saw a light. Come on."

The men quickly moved up the front steps. Briggs turned the doorknob. It was unlocked. He pushed the heavy door open slowly without making a sound. Briggs took out his flashlight and directed the beam to the bottom of the stairs, off to the right of the entranceway. He turned to his men. "I'll go up first. You guys come up behind. No more talking."

Briggs skirted the floor and took the stairs slowly. As he got to the top, he stopped to listen. He heard the sound of someone moving in the room across the hall. The door was closed. There was a small amount of light coming from under the base of the door. Briggs leaned against the wall. He was nervous. He watched his breath mist in front of him. He waited until he calmed down, then, very carefully, he shined his light down past the door. The wallpaper and plasterboard were beginning to peel away from the walls in spots. There was a window at the far end of the hall. Three of its four panes of glass were broken and snow was billowing in from outside. Closer to him on the right was the lower end of a finely carved banister, the stairs that led up to the third floor. Just opposite the stairs was what appeared to be another door leading into the room where Victor and the mayor were located.

He turned to Palin and Kroner, who were peering up through the darkness at him. Briggs pointed to Kroner and then moved his hand to his back. Kroner understood that he was to stay with the chief. Briggs pointed to Palin, then down the hall towards the far door. Palin nodded and moved quietly past Briggs. He made it past the first door into the room before he accidentally kicked a small piece of plaster. The small object slid along the floor, making a noise that sounded like thunder in the quiet hall.

31

"Roland! That must be you," said Victor from the other side of the door. "Why don't you come in, very slowly, and join us."

Briggs shined his flashlight on Palin, who was now looking desperately at the chief. Briggs waved his hand at him. "Get down there," he hissed. Palin moved the rest of the way down the hall while Briggs noisily crossed the hall to the door. "Okay, Victor. I'm coming in." Briggs turned the handle and pushed the door open. The light he'd seen from outside was coming from a small lantern sitting on the far side of the room.

"Of course, Roland, you'll humor me and slide your gun in ahead of you, please. And tell your henchmen that if I see or hear anything unusual I'll kill the mayor instantly."

Briggs looked back at Kroner. "You heard him. Stay put."

"Chief! You can't go in there. He'll kill you, too. This guy has nothing to lose," Kroner whispered back.

"What choice do I have? Stay here." Briggs pulled his gun from his shoulder holster and slid it across the floor to the center of the room. Then, with his hands on his head, he slowly entered. The left side of the room was empty except for some decaying bookcases. As Briggs cleared the door, he gazed upon Victor, standing behind a large wooden desk. He had a knife in his hand. He was next to the mayor who was standing on his toes on flimsy looking wooden chair. His hands were bound behind his back. He had a piece of silver duct tape across his mouth. A noose, tied to an exposed pipe above them, was around the mayor's neck. The mayor was gasping for air.

"Jesus Christ, Victor. Let him go."

"Oh, come now, Roland. After all I've done to get to this point! Don't be ridiculous." Victor firmly patted the mayor's hip. The chair teetered for a second. The mayor set his feet nervously, trying to steady himself.

"You can't get away. I've got the building surrounded," Briggs lied. The mayor didn't do anything to you. It was his father. It's in the past."

"Ah, but there's were you're wrong, Roland. It is only in the past for those like you who don't have to live with the ramifications of what this man's father brought down upon my family and me. The great Superintendent Tatum," Victor said sarcastically. "The dictator. The vilest evil I have ever known. I assume that since you have so skillfully found me out, that you might have an inkling as to what eugenics was?"

Briggs nodded.

"Very good. I must say that my faith in your detecting skills has not only returned, but increased. How did you know to come here? Was it the quote?"

Briggs nodded again. "And we knew you were going by the name of Murman when Kroner found you listed as the beneficiary of Goldsmith's fortune."

"Ah, yes, Dr. Goldsmith. What great memories. He had his stroke and was looking for a caretaker. It was a dream come true. Of course he didn't recognize me and I got the job. I tortured him for years. When I got bored, I forced him to sign the new will. Six months later, I tossed him down the stairs.

"As I was saying, Superintendent Tatum was a zealot. He refused to relinquish the ideas of the eugenics movement, even when most sensible men were. And his power was unquestionable. It took the state of Massachusetts until 1945 to see what a dinosaur this man had become. All too late for my family. And the families of so many others. He sat up here, on his throne, determining the fate of so many innocent people. Thousands of people, all herded into buildings, treated worse than animals, all at his say so."

"He thought he was doing the right thing back then. It was...the way the world saw things. He wasn't doing anything to you personally."

"Exactly, Roland! He didn't even know me. Or my brother, or my sister. In the six years I lived up here, I never met the man. And yet, his signature on a piece of paper condemned my family to hell." Victor's voice was shaking. He paused to regain his composure. "This man's father determined when I got up in the morning, when I went to work, what time I ate breakfast, lunch, dinner. He decided on the clothes I would wear, the health care I received—or didn't receive, and he determined the punishments that I got. And there were plenty, Roland. And all this was supposed to be for our good—to benefit us, make us sick creatures better. And he pulled it off for so many years. Acting like there was some special thing that he was doing, some treatment to improve our behavior. But let me tell you, Roland. There was no secret cure. Only banishment from society, all because of this man's father." Victor pushed on the mayor again, harder this time. The mayor almost fell.

Briggs could see that Murman was getting angry.

"This man's father allowed my sister to be raped and then he let the man who did it walk free. He created the environment that allowed those bastards in C building to get away with the murder of my bother, and he took away my ability to father a child."

Briggs looked confused. Victor saw it.

"That's right, Roland. I tried once to put this behind me. I was even married once, to a wonderful woman. But she wanted a family. We tried. Nothing happened. Later, I found out that while I was here, they tricked me into signing a form allowing them to give me a vasectomy. The marriage was annulled. But this wasn't unusual. There are over eighty thousand people in this country that were sterilized because of the eugenics movement. And those were the documented cases. There were probably thousands of others that went unrecorded. So, you see, this man's father not only took the family I had away from me, he took the family I could have had away too." Victor pushed the mayor again. The mayor swayed dangerously for a moment. He sucked air through his nostrils. "Look at his eyes, Roland. Isn't it wonderful? Look at that fear. They were all like that. All the great eugenics members quivered in fear and I loved it. They all begged for their lives, desperately trying to somehow repair what they'd done to my family and me with a few words of apology. What a joke!

"Look. I understand how you feel. I—"

"You what!" Victor's tone changed dramatically. "I know all about you, Roland, and I can tell you this, you will never know how I feel. YOU know how I feel! Look at you," he sneered. "Your wife killed herself because you didn't give a shit about her. Your kids don't talk to you and you do nothing to rectify that. You sleep with another man's wife! Come on, Roland. You and I are not alike in the least. Don't even try and lower me to your level. You had it all—a family, a life—and you threw it all away. Let it slip right through your fingers. I never even had a chance to taste these things you took for granted. And I've spent my life getting back at the people who took it all away. Destroyed my right to a family. To a life.

"How many people did you kill in the war, Roland?"

The question caught Briggs by surprise. He was still reeling from Victor's words. "Does it matter?"

"Not really. I only bring it up to again show you how we are different. You kill, and you get the Congressional Medal of Honor. The big war-hero, fighting for his country. I kill, and I am labeled a murderer. It's all semantics as far as I'm concerned, Roland. I killed for family, and I would do it again and again. As far as I'm concerned, it is far more honorable than anything you've ever done."

There were voices outside the building. Other officers had arrived.

"Here come the troops," Victor said.

Briggs glanced at the mayor. He looked exhausted. "Listen, Victor, you're entitled to your opinion, but as far as I'm concerned, you're no fuckin' hero. You killed defenseless people. You're a fucking genius, you could have figured out a different way of going about this if you tried. You've got to end this now. There's no way out. You've run out of tricks."

"Ah, Roland. After all this, you still underestimate me. Look at what I was able to do. I befriended this fool and was able to monitor all your actions through him. Whenever I wanted, I climbed into your office and checked out your notes. By the way, I hope you felt that Gowan's murder lived up to your expectations."

"So that's how you did it."

"Yes. It was quite easy, actually."

"Why did you go after Meredith out by the horse barn?"

"For fun more than anything else. But it also solidified in her mind the memory of my standing in Gowan's yard."

Briggs looked at the mayor again. He was losing his strength. "Look, Victor, This place is surrounded. All you have is a knife. What could you possibly do to escape."

"I was hoping you would ask." With that, Victor calmly turned towards the mayor and shoved him off the chair.

"Oh shit!" Briggs started racing towards the mayor. "Kroner!"

Victor ran to the side door just as Palin swung it open. Before Palin could react, Victor sunk the blade into his belly and ran past him. Briggs got to the mayor and hoisted him up while Kroner jumped up on the chair and sawed at the rope with a pocketknife. After a few seconds, he managed to sever the rope in half. He and Briggs lowered the mayor to the ground and loosened the noose. The mayor gasped and sputtered desperately, but it looked like he was going to be okay. Briggs quickly turned his attention to Palin, who wasn't fairing as well. Blood was everywhere.

"Hang in there, kid. You're gonna be all right." He stood and ran to the window, kicking it out with his boot. He looked out and saw some of his officers below. "Did you see him come out?"

"No, Chief," yelled one of them. "No one's been through these doors."

"Fuck! Well he's taken off, so be ready. One of you radio for an ambulance. The mayor and Palin are hurt. Briggs turned back to Kroner. "Stay with these guys. I'm going after him." He grabbed his gun and headed out the door.

When Briggs got to the bottom of the stairs, he threw open the front door.

"Freeze!" he heard Officer Berson yell.

"It's just me, goddamn it. Still no sign of him?"

"Nothing, Chief."

"All right. Hold your positions. He may still be in the building." Briggs ran to the rear of the hall and down the back stairs, just as he had the day he first came upon Richards. He pushed on the door but found it locked. "Damn it! Where the fuck did this bastard go?"

Briggs turned and waved the flashlight beam around what appeared to be a basement. There was old furniture piled in one corner and a stack of wood almost to the ceiling in another. He moved deeper into the basement. As he played the light around a bit more, he noticed some writing on the wall, just beyond the edge of the woodpile. The writing was partially covered with dust and dirt. He moved closer, wiping it away. In white faded letters was the word 'tunnel.'

Briggs peered in behind the pile of wood. There was a small staircase leading down to a door. Briggs took the stairs two at a time. He got to the door and pushed it. It swung open easily. He stepped into a long, dark cement corridor. Briggs' mind quickly flashed back to the day at Snowdon Nursing Home. Maybe all these old institutions had tunnels. He shined his flashlight first to the left and then to the right. The tunnel was long and narrow, about as wide as a normal hallway. There was what appeared to be old gaslight fixtures on the wall every ten yards or so. It was damp and the air was stifling, stale. Briggs listened. Nothing, no movement, no sound. He quickly flashed his light down at the ground. There was a thin layer of dust built up on the floor. Nothing to the left. He moved to the right of the doorway and found what he was looking for, the faintest trace of a footprint.

Briggs bolted down the corridor. It slowly bent to the right. About fifty yards in, he came across another door. Locked. He kept running. The next two were locked as well, but the third one was open. Briggs guessed that he was underneath C building. He slid inside and found himself in a basement very similar to the one under the administration building. He found the stairs leading up to the first floor. He could hear Victor upstairs. He took the steps quickly and listened again. It sounded like Victor was trying to get a door open. Briggs burst through the door and shined his light down the corridor.

"Turn around, Victor!" Briggs yelled, gun at the ready. "Put your hands in the air."

Victor turned slowly and smiled at Briggs. His knife was in his hand. He'd been prying at the lock with it. "Roland, you are *so* resourceful." He dropped the knife and raised his hands. "You wouldn't shoot an unarmed man, would you?"

"Don't tempt me. You wounded a police officer and killed who knows how many others. I don't think too many people would question it if I did."

"I guess we'll have to see." With that, Victor was off again. He bolted to the stairs to Briggs' left and disappeared onto the second floor.

Briggs almost pulled the trigger, but hesitated. "Fuck!" he yelled and shook his head. He started up the steps. He heard Victor's feet above him. He was going up to the third floor. Briggs followed. As he came to the top of the stairs, he felt the cold wind on his face. Another door at the end of the corridor. It was hanging open. Briggs moved quickly to the egress. He peered out. Off in the distance he could hear his men yelling to each other, but the snow was falling so heavy now that he couldn't see the ground. He stepped out onto the roof.

Before he knew what was happening, Victor swooped down from above, violently knocking Briggs to the rooftop. The roof slanted down at two different levels and Victor had been able to jump up to the higher level and crouch on a small ledge above the door. The gun fell away into the snow as Briggs attempted to break his fall. He got up quickly and turned just in time to block a punch. He sidestepped and hit Victor with a sharp straight punch to the face, then stepped forward and caught him solid in the nose with a devastating elbow shot. Victor fell back, stunned. He regained his sense of balance and charged Briggs like a bull. Briggs brought his leg up to throw a front kick, but his footing gave way in the snow and he fell onto his back.

Victor pounced. Briggs had him in the skill areas, but Victor was extremely powerful. Victor began to swing wildly, catching Briggs several times in the face. Briggs managed to get his foot between him and Victor. He pushed hard. It was enough to back Victor up a little. As Briggs tried to stand, Victor stepped forward and kicked him squarely in the ribs.

Briggs heard his ribs crack as he fell backward. He sucked for air. Victor was moving towards him. He again tried to stand. Victor kicked again. Briggs fells sideways, rolled over once, and then felt the roof disappear beneath him. He was falling! He reached out wildly. His right hand caught the rain-gutter and his body swung down and in. The roof's edge extended about two feet out beyond the wall. Briggs' legs crashed into the side of the building. He almost lost his grip. He reached up with his left hand as he spun, missed the drain, spun again, and then caught the edge. He hung there by his hands. The pain from his broken ribs shot through his body. He looked up into the snow.

Victor stood above him, looking down. He leered at Briggs triumphantly. He was breathing heavily. He wiped the blood away from his nose. He knelt down. "Well, Roland, it appears as though I've won again." Victor looked off over Briggs. The voices of the other police officers were getting closer. "You were a worthy adversary, Roland, but like everyone else, you underestimated me. How are those ribs?"

Briggs couldn't answer.

"Yes, I bet they hurt. Hard to talk, isn't it. Well, if you can get up the strength to yell, your men might save you. That is of course, if you can hold on that long. You should feel pretty good about yourself. You did prevent the death of the mayor. If you survive, tell him I'll be seeing him eventually, won't you."

Briggs stared up at Victor for a few seconds longer, then turned his eyes away. He wanted to tell him to go to hell, but he could barely breathe. His fingers ached. He listened to the sound of Victor's muffled footsteps fade out of earshot. For a second, there was silence, and then suddenly there was a booming crash from above that echoed through the storm air for a moment. Then silence again. Briggs looked to his right. He was a few feet away from the corner. There was an old phone line that ran away from the building. It was connected to the wall about a foot and a half below the roof. Briggs heard the sounds of his officers running in his direction.

He looked down for a moment, into the swirling snow and darkness below. "That's a long fuckin'drop," he whispered to himself. He took as deep a breath as he could before he began to inch his way to the corner, sliding his hands along the edge of the gutter. He got close to the cable and, with extreme effort, swung one leg and then the other over it. He hoisted himself up to a sitting position and then, very slowly, he stood on the cable. He was now able to flop back onto the roof.

"Chief! Chief! Are you up there?" yelled Mark Adams from below.

Briggs pulled himself up onto his knees. "Yeah, I'm up here," he croaked. "I'm hurt."

"We're comin', Chief. Sit tight."

Briggs turned his head and looked across the rooftop. He pulled his flashlight from his pocket. The beam fell on a large hole where the roof had caved in. He crawled over to the edge and laid himself out. While peering into the hole, he shined the flashlight onto the scene below. There on the stairs, about thirty feet down, was Victor's twisted body. The school had opened its jaws and taken Victor back into its belly. Briggs slid himself away a few feet and turned over, lying quietly in the snow. He felt the cold flakes hit his face. Closing his eyes, Briggs waited for his men.

32

Late March, 1973. Mark Palin stood in the doorway of Briggs' office. "Hey, Chief, got a minute?"

Briggs had his back to the door, sitting in his chair, looking out the window. He swiveled around. "Shouldn't I be calling you that, now?"

Palin smiled. "That's gonna take a while to get used to."

"Hey, you deserve it. How are you feeling?"

"A lot better. Boy, we're a pair, aren't we? You with your healing broken ribs and me with my slowly healing belly!"

"Well, at least we got our man," Briggs joked. "What's up?"

"I just wanted to say goodbye. And...thank you for everything. I've learned a lot from you. I wish you didn't have to go."

"You wouldn't be able to become chief if I stayed."

Palin pretended to think about that for a minute. "Hmm...
guess you're right. Well, good luck!"

"I thought you'd see it like that."

"Seriously, though, thanks for everything."

Briggs smiled. "You're welcome."

There was a brief silence, then Palin said, "Have you decided
what you're going to do?"

Briggs swiveled around in his chair, again looking out the window. He seemed pensive. "Can I talk to you?"

"Of course, Chief."

"I've been doing a lot of thinking. It came to me that I've spent
most of my life being a pretty self-absorbed person. It's always
been about me. I put myself before my wife and kids and it cost
me dearly. Then, I come up here and start seeing a married
woman—who by the way is a wonderful person—and I took
advantage of her. She was vulnerable and I tried to pressure her
into things she really didn't want to do...couldn't do. It's time for
me to do a bit of growing up."

"Wow! You have been doing some soul searching."

Briggs swung back around and smiled. "Yes, I have. When I
leave here I'm going out to California and I'm going to get my
daughter back into my life. And then I'm going to spend some
quality time with my son, who, believe it or not, wants to go into
the FBI."

"That's excellent, Chief. But how ya going to support yourself?"

"I've saved up a good bit of money. And I think I'm going to
take my friend up on his offer."

"What offer was that?"

"That guy I mentioned, Doug Johnson, he got his program
approved to study violent offenders. They want to take on some
old veterans like myself to help get it going."

"All right! So I'll have two connections within the FBI."

"Looks that way. It intrigues the hell out of me, these people. How is it that their thinking becomes so twisted?"

"You got me, Chief."

Briggs thought for a minute. "Socrates said that evil does not exist. That intentional evil is impossible because when people do evil things they mistakenly think that they are doing good."

"Sounds like our man, Victor Gianetti."

"Yeah, it does. He perceived his acts as heroic. From his point of view, they were."

"You're not condoning what he did, are you?"

"God, no! There is no way one can justify his acts. In the long run, he knew what he was doing was wrong. The fact that he covered it up so well proves that. My interest lies in discovering how these men think. How he created that reality for himself. Hopefully, by doing so, I'll be able to help prevent others like him from doing lots of damage."

"Any early guesses?"

"It's all about personal relationships and the perception of those relationships as far as I'm concerned. Everything that means anything to anybody usually involves others. As we grow up, how we are treated, and, especially, how we see ourselves being treated, seems to create our entire personality—our perception of the world. If one's beginnings are distorted...that is, one's early intimate relationships are distorted, they often will be distorted forever. Their search for intimacy as an adult will undoubtedly be skewed. A few of these people slip over the edge. They lose themselves in their own personal view of how the world has screwed them over—left them isolated and alone. They become angry and that anger mixes with distorted realities and out comes their rage. Intimacy becomes all about gaining power and control over others. And what better way to achieve that than making other human beings grovel and beg for their lives.

The ultimate high for them seems to come through various forms of assault and murder."

"Impressive."

"I don't know about that, but it's a start."

"Hey, did you ever find out if Victor was a real architect?"

"He wasn't. There was no record of his attending any college—not as Gianetti or Murman. He called himself an architect, but the jobs he did over the years were really just renovation and carpentry jobs. He did good work, though. Everyone we talked to said he was very talented. He did a great job on this building."

"Yeah, he did. The place looks great."

Briggs hesitated. "It's funny when you think about it. Old Victor never really mentally escaped that school, and in the end, it took him physically as well." He stood up slowly and grabbed the last of his packed boxes off his desk. "I better get going."

Palin held his belly and stood too. "Well, don't be a stranger, ya hear. Did you get a chance to say goodbye to Kroner?"

"Yeah. He and I went out for a beer last night. He's very excited about moving up to detective. You'll have to be patient with him. He'd only just gotten over the thrill of becoming a cop!"

"I know. He moved up quick."

"He did a great job. And so did you. Next to firing Carr, moving you guys up were very satisfying last acts, for me."

"Thanks, Chief Briggs."

"No problem, Chief Palin."

*   *   *

Briggs put the last box into his trunk and slid behind the wheel. He went to start the Bronco when there was a knock on his window.

He turned to see the mayor smiling at him through the glass. Briggs rolled down the window.

"I just wanted to say thanks one more time. I'm sorry I ever doubted you."

Briggs smiled. "Don't give it another thought."

"Well...good luck. Are you sure you won't stay?"

"No, Sir. It's time for me to go."

"Richards tells me that you and he are going to get together and write a book about this case. Is that true?"

"We're giving it some serious thought." Briggs saw the mayor's face cloud up a bit. "Don't worry, I won't make you out to be a bad guy!"

"Thank God!"

"Did you take care of that little matter we'd discussed?"

The mayor smiled slyly. "Oh, yes. I've talked to the district attorney, who, of course, is a good friend of mine. No paperwork exists to show that the money set aside for Felicia Gianetti's present and future hospitalization came from the money Victor got from the stolen inheritance."

"Excellent! At least she'll be in great hands through 1980. I wonder what will happen to her after that?"

The mayor patted Briggs on the shoulder. "Don't worry. I've talked to Mrs. Tatum. We've decided to pick up the tab after that."

"Really! That's great, Mayor. Maybe you're not such a jerk, after all!"

The mayor smiled. "See, I keep surprising you, don't I?"

"You sure do."

The two men shook hands and Briggs pulled away. It was a gorgeous morning. The sun was shining and the buds were just starting to form on the branches of the trees. The air was warm so he left his window rolled down. As Briggs passed the library, he saw

Meredith and her daughter walking down the steps. He tooted his horn. Meredith looked up and smiled at him. He gave her a wave and she returned it. He turned back to concentrate on his driving. He took a deep breath and let it out slowly. He hadn't smoked since he was hospitalized for his broken ribs. The smell of the earth was heavy in the air. Briggs felt good. He turned onto Rt. 63 and headed for the interstate. He'd be in California in six days. He couldn't wait to get there. He pulled his thermos out and opened it up. He held it out in front of him and toasted the air.

"To new beginnings," he said, and took a big swig of the coffee.